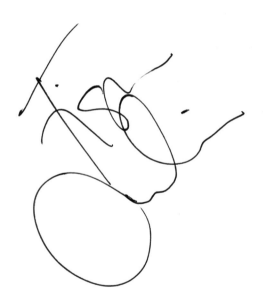

FURY

BOOK THREE OF THE SEVEN DEADLY SERIES

FISHER AMELIE

ETHAN MOONSONG IS
FURY

Fisher Amelie

http://www.fisheramelie.com/

First Edition: May 2015

The characters and events portrayed in this book are fictitious. Any similarity to real persons, living or dead, is coincidental and not intended by the author.

Printed in the United States of America

To Matt,
Finally

PROLOGUE

Anger is a consuming thing, a burning takeover.

It sets up shop in your heart and head and murders anything else attempting to make its way in. Life becomes obsessed with it, clouded with it, engrossed in it. You justify the feeling with delusions that you're owed retribution. You condone thoughts and vengeful acts, feeding yourself with the idea that it's warranted.

But that nourishment comes at a price. It costs you pieces of your soul, your love, your worth. You disregard your beliefs, your conscience. You adopt apathy like it's salvation because you know in your heart of hearts that you would deteriorate into nothing without it. Because you don't want to let it go. It makes you feel powerful, that anger. It makes you feel important. So you will let it eat you alive, consume every part of you until all that's left is hollow revenge.

FURY

And when revenge is finally yours?

The fog will clear and all you'll have gained from it is the insanity of guilt and the blood on your hands.

"Ethan," she warned.

He faced me, the most furious, most livid expression in his eyes, and when he spoke, his voice dropped menacingly.

"Spencer Blackwell, I warned you. I told you. Now I'm gonna get you...when you least expect it."

He eerily turned from us and wordlessly walked to his truck. He got inside, started the engine, but before he drove off, he watched me.

His eyes promised a *furious* revenge.
-GREED

Never take your own revenge, beloved, but leave room for the wrath of God, for it is written, "VENGEANCE IS MINE, I WILL REPAY."
Romans 12:19

CHAPTER ONE

Breathe.

Breathe.

Breathe.

My chest burned with such intensity I could barely stomach it.

I glanced behind me. He was close. My eyes searched my surroundings. Pitch black and seemingly nowhere else to go. I caught sight of a small alley to my left about half a block ahead, ducked within it, and noticed piles of trash amassed against the edges of the buildings. The smell was atrocious, burning my nose.

I threw her onto the ground and tossed what I could over her.

"Don't move," I told her. "Don't say a word. Don't breathe." I peered furiously over my shoulder. "And for the love of God, whatever you do, cover your ears and *don't look*."

Her eyes widened to an impossible breadth and she nodded. She obeyed me and faced the wall. I covered her face as best I could and waited.

Breathe.

Breathe.

Breathe.

My chest rose and fell violently. The rapid *thump, thump, thump* of my heart drummed frantically in my ears. Strapped to my sides rested two sharp blades I'd brought from home, the ones I'd always hunted with. I carefully unzipped my hoodie, crossed my arms, and palmed the knives' handles.

Breathe.

Breathe.

Breathe.

"Đến đây!" I heard, making my pulse jump. My heart leapt into my throat. I crouched, bent my knees, readying for anything.
The speaker, the man chasing us, rushed around the edge of the building but came to a stop when he caught me standing. He smiled cruelly then spoke to me in Vietnamese, words I didn't understand, and steadily made his way toward me. He stopped short once more. His head tilted to his right. His eyes narrowed.

"You messed up," he said in English, realizing I hadn't understood him before and made his way toward me once more.

I shook my head, my tongue too thick to speak.

He was big for a local. I suppose that's why they hired him to do what he did, but no matter. I was taller and built better. I also had something he didn't. I was trained to kill. Animals, yes, but to me he was just that. An animal.

My blood boiled in my veins and the anxious adrenaline was replaced with an absolute hatred, a fury so destructive it frightened me. My teeth gritted in my jaw and I reveled in the pressure.

I knew it the instant he'd made the decision, and all the breath I held whooshed from my lungs. A look of determination flitted across his face, and I could only smile, content in my malice. This visibly confused him, but he charged forward, regardless.

Two feet within striking distance, my short blades pealed with a beautiful ring, and it brought me such serenity. The gun strapped to his back was useless now and he knew it.

I plunged both blades into the sides of his ribs and his mouth opened in shock, his body leaning against mine in support. I held him up with the blades and bent into his ear.

"You messed up," I said, stealing his words.

Blood curdled from his mouth and I removed my blades as he slid to the ground. I bent and wiped my knives on his jacket. His mouth opened and shut like a fish out of water, but I couldn't conjure up any compassion for him. Instead, I stood over him and placed my boot over his heaving chest, pressing as much of my weight into him as possible.

"You will burn in fire so scorching you'll beg for this moment over and over again."

His last breath struggled from his lungs and his eyes went blank. I replaced my knives and kicked the corpse to the side, covering his body as much as I could with garbage. Hoping the smell would hide him and no one would find him for several days.

I turned back to her, fished her from her hiding place, and threw her over my shoulder. "Don't look," I ordered, and she nodded her head.

CHAPTER TWO

Three months earlier...

Ethan

    I heard a snap and the light cracked on, piercing through my closed lids. My head pounded and I groaned then rolled over, pulling my cover over my head to drown out the source of my pain.

    "Get up," a deep voice commanded. "Get up," he continued, kicking my shoe.

    "Dad," I rasped. "I'm hungover and feel like shit."

    He was silent for a moment so I pulled the cover down just enough to see his face. He was not amused.

    "Ethan, watch your language, get your butt up, and find a job." I didn't answer him. I had nothing to say that would please him. "And while you're at it, stop this ridiculous drinkin', son."

I sat up, ran my hands through my long black hair, and wrapped the length around my fist. I sat back against the wall, reveling in how cool it was, and tried not to vomit.

"Did you see them today?" I asked him, unable to help myself.

My dad removed his hat and leaned against the jamb, scrubbing his face with his free hand. "You like to torture yourself," he said, shaking his head and sighing. "You remind me so much of your mama."

The mere mention of my mother sent me spiraling down once more in depression. We'd lost her a few years before and I was still in agony. That, coupled with the fact that Spencer Blackwell stole my girl right out from underneath my nose, was enough for me to drink to excess every night. *I hate him.*

"Are they," I swallowed, afraid of his answer, "are they together now?"

My father sighed again. "Ethan, get dressed."

"Are they?" I asked again, letting my hand drop to my side. My hair slid with it and cascaded down my back.

"You are a stubborn boy. Yes, okay? Yes, they're together. All the more reason to move on, son."

My body suddenly weighed a thousand pounds and I felt my head reeling. So it was true. They were together and they would probably get married and I was going to have to sit there in that godforsaken small town and watch it all happen. I was going to get a front-row seat to my own misery.

I nodded once, rested my hands on my knees for a brief moment, then ran past my dad, shouldering him as I did so and nearly knocking him over before making it to the small bathroom across the hall and retching everything in my stomach into the toilet.

My dad stood in the bathroom doorway shaking his head in disappointment. When I was done, I fell back into the wall. That look shamed me to my core. Any time my dad felt let down, I felt the weight of my disgrace so heavy the only thing I could think to dull the ache was to drink myself into a stupor. It was a vicious cycle.

I let my hair cascade over my face. I heard the old wood floor creak beneath his feet as he left without another word and jumped when the front door slammed. My eyes closed as my head pounded.

The claw foot tub sat to my left so I leaned up and turned on the water, removing my clothing one piece at time. Each movement felt like a hammer slamming into my head.

"God," I groaned. "*I* am an *idiot.*"

I stepped underneath the warm water and stood in silence, letting the water absorb into my hair and seep into my skin. I breathed in the steam. I was miserable. Not just physically, but my heart was the heaviest it'd felt since my mom passed, and I had no one to blame but Spencer Blackwell for that.

The asshole who rode into my life under the guise of helping his sister only to yank what I thought was a stable foundation right out from underneath me. He stole from me, a bona fide thief, and I wanted to make him pay. No, I *needed* to make him pay.

But how?

I finished showering and threw a towel around my waist, stepping from the tub and toppling onto my bed when I reached my room and fell to sleep, not even bothering to dress myself. I fell quickly, fantasizing about my revenge.

I must have slept for hours because when I woke, it was pitch black outside. I rolled onto my side and checked my alarm clock. Eleven o'clock. *Perfect timing*, I thought.

I sat up and tucked my towel around my waist a little tighter, stood, and went straight for my dresser. I grabbed a pair of boxers and socks and put those on before heading for my closet and tossing on an old, worn pair of jeans, a thermal, and an old tee. I brushed my teeth, grabbed my wallet and keys, threw on my boots, and headed toward my piece-of-shit truck.

I knew exactly where I was going because it was where I planned on going every night until I forgot about Caroline Hunt.

CHAPTER THREE

My truck started, but barely, and I tore out of our driveway not bothering with my seatbelt, kicking up dust and rocks as my tires spun against the loose gravel. I'd replaced my stereo because I couldn't stand radio, at least not Kalispell radio, and plugged my phone into the audio cable. Bastille's "Dreams" remake blasted and I turned it up, letting the painful lyrics wash over me, fueling my desire to get plastered as quickly as possible.

I entertained myself with thoughts of strangling Spencer Blackwell with both hands then beating the shit out of him with my fists. *Fucking bastard.* I pulled into the local pub and put my piece into park before tucking my left foot onto the emergency brake.

I disconnected my phone and the stereo went silent, reminding me of how alone I really was. I turned the engine off and absolute silence surrounded me. I couldn't take it. My door creaked with age as it swung open and I slammed it shut, unable not to. The fury raging in my blood was more than I could contain.

Before heading inside, my hand went to the empty space between the cab and the bed and searched for the bottle of whiskey I always had wedged in between. I took a large swig, not wanting to spend too much of my savings on the liquor inside the crap establishment. After all, I was going to need it. Revenge was a costly business.

I took one more swig for good measure and wedged it back in its usual place then wiped my mouth on the back of my sleeve. My hair swung in my eyes. It was still a little wet from my shower, and I thought about tying it back with the extra leather tie I usually kept in my glove compartment but thought better of it. It helped me hide, and I wanted to hide.

I looked around me. The lot was full, but I only recognized a few cars this time, which was good because I had no intention of making conversation. Regardless, most of Kalispell had stopped trying because I'd rarely done any responding since Cricket cut out my fucking heart and ate it raw. The hair was only insurance.

I took two deep draws of air, gulping it down, desperate for it to soothe me but, of course, it didn't. I let each escape my lips in shaky breaths and clenched my fists over and over before deciding to head inside.

My boots crunched the gravel beneath my feet as I headed toward the door. When I entered, I ducked my head toward the floor and let my hair cover me, not that it did any good other than to conceal me. I could still feel the heat of their stares, though, still feel the pity in their gazes. I wanted so badly to yell at them to fuck off, but I kept as much composure as possible. I couldn't get kicked out of the only real bar in Kalispell.

I picked a stool at the end of the bar, the same stool I always did—in the corner and in the back because it was dark. I sat and met Vi's eyes. She sauntered over to me, placing her elbows on the bar top, giving me a clear view of her generous chest. I held back my eye roll.

"Hello, darlin'," she drawled. "You look like shit."

"The usual, Vi," I told her as quietly as I could.

"How 'bout a kiss first?" she asked, leaning in a bit more.

"Christ, Vi, how many times? Huh? Just get me the gosh damn drink."

She laughed. "Already worked up, I see. I like it," she said, winking.

Vi, or Violet, was thirty-nine years old, had lived in Kalispell her entire life, and had worked as a bartender for more than fifteen years. I could tell at one time Vi had been a beautiful woman, but I could also tell she had heard many hollow promises from equally hollow men and that she obviously believed them all. Otherwise, why would she still be there? I watched her tired eyes and her slightly too-forced smile. She had the look of someone who used to be chased but had graduated to the chaser. She looked miserable.

She left and returned with an empty glass and a bottle of Jack. She set the glass on the bar and filled it to the brim. She was being generous. She was always this way. She told me once she hoped I would drink it all away and decide to take her up on her offer. I told her that would be a cold day in hell, to which she only laughed.

"Drink up, buttercup," she said, smiling lasciviously.

"I will," I told the bar top.

I watched the world around me through the breaks in the hanging strands and six glasses later, I was starting to feel numb. I lifted my head a little, feeling slightly relieved, feeling like I could breathe a little deeper now that the ache wasn't so severe. I continued to search the crowd, not knowing who I was looking for.

A quiet but persistent nagging awareness took residence in my chest for some unknown reason as I watched a girl dance on her own in the middle of the dance floor. Others around her paid no attention to her, but she was the first person my eyes were drawn to. I studied her.

Her hair was tucked into a blue scarf, little tendrils peeking through and grazing across her neck whenever she moved. She was extraordinarily tall and her hips and rear end were more indulgent than I'd ever considered. She turned, giving me her silhouette. Her stomach was flat and her breasts were full. She was beautiful, I could tell, even if I couldn't see her fully through the low lights.

"Jeez," I said, swiping a hand down my face. "I've had too much."

But I still couldn't stop watching her. She wore worn jean cutoffs, a fitted button-up with the sleeves rolled up her forearms, and ankle boots. She rolled her shoulders playfully, enticing someone she knew just off the dance floor. Another girl joined her side and they did the robot. She threw her head back and laughed.

This shocked me almost sober. "That laugh," I whispered to myself. "That laugh," I repeated. I knew it but couldn't quite place it.

She took her friend's hand and twirled her around the floor. She was so full of life. So my exact opposite.

She skipped in place and raised an arm in salute to her friend before turning toward me.

That's when I got a good, clear look at her. I gasped and placed my hand on the back of my head, my elbow on the bar top, ducking my head down lower to hide myself further.

Please, please, please do not recognize me, I thought, still watching her from the corner of my eye.

She stood two seats down from me. "Vi!" she said, laughing a little. "Vi!"

Vi turned toward her. "Hey, baby! What'll it be?"

"Can I have a water, please?" she asked, sitting down and releasing a breath of exhaustion. She continued to smile, and it ate a little at my gut.

"Of course," Vi answered and started to pour water into a clear plastic cup. Vi's eyes pinched a little. "Hey?" she said.

"Yeah?" she asked.

"How come I never see you drink anything harder?"

Her face fell a little but picked right back up. No one would have noticed it but me. "I've never had good luck with alcohol," she admitted a bit sadly.

Vi was quick enough to recognize something there that didn't want to be said and let it go with a nod, handing over the water without another word.

"Vi!" someone else called out, and she walked their direction.

The girl took a long drink from her water and set it down, turning toward the crowd and surveying the dancers. A small smile tugged at the corner of her mouth, some private joke she shared with herself.

I looked on her for a long time. Long enough for my heart to calm itself. Long enough to struggle with myself in an internal argument. Finally, I decided I wasn't watching her because I found her attractive, though I knew she was. Only that I was wondering what she was doing there.

She turned around in her seat after catching her breath and glanced at me. For a moment I believed she didn't recognize me, but I was wrong. A second scan confirmed it for her. She leaned in and narrowed her eyes. *Shit.*

"*Ethan?*" she asked. "Is that *you?*"

"Hello, Finley," I answered.

"How are you?" she asked, somehow devoid of the pity I'd often heard in so many greetings since Cricket. I was grateful to her for this.

"I'm fine," I slurred, lifting my head a bit to meet her eyes.

A grin met her lips. "You were always a terrible liar." Her smile fell a little. "What are you doing here?"

"I'm drinking."

She narrowed her eyes. "You hate drinking."

"I learned to love it," I said, downing the remaining contents of my glass, letting it burn.

She looked me up and down, making me feel self-conscious. "But apparently it doesn't love you."

"Thanks," I snorted, acting like I didn't care. But I did.

"You look terrible," she said, ignoring me. "Are you even eating?"

"I'm consuming the daily recommended calorie intake," I hedged.

"Ah," she answered, examining my empty glass. I shook my head and signaled to Vi for another.

Finley narrowed her eyes once more. "Can I get a basket of chicken tenders too, Vi?" she added.

"Sure thing," she said, ringing up Finley's food before grabbing the bottle of Jack and filling me to the top.

Finley examined my glass but didn't say a word.

"What?" I asked, feeling defensive.

"Nothing," she answered, looking at her hands. "Judging me?"

"Not at all," she said and looked me dead in the eye.
This look froze me, and the glass slipped from my fingers and back onto the bar top, spilling a little from the rim.

"I've done that very thing," she said, gesturing toward my glass.

"Drink 'til you're numb?"

"No," she said, "succumb to a vice in order to forget."

I leaned forward, stunned by this admission, and my eyes found hers. "What, Finley?"

She hesitated, started to open her mouth, but someone called her name and she turned around. It was an ex-classmate of ours, couldn't remember her name, the one she'd been dancing with, and I found myself feeling anxious all of a sudden. I hadn't felt anxious in a long time. Hadn't felt anything, really, other than severe pain and shame, in a very long time. *Huh.*

"Finley, Chris is gonna give me a ride back home. You cool?" the girl asked, eyeing me. She knew. The whole town knew about my tumble down the rabbit hole.

"Yeah, Holly Raye. I'll see you tomorrow," she answered, her brows scrunched in confusion. Finley was surprised by Holly Raye's apparent worry which I found odd.

"Okay," Holly Raye said, kissing Finley's cheek. Chris was waiting by the door for her, and we both watched them leave, afraid to speak, our earlier moment gone.

Vi walked up with Finley's chicken tenders and set them in front of her. Her fingers found one but lifted up quickly with a tiny gasp.

"Hot," she whispered, resting her fingers against the side of her water glass.

She let them cool for a few moments and we sat in awkward silence. I wasn't sure what she was still doing there. I didn't have any clue why she had even started to talk to me either. I mean, I knew in high school she'd had a crush on me, but I figured it was long gone. She used to stare at me a little doe eyed, and I had always done my best to be kind to her but not too kind. I'd considered her a friend but nothing more, even if I did take solace in my conversations with her. I'd never admitted that to anyone then, though, not that I was ashamed or anything. It's just, I was in love with Cricket.

Cricket.

The ache in my chest burned deep, a restless reminder of all I'd lost. And suddenly I felt guilty for finding Finley attractive even when I thought she was a stranger. Even after Cricket left me for Spencer.

"You should probably leave," I told her.

She looked at me like I was crazy. "I'll do whatever I want," she said, sitting taller, pitching me that confident Finley attitude I remembered from high school.

"Whatever," I said, then called out to Vi for another round, which she served up quickly.
Finley tore apart a few tenders then handed me half of one.

"Uh, no," I said, downing my glass.

"Uh, yes," she mocked, shoving the piece in my face.

"Stop," I said, swiping it away.

"Eat, damn it," she said.

I looked at her and the expression on her face told me she wouldn't quit, so I roughly took it from her and took a large bite. She bit into her own piece, a smug look on her face. She practically hand fed me every piece in the damn basket, but I didn't care. I knew what she was doing, but it wouldn't work because the liquor resting in my belly was too substantial to be worked against.

"What have you done with your summer?" she asked me.

"This," I said, gesturing to my glass.

"What the hell, Ethan?"

"What, are you my mother?" I asked, immediately regretting those choice of words. I closed my eyes.

Mom. My heart dropped into my throat. *Must remedy that.*

"Vi," I said loudly to her at the other end of the bar. "One more."
Vi walked the length of the bar and filled my glass again, much to Finley's obvious horror.

"Vi, can I get some mozzarella sticks?" she asked.

"Of course, darlin'."
Finley smiled at me.

"I'm not eating those," I told her.

"Oh, you'll eat them."

"I won't."

"You will."

"I sure as hell will not, Finley Dyer."

She leaned closer and my head began to swim. Her signature scent of apples and wild daisies swarmed around me, making my heart race. It'd never bothered me before. *It's the liquor*, I told myself.

"You will or I'm taking your ass home right now."

"You can just kiss that ass, Fin."

"That's the Jack talking."

"No, that's me. I don't want to play anymore. I want to be left alone now."

"You see," she said, settling her elbows on the bar top, "I think— No, I *know* you're lying. Like I said before, you're a terrible liar. I think you've lied so often about wanting to be left alone, though, that you've convinced your head it's the truth, but you can't convince the heart, Ethan. You know why? Because the heart can't ever be lied to, and yours beats the loneliest I've ever heard."

I didn't answer her. *Couldn't* answer her.

"What have you done this summer?" I asked, ignoring her spot-on observation.

She played along. "I've had a temp job here in Kalispell answering phones for Smith Travel, trying to earn cash for my trip."

My brows furrowed. "What trip?"

"I'm heading over to Vietnam for a year."

This shocked me. "What in the world would you go to Vietnam for?"

"Charity work," she answered, making me laugh.

"Why?" I asked.

"Don't be an asshole," she replied.

"No, really, why?"

"I've wanted to do this for close to five years now."

"How come I don't ever remember you talking about this at school?"

"Ethan," she said softly, "let's not pretend we ever really talked in high school deeper than filler conversation."

This wounded me a little, though I'm not sure why. "What the hell, Finley? You and I were friends."

Now it was her turn to laugh. "We were most definitely not friends. I may know everything about you and you may know everything about me because we grew up together, but we were not *friends*. You had a constant bodyguard in Cricket."

I sat up at the mention of her name. "Don't ever say her name again," I gritted.

She raised her hands in concession. "Fine." There was a pregnant pause as she let me calm myself down.

"I talked to you a lot in the classes we had," I offered.

"We talked a lot about the upcoming football games or class assignments. Once or twice, we took the seventy-year-old route and discussed the weather."

I fought my grin. "Okay, so it was always surface observation, but we were kids."

"No, Ethan, that's not what it was."

"Well, you were in love with me," I bravely spit. "I couldn't take it further than just below the shoal." *Thank you, Mr. Daniels.*

"Full of yourself, are we?" she asked. "Listen," she continued, "I had a crush on you in high school. So what? Lots of girls did. But I was, *am*, a human being. You didn't have to treat me like some leper. Trust me, Ethan, we all know who you belonged to," she said.

She stood to leave, but I grabbed her arm. The heated warmth of her skin shot straight to my heart. We looked at one another, wide eyed, our chests panting. I shook my head to recompose myself. "I'm sorry," I told her, encouraging her to sit back down. "I'm— I know you deserved better."

She hesitated but sat back in her seat. I stared at her, a little too intently thanks to the Jack. She nodded once and we sat in a comfortable silence as I had five more shots.

The whiskey made my body heavy as hell, the weight of its honeyed venom deadened the ache inside me.

I sighed and smiled to myself.

"What's so funny?" she asked.

I looked up at her though it felt unusually burdensome and leaned toward her. "I'm going to get them back," I admitted to her.

She narrowed her eyes. "*Who*, Ethan?"

30

"*Them*," I said, bringing a tired finger to my lips. "Don't tell anyone."
I fell back into my chair. I brought my fingers to my empty glass and tilted it, balancing it on one finger. She was quiet for a moment.

"Ethan," she began, whispering, "that's not like you."

I smiled. "I'm not who I used to be, Finley."

"That's a shame," she said, "because you used to be wonderful."

I narrowed my eyes at her. "Do you *know* what they did to me?"

"She left you for him," she said matter-of-factly.

I let the glass tip over onto its side at her bluntness. "Exactly. After all I did for her. After all I was to her. *She* left *me* for *him*."

"She wasn't meant for you, Ethan."

My skin burned with hatred at that statement. "No one is meant for anyone, Finley. You choose someone and then you make a commitment."

She shook her head at me. "You have no idea what you're talking about."

"She chose me, convinced me that she was all in, and I was willing to die for her because of it. She convinced me she actually loved me. I thought she *loved me*."

"She did love you. I believe she, you both really, would have been somewhat happy if Spencer had never shown up."

"Exactly."

"You're not hearing me. You both would have been *somewhat* happy. Neither of you would have been utterly happy."

This infuriated me. "I could have made her happy!" I yelled, earning a few glances from around the bar.

"Yes, you could have made her happy, but not as happy as Spencer does."

My blood simmered in my veins. "You are cruel," I bit.

She leaned forward. "I'm being honest with you. Someone has to since you're not being honest with yourself. I saw them together, Ethan, and she never looked at you like that."

"Stop," I said, gritting my teeth. "Stop."

"Ethan," she said, resting her hand on mine. I yanked it from her. "Don't you want the same thing for yourself? Don't you want forever with someone who burns for you the way you burn for her? You deserve that just as much as she does."

"Shut up," I said, bringing my hands to my hair and fisting it at my ears. I didn't want to hear it.

"Fine," she said, sitting up. She looked around her and asked Vi for two cups of coffee.

I couldn't breathe. Finley voiced everything I'd worked so hard to drown out, I'd attempted to numb. I hated her for ruining the struggle to suppress it. I just wanted to pretend. I wanted my hate, wanted it to live close to me. It was the only thing I felt could keep me alive. I couldn't let her go. I didn't want her to be loved by anyone but me. I didn't want to be reminded that someone else really did love her better than I did, that someone else made her happier. Because I had watched them too. I saw what Finley saw, and my God did I hate Spencer Blackwell for it.

I wanted bitter. I wanted sadness. I wanted my revenge.

When Vi brought the coffee, she set the cups down, one in front of me and one in front of Finley. My hands shook as I reached across the bar and lifted the bottle of Jack. Vi saw me and nodded. Slowly, I unscrewed the lid and poured some into the cup.

Finley pursed her lips and shook her head. I replaced the cap and set it back but I was so drunk, I slipped and spilled the coffee, emptying its entire boiling contents down my shirt and jeans. The heat scalded. I gritted my teeth and closed my eyes, taking the pain, wanting the pain.

Finley and Vi moved as if in slow motion around me, pulling me up from my seat and asking me if I was okay. I swayed on my feet as I let them do whatever they wanted, not paying any attention to them. I was on the verge of screaming, wanting to yell at the world. I wanted them to suffer as I was. I wanted them done. I wanted them to *suffer*. I wanted atonement.

My eyes burned and I gnashed my teeth. I heard rather than anticipated the groaning air that left my chest. My hands shook as I tried to steady myself on the edge of the bar, but I misjudged the distance and fell forward. I felt them try to hold me up, but I was too heavy for them. My face met the lip. A sharp ache filled my head and face and I nearly vomited from the pain. My stomach didn't have room for the liquor *and* all the hurt.

The hurt. Everything seemed uneasy, seemed to suffer. I laid on the floor, in and out of consciousness but holding steady to the discomfort, to the disquiet, to the agony.

Much to my dismay, a pair of cool hands found my face. Suddenly, the tortured pressure left my body in one swift sigh.

"Finally," I exhaled as I drifted toward the black.

CHAPTER FOUR

I woke to the soft sound of breathing that wasn't mine. The room was dark but there was enough light from the crack in the door, creating a soft glow over the walls, enough to make out my surroundings. I felt a warm body next to mine and my heart started to race. I studied my environment, not able to recognize the room I was in. I started to panic.

Get it together, Ethan, I told myself and glanced to my left. It was a thin girl, covered in a comforter. I turned my head a bit to get a better look, trying to see her hair, but I wasn't able to see anything. I wondered if I would be able to leave her bed without her noticing but ruled that out since it was wedged right up against the wall and I would have had to go over her to get out.

I warily sat up, my head swimming from all the liquor. I nearly groaned from the pain as I brought a hand to my face. I winced, pulling my hand back quickly. I'd forgotten about my fall at the bar. I laid back down, my stomach threatening to bring everything back up, and when I did this, wild daisies and apples assailed my senses.

I breathed a sigh of relief. *It's only Finley*. I breathed a little deeper and closed my eyes. I felt the bed move and cracked one lid open. She'd shifted around, facing me, the blanket covering her, exposing her face, and her hair spilled around her pillow. She looked angelic.

Her hand came up and scratched the tip of her nose, but she stayed asleep. Then her hand fell on top of mine and for some reason, my heart rate slowed down and my eyes became sleepy once more. Before I knew it, I was asleep again.

I woke a second time in Finley's room, but this time the room was flooded with light. My face rested against the wall, so I stretched and turned over face to face with Finley about a foot apart. She was still asleep but her makeup was gone, revealing how porcelain her skin really was. Her tawny strands fell across her cheek, ran down her neck, and gathered on the bed, like a coppery river. Her lips were parted. She was undeniably beautiful, even I could admit it. It was the strangest feeling admitting that to myself.

I'd always thought her beautiful, but I was faithful to Cricket and wouldn't let my thoughts trail any further. I reached out and pulled at a strand that had fallen over her eye and tucked it with the rest of her rivulets of hair. She had a wild look about her.

I compared her to Cricket.

Cricket was always polished, her hair perfectly in place and her clothes stylish and refined. She was very well put together and she *never* deviated from it, not even when in the fields.

If I were being honest, it was disconcerting since I was the exact opposite. I've never cared about my appearance. In fact, I'd consider myself the disheveled sort. I didn't even own an iron, let alone a tie. All my jeans had shredded knees. All my undershirts were waffle-knit. All my overshirts were plaid and button-up. None of them were anything but faded. My boots were dusty and my hair was long. I was Cricket's opposite.

My eyes narrowed on Finley.

Finley was more like myself, much more down to earth, much more provincial. This wasn't to say she wasn't intelligent because, from what I could remember, Finley was often the sharpest in my classes.

She had long, wavy hair always pinned half up or full down in charmingly hot disarray, with wisps of hair constantly around her face. Her bright blue eyes were occasionally covered with Holly-esque frames. Her clothes were vintage, probably thanks to a limited budget, and I remembered her frequenting thrift stores a great deal. I thought she still did. She layered unusual pieces together a lot too, wore a lot of odd jewelry. She pulled it together pretty well. You could probably pluck her up out of Kalispell and drop her in New York City or London and she'd fit right in. The only thing that wouldn't have jibed were her bare feet. She was obsessed with bare feet. On more than one occasion, even in high school, I remember her getting sent home from school for not wearing shoes.

I looked back on my memories of her and couldn't remember a time I felt more relaxed. That's what Finley did for me. She relaxed me. She claimed we weren't really friends, but I knew differently. Yeah, I was careful around Finley, but I did pay attention to her. I just never told her I did. I watched her probably more than I should have, probably more than I could have admitted to myself.

When I was with Cricket, I was constantly on edge, nervous about her medical condition. Toward the end, it was all we could talk about. Growing up, Finley was a mini-break from that tension because we talked about the obvious. So Finley may have thought we weren't friends, but our conversations about nothing helped keep me sane, and they meant more to me than she could have ever known.

"Finley," I began, but my hoarse voice broke. I cleared my throat. "Finley," I said deeply from sleep and rough use.

She opened one eye. The surprised look on her face priceless, and I almost laughed for the first time in many months. Except it wouldn't have been the first time, would it? She'd made me laugh at the bar. That shocking feeling sobered me, and I was never more determined to get out of there.

"Good morning," she said, remembering I was there. "Did you sleep all right?"

"I, um, I did," I answered self-consciously.

"Good," she said, sitting up and rubbing her eyes. "Come on," she ordered, throwing off the covers, standing, and stretching.
She wore a huge T-shirt and baggy flannel pajama pants and she looked ridiculous.

She must have seen the expression on my face because she looked down at herself then back up at me.

She narrowed her eyes. "Well, excuse me, Ethan Moonsong!" she ranted. "I'm not a silk pajama kinda gal, okay?" She stood straighter and smoothed the front of her shirt. "Besides, though this shirt may have been made for a robust two-hundred-pound man, it's still M83 and they rock socks, so can it!"

I raised my palms. "Fine."

"Good," she said, relaxing a bit. "Now," she continued, "breakfast. Come with me."

"Uh," I began, "that's cool. I need to get going."

She swirled around, her hair fanning around her. "Nope. Sorry, but I drove you here. Meaning, your truck is still at the bar and I'm not going anywhere without breakfast first."

I kicked my legs over the side of the bed and stood to my full six-foot three. Finley was tall at five-foot eight, but I still towered over her. I tried to intimidate her into taking me to my truck but it didn't work. She only gritted her jaw and set her hands on her hips. We stood there quietly, long enough for *me* to start getting uncomfortable, defeating my purpose.

"Whatever," I told her.

"Good," she said, smiling. "Besides, it's bacon, eggs, and French toast day! You won't want to miss this."

She turned on her heel quickly and bounded down the hall, no doubt expecting me to follow her. "Can it be bacon, eggs, and aspirin day?" I asked, holding my head and following her.

I had to duck my head under her door to get into the hall and her ceilings weren't that much higher. A few more inches and I'd have had to crouch everywhere we walked.

"How do you live here? I'd get claustrophobic."

"I don't have to drop it like it's hot or anything to walk around here, Lurch."

"*Okay.*"

"Sit," she ordered, gesturing to a light blue Formica dinette with chrome chairs.

"Is there anything in here *not* fifty years old?" I asked, examining my surroundings. Apparently she shopped for furniture at the same place she shopped for clothing.

"You gotta problem with my independence, Moonsong?" she said, placing a cast-iron skillet on her enamel stove.

"No."

"I'm an independent woman."

"True," I said, secretly proud of the girl she'd become. Finley had always been poor from what I could remember, but she knew how to work with it.

"Question!" she began, shifting her rear from side to side, which looked ludicrous in her pajamas. "*Tell me what you think about me. I buy my own diamonds and I buy my own rings. Only ring your celly when I'm feelin' lonely.*"

"What?" I asked her, confused.

She turned toward me and rolled her eyes. "Never mind."

"So, uh," I began, "did you say something about leaving Kalispell last night?"

She turned from her task and got a thing of butter from her fridge before returning to the pan. "Yeah, I'm leaving in a few weeks."

"Where are you going?"

"Vietnam."

I was taken aback. "*What?*"

She looked at me with a large smile plastered across her face. "Vietnam. It's an Asian country, full of sweet people, south of China, east of Laos and Cambodia? We went to war there? Ringing any bells?"

"I know Vietnam, Finley. I want to know *why* Vietnam?"

"I'll be doing some charity there. I told you." She went back to flipping the bread on her skillet and the smell of vanilla and nutmeg filled the kitchen. "Get the OJ out, will you?" she asked, gesturing to her fridge.

I stood and did I was told, setting it on the table. I started opening her top cabinets, looking for her juice glasses. "Why?" I asked.

"Because it's delicious and made from oranges and I have to have it in the morning even though it gives me acid reflux like a mother."

"No, why leave to do charity work?"

Her face paled a little. "It's just a place I feel drawn to."

I studied her but her face gave nothing else away. "Cool. That's really cool of you," I told her.

She looked at me and gave me a small smile, letting her armor down a little. "Thanks."

She placed the last piece of bread on her pile and set the plate in the oven before moving on to the bacon and eggs. The smell started to make me feel ill so I grabbed my glass, filled it with cold tap water, and downed it. The fact that I even felt the slightest bit nauseated was a testament to how much I'd had to drink the night before. I knew if I wanted to function at all that day I'd need to eat.

I sat down when Finley pointed to the chair I'd previously sat in. "So," she said, placing a plate of food in front of me.

"Thank you," I told her.

"You're welcome," she responded. She took a deep breath. "So talk to me, Ethan."

I furrowed my brows and swallowed a bite of bacon, staring at my plate. "Nothing to tell."

She pursed her lips and shook her head. "You're lying."

I sighed. "I don't want to talk, Finley."

"Fine. Then I will. Yesterday, I woke up, oh, I don't know, around seven-ish? I ate breakfast, showered, and all that jazz. My hair was doing this wonky thing so I wrapped it in a blue scarf. It looks fabulous today though, right?" She paused for my response, but I didn't give one. "Anyway, I think it does. Where was I? Oh yes, I got dressed and headed over to Smith's to answer the phones. No one called, by the way. And do you want to know why?"

"Why?" I asked, delving into the French toast, which tasted unbelievable.

"Because no one in Kalispell has enough money to travel, dude, that's why."

"How do they stay in business then?"

"It's a mystery, man. A flipping mystery." She took another bite, chewed and swallowed. "Then I collected my check, deposited it, and ran some errands, went grocery shopping, picked up my mail."

"This is all very fascinating, Finley."

"Isn't it?" she asked sarcastically and continued. "I ran into Helen Green on the way to pick up my dry cleaning. Have you spoken to her lately?"

"No, I haven't."

"She told me that her dog had to be put down a few days ago for cancer. Poor thing. She was so heartbroken. I couldn't leave her there in front of the Sip-n-Stop all alone. So I sat next to her as she told me about all the good her dear little Jakie did for her over the years. How he'd fetch her paper and all sorts of

42

things from her room for her. She'd just call out what she wanted and Jake would get it for her. Can you believe that?"

"No."

"Neither could I, but I suppose anything's possible. Let's see. What next? Oh! I haven't catalogued what I had to eat!"

"Enough," I said, setting down my fork. "Fine." A smile so wide formed on her mouth, I could count her teeth. She settled in her seat.

"I'm miserable, Finley."

Her smile fell and she nodded her head in understanding. "I know, Ethan," she said softly.

"And I don't know what to do about it. I'm so angry. So, so angry." I sat back in my chair and stared out her window. "I want to hunt Spencer Blackwell down and do something, something awful to him."

"Ethan, that's just not healthy, dude. I mean, I know anger. I've felt anger, but I did something about it. I felt it taking over me and I decided to let it go. I can tell it's taking you, and you have to let it go."

I looked back at her. "I don't want to," I told her truthfully.

She shook her head. "You're just mourning her and can't deal is all."

"No," I said deadly seriously, "I don't think that's all. I think Spencer Blackwell is the shadiest asshole I've ever met, and I want him to pay for how he wronged me."

"Not any shadier than—"

"I told you," I interrupted, "I don't want to hear her name. Never say her name."

"Fine. It's crazy, but whatever."

It got quiet and we both stopped eating.

"I hate him," I whispered. "I hate what he's done to my life. I had held on to her so tightly, was willing to give her my kidney along with the heart I'd already given. I never thought in a million years that she would do that to me, and I don't think she would have, had it been anyone else. He did something to her. I don't know what it was, but he distracted her from what was real."

Finley sat back in her chair and folded her arms across her chest. "Jeez, Ethan." She sighed. "What did she tell you when you broke up?"
I was surprised by this question. No one had ever asked me about the circumstances surrounding what happened that day in the woods.

My mind went back to the camping trip, to her choosing him over me, to my promise to Spencer that I would get him back when he least expected it.

"She told me nothing," I explained. "She tried to appease me, attempted to let me down easily, but it felt like a cop-out and I wouldn't let her do it. She chose Spencer over me by running to him when I expected her to run to me, literally and figuratively. He stole her and I want my revenge."

"Damn it, Ethan, this is a ridiculous mentality! Life isn't fair. Life is far, *very, very* far from fair. Sometimes it slaps you so hard in the face you fall back, you hit the ground with a resounding thud, knocks the breath outta you, but it's how quickly you stand and fight for the life you want and how you forge that new path that defines you. Ethan," she said, resting her hand on mine, "nothing is so overwhelming, so dreadful, that it cannot be defeated."

"Even a love lost?" I asked in all sincerity,
watching the window again.
"Even *that* love lost."
A bird landed on the sill, its tiny head
robotically searching for food that wasn't there.
"You have no idea what you're talking about."

She stared at me hard, her jaw clenched. She leaned
closely to me to drive her point home.

"Trust me, Ethan Moonsong, I know anger. I've
lived anger, and I had *every* right to seek the revenge I
so badly wanted but hear this, *know* this, *revenge is a
slippery slope*. The eye for your eye never satisfies. You
may achieve your goal but the reward is never as
sweet as you imagined it."

I shut her out. I was unwilling to hear her
words of unburden, of relief. Only, one thing burned
me with curiosity. "And what do you know of anger?"

"Enough," she explained, avoiding eye contact.

I smiled. "It seems neither of us is willing to talk
about what we really want to hear the other has to
say."
She smiled back. "It's high school all over
again."

CHAPTER FIVE

Finley dropped me off at the bar after breakfast, and I waved goodbye as she drove away in her rickety navy blue VW Bug that reeked of oil. I watched her drive away and wondered if I would see her again before she left for Vietnam.

I found it so odd that she would choose Vietnam, not that I knew anything that even went on in Vietnam, but she was proving to be just as tight-lipped about her life as I was. It seemed we had that in common. I was curious, though, about her life, about her attitude about said life. Maybe it was because I considered her more an old friend than she thought me. Maybe it was because I was pathetic and was desperate to hold on to anything that could distract me from the chaotic crappy life that was my own.

I got in my truck and stuck the key in the ignition, ready to return home but was immediately struck frozen mid-crank when Spencer Blackwell's truck sped past me on Main.

My heart pounded, raced with adrenaline, and my palms started to sweat. I turned the key but my truck wouldn't start, and I began to panic.

"Come on, come on, come on," I begged her. I tried again and again to start her but she wouldn't turn. "Damn it!"

I paused, my hand resting on the key, and gritted my teeth. I cranked the key as hard as I could and felt the rush of relief when she turned over and the engine rumbled to life. Tearing out of the lot, I felt invigorated. I didn't have a plan, but I knew I needed to follow him.

I took a left onto Main and spotted him two blocks ahead sitting at a stop light. I sped up a bit so I wouldn't lose him but not so close that he could recognize me. That tingling rush adrenaline gives you tumbled through my veins, but there was a sick feeling in my gut I'd never felt, and I didn't recognize the source. I chalked it up to the drinking and hitting my head from the night before and ignored the sinking feeling it was something else. Instead, I focused on keeping him in sight.

He approached the light at Third and came to a stop, turning on his blinker to turn left. I drove past him but kept him in my rearview then took a left at the next street and another then came to a stop right before Third so I could watch him. His light turned green and I thought he'd turn left but he made a U-turn instead, and that's when I knew exactly where he was going. Ceres Bakery. I took a deep, shaky breath. And I also knew who he was with. Because it was her favorite.

I took a left then a right to get back onto Main, drove past his truck and parked in front of the flower shop she and I intended to hire for our wedding a few stores down. My hands shook on the steering wheel as I contemplated my next move. All sorts of awful, strangely appealing scenarios ran through my head, which scared me.

The truck door slammed closed behind me as I reached for my hidden bottle, unscrewed the lid, and took a swig. It burned on its way down, alleviating that sick feeling in my stomach, albeit temporarily.

Slowly, ever so slowly, I walked toward the bakery. I kept as close to the storefronts as possible. When I reached Ceres, I stopped and leaned against the brick beside the window, knowing they couldn't see me. Carefully, I peered into the window and saw them. Their backs faced me as they ordered at the counter.

"My God," I breathed.

There she was. It was the first time I'd seen either of them since the day in the forest when she chose him over me. It felt so surreal to me. Her hair had grown out a little and she'd gained weight, probably since the transplant went so well. I looked at Spencer. I bet the bastard was her hero. I couldn't help but think I could have just as easily been him. I could have been standing next to her in line at Ceres, waiting for our sweet potato sticky buns, laughing and feeling happy because I was with her.

I thought about what Finley told me earlier that morning. I thought she was wrong. Cricket would have been just as happy with me as she was with Spencer.

I studied them together. She bounced on her heels, talking animatedly, her hair swishing around her shoulders. She used her hands a lot when she spoke. I wondered what she was talking about. I wondered if she thought about me at all, if she gave a shit that she broke my heart, shattered it into a million pieces. She smiled at Spencer and they started laughing.

Apparently not.

God, I hated him. I mean really hated the guy. I looked back at my truck and remembered that I kept my hunting knives in the glove compartment in case my mom's brother Akule, the only one willing to talk to me on her side of the family, wanted to go hunting. He gave them to me for my eleventh birthday. They were beautiful. Two Spartan short swords with leather handles, and I knew what I was doing with them.

Akule is Echo River Indian, as was my mother. She left the tribe when she converted to Catholicism right out of high school, and they didn't approve but Akule was young when she did and he was close to my mom, so he didn't care. He would sneak into town and they would watch movies together at her apartment.

He taught me how to hunt with my hands in Echo River style from a young age but when my mom died, he made it a weekly trip to the mountains. We would spend entire weekends up there up until I turned nineteen and Cricket got really sick.

I looked back at Cricket. She brought her hand up to Spencer's back. He followed suit and tucked his hand into her back pocket, incensing me. Immediately, I walked to my truck and opened the passenger side door. The knives sat in their sheaths in the glove box. I hadn't touched them in months, and my hands itched to hold them again.

I reached for them but paused a few inches from the handles. My hands shook and my heart pounded.

"*What are you doing?*" I asked myself.

I shut the glove box and sat on the bench of my truck, my booted foot resting on the concrete below. I ran my hands through my hair and rested against the back of the seat, shocked I'd been even contemplating what I'd been pondering.

"What were you going to do?" I asked myself. "*Murder* him?"

I felt sick to my stomach I had indeed thought about just that.

"Mom, help me?" I asked the ceiling. "I'm suffering for her and it's literally driving me insane. Please help me figure out how to get over her."

Just then, Ceres' bell above the door rang out and I shoved my foot inside and shut the door. I didn't have time to start the truck, so I laid flat against the seat, hoping they wouldn't be able to see me. I sat up a bit and looked through the side mirrors, my chest pumping oxygen in and out at a furious pace.

They started walking the opposite direction toward the music store. I wasn't going to sit around and wait for them to stumble upon me, so I slid over to the driver's side and started the truck in one turn. I sped out of there, watching them all the time through my rearview.

I needed to sort myself out before I did something stupid, before my hate took over and stupidity started to sound even better to me than it did at that moment. Finley, of course, was right.

CHAPTER SIX

I decided that night I no longer cared to get myself under control. I decided I wanted a drink instead.

"Vi, one more?"

"Sure, darlin'."

I nodded when she set down the glass and walked toward another customer.

"I'm surprised you're in here again," I heard over my shoulder, and I tensed.

"What are *you* doing here?" I asked Finley.

"Lookin' for your dumb ass."

"Why?" I asked as she sat down beside me.

"Oh, I don't know, maybe because I'm an idiot? Maybe because I'm bored?" She sighed. "I don't know."

The bell above the door rang out and we both turned to see Spencer Blackwell and Cricket Hunt walk in holding hands as if they didn't have a care in the world.

I narrowed my eyes and tried to steady my breathing. "What the *fuck* are they doing here?" I asked no one.

My eyes locked in on them as they moved to the opposite side of the large room. They had no idea I was there. They sat together, totally unaware that their mere existence in that moment bruised me more brutally than I'd felt in a long time. I studied Caroline, the palm of my hand absently rubbing at the knot in the center of my chest. *My Caroline.* She had no idea just how much she'd worn me out since we'd broken up, worn my body and my soul. I felt too heavy to carry around since she'd gone from me. Far too heavy. She'd been unintentionally cruel, but cruel nonetheless. So I swallowed back the lump in my throat, a lump she'd put there with our childhood memories, our laughs, our love. The ache. The awful ache she caused me.

I continued to watch her. She was laughing, so happy, and very much in the moment with him. And that's when I saw it. Saw what Finley and everyone else saw. She had *never* looked at me the way she was looking at him, and I was suddenly sick with jealousy and a terrible, terrible hatred. His hand wrapped around the back of her neck and I snapped. My hands trembled on the surface of my glass and I breathed from my nose in seething anger.

Finley whipped her head my direction, her eyes wide. "Let's go," she pleaded.

"Get out of here," I ordered her.

"No," she whispered, placing her hand on my own.

I peered into her eyes. "Just. Go."

I stood up and threaded my way through the bodies. There was nothing planned, no finite idea, but I knew I wanted to get to my truck, the passenger side, the *glove box*. I shoved through the bar door and into the summer night, my blood pumping through my veins. My truck was parked in the space closest to the street, and each footstep it took to get me there felt like an eternity. I clomped through the gravel lot and threw open the passenger door. I'd forgotten that the glove box had been locked. My hand found my pocket to dig out my keys but they were stuck at odd angles, making it difficult or maybe it was that I was too drunk to remove them with any kind of finesse. This made me pause, but my body couldn't catch up with the thought and I pitched forward, my hand clumsily finding the edge of the roof of the cab. I swayed and the memory of his hand on her neck renewed my fury.

"I told you you'd feel my wrath, Spencer Blackwell," I spoke to no one. "And I never break a promise."

I took a deep breath as my fingers found their purchase and pulled out my keys. The key I needed somehow hit home and the lid sprang open, the knives staring at me, daring me. I watched them, waited for them to tell me what to do, but nothing came. They laid still, gleaming in the moonlight waiting for me too, it seemed. I sat in the passenger side seat, one boot still on the gravel, and made the first move. Raising a trembling hand toward the temptation, my fingers felt the cool length of each blade.

The rage still burned in my veins and I felt myself sobering, hesitating. *No*, I kept hearing. *Pick them up*, a voice said, so I did. Their weight felt good in my hands, comfortable. I breathed three breaths before gripping their handles and twirling them quickly in my palms. Even drunk, I could slaughter anything that moved. I was made to hunt. *And hunt you shall*, the voice urged.

I nodded and stood, shutting the passenger side door, tucking the blades into the back of my jeans, and camouflaging them with my shirt. My boots echoed with each step back toward the bar, heavy and dark like the night that surrounded me, like the thoughts in my head.

The adrenaline seared through my body, heightening every nerve, intensifying every sense. My heart pounded like a bass drum in my chest, pressing painfully against my ribs. My skin burned with anticipation.

I reached for the door handle.

"Where do you think you're going?" a voice whispered, startling me.

I stopped, one hand on the handle. "Finley, go home," I ordered her.

She stood from her leaning position against the outside wall of the bar, out of the shadows, and walked toward me. Her eyes seared through me. She came to me, stood closely, the heat from her body enveloping me.

"No, I don't think I will," she told me, looking up into my eyes. "At least not alone."

She stood tenaciously, fearlessly. I noted how much taller she was than Cricket and it was a little bit intimidating to me, like what she said was going to happen whether or not I liked it. I respected her and I didn't know why. I stared at her hard, but she didn't budge. No, instead, she strengthened her own resolve, her jaw tightening with the decision and glared back even harder. She said and did things with such righteous authority, I felt powerless to her. I'd never felt that way before about a woman. It wasn't pushy or irrational, it was simply as it was going to be.

My eyes and face relaxed the moment I acquiesced. "Fine."

Her body followed suit and she nodded once, grabbing my arm and leading me toward my truck. Her hand reached into my jeans pocket, sending an inexplicable electrical charge through me, which I promptly chose to ignore, and yanked out my keys.

"Get in," she ordered and I obeyed.

She threw herself into the driver's side and slammed the door shut, sticking the keys in the ignition and turning only once. The engine started, daring not to further goad her. The stereo kicked on, belting something indicative of the moment we were leaving behind us, full of bass and a sharpness so edgy it echoed through my chest and head.

She shoved the truck in reverse, throwing her arm over the back of the bench, and her stare found mine. It was a solid look, packed full with a storm of unspoken words. Without breaking her gaze, she shifted into drive. She held there for a moment, driving her disappointment in me deep down into my soul before finally looking ahead to the end of the parking lot. *I know I'm toxic, Finley*, I thought, but that didn't stop my mouth from retching awful thoughts.

"You have no reason to be pissed at me," I told her, practically begging her to speak.

She didn't say a word as she pulled out onto the road with more punch than the Finley I knew normally would have, turning toward the interstate. I had no clue where she was taking us, but I wasn't about to ask.

Just make her turn around, I thought. *Tell her you won't do anything.*

I opened my mouth to speak but caught a glimpse of her hair whipping about her determined face from the open windows and forgot what I was going to say. I turned my gaze toward the windshield. The light from the headlights exposing just enough of the road to make me nervous at the speed we were traveling. One hand found the dash to steady myself.

"What's wrong, Ethan?" she asked.

"Huh?" I asked, whipping my head her direction.

"Too fast for you?"

"No."

"Liar," she said, calling me out.

I wiped my palms down the thighs of my jeans. "Slow down," I said, swallowing.

"Oh, now you want to play it safe?" Her eyes narrowed. "You're so selfish, you know that?" she asked. I was taken aback. She'd never talked to me like that.

She leisurely drove across lanes as if traveling more than a hundred miles per hour was completely normal.

"What?" I demanded, feeling alert. The adrenaline had sobered me quickly.

"You're selfish. And stupid. Let's not forget stupid."

My blood boiled. "Whatever, Finley."

"Whatever, Finley," she mocked. "Don't you know I'm suffering? That I'm the only person in the world who suffers? Can't you see that I'm determined to be foolish, Finley?"

"What do you know of suffering?" I asked, incensed.

Wide eyes met mine and her jaw clenched as she pulled over, slamming us to a stop. Her hair flew forward from the force before settling onto her chest and shoulders.

"I know more about suffering than you could ever possibly imagine. You don't know shit! So you got your heart broken. So what! There are worse things, you know. There are things out there that would curl your toes to know about, Ethan."

She stopped, breathed deeply. Her hands white-knuckled the steering wheel as she watched me.

"What- what things?" I asked sincerely.

"I can't say. I *won't* say."

I swallowed.

A few moments passed in silence and her eyes softened. "A broken heart is terrible, Ethan. I know it's terrible, but it's also a part of being human. You're allowed to be tossed about in love sometimes. It sucks but it's not the end of the freaking world. It's not worth a *homicide* conviction."

My jaw clenched at her presumption. "What do you know of a broken heart? Who has ever loved you?" Her hands fell to her lap in a dull thud at my words. Her mouth gaped open in a painful expression, and I immediately felt like such an awful douchebag. I reached for her. "I'm sorry, Finley. I just meant that..."

"I know what you meant," she said quietly, raising her hand to fend me off.

She brought her hands up to the wheel once more and turned on the blinker before heading back out onto the highway.

I knew Finley had been abandoned by her parents. I knew this but I was so absorbed in myself I'd forgotten to think about that before I spoke. Now that I was feeling much more aware of myself, I wanted, no, needed to thank her for saving me from doing something unforgivable. I didn't know where this awful side of me was coming from. The fact that I was no longer living in the fantasy of revenge was more than a little horrifying.

"Finley, I—"

"No more, Ethan. Just, just no more."

I nodded, feeling horrible for what I'd said to her.

We continued on in silence for close to an hour and I figured out where she was headed. Doris Lake. It was her favorite place. Everyone knew if you couldn't find Finley Dyer, it was probably because she was at Doris Lake. It was a sort of haven to her for some reason none of us could figure out.

She took a right on Doris Creek Road and within a few minutes, we were near the trails. She parked and removed the keys from the ignition.

The quiet was deafening but I dared not open my mouth. We both needed that silence, that was obvious.

I was the first to open my door so I slowly walked to hers and opened it for her, reaching out my hand to help her. Her eyes met mine. The few seconds it took her to decide whether she wanted my hand was excruciating.

We were at an impasse.

This is where she decided whether we were to continue this odd friendship of ours.

When she took my hand, I released the breath I'd been holding and simultaneously discovered that I was relying on her more than I dared admit to myself.

I helped her from the truck and closed her door for her, and my heart beat a little bit faster in relief of her choice. I followed her quietly in the moonlight through the trail to Doris Lake, a trail she so obviously knew like the back of her hand. About a mile in, we passed Blow Lake, the little stone bridge amongst the trail as well and in another mile and a half, we'd arrived at Doris.

We'd walked briskly and in silence, so I was surprised when she turned toward me at the water's edge. A single tear fell down her face that reflected in the moonlight. It surprised me how tender Finley could be yet how strong she was as well. She was a dichotomy of marvelous.

"I'm sorry, truly sorry," I told her in earnest.

She sucked in a ragged breath and nodded, then turned her head toward the stock-still surface of the water. The moon mirrored in its round face.

The lake was stunning. Surrounded by staggered mountain peaks, the back of the water was enveloped by a sharp ridge of rock that cascaded down the sides of the lake and peppered with fresh, emerald forest that rounded to the beaches and met us where we stood. The water was so clear even in the moonlight, we could not only see through to bottom of the shallows but also at its deepest in the center of the lake.

"I can see why you would come here as often as you do," I told her.

She turned her face toward mine once more. "Let me have them," she said.

"What?" I asked, confused.

"The knives." She swallowed. "Let me have them."

I closed my eyes briefly in shame and guilt before lifting the back of my shirt and sliding my blades out, then handing them over to her. She took them in her hands and examined them, running her fingers over the blades.

"They're warm," she told no one.

"They were laid against my skin."

She looked up at me sadly. "I know, Ethan." She laid one blade over the other and set them together on the bit of rocky beach we stood upon.

Finley wrapped her arms around herself and slowly began to rock from side to side. I'd seen her do this so many, many times for years but it wasn't until that moment did I realize it was a coping mechanism for her. She swayed slowly as her eyes glazed over, seemingly staring at nothing.

I looked on her, really studied this young girl willing to help me, willing to risk my unpredictable behavior and discovered something. *Finley was a victim*. It practically smacked me in the face now that I'd been willing to pay attention to her. She emanated something. Something terrible. Yeah, she may have been strong as hell but even the strong fall. They're human, after all.

"What happened to you, Finley Dyer?"

She stopped swaying. "Nothing at all," she answered, looking at me with a secret smile, implying that those words meant something else.

I narrowed my eyes at her. "What is 'nothing at all'? Why is that significant?"

She faced the wilderness. "It means I have nothing to say."

I drew closer to her, stood beside her and stared into the same dark abyss. "Your words, they meant something to you. Explain them to me?"

She sighed and faced the beach below our feet. "I was told that phrase very often as a kid."

"Why?" I prodded, interested to know what it all meant.

I surprised myself then because I suddenly realized I hadn't cared about anyone else but myself for a very, very long time. I wondered in that moment whether it was because she took the time to care for me. I wondered if she'd impressed upon me a sense of empathy, despite my attempt at fighting any such human emotion other than the hate I wanted to hold so closely. I could tell she'd influenced me, and I wasn't sure how I felt about that.

"The first time I heard it or rather, the first time I remember it," she began in an almost whisper, "was the day I turned five years old. The school keeps records of the student's birth dates and all that, right? Well, my teacher marked on a big calendar at the front of the classroom each kid's birthday. If it hadn't been for that calendar, I believe I wouldn't have ever known my birthday.

"I can still remember every detail of that thing like it was yesterday. A big green apple with the months all staggered in rows of three. Mine was right at the end. December third. I remember quietly counting the days until I got to the little worm marker that read *Finley*.

"That day, my teacher placed the big button she put on everyone on their birthday on the front of my yellow gingham dress. It was my best outfit. The girl in the trailer next to mine grew out of it and her mother asked mine if she wanted it. My mom said she didn't care, so the woman placed it in my hands.

She shook her head at the memory. "God, I thought it was the most beautiful thing I'd ever seen, that hand-me-down. I took it in my hands and lovingly examined every seam, every pleat, every inch. The front had two feminine little pockets sort of like what you'd see on an apron.

"It was my most cherished possession. I'd put it on when I was all by myself and pretend I was the president," she related, making me smile to myself a bit. Of course Finley wouldn't have been the kind of girl to pretend anything else. "I'd made a makeshift oval office," she continued, "out of the ironing board and an old sheet. Anyway, I put this little dress on knowing that the day was going to focus on me, and I just couldn't wait.

"She placed the button on my dress and I just beamed. Most kids' moms made cupcakes for the class but I guess my teacher knew that wasn't going to happen for me so she brought some herself." A little tear escaped and ran down her cheek. "They were strawberry," she choked, "with cream cheese frosting." She looked at me earnestly and smiled through soft tears. "She even put a tiny candied number five on the tops of each one.

"It was the happiest day of my life. After school, I came bounding up the rickety stairs of my mom's aluminum trailer, eager to tell my mom all about it, but she was gone as she so often was.

"Instead, I hung up my little dress, did my homework, cleaned the trailer because it was expected of me and made a dinner of peanut butter and crackers I'd stolen from the school when I thought no one was looking. The water had been turned off so I went out back and used my neighbor's hose. I washed myself as best I could and went back to the trailer only to discover that my mother had returned home and she was not sober nor alone."

My breath caught in my throat.

"I contemplated," she spoke softly, "just leaving and staying the night at that same neighbor's house but being little as I was, I wanted to tell her about my day."

"Finley," I said, turning toward her and grabbing her forearm.

"It's okay, Ethan. I promise," she reassured me, but I still didn't let go of my friend's arm. "She sat at the plastic veneer table we had with all but one broken chair and as soon as she saw me, I knew I'd made a terrible mistake."

I squeezed her arm gently.

"She stood up quickly, tipping her chair back onto the torn linoleum and almost fell over she was so intoxicated." My skin heated uncomfortably at the thought of the times Finley had seen me shit-faced and I cringed knowing what her memories probably did to her. "She lunged for me but landed on her face, which just incensed her further. She stood and grabbed me and asked me where I'd been. I told her about my pseudo-bath and she slapped me across the face, yelling something about how she thought I was trying to embarrass her in front of her new friend. I frantically tried to soothe her but, of course, it did no good.

"She dragged me to my room and threw me to the floor before walking over to my closet and yanking my little dress off the hanger. She held it in front of me, ripped the pockets and tore it to shreds all the while laughing while I pleaded for her to stop, but she didn't. When she was done, she tossed the dress to the side of the room and staggered a bit on her feet.

"I cowered there on the floor, afraid she would wail into me like she normally did, which made her laugh uncontrollably. She yelled at me to get up so I obeyed. She grabbed me by the shoulders and shook me, tears streaming down my face and said that I meant *nothing at all* to her and I better be careful or she'd sell me and I'd have to go live with the bad men.

"I was five. Barely five, really, and wanted so badly to stay with her despite how awful she was to me because, well, because she was my mother. I had no idea the other children in my class didn't live exactly as I did. Besides, even people who hate their mothers love their mothers."

She shook her head once more. "The first time I'd ever spent the night at someone's house was when I was in second grade. I spent the night at Holly Raye's." Holly Raye. That was the girl at the bar. Our classmate. "She was the nicest girl I'd ever met and her mother was no different. I remember sitting at her dinner table practically shaking in my boots when I spilled milk all over their table. When her mother stood to clean it up, I cowered in my chair.

"The woman looked at me with such pity. She cupped my cheeks and kissed the top of my head and said, 'No use crying over spilled milk, my darling.' That's when I figured it out. That not all mothers were like mine.

"When dinner was over, Holly Raye's mama fed us two huge pieces of chocolate cake and I thought I'd died and gone to heaven. She let us stay up late and watch movies and talk. And soon enough, within a few hours I'd forgotten about my mother and my situation. I'd considered Holly Raye my sister that night. I still do, in fact. Needless to say, I practically lived there after that.

"That's what I did."

"Did what?" I asked softly.

"Stayed at people's houses as often as they'd allow just so I could feel like I was part of a family. So I could learn, teach myself how to be normal, really."

"Jesus, Finley," I breathed, turning her toward me.

I brought her to my chest and hugged her, wrapping one hand around her neck and the other around her lower back. I held her tightly against me, but she didn't cry or sink into me with any sort of vulnerability as I thought she would. Instead, she hugged me back fiercely and I realized she wanted to support me just as much as I wanted to support her and I loved her for it. As much as I hated to admit it, I pitied her for it.

Finley Dyer was as selfless and brave an individual as I could imagine, and even though I could tell she'd only tapped the surface of her past, of her tortured soul, she wasn't going to let that past define her. I don't think I'd ever respected someone as much I had grown to respect Finley.

We broke the hug and faced the water once more.

"Thank you," I said as loudly as my rough voice would allow.

"For what?" she asked.

"For saving me from making a horrible decision. From being the horrible person I've become."

She nodded her head once. "I've been around horrible decisions before, Ethan. If you were as you say you are then it wouldn't have been so easy to defuse you. When you mix alcohol, though, with a perfectly kind individual, that kindness can dissolve quickly. It's toxic in so many ways."

I nodded, letting the shame of her words sink into me. The reality of what I was going to do that night hit me like the atom bomb and my hands began to tremble in fear of what I'd almost done.

"You'll be okay, Ethan Moonsong," she said simply and turned her eyes toward the water once more.

After a few minutes of silence, she started a playlist on her phone and set it on a rock near the shore then removed her sandals and waded into the water. When the water reached the bottoms of her knees, she turned to me and signaled for me to follow her. I removed my own boots and socks but took my shirt off and met her side, soaking my jeans but I didn't care.

"It's tepid," she said, running her fingers over the surface.
I nodded.

She stepped farther into the lake then began to float.

"Come on," she said to the sky, so I obeyed. When I drifted close enough, she hooked her arm with mine. "We're otterific."

"What?" I asked, not able to stifle a laugh.

I could see from the corner of my eye her mouth turning up. "In the water, sea otters latch paws when they sleep so they don't lose track of one another."

"Seriously?"
"Yeah."

I smiled. "When?" I asked after a few minutes of silence, not needing to embellish further.

"Two weeks, three days."

"For how long again?"

"One year."

I thought about that. "That's an incredibly long time. What type of work will you be doing?"

"The toe-curling kind."

A lump formed in my throat. "I'll respect the vague. Just tell me one thing, though?"

"Depends on what it is," she countered.

"Finley, is it dangerous?" I asked.

She was quiet, too quiet, making me nervous, but when enough time passed, I knew she wouldn't be responding, so I had my answer anyway.

"*Finley*."

"Please, let's change the subject, Ethan."

I sighed. "Why Vietnam?"

"Because I can. Next."

"Where in Vietnam?"

"Hạ Long City."

"I have no idea where that is."

"It's far north Vietnam and on the east coast, about two and half hours from Hanoi and about three hours south of China. It's—" She paused then took a deep breath, "It's a heavy tourist area."

My gut tightened at her hesitation. I didn't understand it but it made me nervous as hell. "I'm actually scared for you, I think."

"I'm not afraid of death, Ethan."

"*Is death a possibility?*"

"It is. I'm prepared for it. Plus, I'm carrying hope with me, so I'm cool."

I turned toward her, my left ear sinking into the lake. "Finley, you're not even the slightest bit afraid?"

She looked at me, the lake water rippling from her movement. "Ethan, you can choose to hope or you can choose to fear. Fear is a crippling disease. It takes over and paralyzes. Hope bolsters, motivates. People who fear, die. People who hope, live. Even in death they live."

I let her words sink into me while we paddled closer to shore to prevent ourselves from drifting too far. We did this when the music started to feel too distant. We floated in silence, listening to her dynamite playlist and memorizing the stars and moon.

"Finley?" I asked a half hour later.

"Hmm?"

"You said at the bar that we were never friends in high school."

"Right."

I turned toward her again, our bodies rippling with the movement. "Do you really believe that?"

She sighed toward the stars. "Yeah, I do."

"That's bullshit," I said matter-of-factly.
She didn't respond, but I could practically feel her eyes roll.

"It's bullshit," I explained, "because there's still merit in small conversations. Yeah, we might not have waxed philosophic, but we most definitely talked real life. I think you forgot that. To be honest, those seemingly nothing talks to you meant so much to me." She furrowed her brow. "I needed to talk to someone so badly at that time about regular things, regular life. I was overwhelmed with responsibility then and felt like I was drowning. I found solace in our synoptic talks, Finley. I found worth in the culmination of those

68

hundreds of hours we spent in one another's company. I didn't do that with anyone else." I paused. "You were a soft place to fall," I whispered.

Fragile tears pooled in her eyes and spilled into the lake beneath us. "Don't mistake me," she explained. "They meant something to me as well. I just had no idea they signified anything to you. I assumed you were just passing the time with me, Ethan. It's why I never considered us friends. I figured them as one-sided politeness on your end."

"I was careful around you," I admitted, her crush then an unspoken point, "but I was still vulnerable to you." I was thoughtful for a moment. "I don't want you to think that your friendship was only an escape for me either, though. I need you to know that I counted you as significant." I looked at her and she looked at me. "You're still significant, Finley." I tightened my arm and pulled her closer so that our legs and shoulders touched.

"Thank you," she whispered.

CHAPTER SEVEN

I dropped Finley off at her apartment in Kalispell and headed home around three in the morning. My jeans were soaked but I didn't care because Finley had saved my life. My house was dark, save for the small porch light. That light, in fact, was the only one for fifteen miles all around us, further solidifying just how isolated Montana, I, really was.

The house lights were off as well so I was surprised to hear my dad speak from the sofa when I opened the front door. The television sitting on the old metal TV tray against the half wall that separated the tiny kitchen and the living area was playing a rerun of *Leave it to Beaver*, a reminder of how innocent life could be if you so chose it.

"Hey, kid."

"Hey, Dad, what are you doing up so late?" I asked, startled to see him.

"Waitin' for you."

"Seriously? Shit, Dad, I'm sorry. Don't you have to be up in two hours?"

"First, watch your mouth."

"Sorry."

"And yeah, I have to up in two hours, but I've been trying to talk to you for days now. You come home when I'm asleep and wake up after I leave, Ethan."

I fell onto our twenty-year-old gold plaid sofa and squirmed a little because my knees were practically in my chest.

"I never sit on this thing. Too tall," I offered, grasping for any semblance of normality between us. Normal was something my dad and I never did. Not since my mom died. She was our normal.

"Maybe I should get a new one."

"What for? I doubt I'll be living here for much longer," I told him.

He didn't reply but his chest stilled. I'd surprised him.

He looked at me. "Where're you going then?" he asked before taking a swig from his Mason jar iced tea.

"Not sure," I told him truthfully. "I just figured you'd want me out of here soon, seeing as how I'm getting older."

He took another sip from his tea and set the glass on the ground near his foot. When he did this, he leaned forward a little bit and groaned when he sat back. A little piece of me died when I saw him do this. He was getting older as well and I hated that. Dads were supposed to live forever. So were moms, for that matter. Realizing in that moment that he was indeed mortal, that he was utterly human, made my chest ache in unimaginable ways.

"You always have a home here, son," he finally said, making that ache in my chest throb just a little more stiffly, painfully.

"Thanks, Dad."

He nodded. "Sober, I see."

I laughed bitterly. "So?"

"I'm relieved."

"Yeah, well, you can thank Finley Dyer for that."

He sat up, not so perceptibly that anyone who didn't know him would take notice, but I was keen to my father's everything. He was so subtle in his movements, his words, that if you weren't paying close attention to him, you could miss an entire feeling. I knew from that barely there action that he was interested in this new revelation. For whatever reason.

"Finley Dyer?" he asked. "She that russet-headed girl?"

"Yeah, that's her."

He nodded his head, but I also caught the faintest hint of a grin.

"She's my friend," I offered in explanation.

He could only nod his head again.

I stood because there wasn't anything I could offer him that could explain what Fin's friendship meant to me. He knew what I was struggling with getting over Cricket. He should have known that Finley could be nothing more to me than an earthly salvation. I didn't know why Finley found me when she did but I wasn't going to question it. So I stood because I was done talking.

"'Night, Dad."

"'Night, son."

The next morning, I woke surprisingly early for some reason and decided to cut and clear up the dead tree that had fallen over earlier in the summer in our front field. After watching my father the night before, I couldn't live with myself if I let him do it on his own. If

I was being honest with myself, it was probably also a little out of guilt for all the late nights and late mornings.

I secured my hair as well as bound a worn bandana across my forehead to catch the sweat. I threw on a pair of jeans and boots but didn't bother with a shirt and headed out to the old storage shed at the back of the house to grab the chainsaw and the canister of gasoline.

The tree fell about a quarter mile off and to the left of the house. The grass reached my knees and I felt it slap against my legs as I trudged through the field, the chainsaw balanced across my left shoulder.

When I reached the tree, I discovered that it had only partly fallen over making it sort of dangerous for one person to cut down by himself. I walked around it, deciding to start at the top of the tree and work my way down.

I'd just pulled the chain when I saw Finley's little Bug kicking up dirt and gravel as she turned into my drive. She was about half a mile away from me and I was afraid she'd go all the way down the mile-long drive to our house before discovering I wasn't there. I killed the chainsaw and set it against the trunk of the tree and for some reason I couldn't explain, I started running toward her, raising my arms above my head in that usual way people did when they wanted to get someone's attention.

To my surprise, she saw me and cut through the grass before I'd gotten far from my day's work. She came barrelling a little too quickly toward me and slid to a stop a few feet from the tree. Her windows were down and a song I barely recognized, but knew was from the nineties because it was Finley, came tumbling out. It had a heavy beat and it spilled happily all over the field surrounding me.

She tossed her door open and turned up the volume full blast and jumped out, singing at the top of her lungs. She stood on the hood of her car, her arms raised at her sides, and continued to belt out the tune the only way Finley knew how to do anything, with as much life as her heart could give.

I burst out laughing almost immediately but that didn't stop her. In fact, it only seemed to bolster her. She slid gracefully off the hood onto the field below and came skipping toward me still singing. She grabbed my hands and made me dance with her. I humored her but it was proving difficult because I was laughing so hard I could barely stand. When the song came to an end, she pulled away, her eyes gleaming and her chest pumping from the effort. She playfully fell to the grass, out of breath.

"God, I love that song," she said, smiling.

I backed up and leaned on the hood of her Bug. "I can tell," I teased.

She looked over at me seemingly just realizing that we were out in the middle of my field. "What are you doing out here?" she asked, studying her surroundings.

I gestured to the dead tree. "It fell down a few weeks ago when that big storm rolled across and I've, uh, been meaning to get to it before my dad did."

"That's awfully nice of you," she said, catching her breath.

"Not really. My motivation is guilt."

"Best kind, really," she joked.

"Yeah," I laughed, "the great persuader." I studied her. "Don't have work today?"

"Nope. Well, not during the day. I don't work Mondays through Wednesdays at the travel agency."

"What do you do for cash then?"

"I, uh, work nights at Buffalo's," she admitted, avoiding eye contact.

I fought a smile.

She sat up, fighting a smile of her own. "Whatever, Moonsong! I do what I have to do. I'm not ashamed!"

Buffalo's was the local burger joint. That may not seem that bad, but unfortunately its main clientele were usually between the ages of fifteen and nineteen. Local farm kids rarely get the opportunity to do much other than school and work on the ranches. Needless to say, when they get together, they're, let's call them a rambunctious lot. Oh, and I almost forgot, the manager makes the waitresses there sing and dance to songs from the jukebox on the bar top once an hour. Nothing seedy but, I mean, come on, it's pretty girls in shorts and cowboy boots. You can imagine how much the local high school boys like it.

"I'm not knockin' it, Fin. I just feel sorry for you is all."

Her smile went crooked.

"What time's your shift?" I asked.

"Six o'clock," she answered, standing up and brushing the grass from her shorts and band T-shirt. "It'll be busy but you should come out," she prodded.

"I know what you're doing," I said, walking back over near the tree and picking up the chainsaw.

"What am I doing, Ethan?"

"You're tryin' to keep me from the bar."

"So what if I am?" she asked, joining my side and propping herself on top of the dead trunk of the tree. She looked me dead in the eye.

"I have no plans to go to the bar tonight," I admitted.

She narrowed her eyes. "Really," she stated as a fact more than a question.

I met her eyes. "Really."

"Why not? I mean, I'm glad and all, but I want to know why."

"Because of how close I was to *you know*..." I left the sentence hanging. Nothing more needed to be said.

"Come in at eleven. It's pretty dead by then. I'll save you a booth." She jumped off the tree trunk then tied her hair back. "Let's do this," she said, examining the tree.

CHAPTER EIGHT

Finley helped me by binding up all the loose branches with twine and setting them in a pile as I broke down the dead tree. I felt pretty grimy by the end of it but it also felt so good to use my muscles again. It'd been a while. It was odd to go from a backbreaking type of work to nothing at all in the matter of one day. It was amazing as well as disheartening to have realized that I was more sore than I should have been and it encouraged me to begin working out every day to keep myself up. Finley had gone home to shower and change for work, and I promised her I'd go in to Buffalo's that night.

Inside, I stripped and sat under a hot shower for a few minutes reveling in the burn of the muscles of my back and arms. After, I threw on a pair of jeans and my boots and went to the fridge. It was empty, which made my chest ache. It'd been empty for about five years 'cause my mom was the one who'd kept it full. Looking back, I thought about all she'd used to buy in order to make whatever meals she planned for the week.

Which made me think of something. I left the
fridge open and studied the calendar on the wall near
the pantry.

Son of a bitch.

Suddenly, I wanted a drink. Badly. I slammed
the fridge door closed and paced the small kitchen, at
war with myself. It would have been so easy to head
out to my truck and grab my emergency stash. I could
have just as easily started it and headed toward my
dealer Vi.

You can't, I told myself. *Distract yourself.*

I looked at the fridge once more then grabbed
my keys. My truck started easily for some reason and
the roads never seemed so clear to me. I headed
straight for Sykes Market because that's where Mom
always did her shopping.

When I walked into Sykes, I barely recognized
it. It'd been renovated since last I saw it and that made
my gut ache. Everything changed. Everything. Nothing
seemed to stay the same anymore. All the things I
thought I could rely on, I realized I couldn't.

I grabbed a basket and walked the store, taking
things in. There were only two registers and they sat
catacorner to one another. Behind the registers, I
noticed the entrance to the diner. To my great relief, it
looked much the same. The same red countertops and
blue stools, though a little faded. The same lacquered
table tops and red and blue chairs. But now the lights
shone down on white vinyl flooring instead of the red I
remembered.

I set my basket down on the countertop and sat
on a stool, remembering all the biscuits and gravy I
used to eat there with my mom and dad on either side
of me. My hands glided over the counter and I found

myself breathing deeper from the memory. I remember my dad liking the fact that he could get a cup of coffee for a dime. He mentioned it to us every single time we went there, and my mom would just smile at me and wink when he'd say so, only to agree with him as if it was the first time he'd ever told us.

God, I missed her with the fire of a thousand suns. Losing your mom is a kind of pain you never knew could exist. No one but others who have experienced the same understand with even an iota of comprehension how it desolates you. Their sympathy, although sweet in its intentions, is futile. Because losing a parent is *life altering*. Everything you come to rely upon shatters into such tiny slivers and into such abundance there is no hope for refastening it as it was. Yes, you can lace and reassemble as well as you possibly can, but no matter how attractive the weave, the strength in that foundation is never the same. Its new formation is a fragile, fragile thing despite appearance's sake.

Which is why Cricket's leaving me was so catastrophic to me. I'd come to rely upon her. She was a stable fixture in my world after my mom passed. She *was* my world. I realized even then that it wasn't exactly the healthiest way to cope, but I was young and knew no other way. Besides, no one understood me as well as Cricket did at that time in my life, as she had lost her own mom as well.

I looked down at the countertop once more and remembered all the shared baskets of onion rings and huckleberry bread puddings and nearly froze to my seat. My hands began to shake so I brought them to my chest and tucked them beneath my arms.

"Haven't seen you in a while! Can I get you somethin', hon?" someone asked, startling me. It was Delia Phillips. Delia had been the head waitress there since before I could remember.

I looked up at her and the expression on her face turned from cheerful to worried in the span of a heartbeat.

"You okay, baby?" she asked.

I shook my head and stood up quickly, desperate to escape, nearly tripping over myself to reach the exit as fast as possible. I fought the urge to glance behind me, to drink that misery down deeper. Sykes was haunted now, swarming with the excruciating ghosts of my former life.

I bypassed the checkout counter, tossing my basket on top of the others and escaping out onto the sidewalk. My eyes searched my surroundings. The bank, the post office, the secondhand store. I was enveloped by memories of my mom carting me around to all these places. The memories beat down on me with such a furious pounding I grabbed at my head and squeezed, hoping to force them out. My breaths came hard and fast. I was losing it. So close to losing it all. I didn't know how much more I could take and in that moment, I realized it. The sum of my miserable life came tumbling at my feet in the form of burnt ash. I had nothing left.

I closed my eyes. "There's nothing salvageable," I whispered.

Just when I thought I couldn't think of a single reason to hang on to the small sanity I had left, a warm hand touched the back of my neck, subduing the war brewing inside my head, and I breathed an inexplicable sigh of relief. *Finally*, I lamented to myself.

I opened my eyes and looked toward the owner of that hand.

Finley.

Without thinking, I grabbed her and brought her to my chest, grasping with an almost wildness. For a second, I thought it would scare her and even contemplated letting her go, despite how much I needed her, but it didn't and she hugged me back with the same kind of intensity.

"Finley, I—" I began, but she stopped me by pulling back a bit, her eyes wide and piercing mine with a resounding unspoken *no* before she pulled me back in.

It felt strange yet wonderful that I didn't have to bend noticeably to hug her. I rested my cheek on the top of her head and breathed deeply, my dark hair swimming around her face, cocooning her. The sweet coconut smell of her hair was a balm to my disordered soul. Slowly, painstakingly slowly she pulled away from me and looked up at me. Her hands, her baffling and mysteriously pacifying fingers found my face, pushing my hair back from my eyes. Her palms held my hair back at my temples. We stood there quietly as she examined my face for something. Though I had no idea what she was looking for, I let her do it just to keep her hands on me.

"You're a tortured soul, you are," she finally said. I swallowed but kept my focus on her.

She began to pull her hands away but I quickly grabbed them and placed them around my neck. "No, please," I begged her. She nodded in reply, asking for no explanation.

I brought her back to me, hugging her frenziedly. I asked if I was hurting her to which she replied, "Not even a little."

I kissed the top of her head and she wrapped an arm around my waist, leading me with tenderness to my truck. I noticed that she never stopped touching me, not for one second, even when we were forced into awkward corners and walkways on the way back to the lot.

"You need to get to work now, don't you?" I asked.

"Yes, but you're comin' with me," she answered simply.

"It's okay, Fin. I'll be okay. You can go."
She stopped then and shook her head at me. "What if I told you that I wanted you to be with me tonight? That just knowing you're there will make me happier?"

"That's kind, Finley, but you don't have to—"

"No," she interrupted, "it's a selfish kindness. Just appease me, Ethan."

"Okay," I conceded, happy to be near her.

I walked her over to the passenger side of my truck and opened the door for her. She swung into her seat and started putting on her seatbelt as I was shutting her door. I walked to the driver's side and got in. The key turned and the engine roared to life. I turned left onto Second Avenue and headed for Main and then Ninety-Three on our way to Buffalo's.

"What brought you to Sykes?" I asked her quietly, keeping my eyes trained on the road. Her hand sat on my shoulder, bringing me relief.

"I was making a deposit before heading in and when I was crossing the street, I saw you. I shouted your name a few times before realizing that you were struggling with something and couldn't hear me."

"You must think I'm nuts," I laughed without humor.

"Absolutely not," she answered. I glanced at her and saw she was staring out her window at the passing scenery. A haunted song played on the stereo.

"I don't think it a coincidence I found you today."

"I'm starting to believe it's not a coincidence either. That goes for all of the days you've saved me, actually, and I don't believe in anything anymore," I added quietly.

She squeezed my shoulder in answer.

We pulled into the lot and Buffalo's looked unbelievably crowded. I wondered if it'd have just been better to drop her off then pick her up at the end of her shift.

"No," she said softly, reading my thoughts, "just come in. It's cool. There's a booth in the back corner no one's ever assigned so it can be left open for family and friends of Charles." Charles owned Buffalo's. "He won't care if I use it tonight."

I pulled into an empty space in the far back of the restaurant and we walked in the side door together and I almost turned right around.

Let me explain something to you, something I'd experienced every day of my life. I'm Native American. Mixed, yeah, but with a light olive skin tone, six foot three inches, almost translucent grey eyes, and I have long black hair. I've known since I was little that I didn't look like everybody else. I wasn't the Montana boy next door, and I'd always been okay with that despite the stares every now and then when I was in an unfamiliar place. Occasionally, though, I got taken by surprise even at home.

Buffalo's was packed to the rafters but when we walked in, everyone stopped. Waiters, waitresses, customers, managers. Everyone stopped what they were doing to look at me. But I knew in that moment it had nothing to do with my strange height or dark hair. No, they were staring because this was the first time I'd emerged into public save for the visits to the bar. I was a spectacle. *Everyone look at the boy who just got dumped!* Cricket's and my breakup was the biggest thing to happen in our little town because we lived in a little town and scandals like ours just didn't happen often. And I was the one who got left. I was the one they were curious about.

When you're as tall as I am, it's hard to look conspicuous and the times in which you feel like you're on display that height makes it difficult to shrink into oblivion. I started backing out but Finley grabbed my arm and pulled me through.

"Don't worry, they'll get over it soon," she explained under her breath.
Sure enough, after a few seconds of utter silence except for the jukebox, heads returned to their plates and the staff got busy again. I sighed in relief. Finley dragged me to the booth in the far back corner by the long bar top and made me sit with my back to the wall.

"I'll be right back," she said, giving me a small smile.

I turned around in my seat, peered over the half wall near me and watched her tie her half apron over her cutoffs. She wore this almost sheer, billowy pullover on top of a a white tank top along with a pair of worn-in brown leather cowboy boots with a squared toe. An off-white sock peeked out of the tops of her boots. Her auburn hair was wavy and fell down her back. She stood near a mirror over a few shelves where she placed the messenger bag she'd brought with her. She peered into it and dragged all her hair on top of her head and started jamming pencils into the random pile. It looked absurd but when her hands fell to her sides and she examined herself, the result, I had to admit, was pretty. Tendrils framed her face and neck. Soft and romantic yet practical.

Someone moved behind her I couldn't see because they were hidden in the office behind the open kitchen. She turned and said something to them then laughed. She waved a hand toward me and said something else then nodded her head before heading back my way.

She pulled a pencil out of her hair but it did nothing to ruin what she'd just accomplished. I stared at her in wonder.

"You thirsty?" she asked me when she reached my table.

"Yeah, uh, could I get a Coke, please?"

"Well, gee, I can see what I've got, Beav. Sit tight," she said, winking then heading to another table and taking their drink order.

She approached a third group of four teenage boys and I sat up a little for some reason. They gave her their drink orders and she wrote them down, smiling and patting one on the shoulder. The one in the back corner on the left asked her a question and she leaned over to hear him better because the music was so loud, which made me hold my breath for yet another reason I didn't know. The one she'd patted on the shoulder purposely dropped something on the ground and tapped her on the shoulder then pointed toward what he'd let fall. She looked down and he said something to her to which she just laughed at then headed back toward the kitchen, passing me with a smile.

She got everyone's drinks and spread them in a spiraling circle on a drink tray. She picked the thing up like it weighed nothing and walked our direction again. She set my drink down so quickly I barely saw it.

"Be right back," she said over her shoulder. She dropped off the table's drinks between mine and the boys then moved on to the teenagers, setting theirs down along with a pitcher of dark syrupy soda. She took their orders as well as the middle table's and then came to mine.

"Know what you want?" she asked, running her hand down the top of my head, her pencil tucked between her thumb and fingers, and grabbing a few strands of hair, pulling them softly to the ends. Her momentary touch assuaged my frayed nerves.

"Uh, surprise me," I told her. She didn't question it and walked off to the kitchen.

She returned with another pitcher of soda and exchanged it for the pitcher she'd set down in front of the boys as if she knew they were going to drain it while she'd been gone. She set the empty pitcher on the bar top and the bartender took it from her. She glanced at her next table, looked satisfied then came to mine, leaning over the tabletop and resting her chin in her hand since the booths were set a few feet off the ground for easy access.

"I think you're gonna like what I ordered for you," she said, turning to look over her shoulder at the bartender when he said her name.

"Yeah, Pete?" she asked.

"Grab me a crate of pilsners, will ya?"

"Be right back," she said.

And that's how the entire night when on. About five hundred *I'll be right backs*. She'd brought me a giant bacon burger a few minutes after she'd ordered for me, and I ate the entire thing along with a plate of fries. All the work I'd done that afternoon had caught up to me and I guess I was hungrier than I'd thought I was. That, or it was Finley's oddly mollifying hands. She may not have been able to talk to me that often during her shift but every time she'd pass me, those hands found the top of my hand, forearm, fingers, shoulder, or occasionally my neck.

Around ten, they called all the servers onto the bar top by blaring a siren sound throughout the whole burger joint. I couldn't help but cringe for Finley when she rolled her eyes and climbed on top of the bar with all the other girls. She was on the far end, closest to me, and when "Cotton-Eyed Joe" began to play they all wrapped their hands around one another's backs and line danced. Finley's face looked tired and she wore a forced smile. She hated it and that made me smirk.

She noticed me and smiled genuinely before shaking her head at me. Her dance moves looked rehearsed but sufficient. When the song was over, I stood up and offered her my hand to help her down.

"You looked really into it," I teased her.

"See that girl over there?" she asked, pointing to another server. A girl, I'd noticed, who *really* enjoyed the line dance.

"Yeah?" I answered, curious where she was going with her question.

"Well, see, she has thirty-seven pieces of flair."

I laughed. I mock examined her. "And it looks like you're only wearing fifteen, Fin."

"The thing is, Bob, it's not that I'm lazy, it's that I just don't care."

"You're funny."

"Yeah, yeah, sit down, will ya? Wanna piece of cake, Milton?"

"Nah, the ratio of people to cake is too big."

She smiled. "All right, fine. I'm gonna clean up then. My shift is done. They cut me early."

"Cool," I said, then thought of something. "Wait."

"What's up?"

"Those guys earlier. One of them dropped something on the floor. What was it?"

She shook her head. "Oh, that. Yeah, he elbowed a sugar packet onto the floor and told me I'd dropped my name tag."

"Clever," I said, almost laughing.

"They've got a new one every week."

Finley tossed her apron onto a pile to be laundered, I assumed, then washed her hands for what seemed like the thousandth time that night.

That night's bartender came up to me just then. "You goin' out with Finley Dyer now? She's got issues, you know. I tried it out with her once and she wanted nothin' to do with me."

I eyed him. "And that's why she *has issues*?" I asked. "Because she wouldn't go out with you?"

"Nah, man, I just heard some stuff. So, you goin' out with her or what?" he asked, more curious than casual conversation merited. It was obvious he was still into her.

"No, we're just friends."

"Cool," he said, seemingly satisfied. He started to walk away but stopped and turned back around. "You should be careful around her, though. Remember what I said, she's got issues, man."

I snorted. "Not any more than I do."

"What?"

"Nothing, see you 'round," I said, standing.

"Later."

I leaned against the edge of the booth to wait for her. Finley came around the office corner removing all her pencils and her hair came tumbling down her back. She tossed them all in her bag on the shelf then swung the strap over her head and across her torso, untucking her hair that'd caught in the strap.

She sighed, threading her hands through her hair. "It's been a long night," she admitted, looking sleepy.

"Come on. I'll take you home."

"No, my car's at Sykes remember?"

"No way. I can tell you're exhausted. I'll just pick you up tomorrow morning and take you then."

"Fine," she conceded.

But life rarely makes it easy for you, because my truck had other ideas.

The key turned and the truck began to rumble but died outright. I tried it multiple times but it wouldn't start.

My hands fell to the seat in resignation. I turned to Finley. "Shit, I'm so sorry, Finley."

She laughed. "Nah, it's fine. It happens. What do you think is wrong with it, though?"

"Pretty sure it's just the battery."

"Okay, we'll ask somebody for a ride."

We got out and shut our doors. I felt so bad for keeping her up because of my piece-of-shit truck. I couldn't stop screwing up her life.

"What's wrong?" she asked, studying me when I met her side.

"I just feel like you've helped me out so much but I can't seem to return the favors. Small, though, they may be."

"Life is strange like that, Ethan. There are going to be times where you're wondering what the hell is going on with yourself, when you begin to question your world. You'll be lost as shit but inexplicably someone finds you the moment you're ready to jump from the ledge and helps you stand back up. Holly Raye did that for me once, and now it seems it is my destiny to help you. There are no debts earned or owed when life is cruel to you like that. It's my duty as a friend first but also as a human to lift those who need lifting, to lift you."

"That's so comforting to think about, Fin. Not everyone thinks the way you do."
We began to walk back toward Buffalo's.

"Just because they don't doesn't mean they shouldn't. Besides, people will surprise you sometimes. All we need is for someone to shine by example. People inevitably gravitate towards the good when the good can't be helped but to overshine the awful. It's human nature."

"Many would disagree with you."

"Are one of these many you?" she asked.

"No," I answered, earning me a glorious smile.

"We're bombarded with so much evil in this world on a twenty-four-hour basis that it's hard to believe we're capable of anything but the worst. But all it takes is the conscious decision of one. One person can move mountains."

"What if they fail?" I asked.

She eyed me. "Dig yourself out and move on to the next. Your hands may bleed, but they'll be made all the stronger for the effort. Failures and trials are designed to make you that much more resilient. They callus the weak parts of you and leave the strong."

I nodded my acceptance and we kept walking. A loud pickup truck whipped around the corner. My arm shot out to keep Finley from moving any farther. The truck came to an abrupt stop and obnoxious music came spilling out of the windows as they rolled them down. It was the teenage boys from earlier.

"*Oh jeez,*" Finley said under her breath.

"Hey, Finley. What's up?" the driver asked, eyeing me up and down.

"Hey, Patrick," Finley answered. She gestured toward me. "Ethan's truck's battery died."

"You need a jump?" he asked.

Finley looked at me for an answer. "Thanks, yeah, that'd be cool," I told him.

Patrick drove his truck and parked a few feet from the front of mine, and Finley and I walked back to meet him. There was a guy in the passenger seat and two in the bed of the truck but they stayed put, staring at their phones. Patrick got out and opened his hood while I fished behind the bench for my cables. After we got everything hooked, I attempted the engine but it didn't even turn over once. We decided to let the cables stay connected for a while before trying again.

"So, uh, you guys are together or something?" he asked after a few moments.

What in the world is up with that question tonight?

Finley giggled. "No," she offered, looking at me and smiling. "Ethan and I *are* very good friends, though." She ran her palm down my arm and squeezed when she reached my fingers before letting her hand drop back down. I nearly closed my eyes at the relief her brief touch gave me. Hearing Finley admit that we were friends out loud after our discussion at the lake was yet another balm to my soul.

Patrick eyed me, sabotaging the reprieve her fingers gave me.

"*Oh*," he responded, as if she meant anything other than its true meaning.

"Finley's not that kind of girl," I defended, narrowing my eyes at him. My chest began to burn in anger for her.

Patrick leaned against the side of his truck, looking out into the field behind the restaurant. A small smile laid across his face. I could already tell Patrick was the kind of guy who needed a good ass-kicking to wipe out that annoying cockiness most guys his age developed. Now, I know I wasn't much older than him but, to be honest with you, I'd lived a pretty rough life. Maturity came at thirteen and slammed into me with such ferocity it threw me across the field called experience at astonishing speed. I came up on the other side never really having had the opportunity to revel in anything young. At times, I felt like I was *born* old.

Patrick stared at me hard. "I see."

I was so close to ripping off the cables and telling him he was no longer needed but Finley looked so tired, I couldn't do that to her. Instead, I gritted my teeth and sidled closer to her.

I tried the engine again but to no avail then again with Patrick revving his engine, but nothing.

"I think I just need a new battery altogether," I said with a sigh, running my hands through my hair. "I'm so sorry, Fin."

She yawned then laughed. "It's okay. What do we need to do?" she asked, standing between the driver's side door and me, her arm resting on the window.

"I think we'll need to hitch a ride with dumbass over there."

Finley laughed under her breath then sighed. "All right."

"I'll have him drop you off at your car first, okay?"

"No," she corrected quickly. "No, I think it'll be better if I go with you."

"Finley, you don't have to come with me. I promise not to drink anything tonight."

She smiled crookedly. "It's not that. It's—"

"What?" I asked, furrowing my brows.

"I-I just don't want to go home to an empty apartment."

I studied her, finally deciding she was being serious. "Okay."

Patrick dropped us off at O'Shaughnessy's, our local auto parts store. It was closed but Harv, who owned the store, lived above the shop and wouldn't mind opening up to sell us a battery. It was also nice because it was only seven blocks away from Sykes where Finley was parked.

"Thanks for the ride, Patrick!" Finley shouted as I lifted her from the bed of his truck.

Patrick leaned over his friend to talk to her out the passenger side window. "Uh, I can take you back if you want."

"No, thank you so much, though. I don't want to inconvenience you any more than we already have. My car's just down the road a spell. We'll walk there and I'll take him back to Buffalo's myself."

"Oh, okay," he said, looking defeated.

"Thanks again. Thanks, guys!" she shouted to the others.

We turned around and she waved one last time as we walked up the side stairs to Harv's apartment.

I opened the screen door and it creaked loudly, then I knocked twice. Finley stood one step below me, one booted foot resting on the deck where I stood. Harv didn't come to the door, though. He wasn't there. Or he was asleep and couldn't hear us.

"Are you kidding me?" I asked, my eyes raised toward the night sky.

Finley laughed and started heading down the stairs.

"Oh, well, let's go get the love bug. We can come back and try again."

"Okay," I answered, trudging down the steps she'd just hopped down.

We'd just started out toward Sykes when her cell rang.

"Hey, buttercup," she answered with a smile. *It's Holly*, she mouthed and I nodded. "I'm not at home yet. Ethan's truck battery died and I'm helping out." She listened then sighed. "Yeah. Yeah, I will." She hung up.

"She doesn't like you hanging with me," I said.

"Nah, she just checks up on me whenever I have to leave work late," she evaded.

I smiled at her to which she smiled as well but turned her head toward the sidewalk.

"She hates me," I insisted.

"No!" she denied. "She ... Well, she just doesn't trust you."

"Ah, I see. Well, even if I think she's wrong," I said, elbowing her playfully. "I like that she cares enough about you to worry."

"She's lovely, my Holly. I humor her because she *is* a bit of a worrywart, though. I make it a point to call her when I come home late from work. It scares her otherwise."

"You're a good girl, Finley," I told her, meaning it.

Hearing the words "good girl" tumble from my own lips triggered a memory of my mom, making my chest ache so deep I could decipher each individual cell that made up my broken heart. Each one throbbed painfully. My hand went to my chest and my steps faltered enough that Finley felt the need to reach for my arm.

"You okay?" she asked, concern in her eyes.

My mind went spinning back in time.

"Do you have your backpack, Ethan?" my mom asked.

"Yes, ma'am," a small voice answered back. We walked down the steps of our front porch hand in hand. My dad was standing by his truck loading some sort of tool into the bed.

"We're headed off to school, Daddy," my mom spoke to alert him to our presence and to set the tone of what she expected from him.

"Well," my dad said kindly, picking me up and kissing my cheek. "Be a good boy, son. Listen to your teachers. Make good decisions today. Pray to God for peace during your test today."

"Yes, sir," I said, beaming at him.
He sat me down and ruffled my black hair. My mom kept it short then.

"Oh," my mom playfully complained, "I just combed his hair, babe."

"Excuse me," my dad responded sarcastically, grabbing my mom by the waist and kissing her on the mouth.
I stuck my tongue out and wrinkled my nose in disgust but deep inside, I secretly loved watching them love one another. It gave me happiness, though I didn't recognize it as so then. I just knew it made me feel happy inside.

My dad let her go, smoothing her hair down on both sides of her head and kissing her forehead.

He turned to me then, resting his hand on top of my head. "Love you, Ethan."

"Love you too, Daddy."

"See you after school, son." He turned to my mom. "Love you too, good girl."

"Love you too."

My mom and I walked away toward the end of our lane to wait for our bus. On our way there, I asked her why my dad called her a good girl.

My mom smiled to herself then said, "Does it feel silly to hear him call me that?"
I nodded.

"When your daddy and I first met, he told me he was just a good guy lookin' for a good girl." She smiled at the memory. "We got to datin' for a little bit and one *day he told me he'd found her in me, that he thought I was his good girl."*

"And will I grow up and get a good girl too?" I asked her.

"Yes, you will, Ethan," she answered without hesitation. She stopped me in the lane and held my chin. "You deserve nothing but goodness." She leaned down on her ankles, at eye level. "Good girls are hard to come by, but I think God's got one all lined up for you already. Just keep an eye out for her, right? Treat all girls with kindness, Ethan, 'cause you never know which one will turn into the good girl you're meant to keep."

I nodded, eyes wide. "Yes, ma'am."

I noticed Finley waving her hand in front of my face. "Ethan?" she asked, worry etched over every inch of her face. I wondered how long I'd stood there with her, drowning in the memory of my dead mother.

I blinked once. "Finley," I said quietly.

"Yes?" she asked, her brows furrowed in distress.

"Yesterday was the anniversary of my mother's death. And-and I forgot." My voice cracked at the end. I cleared it to gain composure.

Her loss felt fresh again saying it out loud. The wound of her death ripped back open, exposing my already damaged heart to the harshness of a bitter environment. An environment I'd created on my own. I discovered I'd forgotten when I opened the fridge earlier that afternoon. Its emptiness consumed me in a strange way, as if my body *knew* I'd forgotten. That was when I glanced at the calendar and discovered I'd dishonored the memory of my mom by forgetting the worst day of our lives.

Finley's hands went to her mouth and her eyes glassed over. "Ethan," she breathed.

"How could I forget the worst day of my life, Fin? How?" She moved for me but stepped back when I continued again, her hands fisting at her mouth. "The awful part is I hadn't even realized it was coming up. I couldn't even bother to remember." My left hand laid at my side while my right clenched at my heart, ready to tear it out just to relieve the hurt. I averted my gaze, focusing on a neon sign pulsing in the pitch-black night. "I'm a terrible son, Finley."

My whole body felt overwhelmingly sad. I recognized with that memory that a person may forget a date but they cannot forget a torment. The mind may fail you but the heart never does. Grief etches itself inside the body's stone. It weathers with age as all etchings do, worn by the winds of time, but the remnants are there. They remain and they continue to distinguish themselves. A sculptor would never forget its chisel. It's the curse of the carver.

Without warning, a cool, slender hand found my forearm and some of the agony suffered a little less.

Finally, I sighed to myself, pulling her to me and wrapping my arms around her.

CHAPTER NINE

Harv did sell me a battery that night when we went back, and it was close to three in the morning when I finally dropped Finley at her apartment. She was so exhausted she admitted the loneliness she'd felt earlier had disappeared since her eyes were already half closed. I walked her inside and made sure she locked her door when I left, not that Kalispell was dangerous or anything, but why take chances?

I went home that morning with a fairly definite idea of who Finley was. She was my earthly guardian angel, my little salvation. I'd never tell her as much because who needs that kind of pressure, right? But I most definitely relied on her. The entire drive back, I wondered if I would ever deserve her friendship, how I could ever pay her back for what she'd done for me. I knew that I might not ever atone for it, but I also knew I'd live my entire life aspiring to accomplish just that.

We spent every single day together the weeks before she left for Hạ Long Bay, and the comfort she brought me is an insane thing to try to convey. Finley and I became incredibly close during those weeks. And it was an allied effect I'd never felt, not even, I'm ashamed to say, with Caroline, because with Finley it was in no way forced or ever uncomfortable. There were no motives. We weren't occupied with anything other than being in one another's company. We never needed to explain ourselves because we wanted nothing more from one another other than to care for each other, to rely on each other, to regard one another as the only person who truly understood us. Finley, for lack of a better phrase, was my best friend. Hers was a friendship I'd never had nor ever thought existed. I never thought a friend could be like that.

And just like that, Caroline was forgiven. Because if she had never left me, I never would have found Finley. Finley's friendship meant more to me than the relationship I had with Caroline. My hatred dissipated into a pool of nothing at my feet.

"Pass me that bag, will ya?" Finley asked, hooking her phone to the small speaker she carried with her at all times, and she started a playlist. I reached down and picked up one of the myriad bags on her plastic-covered mattress and held it out for her as the heavy bass of the first song swam through my skin. "No, not that one," she said, pointing at another.

I reached for the one I thought she wanted and she shook her head then tried another without success. "Jeez, Fin, there's a hundred on here. Describe it to me," I demanded as she rummaged through a random drawer.

"The greenish one with the mustard-colored stripes." I grabbed the one she wanted and set it on top of her dresser.

We'd moved all of her stuff into a storage unit the day before and had returned to grab a few things before her flight the next day.

She was packing for Vietnam.

"I can't believe you're leaving for a year," I told her.

She glanced at me and smiled. "It'll pass by like that," she said, snapping her slender fingers.

I smiled in return but I wasn't so sure. Admittedly, I leaned on Finley a little too heavily but it was a coping mechanism. She was a lifeline, more a life jacket than a preserver. Our friendship tugged that closely. She was so pleasant to be around as well. Funny and silly and full of life.

She was leaving for Vietnam in the morning and I was driving her to the airport. I was dreading her absence. Selfish, I know, but I didn't want her to go. If I'd known the kind of charity she was doing, I thought I might have been able to come to terms with it a little better.

"You know, if you just told me what you were doing over there, I might not feel so crappy about dropping you off tomorrow," I said with a bite I hadn't intended.

Her hands stilled as she stared at the top of her dresser and sighed. "Ethan, let it go, will you? If I told you, you'd just force me to stay."

I stood from sitting on her mattress. "That's it. That's enough for me to force you right there."

She shook her head. "You can't stop me," she said, avoiding eye contact, rummaging through a deep bag.

"What if I refused to take you?" I threatened uselessly, inching near her.

"I'd just take a cab, dude."

I stopped a mere few inches from her and sighed, resting the palm of my hand on the surface of the dresser, inches from her fingers. "Fine, but will you at least call me when you get there? Give me the number to check in on you periodically."

Her eyes met mine briefly and something passed between us. Something I couldn't define. My stomach dropped so I backed up a step.

"Fine," she told the inside of the giant bag. "I'll call you and give you the details of where I'll be. Will that make you feel better?"

"Not really, but if it's all you'll give me, then fine."

Finley zipped the top of her bag, resting an arm on top of it. She turned toward me, using her other hand to hold back wisps of hair tumbling about her face from the wind tunneling into the unit from outside.

"I'm ready," she said with a sad smile.

"Are you nervous?" I asked her. There was limited space to move around or even stand so I threw a knee over the mattress to give myself the illusion of room. I was feeling stifled for some reason, overcome by the crowded boxes and disheveled furniture. My chest felt constricted because of it, I thought.

She sat on the plastic-covered mattress then laid back, her feet planted on the floor.

"A little," she said, meeting my eyes and smiling. "A lot, actually." Her eyes glassed over, so I joined her side and laid beside her.

"You don't have to go," I said.

She turned to me and I looked at her. "Yes, I do. I really, really do," she answered.

I nodded, accepting her answer. "You're courageous, Fin."

"I don't know about that," she said, voice low, "but I'm trying."

I realized then I'd selfishly made it harder on her by encouraging her to stay, by giving her a hard time. "I'm sorry I gave you shit. You should go. Go but know that anytime you need me, you just call me and I'll be there for you."

Finley wrapped her hand around mine and we stared at the top of the storage unit in silence.

***

At two in the morning we left for Glacier Park International so she could make her six a.m. flight. It felt surreal that she'd be flying halfway across the world. I almost couldn't believe the day had come. For some inexplicable reason I thought I had all the time in the world to spend with her before she had to go, but like so many things, I was mistaken.

She was quiet most of the ride. Nerves, I thought, keeping her silent. When we arrived at the airport, I pulled into a garage and grabbed a time ticket. We parked and I got her door for her, followed by her bags, except her ridiculous carry-on which she insisted she could shoulder.

I stacked a bag on top of her rolling luggage and we headed for her gate but she stopped in the middle of the pedestrian crosswalk, her hand gripping my forearm. Relief from the harsh anxiety I'd been feeling subsided with one breath. I slowly stared down at those soothing fingers, wishing I could glue them there.

"I'm-I'm scared," she said, her knuckles turning white.

My gaze rose to meet hers. She was staring so firmly at my eyes, it sort of knocked me back a little. I opened my mouth to answer, but before I could, a shuttle bus honked at us to let him by. Startled, we both staggered back onto the sidewalk. I set her bag up to stand on its own and turned toward her.

"Finley," I whispered, sliding my hands between her hair and face and settling my palms against her cheeks and neck. Her hands raised and gripped at my wrists a little desperately. My forehead met hers and my hair slid forward, mingling with her own. "You've got this, Fin. You've got this, and *I've* got you." She took a deep, profound breath, let it out slowly, then nodded. I stepped back a bit, breaking contact save for my hands on her face and her hands on my arms. "Acting bravely doesn't mean there's a lack of fear, Fin. It just means you overthrow it, stamp it down, and toss it in deep with the cowardice."

She took another rooted breath and found that very place. Her jaw clenched and she hiked her carry-on farther up on her shoulder. "Let's go."

We stood quietly at the ticket counter, butterflies taking residence in both our bellies. It was written all over her face. Hers for obvious reasons. Mine because I was scared for her but was trying not to show it.

There were surprisingly a lot of fliers for that early in the morning. Finley had two connecting flights, the first being in Seattle. She'd get there in only an hour and a half but she had an almost nine-hour layover when she landed. When she got her ticket, we discovered we had at least an hour to kill so I grabbed a couple cups of coffee along with a few warm croissants.

I sat next to Finley, who'd removed her flip-flops, of course, and pulled her feet into her lap.

"If Principal Healy could get a load of you, dude," I chuckled, gesturing to her feet.

She rolled her eyes but smiled. "What an asshole, right? Why did he care if I did or did not wear shoes, anyway? He was *obsessed* with trying to catch me without them. He'd rant about how if I hurt my feet on school property, they'd be liable, blah, blah, blah. I asked if he was so concerned about it, why not just let me sign a waiver, and you know what he said?"

"'Where would be the fun in that, Miss Dyer?'"

She did a double take. "How do you know that?"

"'Cause I was there that day, Fin. You wouldn't shut up about how 'unfair slash creepy' he was."

Her cheeks bloomed red. "Oh."

I don't know why, but I liked the color on her. "I agreed with you, though. I thought he was a little too preoccupied with catching you. I remember telling you I thought it was disturbing the amount of joy he got out of sending you home."

"I know. What a douche canoe." She raised her coffee in the air and announced with a terrible English accent, "His mother was a hamster and his father smelt of elderberries!" She brought her hand back down and took a sip of her coffee.

A burst of laughter that'd been growing in me pretty much since she saved my life that first night exploded out of me, deep and guttural. It was the hardest I'd laughed in many, many months, and it was apparently catching because Finley's shining eyes met mine and she joined me. We were both so loud, in fact, a few people stopped and stared. Tears streamed from our eyes. It was junior year bio all over again.

"This is only funny because it's four in the morning," she said, giggling.

"I know," I agreed but kept laughing. After a while, I wiped my palms down my face and sighed. "Henry Kissinger, I've been missin' yer."

She nodded as she ran her fingers under her eyes, wiping away all traces of happiness it seemed because her face sobered quickly. "I *am* going to miss you while I'm gone," she explained.

My face matched hers. "Same here, Fin. Same here." I glanced down at my watch. "It's time."

She looked at me and her eyes glassed over. One tiny tear escaped as she nodded her head, her smile strained.

"Fin," I quieted, my voice dropping a few octaves.

She sucked in a breath. "I wasn't so sad to leave before you turned up," she explained, candid.

I stood and pulled her up to me, wrapping my arms around her slender shoulders. Her hair spilled across the tops of my forearms and I tried to memorize how soft it was, tried to commit to memory the smell and color. It was such an unusual complexion, a mixture between tawny and deep red. It was a spectacular spectrum between bronze and auburn.

I took a deep breath and secreted into that hair, "I'll be honest, I'm glad to know you again." I hugged her tightly. "You're the best friend I've ever had, Fin, in-including Caroline."

She sighed on a bit of a sob and nodded into my shoulder then lifted her head and looked at me, her cheeks wet. "And you're the same for me, actually. Unrivaled." She laughed. "Don't tell Holly I said that. I love Holly like a sister, but you understand me more than anyone ever could, Ethan. Like we share the same sort of insides. As if we're knitted from the same thread."

I pulled her back and studied her. "Go," I ordered softly then added, "before I make you stay." She smiled at me. I bent and grabbed her carry-on and rested it on her shoulder for her.

"Thanks for everything," I told her.
She nodded, kissed my cheek, and left for security, not another word spoken.

A funny, dull pain set up in my chest. My brows narrowed at that and my hand automatically lifted there. I examined my feet for a solid minute before realizing I'd been standing still like an idiot. When I looked up, she was already through. I couldn't find her in the crowd beyond security either.

Missing her already, I turned and headed for my truck.

CHAPTER TEN

When I got home that morning it was still dark and I felt an overwhelming urge to take a drink to take the edge off. I parked my truck beside my dad's, got out, and reached for my spare bottle. I twisted the lid off the top before turning it over, dumping all its contents onto the gravel near my feet, then pitched the bottle with a grunt, my hair tumbling forward with the effort, as far as I possibly could into the field near the tree I'd broken down with Finley. I hadn't had a sip of alcohol since the night we'd gone to the lake, and I didn't plan on stopping there. She may have instigated the quit, but I would be the one who would keep it quitted. She'd reminded me I was capable of anything. Capable of horrible things, as any human is, but also of good, honorable things.

My boots bit at the gravel beneath me as I approached the porch. I bounded up the steps onto the wraparound and reached for the handle but before I could pull open the screen door, my dad pulled open the front door, startling me.

I swung back on my heels and stood still as he swung open the screen door, inviting me in.

"Hey, Dad. Surprised to see you up this early. It's your day off, yeah?"

He nodded and I ducked to enter the house. "I got up to use the restroom a few hours ago and didn't see you in your bed. I was wondering when you were coming home."

"I was home," I explained, heading for the fridge for some orange juice. "I just got up early to take Finley Dyer to the airport. Want some?" I asked, holding up the carton.

He shook his head and fell down into his chair, clicking on the television. "Where's the Dyer girl goin'?" he asked, stopping on a rerun of *Cheers*.

"Vietnam," I said, that ache in my chest flaring up. I took a sip of my orange juice, desperate to relieve the sore and unfolded myself uncomfortably across the couch.

"*What?*" he asked, meeting my eyes and surprising me. This was more emotion than my father usually showed.

"She's doing some charity there," I explained.

He nodded approvingly. "Good for her," he said, tossing his head to the left once. "Glad she turned out as well as she did."

"How do you mean?" I asked, sitting up a little, considering his thoughtful expression.

"Hmm?" he asked, distracted by the TV.

I set down my cup. "You said you were glad she turned out well. What did you mean by that?"

"Well, she was taken away from her mama when she was little. It was a scandal then. She seems to be doing well."

My heart beat harshly in my already sore chest. "I didn't know she was taken from her mom. I thought she'd been abandoned. Why is Finley turning out well such a surprise, though?"

He looked at me with curious eyes. "'Cause of what happened."

I sat upright this time, my left hand clenching the back of the sofa and my breath catching. "What-what happened?" I asked, not really wanting an answer.

He continued to stare at me like he couldn't figure me out. Understanding dawned on him and he settled in his chair restlessly. "I don't wanna gossip," he said, raising the remote.

I scooted to the edge of the couch. "Dad, this is important to me. I won't spread it around; I just need to know what you're talking about."

He deliberated a moment, deciding something. His tense expression fell when he'd made his decision then he turned away from me, avoiding eye contact. "Her, uh, her mama got drunk a lot," he began. I'd known this already. "And, uh," he hesitated, which he never did, "I guess she would bring all sorts of men around she'd meet at bars."

"*Yeah?*" I asked, ready to scream at him.

"Well," he sighed, "I guess these men would do things to the little girl and the mother would either pretend she didn't see them or, in my opinion, got paid for them."

My breath whooshed from my chest and my eyes burned. I fell back, stunned to learn what I'd just learned. My stomach churned with disgust for Finley's mother and the sick bastards she'd brought into Finley's home. Memories of Doris Lake came flooding to my mind. Memories of things her mom said to her. *Nothing at all.* Her threatening her to give her to "the bad men." I felt more sick than I ever had, repulsed by the mere *ideas* of her abuse. *Imagine living them?* I asked myself. My skin heated to an unnatural warmth and hate poured out of me in droves, making my whole body tremble.

"Did they catch them?" I asked Dad.

"No, son, I don't believe they ever did."

"So, they just got away with doling out fates worse than death, did they?"

My dad's eyes bored through me. "No one gets away with that, Ethan. No one."

I took a deep breath through my nose.

I stood up, forgetting my orange juice, and clomped across the aged wood floor, each step creaking under my weight. When I reached my room, I pulled my laptop out and pulled up a search engine. I had no idea what I was looking for in particular so I typed in "charity organizations Hạ Long Bay" and pressed enter.

It yielded me a dozen or so links so I began clicking through each one trying to decipher which one I thought Fin would have chosen. The first two were environmental, which I didn't think was Fin's path, seeing as she had mentioned she could relate to the charity itself and I didn't ever remember her speaking about it like it was high up on her radar. I knew what kind she would have chosen but, to be honest with you, I was praying it was something else. I caught a few pictures of Hạ Long Bay and couldn't believe how freaking awesome it looked. *No wonder it's such a tourist destination.*

The third link took me to a site dedicated to feeding the impoverished. I set this one aside to investigate further and was just about to click the fourth link when my phone chimed. I had a text message.

landed in seattle, it read.

I gulped down the flurry of questions settling at the tip of my tongue and wrote instead, ***how was the flight?***

I set my laptop to the side and moved to the edge of my bed, my leg bouncing up and down, my phone in my hand, waiting for a reply.

uneventful can't believe i have almost 9 hours here

I typed out about a million replies but erased them all. I had no idea how to talk to Finley anymore. I couldn't believe what an absolute douche I'd been to her and wondered how in the world she still wanted to be my friend. I'd said some of the most insensitive things you could possibly say and she took it like it was nothing, which made my chest throb.

tired? I asked.

nope. wanna play a game?

always, I teased, feeling anything but playful. Finley was out there doing something good for the world. I didn't have the luxury of not being generous with her. It was the least I could do.

ever heard of galcon, she asked.

Knowing Fin played this game did something strange to my insides. "You are surprising, Finley Dyer," I told no one.

you're such a dork, I replied instead of the truth.

ba ha! I know but it's so fun. just DL it.

112

I have it, I admitted.

A few minutes passed without a response.

okay, fellow dork, i'm in upsilon-2, come find me, she finally answered back.

We played for at least two hours and when all was said and done, we ended up dead equal. My phone rang.

"You summa ma' beach!" she exclaimed when I answered, making me laugh.

"Thought you'd have the upper hand, eh?"

She sighed. "Yes, actually. I am a *rock star* at Galcon. You've stolen a little bit of my thunder, dude."

"Sorry. Not sorry."

"I'm a little flabbergasted, man. I've been on the leaderboards for, like, ever. I thought I was going to school you."

"Please," I began, then paused, "wait, did you say you were on the leaderboards?"

"Yup."

I was skeptical. "What name?"

"TailfFin96."

I couldn't believe that. "You are screwing with me."

She laughed. "No, why?"

"I'm Tatooine436."

"Shut—the—truck—up! You're Tatooine436? I feel like punching you and kissing you at the same time."

I laughed. "This is wild." We'd been trading the second and third spots for months now and I had no idea.

"I'm a little flustered about this," she admitted.

"It is a pretty crazy coincidence."

She was quiet a moment. "Crazy is right. I wonder if the number one spot is, like, Patrick or something."

"Jeez, I hope not."

We laughed and talked the entire day. I even took her with me on a few errands and then to pick up lunch. We ate together with half the country separating us.

"Ethan," Finley said after a lull.

"Yeah?"

"What are you gonna do with your days?" she asked. I could tell she was worried.

"I'm gonna get a job, Fin."

"And?"

"Then, well, just take it one day at a time, I guess. I tossed my secret stash today. I'm going cold turkey."

"Good," she said, sounding relieved.

I let the silence set up my next question.

"Fin?"

"Uh-huh?"

"What's the name of the, uh, charity you're going to work for?" I asked as effortlessly as I could.

"It's called Slánaigh," she answered. "It means 'to safeguard' in Irish."

"That's cool," I offered with no other questions.

I had no idea what she'd said, which frustrated me to no end. It sounded like *slunug* with the "s" dragged out a little and the "g" had a slight hard "ch" sound like the "ch" in Bach. I knew I wouldn't even be able to guess how to spell it if I tried, but I didn't want to press her to find out. It would alert her to my possible snooping, and I wanted her calm for her eleven-hour flight to Seoul. Plus, she'd gone to such efforts to keep it under wraps from me.

Finley had to get off the phone at noon because she thought it would take a while to get through customs. When I let her go, I returned to my search. I perused through countless links searching for anything that sounded close to *slunug* but I had no such luck.

I fell asleep searching and woke when I heard Dad's footsteps in the kitchen.

I leaned against the doorjamb. I'd taken off my shirt but had fallen asleep in my jeans. "Dad?"

He looked over his shoulder and seemed surprised to see me. "Yeah?"

"I'm, that is, I think I'm gonna try to get a job today," I said, wrapping my right hand around my left bicep.

He looked down at the bacon sizzling in his pan and nodded his head. "That's good, son."

I walked into the kitchen and sat at the table, my legs stretched forward and crossed at the ankles, my hair settled on my bare arms and chest.

"Why kind of work you think you wanna do?" He looked up at me. "Need ranch work?"

I shook my head. "Nah, I think I'm gonna try something different."

He flipped the bacon over and stirred his scrambled eggs. He gestured to his food. "Want some?"

"No, thanks."

"So, what kinda work you want to do?" he asked.

I shook my head. "I'm not really sure, actually." I remembered something out of the blue. "I know this park ranger over at Glacier National Park. He told me

I'd be perfect for a position they had open. They need someone who knows the land, can climb, etc."

My dad nodded his head. "Sounds made for you."

"It kind of does, actually."

He plated his food and sat next to me. I tucked my legs up and leaned forward, resting my forearms on the corner of the table and drumming a beat on the tabletop with my fingers. My legs were too long and fit uncomfortably beneath the table. I had to arrange them in the same odd way I did when my mom made me sit for meals before she died. I hadn't sat at that table for years.

"It's good to see you this early," my dad offered up in a rare moment of emotion. My fingers stopped drumming.

"You too, Dad," I told him. "You know, I haven't had a drop to drink in over two weeks."

He looked up at me. "I can tell," he said in that gruff voice of his. He took a bite of eggs and swallowed. "It's that Dyer girl."

I nodded my head in that same way my dad did and wondered if it was an inherited trait or a learned one.

"She's pretty spectacular."

"Love her?" he asked, shocking me.

I choked on nothing, sitting up. "What?" I asked when I'd gathered myself.

He bit into a slice of bacon. "Do you love her yet?"

I furrowed my brows. "What on earth would make you think that?"

"A man doesn't quit the drinkin' caused by one woman unless there's another worth stopping for."

My eyes bugged wide. "Finley and I are just friends, Dad."

His fork stopped midway to his mouth. "No such thing," he said. His fork found his mouth again.

I laughed. "You're outdated, old man."

"Bull corn," he said, shocking me further. I was beginning to wonder if I knew my dad at all. "Men are still men, boy. That God-given drive's always gonna be there."

I shook my head at him and sat back, unfolding my legs and stretching them out. "I promise you, we're just friends."

"I don't believe a word. You're just foolin' yourself."

He had no idea what he was talking about. I knew what Finley was to me.

"I'm not jokin', Dad. She's the best friend I've ever had."

"You don't think your mama and I weren't best friends? Boy, she was my matchless friend. Nobody could touch that ever. Still can't."

Talking about my mom made me ill feeling. "You mean you were friends before you started dating?"

"No, I just meant that's how it should be. Your wife should be your best friend. Always."
My brows narrowed at him.

"I don't think of Fin like that, though."

"Why not?" he asked, leaning back in his chair. It squeaked with age. He picked up his coffee cup and took a sip.

"'Cause," I offered weakly. "Trust me, we just don't."

"Is she a pretty girl?"

117

I rolled my eyes in answer.

"Well, is she?"

Admitting this wouldn't help my case any but I wasn't going to lie. "Yes, she's drop-dead, actually."

"Well, now," he said, a small grin laid across his lips, "what's the issue then?"

I let it lie. There was no explaining what Finley meant to me. He didn't understand that I couldn't cheapen how I felt about her with letting something like an attraction take precedence.

CHAPTER ELEVEN

I glanced up at my clock and noted the time. *Finley should be landing within fifteen minutes.* I never asked her to but I was hoping she'd call me once she went through customs. I paced the living room a little once Dad had left, imagining the worst, for some reason. *Damn, dude, you're paranoid.*

Finally, an hour after she was supposed to have landed, I got a call from a random number and picked it up on the second ring like a stalker.

"Hello?" I answered.

"Hey," a groggy-sounding Finley greeted.

I breathed a sigh of relief. "Fin, so glad you called."

"I figured I'd ring you here so you wouldn't worry."

"That's considerate, Fin."

She giggled but it sounded a little muffled. "That's me. Miss Magnanimous. I'm gettin' T-shirts made." I laughed, happy to hear her voice. I couldn't believe I'd have to wait a year to see her again. "Listen," she said, breaking up, "my connecting flight

119

from Seoul leaves in half and an hour and I want to pee and grab something to eat."

"Go then," I ordered. "Call me when you get to Hanoi."

"I will. Thanks, Ethan."

"For what, Fin?"

"For caring as much as you do."

I grinned from ear to ear. "Shut up, Fin."
I don't know how but I could hear her smile and she hung up.

A hard stone settled in the pit of my stomach. With as secretive as she was about everything, I knew there must have been something about what she was doing that was extraordinarily dangerous, and I didn't know what to do with that. I walked toward my room, ready to reach for my laptop. I spent about one minute that morning toggling back and forth between trying to decide whether I should search the Internet for information on Finley's case. I decided I wouldn't betray her that way. I decided, if she wanted me to know, she would tell me, and with that, I showered and dressed.

I paced the living room, ready to text that ranger at Glacier but couldn't bring myself to do it, not when I knew Finley might be doing something crazy, even if it was to help others. I gave in and picked up my laptop, bringing it to my knees, and pulled up a search engine. Fin had said that the name of the organization she was helping was an Irish name meaning to safeguard. I searched an English-to-Irish dictionary and clicked the first link. Four little boxes pulled up and I chose the English translator, typing in "to safeguard."

The word *Slánaigh* fell at the top of the results. Beside it was a small sideways triangle, indicating you could hear how it was pronounced so I clicked it. A man's voice came on and his interpretation sounded like the "slunug" I recognized from Finley.

With shaking hands, I highlighted the word "Slánaigh" and pasted it along with "Vietnam" in the search bar, clicking enter.

There it is.

I clicked on the link to the site and was greeted with hauntingly sad images like a punch in the stomach. Children. Children but their eyes had bars across them to protect their identities, I decided. The headline read, "Stop Child Sex Slavery."

Like that, my world tipped on its side. I felt my breath catch in my throat. I understood why Finley would have wanted to help this cause and I even understood why she kept it a secret. Revealing that the issue hit close to home for her and would have been an admission of her past and she wasn't ready for that. I understood it but I didn't like it. I didn't like it because it was extremely dangerous.

I read their mission statement and cringed, imagining Finley reliving her past. Not being able to stop there, I read their journals, the articles, the personal accounts of survivors and volunteers alike. The men who ran these sex trade circles weren't just the sick of the sick, you guys. They were devoid of anything resembling humanity. They were violent beyond violent. They weren't afraid to murder those who got in their way. They bribed the media and police and they were successful. They were incredibly successful.

I felt utterly ill to my stomach. I couldn't believe I'd let Finley go, that I'd actually *driven* her to the airport. If I had known, I would have stopped her. If I'd known, I would have found another solution for her to feel like she was accomplishing her goal. The idea of her over there risking her life was too much for me.

I let out a shaky breath and stood from my search. The urge to drink was something fierce. Instead of heading to Vi, I decided to put on a pair of running shorts, a pair of sneakers, and go running. I pushed down the overwhelming call to the bottle and headed out onto the outskirts of the fields, running like my life depended on it and as the sweat dripped down my back and chest, I decided something had to be done for Finley.

I needed to bring her home, take her away from the danger, protect her. I *needed* to do this. I needed to save her as she saved me.

And so I ran. I ran away from my addiction like my life depended on it. I'd imagined I was running to Finley and suddenly I'd never had such endurance, never wanted anything more in my life. She'd become more important to me than myself. Nothing would sever that friendship, nothing.

After running hard for close to an hour, I went back home, showered again and sat on the bed with every intention of looking up details about the search-and-rescue position Seth said was available at Glacier, but apparently I'd fallen asleep without realizing it, which was a disconcerting thing. I was awakened by the sound of my phone ringing. I shot up with a confused feeling, glancing at my surroundings and realizing my phone was going off. Searching through the sheets, I found the phone, sliding the answer button.

"Hello," my voice rasped.

"Is Ethan there?" Finley asked.

"Fin, it's me," I said, my voice scratchy from sleep.

She laughed. "I barely recognized you. You already have the deepest voice ever so when Vin Diesel on molasses answered I was like *what*!"

I smiled and shook my head. "I, uh, fell asleep. Didn't mean to. It just happened."

"Yeah, well, I'm envious as hell. I've been flying on an airplane for almost twenty-four hours, dude, and I'm about to go Joaquin Phoenix on someone and strangely rant about frogs and other nonsense."

A burst of laughter eked out of me. "You're deranged, Dyer."

She sighed. "I know. Hey," she went off without warning, "wanna hear something trippy?"

"Always."

"It's, what, two-thirty on a Friday afternoon there, right?"

"Right."

"It's two-thirty a.m. *Saturday* here. Can you believe that? I'm in the future, dude. I'm seriously here on Saturday and you're still in the middle of your Friday."

I grinned. "Far out, Fin, or should I say Marty?"

"Yeah, I'll be Marty and you can be Doc."

"It's a deal. Hey," I said, following her lead.

"Hey what?"

"I, uh, I found out where you're working," I threw out there, wondering how pissed she was going to be.

"How in the world did you do that?" she asked, her voice an almost whisper.

Apparently very pissed.

"Listen, you were just so secretive I couldn't stand knowing if you were in real danger or not."

"I repeatedly let you know how I felt about that, Ethan. If I'd wanted you to know, I would have told you."

I wanted to explain that I *had* respected her privacy by not researching what had happened to her as a little girl, but I decided to keep that little gem to myself.

"Fin, I'm sorry. I really am, but keeping me in the dark is, well, frankly cruel. Imagining where you were and what could happen was playing dirty tricks on me."

She sighed, obviously angry with me. "Ethan, this feels so…"

"So?"

"So rotten! Why couldn't you have done the decent thing and just respected that I didn't want you knowing?"

"I think the only reason you didn't say anything was because you knew you could get hurt, Fin. Keeping me in the dark about something like that, that's not cool, dude."

"If I'd told you, you would have stopped me from going, right?" I didn't answer. "Well?"

"Well *what*?"

"If I had, would you have stopped me from going?

"I don't know," I lied.

"Lie!"

"Finley, it just would have been cool to have at least been informed. I felt like I was blindsided today. I'm-I'm worried about you."

I could hear her slight breathing as she considered what I said. "I know that, Ethan, but this-this is something that has to be done."

"Not by you, it doesn't."

"What the heck does that mean? You don't think I'm capable of helping?"

"You are," I insisted, meaning it. "It's just that, well, what if you get into a situation where you can't defend yourself?"

"I'll be with plenty of people always," she explained.

I breathed through my nose, frustrated with her. I don't know what I was hoping she would do or say by approaching her the way I had. I decided to come out with it.

"I think you should come home."

She growled, actually growled. "Ethan Moonsong, you are about two seconds away from me hanging up this phone."

"Finley, I'd like it if you could come home," I asked as nicely as I could.

She laughed a little hysterically then lowered her voice. "Seriously, you are ridiculous. I'm wearing twenty-four hours' worth of plane, which is not helping my nerves at all, not to mention the little fact that I had this trip planned way before you re-entered my life! And Ethan? I love you and all, but you can't dictate what I do with that life. I'm already here, and I'd appreciate it if you could just get on board."

Shit. "I don't know if I can do that. I'm scared for you, Fin."

She sighed. "I understand. I do, but I *need* to do this. Need it like a thirsty man needs water, Ethan, and there's nothing you can do to stop me. I need this more than you need me home. I'm sorry, but this door is closed."

"Finley, if you can die, it's not worth it."
Things got deadly quiet. So quiet I'd decided she'd stopped breathing.

"Some things are worse than death, Ethan," she finally said with eerie calm.

"I've lost my mom, lost Caroline, Fin, and I'm tired of losing." That was a low blow and I knew it. I opened my mouth to recant it but she stopped me by speaking first.

"This isn't about you, Ethan. It never was."
And with that, I heard a click and shortly after, a hauntingly empty beep.

I cursed, wishing things hadn't ended as they had. I blamed myself because, well, it *was* my fault.

Two days passed and I hadn't heard from Finley. She didn't call me with a number to reach her or email me she was okay. I had overstepped and I knew it. My caring for Finley didn't give me the right to demand things from her.

The morning of the third day, I'd greeted my dad in the kitchen. It was his day off.

"Hey, Pop, what's up?"

He turned toward me. "Oh, nothin'. Fixin' to make some breakfast. You want some?"
He was dressed in his customary Wranglers and worn boots, as if he was going out, but his hat laid on the table.

"I've got a better idea," I said, and he narrowed his eyes in question. "Let's go eat at the counter at

Sykes." His eyes popped open in surprise but relaxed almost immediately.

"Okay," he said softly.

"Just let me grab my boots."

He nodded his head.

I ran to my room and threw my boots on then met him in the living room. He held the door open for me and I ducked under the frame and onto the creaky wraparound porch. We walked silently to his truck, and I got in the passenger side. It'd been several months since we'd ridden in a car together. It felt like years. I buckled myself in and lazily lifted a foot, resting my ankle on the knee of the opposite leg. When Dad got in, he glanced down at my feet, shaking his head.

"Why don't you wear real boots?" he asked me, starting the truck.

I looked down at my brown leather combats. The top of the tongue was worn and flopped out a little. I didn't lace them to the top of the boot because they felt too constricting so I stopped the laces at the ankles. I usually tucked my worn jeans into the top of the boot because it felt practical working in the fields. I smiled to myself. I'd seen a few commercials that showed men in New York were doing the same thing, but I doubt their motivations were the same.

"Cowboy boots feel ridiculous on the foot to me. Besides, I'm a bit more rock'n'roll than country," I admitted, staring out the passenger window.

He shook his head but smirked.

We got on the road and I rolled my window down. The ride to Skyes was quiet. I used the time to think about what I could do about Finley. She wouldn't call me and although I'd considered calling her, I'd quickly decided that would offend her. She didn't like me stepping on her independence. I got that. I didn't want to *force* her to come home, necessarily, I just didn't want her in danger, and since I was used to demanding things from the people I cared for, I didn't think it an unreasonable a request. I thought her outright refusal an overreaction. *Wasn't it?*

Something dawned on me.

I looked at my father. "Dad?"

He glanced at me then back on the road. "Yeah?"

"Do you think I'm a control freak?"

"Yes," he answered without hesitation.

The swiftness in his answer stung. I wrapped my arms around myself. "Seriously?"

He nodded and I thought that would be the only response I'd get, but he spoke again. "You've been like that since... Well, since your mama passed, son."

That wasn't what I had expected him to say. I figured he'd come back with some smart-ass answer. Delving into my psyche was not only *not* welcome, it was about to get shot right the hell out of the dang cab. I'd immediately regretted bringing it up and wished I'd kept my distance that morning instead of encouraging the little walk down memory lane. No doubt bringing Sykes up stirred up all kinds of retrospection...on both sides.

I sank into myself a little, wondering if Dad had wanted to talk about Mom. Frankly, I didn't want to do it. I wasn't ready. I knew I'd never be ready, ever. My chest throbbed, even my skin seemed to retreat into itself. The mere idea of my mother made me shudder. I missed her with a violence I couldn't quite voice. I yearned for her with a frightening ferociousness.

I bit down hard, my jaw clenching, refusing to acknowledge the excruciating torment that was the absence of my mother.

But my father had different ideas. "I'm sorry for you," he said quietly.

"I can't talk about it yet, Dad."
He looked at me with pity.

I stared at him hard. "No! Don't do that. Don't you dare do that!" His eyes softened, turning almost glassy. I turned toward the window. "Don't, Dad. Just don't."

I heard him swallow. "If you're not ready to talk about it, Ethan, it means I've done you quite an injustice."

Light tears leaked from my eyes despite my best efforts. "No," I insisted. "Stop."

"I didn't know how to handle your grief because I was blinded by my own. I failed you and-and I'm sorry for that."

"Stop," I begged. I sighed, trying to keep myself in check. I dragged my palms down my face then back up again, tugging at my hair to distract myself.

My dad shook his head and focused on the road. "Poor boy," I barely registered, sending the pain spiraling deep into my belly.

I let anger rise and take over. I clenched my jaw, steeling myself. "Don't feel sorry for me," I demanded, my fists balling. "I'm not one to pity, old man."

He looked at me and his eyes told me he disagreed. He nodded his concession, but it did nothing to settle my unease. I was a control freak with mommy issues. I was pathetic, yes, but I didn't want anyone's pity, not even Dad's. I was going to tow my grief alone because it was what I was comfortable with. To me, nothing beat familiarity, even if the familiar was agony.

CHAPTER TWELVE

We sat in silence at Sykes, Delia buzzing about behind the counter. She eyed us warily, probably reading our body language. Correction, *my* body language. I was tense because my dad kept looking at me like he wanted to hug me, and I wanted to run the other direction. I loved my dad more than I loved myself but I couldn't wrap my head around this newfound revelation of his. I was accustomed to the quiet, minimal conversationalist dad. Not that he'd been talking my ear off or anything, it was just more than I was used to hearing.

Delia approached us cautiously. "Can I get you boys anything else?" she asked.
We both shook our heads and she walked off.

"Have you talked to the Dyer girl?" he asked out of nowhere.

"Not really," I admitted.

He took a sip of his coffee. "Why?"

I sighed. "Because she's pissed at me."

My dad winced. "Why the language, Ethan?" he asked before continuing. "What did you do to her anyway?"

I stared at my plate, pushing eggs around with my fork. "I sort of demanded she come home." His cup clinked on its saucer, startling me, and I looked at him.

"Why would you do that?" he asked.

"I found out the place she's volunteering at is dangerous. Like, *she could die* kind of dangerous."

He took a deep breath and let it out slowly. "Why would she take a risk like that?"

"Because it's incredibly important to her. It means something to her."

Understanding dawned on him and he shook his head. "That poor girl."

I found myself feeling defensive. "You don't have to feel sorry for Finley, Dad. She's literally the strongest person I know. She helped me out of the dark hole I'd dug for myself and that was a feat, let me tell you."

He nodded. "I'll be grateful to her forever for that. I tried so hard to help you, Ethan. I'd wished every day I could have fixed it for you."

"No one could fix it for me but myself, old man. She just made me see what I'd been so blinded by. She's an enlightener. I don't think anyone else could have done it."

He looked at me, his lips pursed in a thin line, his brows furrowed. "You should contact her then and apologize."

I shook my head. "I don't think so. She was peeved I'd found out where she was. If I called, I think she'd flip. If she wanted to talk to me, she'd have called already."

He sat up in his stool, folding one arm under the other and using his free hand to roll the broken paper binding that had bound his utensils together.

"How dangerous is it? This thing she's doing?"

I looked at him square in the eye. "The organization's leader is being hunted by his opposition and the government there isn't really doing anything to help him."

He squeezed his eyes together and shook his head. "You should go there. Protect her."

I looked at my dad like he was crazy. "*What?*"

"Ethan," he spoke steadily. "She needs to do what she's doing. You obviously care for her. You're very *capable*, son," he said, emphasizing the word *capable*, implying something else unspoken. "You also don't have anything going on right now. Take your savings, buy a one-way ticket and get gone, boy."

I stared at my father, realizing for the first time that although he was a steadfast, quiet man, he was no fool. He observed with a keen eye. He memorized and analyzed. He would have been quite an asset, I believed, to the FBI or CIA.

And he was right. I was very *capable*. I knew if I went to her, I could most definitely guard Finley. I could help her fulfill this insane desire of hers.

I let out a deep, even breath. "You're right."

CHAPTER THIRTEEN

I'd sat at the airport in Seattle for seven hours, desperate to board my plane to Seoul. I couldn't believe I was flying to Vietnam. Once I'd decided to do it, I didn't hesitate. I knew if I hadn't bought the tickets, I'd have convinced myself I was overstepping, so I just purchased them without thinking. I tried calling Finley but she didn't answer and the place she was working at, Slánaigh, didn't have a direct line that I could find. It was almost completely unheard of, I'd discovered. I assumed that was because they didn't want information about where they were, etc., getting out to the ones they opposed.

I'd just nodded off in my plastic, uncomfortable bench airport chair, when I heard them call for my flight. My nerves immediately shot off like a rocket, adrenaline waking every single fiber of my body. I stood in line, jittery and, frankly, from the expressions a few people around me, I'm pretty sure they thought I was up to something. When I made it to the front, I handed the woman my ticket, she scanned it and gestured with a swift flick of her hand for me to move forward.

The flight over the Pacific, was uneventful, though long as hell. When I landed in Korea, I realized what a douche I must have seemed to Finley when she'd called me. I was dead tired and irritable and couldn't believe I only had a two-hour layover before I'd needed to be on yet another plane to Hanoi. That flight, thank God, would only be four and a half hours, a bit more tolerable than the eleven-hour flight to Seoul.

Once I'd de-planed, I passed by a row of pay phones, recognizing them as the ones Finley must have rang me from. When I passed the last phone, I had a vision of a tall, earthy, beautiful Finley leaning against the platform the phone sat on, twirling her hair around her index finger as she so often did, talking to me. I smiled to myself. *Fantasizing about her?* I shook it off. *Pretend. Pretend. Pretend.*

I boarded the plane to Hanoi with little to no plan on how I was going to find Slánaigh once I got to Hạ Long City. I wasn't even sure I'd be able to find her the morning I landed. I knew the locals would either have no idea what I was talking about or, as I more strongly suspected, would act like they didn't know. Because of this, I prepared myself to stay the night in a nearby hotel if I had to.

My first impressions of Hanoi was that their airport didn't differ all that much from any you'd find back home. It was clean and architecturally similar and they were also kind enough to have an English translation on all their signs, which helped with how nervous I was already feeling. I could not believe I was in Vietnam. *Finley's gonna kill you, dude. Like, kill you dead.*

I stood by my baggage claim area hoping to see my bag as quickly as possible. It helped that I was a foot taller than those around me. It didn't help the anxiety coursing through my veins that all those eyes were on me, though. *Yes, yes*, I wanted to say. *I'm a behemoth*.

Thankfully, my bag was the second out on the conveyor and when I excused myself, the other travelers parted like Moses and the Red Sea.

"Great, I'm a novelty," I said to no one.

Three preteen girls gasped then giggled, their hands glued to their mouths, when I smiled at them in a friendly gesture. They began speaking a mile a minute in continuous tittering, eyeing me like they'd never seen anything like me before. I retreated into myself as I grabbed both my bags and swung them onto the floor below. I turned to make my escape but there was nowhere to turn. Bodies filled every square inch around the revolving carousel.

"Jeez," I said, unsure of what to do, but with that one word everyone around me scattered. "What is going on?"

"They're afraid of you," a chuckling man with a thick accent beside me answered.

"Why?" I asked.

"Have you seen you?" he answered, his eyes popping open in mock surprise.

"I'm tall, but that's not *that* unusual."

"It's not just your height," he explained, eyeing the revolving bags for his own. "It's your size."

I looked down at myself desperate to see what they saw. I looked around me. No one was taller than five foot five or so, but they were also very lean, thin. *Ah, I get it.* I was the proverbial American male to them. Broad shoulders from working the fields for years and all that comes with it. I'm sure my hair didn't help either.

I threw my bags over my shoulder to the delight of the group of preteen girls which made my eyes roll and headed toward a sign that signaled exchange services. I converted a hundred American dollars into, I shit you not, two million one hundred twenty-one thousand five hundred Vietnamese dong.

The exchange agent spoke English, so I took advantage. "Excuse me, do you know the best way for me to reach Hạ Long Bay?"

"There are many options," she explained, rummaging through a pile of pamphlets on her desk and pulling out one what looked like a schedule. It was in Vietnamese, though. "There's a minibus that leaves here in half an hour that goes to Hạ Long City. You can also rent a taxi or motorbike."

"How far away is it?" I asked, considering the taxi route.

"About one hundred forty-five kilometers. By taxi, it would take about two and half hours. The minibus is less expensive but an hour is added onto your trip."

"How much for the taxi do you think?"

"Around eighty-five American dollars."

I inwardly sighed. The idea of getting on yet another contraption full of strangers for hours made me cringe, but I didn't have the cash for the taxi. I spent most of my savings on the plane ticket and the rest I had saved to support myself the months I would be there with Fin.

"Where's the minibus at?" I asked.

She pointed me in the direction of the little station. I needed to find the bus that read Hạ Long City and I could pay the driver, she had explained. I dragged my canvas luggage onto my shoulders and huffed it to the bus terminal as quickly as possible. I apparently had less than fifteen minutes to get to the bus or I risked waiting another two hours to catch the next one. And the terminal was ten minutes away. That fact panicked me. I'd had enough of traveling.

When I reached the minibus, I was thoroughly out of breath but I got there in less than five minutes carrying two fairly heavy canvas duffels. There was a line of people so I joined in, dumping my bags at my feet.

I read the fare was two-hundred twenty thousand dong. I did a quick calculation in my head and realized it was only about ten dollars, which relieved me. Nervous butterflies took residence in my stomach at the thought of seeing Finley. I couldn't decide if it was because it was just the thought of seeing her or if I was afraid of how *she'd* react to seeing *me*. A little of both, I finally reasoned.

I paid the fare and boarded the bus, catching a window seat in the very back. As we left the airport, the lulling chatter of the passengers around me subdued my unease and I took in the country that was Vietnam.

Right off the bat, I thought it a magnificent place. The people were beautiful and stylish and the land seemed to match them. I got a kick out of the fact that their street workers wore those conical leaf hats. Later, I would find out they were called nón lá. There were motorbikes *everywhere*. I winced when I saw a very pregnant woman on one but I supposed that was normal for their people.

Entering the highway was beyond scary. Instead of the entrance ramps I was accustomed to, it was a free-for-all from what I could tell. I'd noticed incessant honking since we'd left the airport and it seemed even more outrageous in the cluster of vehicles trying to maneuver past one another. I sat up, white-knuckling the seat bar in front of me. When we got through, I looked around me and almost burst out laughing at all the slack Westerner jaws with their wide eyes.

To me, the highways and regular city streets weren't at all different. The speed limits seemed the same to me but then again, I couldn't read the signs indicating the rate. Though we did share the Roman numeral system, it was hard to guess what meant what.

We had reached the city proper in under an hour and the driver had explained in broken English that we would be stopping for a half hour break so they could refuel and we could eat something or shop. When I left the bus, I was *amazed* at the bustling life all around me. It was intimidating to say the least. Strangely, they carted around massive amounts of cargo on the back racks of their motorbikes. What looked like a giant sphere worth of wicker baskets came barreling through everyone, surprising me, and making me laugh. The woman driving the small motorbike looked on a mission. Cars, motorbikes, and bicycles alike shared the streets in a chaotic battle to further their efforts. Horns bombarded my ears like buzzing bees. Every inch of the Old Quarter seemed to hum, actually. Small alleyways were packed with people and street vendors.

The street food alone, I could tell, was enough to warrant a visit to Vietnam. Each peddler seemed to specialize in their particular fare. Later I would discover just how in love with the food I would become. From the obvious but wonderful Phở bò with chili sauce to the Cơm tấm or broken rice to the Xôi or sticky rice. The popular Bánh mì or baguette and the gỏi bò which is a papaya salad you would die for. Vietnam is a type of food heaven.

I jutted down a popular alleyway where I happened upon a drive-in ice cream parlor. People sat perched on their motorbikes or scattered around talking and eating. I was enthralled by it all.

I passed a long stall full of eaters and came upon some sort of fresh food market. Loud voices carried through and around me as I sort of turned about and absorbed my surroundings. I hadn't any clue how incredible the culture of Vietnam was, and I was mesmerized.

I left the alleyway I was in and followed a main street past incredibly narrow shops chock full to the brim, even spilling onto the sidewalks, with merchandise to purchase. Many of the shops were so compact, I couldn't even stand upright in them. It was a claustrophobic's nightmare but also entertaining.

Amid the shops sat small sections of tables and stools between street vendor setups that sat so low to the ground I thought they were there for children until I saw full-grown adults perched on the stools, chopsticks in hand, laughing and eating.

I paid a dollar and a half for a bowl of Phở that came with a fried spring roll that practically melted in my mouth. I stood beside the street vendor, holding my bowl and chopsticks, smiling like an imbecile unsure of where I was supposed to go or do once I'd received my food. She laughed at me and signaled toward a girl who looked like her daughter. The girl marched over to me, forcefully sat me in a shallow stool made for a four-year-old very near the curb and barked Vietnamese at me but smiled, so I assumed it wasn't a death threat. Motorbikes zipped past me. It was scary and not relaxing in the least, but I wasn't about to argue with the girl because I could tell everything I was experiencing was Vietnam.

The girl left then returned with a bottle of chili sauce and a small bowl of cut limes. She took my chopsticks from me and I watched as she ran the limes up the length of each chopstick, handed them back to me, then ran off again.

If you had told me a week before that I'd be sitting on the side of the road in Vietnam with a bowl of Phở on a stool made for a baby, I'd have had you committed. I wasn't well versed with a pair of chopsticks but knew that practice made perfect, so I laughed at myself and dug in. I noticed that the locals didn't let their mouths touch the sticks, which truly boggled my mind. I attempted it but was not that successful. I was a fumbling idiot at first but by the end of the meal, I had them down pretty well.

Refreshed by the food and the people-watching, I headed back to the minibus right about the time everyone else was arriving. Once I stepped back on that bus, though, the tension began to build. *Two hours until I see Finley.*

The drive to Hạ Long City was nothing short of surreal. The vegetation was so different from what I was accustomed to and it drew my eye. It was probably one of the greenest parts of the earth I had ever seen with tall, plush trees and grasses tucked against buildings and roads. It was as if life found every nook and cranny and shoved themselves inside.

The buildings were scattered in clusters and stacked high with homes and shops. The land was incredibly well farmed. I don't believe any of it went to waste. I could tell there were no bureaucratic restrictions on what could be grown and by whom. I believe the same applied to the street vendors in Hanoi.

Close to Hạ Long City, I could just make out the outline of Hạ Long Bay and my gut clenched a little. I was close to Finley. When we entered the city there was a massive cable-stayed bridge connecting the two mainlands called Bãi Cháy Bridge according to the driver. To me it resembled a giant geometric spiderweb of daunting metal cables that reached high into the sky. I half expected a matching spider to come crawling along the bridge's metal spindles.

When we came to a stop outside a small street sign, I jumped out as quickly as I could, desperate to get my luggage and start my search. The driver started unloading bags and setting them in a line on the sidewalk. I was still searching for one of my bags when he drove away, leaving us all a little bewildered. When he did this, though, he cleared our view of the bay and it took my breath away.

Jagged, gargantuan lime islands jutted up and out creating a cascading look across the surface of the clear, blue ocean. On the tops of each were thick layers of lush green vegetation and they seemed to follow a pattern of winding rows, as if a giant dragon was diving in and out of the water, only its back cresting the water. It was utterly breathtaking. I had no earthly clue just how important it was for me to see this part of the world, and I was so glad I'd followed my dad's advice. Giant wood Asian cruise ships called junks peppered the water with their massive webbed sails made of bronze-colored canvas.The sights were a once-in-a-lifetime view, and I was altogether overwhelmed I'd had the opportunity to witness them.

I drank it all in one more time, shook my head, then found my second bag. I had no idea where to start. I turned around and noticed a little tea shop on the corner. Deciding that was as good a place to start as any, I marched in, and up to the counter.

"Excuse me, I'm sorry, but do you speak English?" I asked.

The man shook his head but held up a finger to stay me. He escaped to the back, having retrieved a young woman about my age.

She smiled at me and asked, "Can I help you?"

"Hi, yes, I'm, uh, searching for a place called Slánaigh. Are you familiar with it?"

When I mentioned Slánaigh, both their eyes widened and the old man started shouting at me so vehemently in Vietnamese, I nearly bolted for the door. The girl said something to him that made him silent, but he eyed me like he wanted to nail me to the floor and use me for target practice. He started to pull back toward the curtained area the girl had appeared from but before he fully disappeared, he looked back once, narrowing his eyes. I flinched.

The girl looked at me. "I'm sorry, my father, he is... Anyway, why are you looking for Slánaigh?"

"You've heard of it then?"

She looked behind me, contemplating something, then turned back toward me. "I don't know. Why are you looking for them?"

The ol' merry-go-round, eh? "I'm looking for a girl that works there. I need to get in contact with her."

The girl stared me down so hard I felt like bolting again and starting fresh somewhere else. After a few agonizing seconds, she finally spoke.

"Who do you work for?" she bit. Her eyes narrowed at me.

"No one. I'm just looking for my friend."

"Did Khanh send you here?"

"No," I insisted.

"How do you find us then? Why this shop?"

"I swear, I didn't know you were connected with them. I just flew in from the United States and took a minibus straight here from the airport. I was dropped off right there," I said, pointing at where the bus had sat.

The man came back from behind the curtain yelling again and my skin started to burn hot with the apparent accusations. I lifted my hands in surrender as the girl shoved the man back through the curtain. She turned back to me.

"Listen," I said, "my friend only mentioned the name Slánaigh and that it was here, near the bay. I know the work she's doing can be dangerous so I wanted to come help her, protect her."

The girl's eyes narrowed at me. "Why didn't you call her?"

"She's mad at me. I tried, trust me. She doesn't even know I'm here."

She watched me again for a long time as if she was trying to decide something.

"What's your name?" she asked.

"Ethan Moonsong."

"Stay right there," she ordered, jabbing a finger my direction. "Don't move. If you leave, I'll know Khanh sent you."

I nodded wondering who this Khanh guy was.

She parted the curtains to the back and I could hear her and the older man yelling back and forth. It got quiet for a moment then I heard her talk again but this time it sounded one-sided, like she was on the phone. I wished I spoke Vietnamese. I heard my name spoken once and then a pause, what sounded like agreeing, and finally I heard a receiver click.

She returned to the counter. "Your friend will be here soon."

CHAPTER FOURTEEN

I paced the sidewalk outside the tea shop, wondering if I'd made the right decision. *No, you're here for a reason.* I repeatedly ran my hands through my hair then tucked my hands under my arms, fidgeting. The girl from the tea shop came out, carrying a steaming cup of green tea.

"You need to calm down," she told me, handing me the cup before heading back inside.

I took one sip of the tea out of courtesy and set it on one of the tables outside the shop. I wrapped my hands around my triceps, hunching my shoulders, my head laid low, watching every step I took. Back and forth. Back and forth. Back and forth. Back and—

Finley's shoes fell into view, stock-still, and I slid to a stop, lifting my head to see her face.

I opened my mouth but her posture struck me silent. Her hands were planted on her hips, her eyes narrowed, lips thinned.

146

"What are you doing here?" she asked with an eerie calm.

My hands fell from my arms, dangling at my side. My hair blew with the wind across my chest and lifted off my shoulder, as if the fury she wore so clearly on her face affected the nature I stood in. I'm not gonna lie, I was scared of her. I was half a foot taller, probably had eighty pounds on her, and could lay out any man who crossed my path, but the girl who stood in front of me terrified me. *Never had this happen*.

"Did I stutter, Moonsong?" she asked with fearsome eyes.

I fought a small smile then shook my head to defeat it.

"Listen," I began and her eyes narrowed into fine slits. "I'm not here to bring you home."

She leaned back on her heels when I said this. I hadn't realized she'd reached up on her toes. She looked like she was ready to sock me right in the mouth.

"You're not?" she asked, still seething.

"No, I'm here to help you. Seriously. I figured if you wouldn't come home, I'd come to you."

Her hands went to the top of her head which, from what I remembered in high school, was a bad sign. "Help me? What are you *doing* here, Ethan? There was a very real reason I didn't tell you very many details. I didn't want anyone interfering here. I made it clear multiple times with you in Kalispell *and* on the phone that I needed to do this alone. It's none of your business!"

My blood began to boil and my hands found my hips. I leaned over her and she had to strain her neck to look up into my eyes but she stayed stalwart much to my delight, though I wasn't gonna tell her that.

"Yeah, well, when you go traipsing off, doing extremely dangerous things, I make it my business, Fin! Now I'm not saying I'm gonna make you come home. I realize what a douche I was in asking that of you and I'm sorry for that, but you can't expect me to stand by while you risk your life! I'm gonna stay whether you like it or not. Just as I can't make you do what you don't want, you can't make me. If you want me gone, you're gonna have to drag me out of here!"

I lifted my arms, palms out, beckoning her to try it.

Finley took a deep, scary breath then pushed me as hard as she could, shocking me, despite the fact that she didn't even move me an inch. She crawled up my body with her legs and wrapped her arms around my neck trying as hard as she could to drag me down. I had no idea what she was trying to accomplish and thought it was hilarious so I started laughing which pissed her off even more and she worked doubly hard to bring me down.

"Come on, you big bastard, why won't you fall!" she said, making me laugh even harder.
She punched me in the shoulder in response, tugging at my clothing and attacking me with every means possible. Her nails dug into my shoulders a little and I winced but tried not to show it. She fell back to the ground, huffing and puffing from her effort, then kicked me in the foot, which earned her a gigantic smile. She fought a grin of her own.

"Stop it, you jerk!" she yelled, swiping a bombshell wave from her face. That grin she fought was starting to crack through and she bit her bottom lip to keep it from slipping further.

I started chuckling again which enraged her and she went for me again, shuffling her feet back and forth, pathetically throwing punches at me. I caught each one without any effort at all but after about ten I'd had enough. I grabbed both her hands, spun her back into me and pulled her arms around herself in a sort of restraint. Her hair draped in her face and with each breath, a strand would tumble away from her face gracefully.

Laughing, I whispered in her ear, "Are you done?"

She huffed. "No," she stubbornly bit, making me smile.

I looked over at the tea shop window and noticed the old man and young girl watching us. The old man didn't look pleased, with his arms crossed in front of his chest but the girl looked at us with the slyest grin on her face. Finley noticed it too.

"It's not funny, An!"

The girl laughed like that's exactly what it was, which I agreed wholeheartedly. She led the older man away from the window, and I turned back to my prisoner.

"I'm going to let you go, Fin. Are you going to hit me if I do?"

"Yes," she admitted with edge.

"Fine," I told her, gripping her arms tighter. Not enough to hurt her but enough to make her uncomfortable. I'll admit it out loud, I liked the power I held over her. I'd never harm her but I did get a kick out of how much it bugged her. For some reason, I liked to get under her skin. Childishly, I wanted under hers the way she'd delved beneath mine. I wanted some sort of sign of agitation from her, anything that showed me I affected her. I'd take whatever, just to know I stirred her in any small way. "You can just stay in this position then."

She stamped her flip-flop clad foot on top of my boot, causing me to snort to which she whipped her head my way. Her eyes narrowed. "I'm no longer a fan of yours," she told me.

I don't know why I did it but I leaned forward, resting my forehead against her temple. "Yes, you do," I told her. "You're putting up this fuss, but I know how scary this all is for you. I can see it in your eyes, Fin. You're glad I'm here but you're too proud to admit it."

"Am not," she maturely retorted.

"Are so," I played along.

"Not."

"Are. Admit it and I'll let you go," I *also* maturely said.

"Never. Not if we have to stand here all night," she gritted.

"Fine," I said, unexpectedly spinning her out.

She stumbled, but I caught her in my arms.

She pursed her lips. "You're a pain in my rear."

"Yeah, well same goes."

She straightened out her clothing and shoved her hair away from her face before looking me dead in the eye.

"Ethan, I don't like that you're here."

"That may be, but I guarantee you're still glad I'm around."

"That makes no sense."

"It makes perfect sense to me, Fin. You can dislike something yet still see the good it can do for you."

A muscle in her jaw ticked. "Get on the bike," she ordered.

I turned my head to find a small red motorbike on a stand near the curb. "You can't be serious."

"Oh, I'm serious," she said with a venomous smile.

"I'm too tall for that. Too big for that."

"Welcome to Vietnam, idiot," she said, making me smile inside. I felt relief she wasn't demanding I left. I would have gone, despite what I'd told her, if she'd truly asked me. I was happy, beyond happy, she hadn't insisted.

She walked over to the bike, acknowledging me no further, and sat down, pulling a helmet over her head.

I followed her with my bags and strapped them to the back of the bike's rack. "Let me drive, Finley," I said, fastening a bungee cord.

"No," she said, starting the bike.

"You don't understand, Fin. If I get on the back of this bike, I'll displace the weight even worse than these bags already are and we could be driving in the middle of the road and fall backwards."

She stared at me like she couldn't stand me but scooted back. I threaded a leg between her and the handlebars and sat. The whole motorbike sank a few inches.

"You're leviathan," she commented, and I burst out laughing.

My laughter was cut short, though, when Finley wrapped the palm of her hand around my forearm to situate herself. I sucked in a breath at its calming warmth.

Finally, I exhaled inwardly without thinking.

Relief filled my constricted chest, and I felt like I hadn't breathed in days. My left hand instinctively found her right and my fingers curled into hers. We looked at one another, and my antagonism and her anger dissipated into thin air. She nodded in understanding and squeezed my hand. She tucked both her arms around my chest, and I ignored the tight feeling in my gut that gave me. *Don't, Ethan.*

"This way," she said, pointing toward a little winding street.

I nodded, pulled us out into the vacant street and followed her outstretched arm. She guided me left then right, around a looped entrance and onto Bãi Cháy Bridge. The view atop that bridge was extraordinary as the junks floated amongst the blue bay surrounded by the bobbing fishermen in their small pump boats donning their traditional nón lá or leaf hats. It was more than an exceptional sight. I smiled to myself, looked down at Finley's hands, and tried to come to terms with how strange my life had become and how, surprisingly, I wouldn't have changed it for anything in the world.

That's when I remembered Cricket and recognized that I hadn't thought of her really since I started hanging out with Finley. The dire, horrific heartache I thought would have taken residence in my chest forever had only camped out for a while then moved on to better things. I felt a little terrible about that. I mean, I had been in love with Caroline. I should still be mourning her loss, but I couldn't muster up even a mock wound. I held no interest in the idea and that wasn't just something I thought was possible, it was something I would have bet my life would have never left me.

I looked down at Finley's clasped hands and my heart skipped a beat, then a slow burn pooled in the pit of my stomach.

CHAPTER FIFTEEN

Slánaigh wasn't anything like I thought it would be. Isolated on a bit of narrow beach in a secluded stretch of land that jutted out into the bay, it sat with its back tucked against the tip of the small peninsula. Three sides of a two-story, split-level bungalow were surrounded by dark, churning water and tall, thick, swaying palm trees.

The house was painted a seafoam green like so many of the homes native to the area and sat on tall stone stilts that prevented the overflowing tide, if the bay should ever flood, from ruining the home. A zigzagging staircase crawled up the front to a large natural wood deck that wound around the entire beach house. There was a roof made of what looked like flat discs of light terracotta washed out from years underneath the scorching sun and were stacked on top of one another like the scales of a fish. All the windows were open and large white drapes blew in and out of their frames with the sea wind. It was beyond picturesque.

We followed a winding seashell gravel drive slowly so as not to kick up the natural entrance and Finley directed me toward a line of motorbikes. I parked next to the bike farthest to the right, nearest the staircase that reminded me a lot of the natural woods I would see at home but bleached stark white by the sun. I let Finley get off, then followed her lead.

She removed her helmet and wrapped the straps around the handlebar. She set her clothing to right before looking at me dead in the eye.

"Please be respectful," she began. I opened my mouth to argue that she knew better than to ask that of me before she cut me off. "I only say this because I need your head in the game, Ethan. We need to talk. Like, seriously talk, but until then, I need you to be aware of everything you do here. These girls have been," she paused, taking a deep breath, "through a lot. Just be calm and quiet at first while I introduce you to Father Connolly and the rest of the staff. The girls watch everything." She stopped and stared at me.

I realized she wanted a response so I said, "I'd do anything you asked of me, Fin." I told her that in all sincerity, which earned me a strange look I'd never seen on her face. I didn't know what to make of it, but it made my heart pound in my chest. I studied her as her mouth parted under my scrutiny. I struggled with the urge to reach my hands out, wrap them around her face, and study her lips with my thumbs just to learn what they felt like. *Whoa, where did that come from?*

I glanced away from her to get control of myself, closed my eyes and fought to gain hold of what I knew was beginning to happen. I was starting to let my startling attraction for her tear at the facade I so carefully built. I didn't need to be attracted to Finley.

She needed a friend and a friend only from me, but the allurement there was undeniable and beginning to crack through with definite ferocity. I imagined the chemistry as something tangible, placed it in a box, and locked that box in my mind.

When I opened my eyes and glanced her way once more, Finley watched me with curiosity.

"I'm ready," I told her without explaining my odd reaction.

She took a deep breath and nodded.

CHAPTER SIXTEEN

Finley

Ethan was in Vietnam.

Ethan.

Ethan Moonsong was in Vietnam, standing just a few feet from me in all his gargantuan glory.

I was in the middle of teaching a few girls how to braid hair when Father Connolly approached me with his constantly changing cell phone saying it was An at the tea shop in town and she was asking to speak to me, which was beyond odd since An only emailed me, even if it was something important. I'd corresponded with her for months before I'd arrived in Vietnam. An and her dad were the only ones Father gave his numbers to. Those in the city, when they would hear any sort of report, or see anything suspicious, would ring An up and An would then call Father.

When she told me whom she had found on her doorstep, I had to have her repeat it twice. *Twice.* Panic had crept up my neck for several terrible reasons. One, Ethan didn't know what work we were doing there and two, he didn't know I was doing the work because I could relate to those girls more than he could possibly understand.

My hands trembled in anticipation, in ill-feeling expectations.

"F-follow me," I said, my words fumbling on my tongue.

I led him up the winding staircase up to the main house, the wood creaking beneath both our feet, an uncomfortable, heated warmth invaded my body. I had no idea how I was going to explain it all to him, and I felt sick to my stomach, unnerved, and terrified.

The shadow of his huge body fell across my back, enveloping me and the ground around me, making me uncomfortable and yet, strangely, feel as if he belonged there both at the same time. I could sense the temperature of his skin even from a foot away and it was several degrees above mine, scorching the back of my neck, the tops of my shoulders and head, and the entirety of my back. I wanted to regress, in more ways than just falling back into his chest. I wished to let his stride meet mine, to let him clutch me, soothe me, let his skin recompose my own, but I couldn't. This journey was meant for me to walk in solitude. I wouldn't ask for his shelter, not in this place. After all, I wasn't the one who needed shielding.

I pushed up the last step and walked across the boardwalk to the center of the house, pausing at the door, one hand on its handle. I felt Ethan reach my side and I took a deep breath, meeting his stare.

"Ethan," I said, my breath hitching, but there was no need to continue because he raised his hand to the back of my neck, squeezing softly. The second the palm of his hand touched my skin, I calmed, my trembling breath evened out. I nodded then pushed through into a room full of shining, beautiful faces, but the second Ethan stepped through, their expressions changed from happiness to fearful anxiety, making me queasy.

Immediately, I held my hands out, pressing the air in a sign that there was nothing to worry about. I fell back, wrapping my arm around Ethan's back and placing my free hand on his forearm closest to me, and I smiled a happiness I didn't really feel. Because I knew their anxiety. I'd tasted it myself many, many times. Anytime, really, my mother would bring home a man, so I recognized that fear.

My hand glided up and down Ethan's forearm and I squeezed him closer to me, showing them what a dear friend he was to me. I did this because they trusted me. I did this because they knew their trust of me could extend, bend, and spill over to whomever I trusted. And I trusted Ethan. With my life. With a past full heart. With my now empty one. With my skimmed surface secrets. It was implicit.

My fingers pressed into the skin of his arm but he stood stock-still, honoring my earlier request.

"Ethan," I said, introducing him to the girls and resting my cheek on his shoulder. "This is my Ethan, girls."

Sister Marguerite stood from her seated position, set down her darning on her chair, and confidently, the only way Sister Marguerite knew how, strode over to us, extending her hand to Ethan. I unwrapped myself from Ethan's side and let him take her hand.

"Nice to meet you, Mr. Moonsong. I've heard so much about you." Ethan looked at me briefly at the mention that I'd discussed him with her.

He turned to Sister and smiled his lopsided grin, bent slightly at the waist, no doubt to reduce his imposing height, and squeezed her small hand in both his massive ones. "Please, call me Ethan. It's nice to meet you as well," he answered her, his dark timbre resonating throughout the room.

His daunting presence had startled a few girls, and they had run from the room, but the remaining girls seemed entranced by him, their expressions finally softened by his apparent unclouded and soothing voice.

Ethan was an imposing force with his booming height, his long, dark black hair, bone-colored skin that stretched across his definitive cheekbones, Romanesque nose, and his light grey eyes. His presence was more than intimidating, it was borderline terrifying, but when he spoke... when Ethan *spoke*, all reservations, all hesitancy you felt over the impact of his striking existence dissipated into dust on the floor. He spoke with a softness, with a deep quietness that was in direct opposition to his sharp looks. He spoke with such a pacifying ease, you couldn't help but feel protected.

And that was what Ethan emanated. He radiated the word *shield* and all that embodied. His name was synonymous with protector. You could *feel* what he was put on this earth to do. Protecting your body with his and all the while soothing your soul with his mollifying speech, these were his callings. You knew his words were not spoken unless there was one hundred percent certainty that they could be kept, that they were meant with a genuineness so sincere, and that he would do all those things even at great cost to himself because when Ethan spoke, he meant it.

Sister Marguerite's shoulders relaxed and her eyes crinkled with her smile. "Come sit, please," she asked, her French accent heavy in each word.

The first day I'd arrived at Slánaigh, I remembered wanting to sit at her feet just to hear her speak with her lilting, lovely accent, her back-of-the-throat consonants. She and Ethan had that in common, if for very different reasons, though. Sister Marguerite's words were beautiful. Ethan's were beautiful as well, but his had the added benefit of naturally, as if of their own accord, easing the worn edges of the listener's heart.

She led him over toward her chair, her rosary beads singing in clinking charms as her heavy skirts swished side to side, and gestured to the wooden stool beside her. He sat with her, hulking beside her tiny four-and-a-half-foot frame.

As she picked up her darning, the sounds of the girls going about their business once more resounded throughout the room again, including, this time, a little giggling. I watched Sister Marguerite keep one eye on her needle and the other on our visitor.

"Why have you come here, Ethan?" she asked.

Ethan smiled at me and I couldn't help but grin back. He cleared his throat. "I came to help, to protect my very good friend."

Sister looked up at him, learning him, seeking something deeper in his words, but I didn't know what. "Do you know what it is we do here?" she asked, twisting my guts into knots. My hands shook, waiting for his answer, and knowing that her response would reveal what I had longed for, worked so hard for him never to have discovered about me.

Ethan looked at me with deliberate slowness, his eyes piercing my own. "You save children from slavery," he whispered in answer, his gaze still on my face.

All the breath left in my lungs rushed out through my nose, my body rocked back, as if his words held weight and when they reached me, pushed me back on my heels.

He knows.

My eyes stung with a shame I hadn't felt since I'd been a little girl. Ethan knew my dirty secret, my dirty past, inflicted upon me by the same type of men I'd hoped to save the girls sitting around me from ever knowing again. I was at Slánaigh to cleanse myself, purge myself, of every single touch I'd ever received that had never been welcome. Those moments I'd never get back, the ones that had been stolen from me, the moments I was supposed to give to the name of my choosing. Slánaigh was my therapy's end point. A time I would dedicate toward forgiving the things that had happened to me and when my year was over at Slánaigh, I would continue to give to them with time, energy, and money, but never for those reasons again. This single trip was a self-imposed border, one I would never, ever cross again.

But he knows.

A single tear slid down my cheek so excruciatingly slowly I could sense every creeping roll, every shifting inch, desperately convincing me to recognize it. It begged me to swipe it away so I did so with the back of my hand and let my hair fall forward. I avoided both their gazes as they returned to their conversation, unaware of my secret torment.

"Yes, we rescue children here from a fate worse than death," Sister Marguerite spoke with sincerity.

"I am here to help you," Ethan added again with that dogged earnestness. "And I will do it, whether you want me to or not, if I have to camp outside this house on the lane, I will be there for every trip, every investigation."

I peered their direction once more, noticing Sister Marguerite's hidden smile of amusement. "No need, young man. We would never refuse the help of anyone worthy of helping, and Finley has assured us that you are."

Looking surprised, Ethan glanced at me with wide eyes, his expression unreadable. He turned back to Sister Marguerite, "Well, thank you for allowing me to stay."

She leaned toward him and lowered her voice, "Prepare yourself then, Ethan Moonsong."

Confused, Ethan only nodded.

I needed to talk to him, take him somewhere I could really talk to him.

"Sister Marguerite, do you mind if I take Ethan down to the shore for an hour before dinner? I want to explain a few of the, uh, delicacies of the girls here," I asked.

"I believe he should speak to Father before you do that, though," she answered.

"Father's gone out to talk with an informant then visit An and her dad. I promise as soon as we see him back, we'll talk to him."

She looked at me then nodded, returning her attention to her work.

"Ethan," I said, his name thick on my tongue. I swallowed.

I started walking around the small groups of girls on the floor and made my way toward the door. Before long, I could feel the temperature of Ethan's skin near my own and I nearly cried at his proximity. Knowing what I was about to reveal to him had me feeling sick to my stomach.

I pushed through the door and onto the boardwalk then down the winding staircase. As soon as my feet hit path, I abandoned my flip-flops, and took off running toward the shore, my breath panting as I passed through the grove of thick trees that canopied the path to the ocean. When I reached the beach, I fell to my knees within the shadow of a tall crag covered in green. My hands felt sand and I realized I'd fallen forward, my gut aching in a sorrow I hadn't let myself feel in years.

I sensed Ethan's heat once more hovering over me. "Why did you have to come here?" I asked in sobbing gasps.

I felt him fall beside me, his arms encircling me, soothing me against my will.

"Stop!" I demanded, throwing his arms off me. "I don't want to be comforted, Ethan! I want to feel every inch of pain. I need to feel this."

"You don't have to suffer anymore, Finley," he said quietly in my ear.

I whipped my face toward his, startling him. "Don't you get it? I want to feel the pain again, Ethan. I know if I can just see it, feel it, I can grab it with both hands and hoist it away from me. I know I can do this. I need to do this."

He pushed off his heels, sitting back, and looked out into the bay, his hair whipping behind him with the ocean wind. "I don't want you to hurt anymore," he told the air around me.

Tears streamed down my face. "It's not for you to decide," I told that same air. I sat back, my legs tucked beneath me. "Couldn't you leave it alone? Why couldn't you leave it *alone*? I didn't want you to know that side of me. Ever." I turned to him, to look at his beautiful face.

He returned the stare. "I want to know every side of you, Fin," he said. "I want to feel what you feel. I want you to know that I care enough about you that the things of your past aren't what define you, and I want to suffer alongside you. I want to help you as you've helped me."

His words made a sob break through. "You don't owe me anything, Ethan."

His eyes burned in anger. "I owe you everything."

"If you're here to pay off a debt, don't worry, you're free and clear."

Ethan buried his face in his hands then dragged them down his cheeks. "Stop it, Fin," he chided into his palms before dropping them. "It's insulting. I'm here because you're my best friend in the whole world and I would be here regardless of how you've helped me. I would be here if I owed you nothing at all."

I felt so much anger inside. I was furious at him for not respecting me and staying behind. Furious that he knew about my dirty past. Furious at my mother.

Furious at the men she brought to our doorstep. I was just so *furious*.

"You shouldn't have come," I gritted, fisting sand in my palms. I turned my red-rimmed eyes his direction. "I'm so tired of feeling powerless, and your being here just shows me how little you respect me." I paused, deliberating my next words, knowing they would be irreversible, knowing they would wound poor Ethan, but the venom slipped out anyway. "You're no different than the men who hurt me as a child. Forcing me to do things against my will."

And as I'd predicted, as soon as the words slipped from my mouth, I regretted them. Ethan recoiled as if I'd hit him, his breath rushed out of his mouth in defeated sadness.

"Ethan," I said, my voice trembling. I reached for him, but he pulled back from me, leaving me feeling so alone I thought I'd drown in the black hole I'd created for myself. "Ethan," I repeated, his face looking so distraught, I felt like vomiting. "Please," I said, hating myself. I lunged for him but he stood, wavering on his feet before turning his back on me and heading down the path through the trees back toward the house.

I fell on my side, the sun-warmed sand against my cheek, but I felt so cold, so dead inside. Being at Slánaigh woke feelings inside me I had thought I'd come to terms with. I'd convinced myself I was healthy enough to be there, but I knew in that moment I wasn't. I knew I'd made a mistake in sending Ethan away with such a hateful accusation. An accusation I didn't really feel, not even in the slightest bit because Ethan was nothing like the men who'd stolen from me. He may have had his downfalls but they weren't mortally wounding. He loved and wanted to love, and I shoved that in his face.

I felt myself shake I was crying so hard but I couldn't hear or see or even taste the world around me. I could only feel, and I had no idea how long I'd been there before a shadow crossed over my face. If I'd had all my faculties, I would have looked up, seen the man before me, but I didn't have the energy. I had lost the one thing I thought I'd always had, the one thing I'd prided myself on always possessing. I had lost hope.

A thin blanket crossed over my body and I closed my eyes, waiting for whatever, not caring of what that whatever was. Abruptly, my body was hoisted up into someone's lap, the blanket wrapped around me, and then that someone sat in the sand.

"Shh," the voice consoled me as I realized I was still crying. "I have you now."
The voice was Ethan's.

I was convinced it was my imagination, but I didn't care so I told him, "You're not like those men. Not at all."

"I know," his deep voice reassured me.

"If you were really here, I'd tell you that I feel so very alone."

"You're not alone."
A few tears escaped at his words.

"If you were really here, I'd tell you that I talk a big game, that I can only give the sage advice I know I'm supposed to follow myself but can't."

"I know," that lovely voice told me.

"If you were really here, I'd let you know I'm cut so deeply there aren't sutures sturdy enough to stitch me back together again. If you were really here,

I'd tell you that I'm ruined. My mother ruined me. Those men ruined me, Ethan. *I'm ruined*."

"Nothing could ever bring you to ruin, Finley Dyer. And because you are so permanent, I will sew you together again. You'll see the seam will only make you stronger."

I so desperately wanted his words to be true. But how could I believe him?

He wasn't really there.

Minutes passed and passed and passed.

Hot skin touched my hand, tempering the storm brewing within my soul.

My eyes opened slowly to find Ethan's face. I raised my fingers to meet his cheek and he smiled down at me, making my eyes burn.

"You didn't go."

"No, Fin, I didn't."

I choked back a sob. "But I clobbered you."

"Please, Finley, you only hurt my feelings a little, and how many times have I done the same to you and you've always come back at me tenfold, saving me from myself? I'm here because you taught me that people aren't always as they seem. Just as I am not always as I seem, you are not always as you seem."

"I'm so grateful you've come back."

"I'm so grateful you've come back for me too."

"You are the most perfect friend for me," I told him, huddled against his chest.

He laughed, tucking me even closer. "Agreed."

We sat, him holding me, in the sand until it got dark, time an irrelevancy. We sat until I could feel myself come back a bit, until my heart beat with a regular rhythm.

"Ethan," I said quietly, afraid of my own voice, it seemed.

"Yeah."

"What happened to me as a little girl," I began, but he cut me off.

"I don't need to hear anything, Fin. I don't need the details, I just need to know your pain."

"I feel run through. Like someone has taken a sword, dug it into my belly and out the other side."

I felt Ethan's body sag as his eyes closed and his breath rushed over his lips.

"Let me guess. You feel exposed, vulnerable, numb yet still feel everything acutely."

"Yes."

He squeezed me. "I am going to help you heal, Finley."

"I know you are."

"Tell me," he said. "Tell me what we're doing here."

This was a moment I'd been dreading since I'd seen his beautiful face outside the tea shop.

"Hạ Long Bay is a tourist attraction, lots of Westerners and the like." He shifted, obviously uncomfortable by the words he knew were coming. I swallowed. "They come to see the wonders of Hạ Long Bay, its beauty, its rarity, its gorgeous people and amazing food, but with those extraordinary wonders come equally extraordinary horrors." I couldn't say any more so I kept silent, letting the truth sink in.

"How bad is the problem?" he asked, after some time.

"Worse than you could imagine."

His eyes squeezed shut. He looked as if he were wishing the problem away with every ounce of his being, and I loved him for that.

CHAPTER SEVENTEEN

Ethan

My fragile Finley.

"We should head inside. Sister Marguerite was wondering what I was up to when I asked for this blanket. I don't want her to think anything *untoward* is going on."

Finley laughed, making my heart skip a beat in relief. "Well, let's go unburden her."

I shifted Finley's weight and she made a move to stand but I wrapped my arms around her, lifting her easily as I stood. She gasped, stirring my heart even further.

"I've got you," I told her.

"I-I know," she stammered. "I just was-wasn't expecting you to lift me like that."

I started walking up the path through the trees again, carrying her with me. She squirmed.

"Stop it," I told her.

She smiled softly. "Aren't I kinda heavy?"

I laughed, loudly this time. "You weigh nothing to me, Fin."

She rolled her eyes but accepted it, which made me happy. She'd felt so delicate to me in that moment I couldn't bring myself to let her walk. I knew Finley was strong, knew it very well, but I could not let her carry more weight than she so obviously was taxed with already, and I felt as if it was my fault. If I'd only listened to her, if I'd only stayed away, maybe she wouldn't have reopened her wounds and her experience at Slánaigh wouldn't have had to be as painful. Then again, even knowing what I knew then, could I have let her walk alone at Slánaigh? No, I knew I was there for a reason.

I set her down at the foot of the winding staircase and walked side by side with her up to the boardwalk and to the front door. I had yet to meet Father Connolly.

When Finley let me through, the main room I'd seen all the girls in earlier was empty, and I finally took in the room itself. Rather large, it contained several sitting areas as well as table areas. A few of the tables had what I could only assume was schoolwork on top but it was in Vietnamese so I couldn't tell for sure. There were dolls, books, and building blocks covering almost every square foot of the floor.

Suddenly, I remembered the anxious looks of all the girls in the room and realized that each one of their innocent faces was there for a reason. I felt ill knowing their reason for finding solace at Slánaigh.

"Ach! Who's this at me door?" I heard a man yell from behind me.

Finley and I turned around to greet a slim, elderly-looking gentlemen in a black cassock standing five foot eight or so with wild chin-length grey hair, long beard that met his chest, bulbous nose, and permanent laugh lines crinkled around his eyes. He sported a long, dark ancient-looking walking stick with weathered knots along the thick collar. It looked to me like more an accessory than an actual needed aid, though, because he swung it toward me on obvious sure footing, lifting his cassock a bit and exposing, surprisingly, a pair of black Chucks. He reminded me of a modern-day Gandalf with shorter hair.

Finley smiled at him. "Father Connolly, this is my friend Ethan. The one I told you about."

He set the walking stick at his side, his weathered hand resting at the rounded handle, and smiled at me. "You're Ethan, are ya?"

"That's me."

"What ya waiting for then? Come here, son," he said, waving me over to him.

When I came to stand near him, his eyes bugged and traveled up to my face. "Ach! But ya are a big beast, ya are!"

I tried not to laugh. "I guess."

"You're treelike an' that ain't the half of it, boyo." He examined me for a moment, deciding something. "Fine then. You'll do. Ya can stay with me on the houseboat."

I was confused by this and looked over at Fin. "Houseboat?"

"Father stays off property for propriety's sake but also for the protection of the girls. He's a wanted man," she added seriously.

Father laughed. "They come for me, they do, but they never get me! They get close but never close enough, they do," he said, swinging his walking stick wildly, making me step back. "Ach! But it is the price I pay for the work we do here." He set the walking stick down then smiled at me as if he just noticed me. "What say ya to a bit of supper, son? Finley?" he asked her as well, before turning toward a hallway.

When Father Connolly was a bit ahead of me, I asked who comes after him but she just shook her head with a look that promised she'd tell me later.

We followed him into a room filled with young girls ages five to probably seventeen as well as Sister Marguerite and a woman I'd yet to be introduced to. I glanced down at a girl who was no more than a baby, really, and my blood burned with a horrible, terrible need to find the men responsible for putting her into the girls' home. I closed my eyes and took two steady breaths to regain myself, to remove the red from my vision, when a hand met mine and my heart steadied itself. I looked down at my right and saw Finley. She nodded in understanding, like she knew, like she could feel what I felt, and I knew then that my enraged reaction wasn't just a product of being me, of being *that* Ethan, it was a product of being human.

The woman I hadn't been introduced to yet walked over to Fin and me, holding her hand out.

"Ethan, I presume?" she asked.

I took her hand. "Yes, ma'am."

"Ethan," Finley began, "This is Dr. Nguyen. She's the on-call physician and surgeon for Slánaigh."

"Nice to meet you, Dr. Nguyen," I said, smiling.

"Nice to meet you as well." The doctor gestured toward a table with the other adults and we followed her. "I understand you come from Finley's hometown?" she asked without a trace of an accent.

"Yes, ma'am. Well, from Bitterroot actually. A town a little ways from Finley's Kalispell but close enough that we all blend nicely."

She smiled as we all sat. "How do you like Hạ Long Bay?"

"It's one of the most beautiful places I've ever seen," I told her.

She began passing around huge ceramic bowls just as three busy-looking Vietnamese women went bustling around the tables, laying down burners with pan-fried spiced fish, heaping plates of green herbs and vegetables, as well as large bowls of rice noodles and small ramekins' worth of a light brown sauce. One of the women placed a setting in front of Finley and me. I watched, fascinated, as Finley dumped the bowl of herbs into the hot pan. I recognized dill, scallions, and assorted herbs as well as smelled turmeric and garlic. It was such a different dish than I was accustomed to, but it looked and smelled delicious.

"How do you know to do this?" I asked Finley as she took my bowl and filled it with noodles.

"I don't really. It's what they have for dinner every night, and I've only watched them a couple of times.

She handed me back my bowl and I studied her myself. She piled the now hot herbs and fish as well as a little bit of oil from the pan on top of her noodles then sprinkled crushed peanuts and red chilies on top. I followed suit, copying her every move, feeling out of my element.

"Now, the pièce de résistance," she said, taking the bowl of light brown sauce.

"What is that?"

"Shrimp paste," she answered matter-of-factly. I felt my eyes bug and she giggled. "It's much better than you think," she said, offering to pour some for me.

"I'm trusting you on this, I guess."

"Duly noted."

She poured some over my noodles with the flat-bottomed spoon I'd seen at Asian restaurants back home then set the bowl down.

I stared at my bowl.

"The trick is to get a little bit of everything with every bite."

"Here goes nothing," I said, picking up my chopsticks and gathering a bite.

I clumsily shoveled it all in my mouth, causing a few of the girls around us to giggle, and swallowed.

"This is amazing," I told her.

"I know, right?"

"What is it?" I asked, gathering another bite.

"It's chả cá."

"Chả cá," I repeated, testing out the language.

"It's a very old dish, " Dr. Nguyen added. "Do you like it?"

"Very good," I told her.

She smiled and went back to her bowl.

We all ate in silence for a few minutes before Finley leaned over her own and whispered, "How did you find me?"

"It's embarrassing," I confessed. "I, uh, took the creepy route and just started remembering little details from our phone conversations, piecing them all together with random searches." She sat back, her eyes watching me. My shoulders hunched under her scrutiny. "What?" I asked.

Her eyes narrowed. "Nothing," she lied.

"Did I just freak you out or something?"

She cleared her throat after a bite. "Uh, no, it's just... You're quite clever, Ethan."

I beamed at her compliment. No one had ever called me clever. I'd always been defined by my height, my ranch-hand abilities, my knowledge of the mountains, and especially by my expertise with my double swords, which I'd only remembered to pack at the last minute. No one saw me as anything other than the physical force I was.

"Thank you," I told her, shocked by how badly I'd needed to be recognized as more than muscle.

"No one's ever called you that before," she said matter-of-factly.

I dropped my spoon in its bowl and stared at her. "Never," I answered after a moment's pause.

She stared back, "How is that possible?"

I didn't know how to answer so I just watched the expressions change on her face from disbelief to empathy to something else I didn't recognize, something I was burning to decipher, though.

"Ethan," she whispered.

That single utterance turned the room invisible. Suddenly it was her and me. Finley and Ethan.

"Yes?" I asked her softly, my voice dropping an octave, surprising even me with how deep, how raspy it sounded.

Her eyes softened, glistening with unshed tears. I reached across the table, running the back of my hand across her porcelain cheek. One single tear fell as she tucked her face into my palm, so I swept it away with my thumb. I pleaded with her with words unspoken, begging her to stop hurting. My hand slid down her face to her neck and rested there. I let my skin soothe her, hoping my touch helped her as much as hers helped me.

"It's like a balm for a blistered burn, Ethan," she answered, making me wonder if I'd spoken out loud. She must have read the confusion on my face, because she explained, "You wear your words, Ethan. In every pained expression, I feel your meaning. I've seen what my skin does for you. Know it works for me as well."

My fingers threaded through her hair at the top of her neck, the weight of that revelation burying itself in my chest with a permanent ferocity. My stomach flipped on itself. *Check yourself, Ethan. She needs you more than you need to fall in love with her. And you're starting to.*

With a slam, I shut that door, checked my expression, letting my hand fall to her shoulder, squeezing in the friendliest way I could think how. *Don't think about standing up. Don't think about the fact that you want to stand, walk over to her side of the table, and take her in your arms. Don't think about it. Don't.*

I rested my forearm on the edge of the table near my bowl and smiled at her but when my eyes met hers, she wasn't smiling. She looked scared, actually, and I wondered if I'd offended her. I opened my mouth to speak but the moment passed when her eyes broke our gaze and she reached for her spoon. Deflated for reasons I couldn't fathom, I followed her lead, picking up my spoon again.

When I looked up, everyone was busy eating, seemingly unaware of our exchange. Everyone, that is, but Sister Marguerite. She sat with her hands folded on the table, watching me closely. Her eyes met mine and I wondered if she was upset that I'd touched Finley but when one brow shot up, her expression said that she had my number. Frightened that she might blow my cover to Finley, I shook my head at her, making her grin. I practically fell into my bowl, desperate to erase that moment but knowing how disappointed I'd have been not to have known Finley's skin one more time. Any touch I got or received from Finley was a windfall I didn't think I could live without, and every single touch since that first was building my addiction to her.

Check yourself, Ethan Moonsong. Don't worry, I answered myself, kicking that ajar door shut with every ounce of strength I had.

CHAPTER EIGHTEEN

After dinner, Father Connolly ushered me through the front door without a real opportunity to say goodbye to Fin as he said he needed to "bed early and rise early." When I ducked under the front door with my bag, I looked back to see Fin, standing in the middle of the room, facing the door, her arms wrapped around herself, rocking back and forth from foot to foot, making my stomach drop. Her go-to coping mechanism. I pierced her eyes with a gaze so fierce she stopped rocking, staring straight back at me, her mouth parted. I nodded slowly at her, reassuring her that I was here, that I was there with her.

Her breath noticeably steadied and she nodded back. When I turned away from her, it physically hurt. I gripped the fabric of my shirt near my chest, pressing to relieve the screaming need to protect. I wanted to run back to her, stay with her, but Sister Marguerite would have shooed me with a broom right back out so I continued on, ignoring my instincts. Men weren't allowed on property at night so I fought the urge and followed Father to the houseboat down the shore.

We walked the sandy path through the canopy of trees and came upon the beach where Finley and I had sat earlier that evening. As we passed the spot we sat, I recognized the indents of our bodies in the sand highlighted in the moonlight. For some strange inexplicable reason I wanted to run to that spot, kick the sand, shatter the imprints of our bodies as if I could physically remove the pain that had buried Finley there. The ghost of that ache lingered there so I turned my face from it and caught up to Father since he'd gotten a bit ahead of me.

"...and it rocks a bit but have no fear, it's nothin' but nothin'," I caught him saying, confusing me.

"I'm sorry, Father?"

"The boat! The boat, boy. I been talkin' to ya 'bout the boat."

Caught up. "Oh, I see. Sorry. Yeah, so it rocks a bit. That's okay."

"Don't worry yourself none, son. Unless ya see water on the floor, then ya might want to jump ship," he said, laughing. I wasn't sure if he was joking, though. "Oh!" he continued, "We canna be on the same soide of the boat at any point 'cause she'll sink a bit an' that can cause a bit o'trouble."

"Watch for water. Stay on opposite sides. Got it."

"We can share a room, you see, but we have to dance a bit. You on one soide, yeah, an' I on the other."

"Check," I told him, earning a smile from him.

He looked up at me again. "You are a right big one, aren't ya! Yes, I believe you'll work nicely here," he said, patting my arm.

"Thanks," I told him, glad he could use me, glad to feel useful.

A few hundred yards from the main house, I noticed a hidden bend around the shore, the ocean dipped into the land a bit then spit itself back out and within a veil of foliage, a few twinkling lights shone through. With familiarity, Father brushed back the greenery revealing a hidden alcove beneath a small waterfall. In front of that waterfall sat a small bobbing houseboat. Looking at it, I thought there was no way it could hold my weight, and I certainly could never stand inside.

Father skirted around the sandy path and stepped onto a small six- or seven-foot dock to the houseboat's front door.

"Uh, Father?" I said, hesitating as I tested my weight at the edge of the dock.

He whipped around, his cane flailing with the movement, almost pegging me in the knee. *Father and his cane were lethal*, I thought with a grin.

"Hmm?"

"I don't think this thing will hold me."

"Have faith, boy," he said simply, turning back around and opening his door. Cautiously, I followed him, placing one foot down and letting my weight bare down before lifting my remaining foot from solid ground. I stood still, waiting for something to happen and when it didn't, I took another wary step forward. The water beneath the dock rippled but it held me.

"Comin'?" I heard from the door.

"Yes," I answered, walking to the door and ducking inside. The roof was a lot higher than I'd thought it was at first. I found I could stand up straight, but the top of my head grazed the ceiling. I'd have to be careful of fixtures but all in all, I thought it was doable. I'd lived in worse.

"'Tis moine," Father said, gesturing to a small room just off the main room. Essentially it was a six-by-ten-foot room worth of a living and a kitchen. Another door laid opposite his on the other side of the living space. "Toilets," he said, pointing to the other door.

I looked around. "I've got the couch then?"

"No, lad," he said, leaving out the front door again so I followed. I hadn't noticed it until Father had stepped down, but the entire boat had a narrow wraparound path. Following it around, we came upon a small floating room of sorts connected by another narrow wood dock. We followed that dock and he opened the door into the simple room.

"It used to be a boat slip but we added a floor and a bed for the odd guest."

"Cozy," I said, meaning it. The room was maybe five-by-seven feet but there was room for a bed and a sink as well as a small table. I set my bag on the bed.

"Lights out, boyo," he said with a jovial smile. "Don't forget ta say yer prayers."

I hadn't the heart to tell him I wasn't the praying type. "Sure, Father," I told him, stretching out my hand for him. He shook it and I thanked him for the room to which he promised me I would earn it, so I smiled. He left and I heard his slight steps and cane as he reached the main house, the door closing behind him.

I sat on the edge of the slight bed and for the first time since I'd arrived wondered how it was I'd found myself sitting on a bed inside a boathouse in Vietnam. It was so far away from where I'd thought I'd be right then. If anyone had asked me six months earlier where I'd been right that minute, I'd have told them dead, drunk, or in jail... and I'd have meant it. I marveled at the turn my life had taken.

A passing motorboat rode by off the main shore, probably unaware there was an entire houseboat hidden behind the hanging veil of foliage near the beach. I felt the effects of its wake bob my floating room up and down, up and down. I kept hearing the hollow thump of wood hitting wood so I peeked out to find a small, rather beat up dinghy attached to the side of the dock just outside of my door.

I studied the small boat and wondered if it could get me to shore quietly without Father finding out. I wanted to find Finley. I needed to see her, really, but I also knew I didn't want to betray Father's or Sister Marguerite's trust. Just as quickly as the thought entered my mind, it'd left. I wouldn't jeopardize my situation because of some selfish want to see Fin, no matter how much I worried for her.

I wasn't completely convinced but I'd have to get used to it. I fell back on the tiny bed, my legs dangling, trying to distract myself from entertaining thoughts of checking on Fin. Every few minutes, I'd justify leaving only to convince myself again that it would prove dire if I was caught. I didn't want to sabotage her. She'd spoken for my character, after all.

Finally, I felt myself dozing as the adrenaline of the day wore off. I was more tired than I'd realized. My eyes closed before I even had a chance to remove my clothing.

CHAPTER NINETEEN

I woke to knocking the next morning, groggy from lack of acclimation to the time difference.

I cleared my throat but my voice still came out raspy, "Yes?"

"Up, lad, we've work ta do," Father Connolly's voice commanded.

I scrubbed my face with my hands to wake myself and sat up, the bed creaking beneath my body. My knees ached from hanging off the bed the entire night. When I crashed, I crashed hard.

I stood up too quickly and the entire room tilted back and forth in the water. "Whoa," I said to no one. When the room steadied, I grabbed a pair of boxers, tattered jeans, and a black T-shirt, heading toward the main houseboat to grab a quick shower. I opened my door and realized it was still pitch black, not even a sliver of dawn hinted on the horizon.

When I walked in, Father was sitting at the small kitchen table, a paper in hand, already showered and dressed but in regular clothing with a ball cap on his head.

"Early, no?" I asked.

"It's four a.m.," he explained, sipping from a coffee cup.

My eyes widened. "Four!" I exclaimed, unable to stop myself.

He laughed. "Yes, boyo, sin does not wait for the sun to rise," he explained, sobering me.

"I see. I'll just shower then."

He gestured toward the bathroom door and I let myself in. Barely able to close the door behind me, I absorbed the size of it. I took stock of a sink and nothing else. *Where the hell is the shower and toilet?* Upon closer inspection, I noticed a ceramic-like bowl lodged in the floor.

"What in the world is that?" I said out loud, making Father laugh outside the door.

"Figure it out, lad!" I heard from the other side of the door.

This was the toilet then. In the airports, they'd had American-style bathrooms and I didn't even think about it. I looked around the room and saw a nozzle attached to the ceiling in the corner of the very small room. *You've got to be kidding me.* The entire bath was the shower, toilet, sink.

I bit the bullet and started to undress, pinching the door open to throw all my clothing on the sofa right outside.

"Here goes nothin'."

I started the shower and yelped, inciting yet another riotous Irish laugh on the other side of the door. The water was freezing. I looked at the nozzle and noticed there wasn't a hot option. Meaning, I was in hell. A perpetual *Groundhog Day*-esque experience. Cold showers every day? *Fine. For Fin.*

I dressed as quickly as I could without getting my jeans wet from the tile below then sat on the sofa in the main room to put on my socks and lace up my boots.

"That was quick, lad, for one with such long, flowin' hair."

I grinned at the ground, tying one boot on. "Is that a dig, old man?" He laughed in answer. "I'll have you know my mom's Native American, sir. I'm a halfling of the Echo River Tribe," I teased.

"And ye da?"

"White as a sheet," I deadpanned.

"That explains it," he said with a smile, leaving it at that, then standing. "Are ye ready?" he asked me.

"Men don't ask other men if they're ready unless there's something to be ready for."

Father nodded slowly in agreement. "Then ready yeself, lad."

He lead me out of the houseboat, over the dock, and down the beach toward the main house. Just as we'd crested the canopied trail, I could see Finley's silhouette in the distance. I had to fight the urge to run to her like a little boy. My hands fisted and opened many times, resisting the impulse. When she turned toward us, though, I couldn't help myself and started walking much faster than Father to meet her side. *Check yourself, gosh dammit!* I stopped briefly, my eyes closed tightly to gain control of myself, before I fell back to meet Father's stride.

Finley

Ethan walked toward me eagerly when he recognized me, stopped, then fell back with Father,

187

setting me on edge for reasons I didn't know. My stomach rose and fell in quick succession at the sight of him. Nerves, no doubt, though something else seemed to nag at me.

"Ethan," I breathed. Although I had to have known he couldn't hear me, his name escaped my lips without volition.

Lean and muscular, Ethan sauntered toward me, his head down, hands shoved in his front pockets, the muscles in his arms highlighted by the action. His hair fell side to side with every stride, and my belly began to burn with something I'd never felt before, making me even more nervous than I already was. I silently begged him to pick his gaze up and share it with me but he seemed entranced by his own steps.

Finally, he looked up and I caught his eye. The look on his face confused me.

"Hey," I said breathlessly, my heart beat erratically. *What is wrong with you?*

He jerked his chin up in greeting the way all guys do, keeping his hands in his pockets. I reached out for his forearm but at the last second reined my hand back in. *Why are you acting so freaking weird, Finley?* I had no answer for myself.

"Hello, lass," Father said in greeting, seemingly oblivious to my awkwardness.

"Father," I addressed him with a smile, watching Ethan from the corner of my eye.
He studied the ground, toeing the shell gravel back and forth, distracted.

All three of us stood in a circle for a moment while Father checked his pockets for his cell phone.

"It's right here," I told him, handing it over. "You charged it in the kitchen last night, remember?"

"Ach! Daft me! Thank ya, girl." He took a deep breath and looked on both of us before turning to Ethan. "Ethan, ye'll observe us today. When I feel yer ready, lad, I might use ye ta fish one out, but 'til then ye watch us. Ye on it, son?"

"Yes," he said, nodding his head in earnest, making me proud to be his friend.

"Roight," Father said, smiling, "we're headin' for Hanoi today, a bit out o' Finley's comfort zone," he began. I opened my mouth to object but he only talked over me. "Now, Finley, lass, ye'll do just fine. An's heard o' bit o' rumblings an' we're only gon' to speak wit' folks."

I nodded my answer and turned to Ethan, whose face looked even paler than usual. Without a second thought, I threaded my hand through his arm. It rested closely to his side because he kept his hand in his pocket. If it had been any other boy, I would have felt rejected but the expression on his face, I noticed, was no longer pained, so I kept my hand right where it was.

It was so odd to me that my touch was just as soothing to him as his was to me. His head lifted, his hair no longer shielding so much of his face. He looked on Father Connolly calmly as he spoke to him about our MO but I observed when he pinned my hand even closer to his side, as if he needed the weight of our contact to deepen. He was nervous. I squeezed his arm to reassure him, which earned me a long side glance. My stomach clenched at his look. *Uh-oh*. That familiar pang of yearning, that deep want for Ethan when I was in high school, crept back into my soul and I had to remind myself why I was there, my mission, and that it was not the time to focus on anything else but that aim alone.

Father Connolly started his scooter so I followed his lead, putting on my helmet and handing Ethan his.

"You'll have to drive again," I told him, avoiding eye contact.

"Oh, yeah, okay," he told me, straddling the small bike.

He started the motorbike, backing it up to idle beside Father's. My heart began to beat an irregular rhythm as I approached him. A gust of wind blew a bit of cologne my way. The scent was signature Ethan, a little bit of sandalwood and a mixture of other scents I couldn't quite put my finger on. The smell made my stomach sink, reminding me of high school all over again.

But Ethan didn't want you in high school, Finley, remember? In fact, he made it quite clear that he's just your friend. Stop torturing yourself!

I checked the old feeling bubbling up and sat behind him. I brought the inside of my bare thighs to the outside of his jean-clad ones and it proved to be fatal, making me feel almost sick with the memories of him sleeping in my bed that night back in Kalispell.

What Ethan didn't know about that night was he'd talked in his sleep.

"*I didn't know it was you,*" he'd told me with closed eyes that late night.

I assumed he was talking about Cricket Hunt so I ignored him and rolled him over onto his side toward the wall. He groaned in pain from his head wound and laid back again, flat on his back, his broad chest heaving with deep breaths.

"I didn't know it was you," he'd repeated, mumbling something about dancing and Holly's name.

I couldn't help myself. *"Who did you think it was?"* I'd asked him, not really expecting him to answer.

"The most beautiful girl I'd ever seen," he told me in his sleep, shocking me.

He's drunk, I told myself.

"I wanted to know you," he told me. *"I didn't want to know you,"* he continued, confusing me. *"I wanted to touch you. I wanted to touch you. I would have died just to touch you. One time. I would have needed just the one time."*

He'd stopped talking at that most inopportune moment. *"Ethan?"* I'd asked again and again with no response. He was out. His words did things to my stomach, things I'd never felt before, things I would never be able to admit to anyone. I'd turned over on my side, fighting all my old feelings for him, those long and buried feelings, finally falling asleep, reassuring myself he was only drunk. *Swallow the butterflies, Finley. Swallow the butterflies.*

Carefully, oh so carefully, I wrapped my arms around his ribs. His stomach muscles contracted when my hands touched him and I swallowed.

"Ready, ye two?" Father asked, unaware of my secret torment.

We both nodded, then Ethan breathed deeply, glancing over his shoulder, his eyes meeting mine in a sideways glance. "I got you," he whispered, his hand resting over mine briefly, sending me reeling as we took off. The almost three-hour trip into Hanoi was agonizing on so many levels. The proximity between us was too much for one person to endure, and it didn't help that the ride itself was physically exhausting, causing me to lean into Ethan for support after a few miles. My ear flat against his back, I could hear every breath, every tortured heartbeat.

Ethan was *indeed* a tortured soul, there was no doubt in my mind about that. I'd always saw that in him, always. I knew his struggles. It was what made me think we'd had so much in common when we were younger. It takes one to know one.

We arrived in Hanoi around eight and the traffic was saturated as usual. The city had been awake for several hours, already having lived an entire day before we'd reached the outskirts. Ethan followed Father Connolly to a nearby street vendor and we shoved our motorbikes as close to the curb as possible, tangling them in with a hundred others, before getting off and standing them. I tore off the bike as quickly as possible, earning me an odd look from Ethan.

I shrugged. "Rough ride," was all I could offer.

He nodded in agreement but I was sure my ride was rough for an entirely different reason than his.

"Phở?" Father asked, making us both grin at one another.

If you ever want to hear something truly knee-smacking, ask an Irishman to speak Vietnamese. *Feckin' highloirious, boyo!*

We ordered our soup and all three of us sat hunched on the tiny available chairs close to the building wall just outside the shop. Ethan crouched down on his haunches, foregoing the chair altogether.

He looked at me. "I'd just break it," he explained, smiling.

I smiled back. "They're made for American kindergartners, really. Don't feel bad."

"I don't," he said with a shrug and another grin, reminding me that his size contributed to who he was. He never made excuses for it nor gloated over it. It was what it was. *And it's breathtaking*, I thought then immediately chided myself.

Out of the corner of my eye, I spied a woman acting strangely, looking over her shoulder a hundred times, memorizing the people around her. I suspected she was An's contact but I wasn't sure so I continued eating without catching her attention. Besides, the last thing I wanted to do was notice her if someone really was watching us. She'd be dead before she crossed the street to us.

So I drank the broth of my soup slowly, eyeing my chopsticks as if they were the most fascinating things in the world, and before long, a shadow fell over our tiny table and all three of us looked up.

"Xin lỗi cho hỏi?" *Excuse me?* She said it quietly, hesitantly.

"Yes," Father replied in Vietnamese, but this time I didn't find the humor in his accent.

They continued to have a conversation and I could only catch bits and pieces. Words like *girl, men,* and *lost.* Ethan and I had set our bowls down to listen as if we could understand what they were saying, both of us on edge. I turned my head to look at Ethan, studying him, scrutinizing him as his eyes widened in alertness, his muscles bunched beneath his skin, flexing as if he could jump twenty feet any direction he chose, and I believed he could have. My gut churned with nerves. The soup had lost its soothing charms.

I watched Father and the woman in animated conversation, wishing I'd had any clue as to what they were discussing. I looked around me, at the people living out their morning, bustling to and fro, getting from point A to point B. It all looked so innocuous, so commonplace but something, I don't know what, was telling me to flee. For some inexplicable reason, my chest tightened, my breath quickened, my skin crawled.

"We have to leave," I said suddenly. "We have to leave, we have to leave," I kept repeating, but Father was too deep into his conversation with the woman in front of him. "We have to go, Ethan," I said, standing up. Ethan followed my lead, standing but keeping his body between mine and the street. I tugged on Father's shirtsleeve. "Father, I have a weird feeling."

He looked up at me. "'Tis it, my choild?" he asked, his voice rising an octave in curiosity.

"Tell her we'll contact her later. I have a sick, paranoid feeling we need to leave."

Calmly, Father stood. "I don't believe there is anything to worry 'bout, lass, but I won't make you stay here." He turned to the woman and explained. She nodded quickly, turned, and sprinted for the street, the same direction she had come from.

"She said to meet her at her apartment. 'Tis just down the road a wee bit," he said, bending to reach for his helmet.

Just then bullets rang out in rapid succession. Screams joined the chaos, but before I had time to do the same, I was whisked into someone's arms, cradled like a child against a big chest. I looked up and saw

Ethan's steady expression, his warrior-like countenance. His was a look of a man who knew *exactly* what to do.

I watched spellbound as he hoisted me up and around the metal counter of a nearby street shop. He left briefly and the fear crept back, the noises rose tenfold. Suddenly, Father was spun in front of me as if he weighed nothing, his cane fell with a clatter upon the concrete floor, adding a sharp echoing thud to the disorder as women, men, and children went diving into tight places, begging for a safe haven from the spray of bullets.

"Ethan!" I screamed when he stood back up as if he intended to go back into the line of fire. "No, Ethan! No!" I yelled desperately at the top of my lungs when he kissed my cheek quickly and gave me a piercing look that confused me.

He went bounding into the fray, me screaming after him to come back as Father dragged me back behind the counter.

"No, lass! Stay put!"

I raised my head, my gaze barely breaking the top surface of the counter to search for Ethan as Father signaled families to give him their children to hide behind the metal counter in his stead. My instinct told me to run after Ethan but I knew I had a duty to protect the children around us. Protecting children was the reason I was there. So I pulled at as many kids as I could, tucking them into one another like a can of sardines, desperately pushing my racing heart and the reason it raced to the back of my mind.

Ethan was out there with the gun. A million thoughts raced through my mind. Why didn't he stay there with me? What was he hoping to accomplish?

How could he risk himself like that? Didn't he know how much I needed him?

I'd reached for a toddler just as the bullets died down to a complete halt. We all stood still, quiet, waiting. When I was sure the bullets were no more, I bounded up, ignoring Father's heed to stay. I ran out into the ghostlike street, such a dichotomy from what it had been not a minute before, and searched for Ethan. My eyes scanned then fell upon Ethan knelt beside the woman we'd been talking to, giving her mouth to mouth, pumping her chest, working furiously to revive her.

"Father!" I yelled into the shop. "They shot her!" I screamed.

He bounded up, hobbling toward her felled body in the middle of the empty road. He fell beside her, checking her vital signs. The resigned expression that came upon his face let me know she was gone and that Ethan was working for nothing.

He put a hand on Ethan's shoulder. "Son, she's gone," he said, stopping Ethan's pumping hands. Ethan pulled back, his whole body trembling with the adrenaline no doubt leaving his body in droves.

Father closed the woman's eyes, made a sign of the cross on her forehead, took her hand, and prayed silently for her. Ethan stood, still shaking, and sprinted the ten feet between us.

"You okay?" he asked, his eyes roaming my body along with his hands, searching me for injuries.

"Not a scratch," I whispered, my body jerking left and right as he checked me over.

He finally stood straight, raking an unsteady hand down his face, the only tell that he was even slightly human. His sleeve had a streak of the woman's blood on it.

"You saved us," I said, stunned.

"What?" he asked, scrutinizing the area around us. "Come on, let's get indoors," he said, grabbing my arm. Over his shoulder, he said, "Father, let's get out of sight."

Father finished up his prayer, crossing himself, covering the woman up with a shawl she'd been carrying, and followed us into the street shop Ethan had hidden us in when the bullets had first sounded.

"You saved us, Ethan," I told him again.

"I did nothing of the sort," his calming voice soothed.

"You were-you were amazing. The way you moved," I told him, almost in disbelief that anyone could naturally move that way.

"I'm just a skilled hunter, Fin, and I've warrior blood," he explained away as if it was perfectly normal that he picked up two grown people and maneuvered them with a litheness I'd only ever seen in animals.

I remembered watching Ethan play football in high school with the other boys and thinking he moved with a skill that could never be taught, a skill that could only come from blood, from the memory of ancestors and the repeated, graceful movements that came with the heritage training he'd always seemed to be gone over the weekends for. It showed then and it showed in that moment.

"You were amazing," I kept repeating, at a complete loss for words.

He stood stock-still, staring, his eyes narrowed, examining me, searching for something but I wasn't sure what it was he was looking for. "Thank you," he said deeply, his voice as immovable, as solid as ever, then relaxed his face.

"Come ye' two," Father said, motioning us toward the opening of the shop.

When we emerged, people started gathering around the dead woman, others fled, and others went about their business as if shootings were an everyday occurrence, which they most certainly weren't.

Sirens sounded through the streets as an ambulance and police car drove through the crowd to reach the woman.

"I want ye two gone," Father said to us both.

"What?" I asked, my heart starting to pound in my chest again. "Why?"

"Because I don't want either of ye questioned, that's why, just in case these officers are bought an' paid fer."

"Then let's go," Ethan said, grabbing my hand and encouraging Father to walk ahead of him.

"No, lad, I'll be stayin' here."

"I won't leave you behind," Ethan told him.

"Do as I ask, Ethan, please," Father asked kindly. "I've done this many a time an' t'was a sacrifice I's willing ta take when I came ta Vietnam, but I canna get out, lad, if you're sittin' in the cell wit' me." Ethan's jaw clenched but he didn't argue. Father gave him his cell phone and the keys to his scooter. "I'll ring ya here, lad, regardless what happens." Father laid his hands in reassurance on both our shoulders before turning us around and scooting us forward. "Now get!"

Ethan squeezed my hand once then dragged me into his side and walked briskly away from the chaos. People were yelling, stalled cars and scooters were honking their horns, unaware of the scene ahead of them, as I glanced behind me once and noticed that Father was talking with his hands as two policemen interviewed him. Ethan tucked us in between a building and tree about a block south so we could watch without being noticed.

My hands fell to my sides and I looked down, pondering them as they shook. My adrenaline was still pumping, and I felt sick to my stomach. I had an eerie feeling in the pit of my belly as I watched the exchange between the officers and Father. He was usually an animated guy, but he rarely got irritated. He kept raising his hands then pointing to where we sat. He tried to signal for the shop owner to come over to him but his hands fell in disappointment when the man shook his head.

"The shop owner's not going to vouch for him. We have to help him," I said, walking forward.

Ethan stopped me by grabbing my arms and pulling me against his chest. He spoke low in my ear. "They will only take you with him, Fin. They have no intention of finding out what really happened."

"How-how do you know?" I stuttered, scared.

"Because they don't work for the city. They may wear the uniform but they're bought, just like Father said."

"What do we do?" I asked, panicked. "Should we follow—" I began.

"Wait," he whispered in my ear, stopping me.

We watched as they cuffed Father, his cane clanged to the street below, and roughly shoved him into the back of a police car. Ethan's arms wrapped around my chest, bringing me closer, clasping me tightly to him, as if his holding me could prevent me from being torn away by invisible strings. He held me with such intensity, such fury, I knew nothing could've severed his tether. I also knew he was unaware of his protective stance because his eyes were intent on the scene before us, seemingly intent on the world around him. It was instinct. I silently thanked him because I'd never felt as secure as I did in that moment, whether or not he was aware of it.

Once the police had driven off, Ethan looked down at me, finally aware of the way he was holding me. He released me and I suddenly felt cold, which then made me extremely uncomfortable. *Stop it, Finley*, I chided myself.

"Sorry," his deep voice soothed. He averted his eyes, grabbed my hand, and we sprinted for the scooters, skirting the traffic jam surrounding the taped-off section where the woman once laid.

I could not help but stare when we approached the dark red spot in the road and my gut clenched.

"Don't look," Ethan's steady voice prodded, wrapping his arm around me and bringing me into his side. I tucked my face into his shoulder but couldn't shake the image of the dark, wet pavement or the lump of human beneath tarp. It would forever be seared into memory.

CHAPTER TWENTY

Ethan

I guided Fin to the scooters and gave her the keys to one. I read her expressions, her body language. She looked shell-shocked.

"You okay?" I asked her.

"Of course," she answered, meeting my gaze, lifting her chin up like a badass, making me burn with pride at her strength. "We should probably call Sister Marguerite and let her know what's going on. I have no idea where the local jail is here, and we'll have to rely on her to tell us what to do."

I nodded and handed her the phone. Her fingers were trembling as they reached for it so I took them in my own and held them there. "Fin," I said steadily.

"Yes," she breathed, making my heart beat erratically.

I swallowed, opened my mouth to speak to her, to say anything, really, just to continue connecting with her but found nothing. I promptly shut my mouth, wishing I could spill my feelings to her as readily as she seemed to be able to spill them to me. I knew I wasn't the most vocal person in the world. It seemed I'd inherited that particular trait, but it didn't mean I didn't have anything to say. I just didn't know how to say it.

"You don't have to," she told me.

"What?"

"You don't need to say anything to me, Ethan. Your touch is comfort enough," she answered, reading my mind.

"I'm not good with words," I told her. "I-I've always been this way. So many times I've wanted to tell you something and just as many times, it seems, fear locks me down."

"You have no need to fear anything with me," she whispered.

I circled the rear of the scooter to stand in front of her.

"That's just it, Fin. I'm not afraid of anything, not even death, but you? You I'm afraid of."

She sucked in a breath, took the phone from my hand, breaking our soothing contact, placed it in her shorts pocket, then threaded and wrapped her thin arms around my waist and rested her face against my chest. She made me wish I could touch her every minute of the day for the rest of my life. It was such a mollifying, soothing, relieving thing, our touch.

But I'd be lying if I didn't mention how it did insane things to my stomach, burning me slowly down to my toes then back up again. Her proximity made me want to touch her places I wasn't allowed to touch. To run my hands along the small of her back, my thumbs across her lips, kiss the line of her jaw, and taste her mouth with mine, but that kind of contact would only be a fantasy of mine. That contact was too intimate for friendship, too forbidden. So forbidden. So remarkably forbidden.

Yet, despite its risky side effects, I knew I'd hover just above that invisible line drawn in the sand, knowing I wasn't allowed to cross but toeing the water nonetheless, testing my boundaries because I was falling in love with Finley Dyer and that's what men falling in love do. They're gluttons for punishment.

I dragged my fingers across her shoulders, applying the slightest bit of pressure, and rested my hands on the sides of her neck before leaning forward and kissing her forehead. I heard a quick intake of breath and for the briefest of moments believed it'd been for me before hearing two scooters near us colliding in a minor fender bender. I turned to realize she'd seen it coming and felt disappointed in myself for hoping.

The drivers began arguing in Vietnamese, shattering our moment. Fin pulled from me, grabbed the phone, and dialed a number. I sat in silence amongst the clattering street noise, absorbing the constant movement around me, bewildered by the fact that a woman had been murdered in the street not half an hour earlier and life, with its harsh, severe insistence to continue on, propelled and shoved its way over her death site, over her memory, her life's blood, never ceasing, never stopping. I was sickened by it all yet, at the same time, it peculiarly consoled me.

Had you not just diverted your own attention from her death as well, Ethan? Had you not just fantasized about touching Fin? You're no different. No less human. No less flawed.

And yet... we may have difficulty controlling our instinctive thoughts, but we do have a level of self-control that shapes us into the compassionate, empathetic people we should always strive to be. I wasn't necessarily condoning their quick abandon of the woman in the street, because it made them human. As Fin had once said to me in class back home, "If you judge people, you have no time to love them." She was quoting Mother Teresa. So who was I to know those people's inner thoughts?

I watched a woman, extremely pregnant and on a scooter, her gaze was somewhere else, her mind as well, I thought. I soaked her in. Who knew what her life was like? I imagined her desperate to get home as quickly as possible to relieve the neighbor watching her other children. She would pick them up next door only to bring them home, set them down in front of a television, so she could get whatever work she could get done before her body gave out from sheer exhaustion.

Those desperate people with their desperate stares and eager scooters were human. Very, *very* human.

I turned toward Fin. She was talking to Sister Marguerite, nodding her head up and down as if she could be seen by her. Occasionally she would interject with a yes or no. I watched her beautiful face. Her eyes widened.

"Sister, I'll have to call you back. I think Father's trying to reach me." She lowered the phone, pressed a button, then brought it back to her ear. "Hello? Oh my God, Father, are you all right?" She paused, looked at me, and said, "Thanh Nhàn Ward Police. Thanh Nhàn, Hai Bà Trưng. Hanoi." I nodded, trying to remember everything she said. "Father, are you—" she began, but her expression fell. "They cut off the phone," she explained, tears glistening in her eyes.

"It's okay. Thanh Nhàn Ward Police. Just remember that." I looked around me and tapped the shoulder of a guy about our age. "Excuse me? Do you speak English."

He smiled at us. "Very little," he offered.

"Do you know where Thanh Nhàn Ward Police Station is?"

"Uh, yes, not far." We pulled a map of Hanoi up on Father's phone and showed it to him. He found it easily when he typed the station's name into the search box.

"Thank you so much," Fin told him, and he waved goodbye as he went on his way. "I would have had no idea how to spell that," she admitted. "I feel powerless."

"You're not. Not even close," I told her honestly.

We both determined the easiest route before putting the phone away and getting on our scooters. We meandered the maze of cars and other scooters, almost ramming into each other once or twice, when someone would try to edge beside us, screaming in Vietnamese. The police station was nestled in a shady-looking street, full of dingy shops, meandering people, and yelling motorists. There was one thing I could say for Hanoi: it was chaotic. The citizens here seemed at peace with it, obviously comfortable, but coming from a laid-back area like Bitterroot where a honked horn was almost unheard of, this was overpowering.

The chaos, the murder, Father's arrest. Falling hard for Finley. All of it was proof that my trip to Vietnam would never, ever be dull. I glanced over at

Fin and followed the lines of her face, gleaming in the sunlight, the creased worry lines at her eyes, the constant biting of her lower lip, and my heart sank.

Stopped at a rare red light, she spun her head toward mine. Her hand shot toward me, resting on my forearm, her expression relaxed. "I'm glad you came!" she yelled over the din of passing traffic, surprising me. "I know I didn't seem like it, you know, before, but I'm-I'm so glad you're here!" She squeezed my forearm, and that soothing warmth crept into my heart and into my soul like a shot of whiskey, heavy and beautiful.

When the light turned green, we cut across a blur of traffic and edged down the street that housed the station. We stopped a few blocks away and turned off the bikes.

"I need to call Sister back," she told me, pulling the phone out of her pocket and dialing.
We waited for her to answer.

Fin's brows rose. "Sister, yes." She paused. "Thanh Nhàn. Not sure if I pronounced that right. Do you know it? Oh, okay. Yeah. Fine, fine. Okay. Bye." She paused yet again, a slight smile appeared. "Yes, ma'am." She hung up. "She's sending a contact here. She doesn't want anyone to know our faces."

"I see," I said solemnly. We were quiet for five minutes at least before I couldn't take the silence anymore. "This is serious shit." She nodded in answer, her bottom lip stiff. "We could die."

"We could," she answered, looking at me in earnest. "Does that make you want to run? You know I wouldn't judge you if you left, Ethan. I'm glad you're here, but I wouldn't make you stay."

"I meant what I said. I'm not afraid of death, Fin." I let our earlier conversation settle in the pit of my stomach. "I'm not afraid of anything." *Except for you*, I let hang in the air this time.

Her mouth opened but closed at an approaching man on a scooter who sidled up beside us.

"Finley," he offered in a thick Vietnamese accent.

"Yes," she said kindly, but her body language implied she was on alert.

"Sister called me to retrieve Father. She says you go home now."

"Uh, okay. She doesn't want us to ride home with Father?"

"You could be followed," he answered, holding his hand out for Father's keys. She handed them to him then got off the bike. "Go," he said before zooming off without further conversation.

"Hop on," I told her, and she obeyed. "I remember how to get to the highway. I'll have to backtrack a bit, but I think I can get us out of here."

She nodded against my shoulder, sending a thrill into the pit of my stomach, and we took off.

CHAPTER TWENTY-ONE

Ethan

The woman who died giving us information was named Kim Banh. She was the unmarried sister of one of the kidnappers she died trying to expose. I only wish I was joking. The asshole had his own sister *killed*. The danger we were in was very real, very heartbreaking. Life meant nothing to these people. Nothing.

Attaching a name to her added the solemnity to her death I'd been seeking and that night, after Father got home and said Mass in her name, I went to bed examining a conscience I'd tried very hard to keep a tight lid on since my mother had died. Scrutiny was unheard of in my head. I wouldn't have allowed it because that would have meant answering for my sins, answering for all the horrific things I had done, or rather not done. A failure to act in right is a failure to do right. It's an uncomfortable settling in the gut, that knowledge. Every time I ignored someone who could have benefited from my help was the equivalent to slapping my mom in the face, and I felt ill to my stomach.

Then it dawned on me...

Maybe coming here won't just be for Finley.
Maybe I was destined to come here for myself as well.
Maybe this is a time for Finley to heal the gaps stamped
through by her thieves and maybe this is a time for
retribution on my part. Maybe I'm here to shed my false
complacency.

I was convinced.

And renewed.

The next morning, I was awakened by the
sudden need to see Finley. I jumped into the shower,
dressed, and ran across the shaky dock from the
boathouse, over the stretch of beach, and through the
grove of trees up to Slánaigh. I peered up onto the high
wraparound porch and my heart stopped by Finley
standing barefoot in a long, stretchy, formfitting
lavender skirt and white tank top, her hair flowing in
the sea breeze. She was watching the water in the bay
but her eyes cut to me. Her hand lifted to shield herself
from the sun. She smiled and waved and the gesture
shuttered and jolted my heart into a steady beat once
again.

Remembering myself, I smiled and waved back.
She turned, presumably to come meet me at Slánaigh's
front door. I found myself sprinting to see her, which
admittedly was uncool as shit, but it was hard for me
to care in the moment. When I bounded up the
winding staircase, I was breathless, but not from the
effort, no, from the beauty that was Finley Dyer. She
wore her heart on her sleeve, and it had never looked
lovelier to me.

"Finley," I panted.

"Hello, Ethan," she said, but the jaw-dropping smile that followed after stirred my insides into mush.

"Come, we have lots to do," she said, leading the way into the main room from the front door.

Girls were scattered everywhere, working on what seemed to be school lessons. Sister's skirts swished back and forth across the wood floor as she quietly made the rounds around the girls, checking work and offering help where it was needed. She looked up at me and smiled before continuing on.

"Through here," Finley said, guiding me toward the kitchen. "There are a couple of new girls who came in last night, stolen away, it seems, from who knows where because they've barely said a single word since they've arrived. The only name they keep mentioning is Khanh's, but there's no news there since we're already aware of how broad his filthy scope reaches. Anyway, we're staying close to home today because we suspect there might be a little cell where the new girls came from close by that may be housing at least ten more girls between the ages of eight and sixteen." My stomach sank.

Fucking eight years old. My hands trembled at my sides. It was noticeable enough that Finley grabbed the one closest to her and squeezed.

"Ethan, it's why we're here. We're here to help."

I nodded, not wanting to voice my real thoughts for fear she would drop my hand and demand I leave the house out of revulsion. Because what I really wanted to say in answer was that I didn't want to "help." I wanted to annihilate the asshole men who put little girls up for sale into such a bloody pulp not even their dental records would identify them. I wanted them gone, never to harm another girl ever again.

"Ethan, lad," I heard at my immediate right.

"Hello, Father," I answered.

"So ya've heard, have ye? We're leavin' this moment ta see if we'n find this cell out. I mean ta have ya by me, boyo. Ya did well yesterday, and I think ya do well today. Just keep yer head 'bout ya."

"Yes, sir," I told him.

"Keep yer wits 'bout ya', boyo, t'ain't to be easy," he drove home.

My stomach plummeted at my feet, but I nodded my head in reply.

We set out as we'd done the day before, but this time we only went a few miles away into the city proper, eventually parking our scooters at the back of An's tea shop. I had to duck my head to get in through the door and memories of a cantankerous old man assailed me.

"I see you've survived," An teased me as she hugged Finley.

"Barely," I said, glancing at Finley, unsuccessfully biting a smile back.

Finley rolled her eyes at me.

"Here, come, sit."

She ordered all three of us to a table near the front. An's father came forward through the curtain separating the back and his eyes widened when he saw me. He started to shout in Vietnamese. He rushed me and I stood, falling back against the concrete wall behind me.

"Father!" An shouted, but her tone negated her actions because she kindly grabbed his arm and guided him back from where he came.

An emerged once more. "I'm so sorry. He doesn't like you," she laid it out.

"I can see that," I said, confused. "But why?"

"He says you are not as you seem."

"What?" I asked, my blood running cold.

"He says you are not all that you appear to be."

"Not true," Finley said, coming to my defense.

"I didn't say I agreed with him," An laughed. She left the table once more to retrieve a pot of tea.

"He just doesn't know you, Ethan," she explained away.

Or maybe he does. No, no, no. I am exactly who I appear to be.

I looked over at Father, distracted by his own thoughts, and writing feverishly in a notebook he'd brought with him, his plans and ideas.

"Father," I called, but he didn't hear me. "Father," I repeated. This time he looked at me. "What is it we need to do?"

"Well, yer bait, son."

"Bait," I copied.

"You'll disgoise ya'self slightly. A hat, maybe, an' we'll fish 'em out, we will."

"Of course," I said, not hesitating. *Anything to save those girls*, I thought.

"Ye'll be all by yer lonesome, though, at the start an' we'll have a meetin' place, see, an' you'll come to us wit' their location. If ya feel o'erwhelmed, boyo, ya walk."

"I can do this," I told him.

"No, if things be too dangerous, son, ya walk. I won't have yer immortal soul on my conscience. Ya walk t'at the first sign o' danger."

"Of course. I'll be very careful, Father."

"Aye. Wait til they 'proach ya, find out where they are, politely decloine, then come ta us. We'll do the rest."

Just then three Vietnamese men came to the table and shook Father's hand. Father introduced them to us as a few local men who like to help on their days off. Apparently there were at least twenty locals who volunteered to help Father and his organization, not to mention the hundreds of peeled eyes and ears who kept him informed of anything they came across that could be of use to him.

I looked on these men. Two were over the age of forty and one was closer to my and Fin's age. I'd find out later that the two older men were brothers who fished the bay for a living, and the younger guy worked in a local shop. The younger guy's name was Phong and his sister had been missing for two years. He suspected she'd been taken from Hạ Long to China to be sold further from there, but he wasn't going to give up looking for her locally or stop helping other girls who shared her fate.

"When was she taken?" I asked him as Father readied the older men with our plan.

Phong spoke perfect English, a shop necessity in Hạ Long for the tourists. "Twenty months, five days," he answered.

"I'm so sorry," I told him.

"Me too," he said, staring off into space.

I tried to imagine what it was like to lose a sibling, the despair Phong must have felt on a daily basis. I could see how cathartic it could be to dedicate your time to Father's organization. I bet it was the only way he could feel productive toward retrieving his sister.

We stood when Father, Finley, and the two fishermen stood.

"Here," Father said, holding out a nón lá to me.

I laughed a little. "You can't be serious."

He smiled back. "Have ta hoide that pretty hair of yers some way," he joshed.

I burst out laughing. "Touché, old priest. Touché."

I wrapped my hair back and placed the conical leaf hat on my head. All the men started chuckling.

"What? You've never seen a six-foot-three-inch Native American in a nón lá before?"

"No, I certainly haven't," An chimed in, grinning. "They'll definitely see you coming."

"But will they remember who I am?" I asked her.

Her eyes narrowed at me. "No, I don't think they will. You're hidden well."

"Which 'tis the point," Father added with a slap on the back. "Now we'll be but a block from ya always. Are ye ready, lad?"

"I'm ready," told him. I kissed Fin's cheek, letting the tingle from her skin calm my heart, and strode toward the door.

I could feel I was being followed but shook off the feeling since I knew my followers. I meandered up and down the streets of Hạ Long, constantly being called to random shops, their owners eager for a sale, but it wasn't until two hours in that I caught the eye of a man shuffling around a corner sidewalk, shifting his eyes from tourist to tourist. Every now and again, he would approach someone and speak to them. I knew exactly what he was doing.

I crossed to his side of the street practically begging him to approach me. As I neared him, I feared he wouldn't but just as suddenly I heard him say, "You like young girls?"

Bingo.

"Huh?" I played dumb.

"You like girls?" he asked again.

"Maybe," I said, avoiding eye contact.

"I got girls for you. Only twenty dolla. Young girls for you."

I didn't answer, afraid I'd lose myself and just choke the guy out right there. He mistook my hesitation as a yes.

"This way," he said, guiding me by an arm. I yanked it out of his grasp, pissed beyond belief that the guy touched me. He shook off my aggression, desperate for the sale. He pointed toward an alley at a door hidden at the end butted against a perpendicular building.

I followed him to it. He knocked twice and a man pulled it open. He screamed something in Vietnamese and two little girls around twelve and thirteen, in T-shirts, shorts, and messy hair jumped to his command, standing before me. Neither would make eye contact with me, and my gut ached to snatch them from him and run.

"How much again?" I asked.

"Twenty dolla."

"I don't have that much," I told him, now that I knew where to point the team.

"Fifteen dolla," he haggled as I walked away. "Ten dolla!" he yelled.

I practically sprinted away, not really knowing where it was I was going but knowing I had to get away from that man as soon as possible. I ran down the street, took a left at what felt like a major intersection, somewhere I knew it would be easy for Fin, Father, and the volunteers to hide easily and start searching the crowds. My chest pumped in anxiety, in fear for the girls who laid beyond that door, and the creeping, violent urge that settled so comfortably in my heart. I needed Finley. Anxiety melted into sheer panic as I searched through the people, shoving where I needed to, desperate to find her.

"Ethan," I heard someone breathe beside me. I yanked the leaf hat from my head and stared at her. There was a brief moment of pause between us before both our hands found one another's faces. *Finally*, I breathed. I hugged her to me tightly, still not feeling like it was close enough. After looking at those girls, I didn't think it would ever be near enough.

"I know where they are," I told her ear.

"Then let's go," she said, snatching my hand and leading me toward our group.

We twisted our way around the crowded street.

"Did ya find it, lad?" Father asked.

"Yes."

"Lead the way then."

I took them all a block from the alley, not so close they could find us out but close enough they could differentiate which alley I was referring to. The original man who'd seeked me out wasn't there on the corner, making me nervous.

"The guy's not there," I told them. "He was just there a minute ago."

"He could have sold to a tourist or possibly suspected you and bolted. We'll find out which one," Phong explained.

We waited a few minutes and sure enough he came back out into the street in search of his next sale.

"What do we do now?" I asked.

"We call a contact of Father's at the police."

"I thought the police were bought," I observed.

"Not all of them," he said.

A Detective Tran showed up a few minutes later, and he introduced himself to us. He instructed Finley and me to stay hidden where we were while he and Father and the volunteers surrounded the building as he waited for a warrant.

"Do you really need a warrant when the guy showed me the girls?"

Detective Tran sighed. "Yes, unfortunately."

Finley and I didn't utter a word while we paced back and forth on the sidewalk down the street, waiting. And waited. And *waited*. It was taking so long that Phong was told to give us an update.

"What's going on?" Finley asked him, her nerves frayed.

"The judge is asking for more evidence than an open solicitation."

"What in the hell? I saw two girls there."

"Some judges want more concrete evidence of illegal sex trade other than an offer," he explained.

"What else could they possibly produce?" Finley asked, both her hands on top of her head.

"They want Detective Tran to see the girls. The only problem is that Detective Tran and Father are both known by sight to this world. There's no way they will open the door for either of them."

"Then we break down their gosh damn door!" I yelled, frustrated beyond belief.

"We can't," Phong explained calmly.

"Wait, so what are you saying?"

"We have to try and come back at a time they're not expecting us," he answered.

I couldn't believe what he was saying. "You're not serious," I deadpanned.

"As a heart attack. They'll be gone soon anyway, so the whole of today was pretty much pointless."

I looked at Finley. Her face stricken with grief for the little girls trapped inside.

"No, there's no way I'm leaving without getting those girls out. No way."

"Ethan," Phong said sadly. "We'll try again. We'll keep trying."

"Unacceptable," I told him, my blood raging in my veins. "*Unacceptable*. There are little girls in there, Phong. Tiny girls," I explained to him.

"Ethan," he told me with glassy eyes, "I *know*." My heart tore in two for him.

I nodded once at him in recognition of his staggering loss. There was nothing I could possibly say to him to drive that sorrow home any further for him, nothing I could tell him that could appease him even in the slightest bit.

"But I cannot accept this," I told him.

"We don't have a choice, Ethan. We're prisoners to the system here. We've tried forcefully taking the girls and it resulted in years of litigation. The police are bought and paid for, even a few judges. You get arrested by a bought officer and you're done for. Father is in mounds and mounds of legal trouble already. Father, you, me, Finley, what good are we to these children if we're locked in jail?'

"But," I began to tell him, but my objection lost its steam. I couldn't argue. It made perfect sense and yet no sense at all. "What a disgusting world we live in," I told Finley, reaching for her hand.

She nodded and took my hand in hers, squeezing it. I calmed down as we stood in silence.

"We're forced to live within the confines of laws inflicted upon us by a society that knows nothing of right and wrong," Finley spoke to the ground, breaking the sad quiet. "Laws that obligate us to fight our natural instincts. It's ludicrous."

Father, Detective Tran, and the fishermen joined us down the street from the alley they'd been guarding.

"'Tis not to be today. Tomorrow," Father exclaimed with a sigh, leaning against a shop wall, his cane tucked into his side. He shook the hands of each of the volunteers, including Phong and they departed to their homes.

"Detective Tran," Finley said, offering her hand. "Thank you for coming so quickly. I know it was your day off."

"Of course," he told her, shaking her hand. "Father," he said, nodding at him. "Ethan," he acknowledged before heading off into the crowd. All three of us stood quietly for a few moments.

"I feel like I've failed," I told them both.

"Never, ever feel loike that, lad," Father admonished in kindness. "Yer here, yer workin' for the good of our Lord. We'll keep troyin'."

We picked up our scooters at An's and made it back to Slánaigh just in time for dinner. We walked through the front door where the girls were lounging about reading and playing. Sister was sewing in her rocking chair. Her eyes lifted when we entered, hopeful in their bright loveliness. Finley shook her head at her and that life died down, making my heart speed up in disappointment.

These people who worked here, these quiet, unassuming human beings with their blazing, vivid souls cared deeply for the hurt and forgotten children of this country. You could see it in their efforts, their dogged attempts at retrieving and healing the broken young of Vietnam. They were rock stars, and no one would ever know who they were. In fact, the world would make it its life's goal to keep them in the shadows, but the ironic part was that they cared nothing for recognition. Their motivation was to fix wrong, to alleviate the burdened souls who had been wronged.

My heart clenched for Finley. I looked on my beautiful friend. If only I could have known her then when she needed me as those girls that day had needed me. If only I could have fought for her, wrestled her demons, the tangible and intangible. I would have shredded them to pieces, obliterated them.

"Let's take a walk at the beach," she told me. "Sister, we'll be down by the water."

"But dinner, Finley," Sister protested.

"Mind waiting?" she asked me.

"Not even in the slightest."

We obeyed Sister out of respect, but I don't think either of us had much of an appetite. We both sat at the table, dejected from the day's activities, shoveling food into our mouths just to avoid questions later. We helped clean up and Finley also assisted the other volunteers in putting the girls to bed, a task I happily was not allowed to participate in. Fifty screaming, giggly girls is right up there on top of my that's-okay-I'll-sit-this-one-out list.

It was close to nine o'clock in the evening when Finley finally emerged.

"Tired?" I asked her.

"Not really," she admitted. "Too jazzed up, I think."

We left Slánaigh, paced ourselves down the winding staircase but took off when our toes hit sand, Finley's-flip flops abandoned at the start of the path, sprinting under the grove of trees bending to the wind. We ran hand in hand until our feet met the lip of the water, warm from baking in the day's sun.

Winded, Finley turned to me. "I wish we could have saved them. It would have been so different if we could have just saved them," she said, bursting into a sob at the end.

"Fin," I whispered, grief-stricken for those girls and for her.

She broke down unselfishly for them, and I wished I could have done something for her then. Swiped my hand and made good of all the bad, but that is not real life as I was painfully becoming more and more aware of.

I sat her in the sand and moved beside her. We laid back, hands linked, staring up into a starlit sky.

"It's not all bad," I told her, gesturing at the stars.

"What?" she asked, her tears having dried.

"I know earlier I declared the whole of the world disgusting, but I don't really feel that way, Fin. It's not all bad. Right now, as we stare up at the starlit heavens, I can see the beauty in it." *When I look at you I see the good in this world.* "We have to see hope here," I told her, "or I don't think we're going to survive it."

"I can't see it right now," she confessed. So I did the only thing I could think to do, I nodded in understanding.

She turned toward me after a few moments of contemplation, her side digging into the powder sand below us, and I followed her lead. Lifting my cell from my pocket, I turned music on and let it lie above our heads.

"What is it about us and water?" I asked her, making her laugh.

"And music," she countered.

"And music," I gave in.

"How far we've come."

"How far indeed," I agreed.

"We're not kids from Bitterroot anymore, Ethan."

"I don't think we were ever really from Bitterroot, Fin. We never really belonged to anyone, ever."

"Confession?"

"Aye, my choild," I said, pathetically parroting Father's accent.
She hit my shoulder but giggled anyway just so I wouldn't feel bad, I think.

"I want to belong somewhere...to someone."
My heart leapt into my throat. Was she asking me? *Me!* I wanted to shout. *Me! Belong to me, Fin. Please, I'll be your home.*

But the moment passed in strained silence, fading behind me in a cowardly fear. Fear of rejection, fear that it would change everything, and a fear that if she left me, I wouldn't recover. In there laid the drama.

I was falling in love with Finley Dyer. Three-quarters fallen if I had been really honest with myself, but did I want to make the final leap? Although I had been quite over Cricket for some time, I knew what it felt like to hurt from love, and my word, was the pain acute.

I let her words lay there, though they begged for a response. Instead, I reached across the sand and wrapped a strand of hair around my index finger, twirling it over and over until I couldn't feel wear my finger started or her hair stopped.

That night I walked Fin back to Slánaigh before retreating to the houseboat, laying on the bed they had given me and wondering how in the hell I was going to change the fate of all those girls, how I could make enough of a difference that my life would eventually feel worthy of existence.

CHAPTER TWENTY-TWO

Turns out there was incredible beauty in the world as evidenced by the girls already residing at Slánaigh. They were cheerful and kind, generous and sweet, funny and even a little bit ornery, which, I confess, was my favorite part about them. They were constantly playing tricks on everyone. I say "tricks" but it was all in good fun and never anything mean. It showed me just how much they were embracing their lives, and it gave me such utter hope. For them. For Fin. Even for *me*.

During the day, Fin and I would help Sister out, occasionally going out with Father as well, but our "hunting trips" mostly consisted at night.

Our fourth week there started out as any other would, we hadn't heard much by way of our "eyes" or "ears," but late in the evening, we'd gotten wind of another active cell near the city proper and we aimed to find them out.

Phong was able to come along this trip as well as four other regular volunteers, Finley, me, Father, as well as Detective Tran, whose hand rested on his phone, ready to request warrants. We'd fallen into a comfortable rhythm using me as bait, my hair tucked back in a man bun and a nón lá on my head.

"You look like a really badass dark Raiden," Finley told me as we readied ourselves at An's. This made me ridiculously happier than a little kid so I smiled like a gigantic idiot, which made her laugh.

"What?" I asked, a little offended.

"You're just so..." she began.

"*So?*" I prodded.

She considered me for a moment before her face sobered, making my heart race.

"Nothing," she finally rasped in answer.

I swallowed. "*Nothing.*"

"Nothing," she whispered, putting some distance between us, and trust me when I say that I felt the space keenly.

"Oh, okay," I stammered.

She smiled timidly at me and I returned the favor in kind.

"Are ye ready?" Father asked us.

We set free into the night and lost ourselves in the methodical canvassing of the city as we swept the streets. The only thing we'd improved upon was connecting two cell phones. I kept a Bluetooth headset in my ear, hidden away from prying eyes. I had hours' worth of one-sided conversations with Finley night after night and, frankly, it did nothing but make me even further enchanted with her.

"Check, check. One, two," she teased into my ear. I glanced over my shoulder and smiled at her. "I kind of like that you can't answer me. It makes me feel powerful. A very rare thing when it comes to Ethan Moonsong." I shook my head as imperceptibly as possible. "Oh, don't like that, do you?" she flirted. "Hey, remember that time our junior year of high school when I caught you looking down my shirt?" I choked on nothing and fought a smile. I did not do that. At least not where she could have noticed anyway. *Did I?* "You don't think I knew you'd done it, but I knew. I could feel the heat of your eyes even then," she told me, wrecking my concentration. *Even then?*

She'd flirted with me like that every time we'd gotten on the phones for our scouting, but I couldn't ever tell if she was serious because it was doused cold with metaphorical ice water the second we'd stand close to one another afterward. She was driving me insane. It was the good kind of insane, though. The kind of insane where you happily welcomed the madness because the torture was too incredibly sweet to forego.

I shook my head to regain my thoughts and a sense of purpose. She stole that so readily from me without even realizing it. She made me suffer in ways she couldn't possibly comprehend. *Make me suffer, Fin. Please make me suffer,* I thought, imagining her lips.

"Twelve o'clock," she told me, shocking me out of my thoughts and alerting me to a group of white men lingering around a man we'd come to recognize as a trafficker.

I nodded that I'd seen them and crept near, shadowing them as silently as possible.

"Only fifty dolla," I overheard the trafficker say.

"Get outov 'ere," a drunk American slurred.

"Okay, no fifty dolla. Forty dolla."

"We don't negotiate with terrorists, you sick bastard," an obnoxious boy answered.

Four American men stood in a cluster, trying to read a digital map on their phone. *Drunk and lost. Smart,* I thought.

"Only forty dolla," the trafficker repeated.

One of the boys made a move like he was going to hit the guy. Finally, he got the message and made his way down the street approaching other tourists and getting turned away. I made my way closer to him, edging around people until I was in stride with him.

"You like girls?" he asked me with their usual opener. I didn't answer him, baiting him further. "Only fifty dolla."

"I only have forty," I said low, disguising my voice.

"Forty! Yeah, yeah! We do forty! Come," he said, taking a right at the next intersection. He tried to corral me with one hand while pointing toward our destination with the other.

"How young?" I asked him.

"Young. Very young," he replied.

I clenched my teeth as he led me down a narrow path between two shop buildings. At the back there was a door. There was always a door at the back.

"In here," he told me. "Just in here."

"No, I'm not comfortable going in there," I told him and turned back around.

"No," he said, snatching at my sleeve.

"Don't touch me!" I roared at him, making him shrink into himself.

"Sorry, so sorry. Only forty dolla," he offered, determined to deal at whatever cost.

"I said no." I twisted around him and made a move to leave the narrow passageway.

"Thirty dolla," he counteroffered, disgusting me.

I burst onto the main street.

"Are you okay?" Finley asked me when I reached the curb, concern in her voice.

I'd forgotten she was there.

I nodded, searching the street for her face but found nothing. *Good, they're hidden well.*

"Detective Tran is getting a warrant now. The men are assembling. Father says to come meet me."

I looked around me, searching for her soothingly beautiful face.

"I'm here," she said, "by the only tree on the street."

I spotted it almost immediately, basically pushing people out of my way to reach her.

"Almost," she said, but I wasn't sure if she'd intended to speak aloud.

I spotted Finley, leaning against the trunk, hidden in the night shadows of two buildings and the cover of the tree. She'd found the perfect spot. I yanked back my nón lá and it rested against my back, the strap lying against my throat. She held out her hand to me. Greedily, I grasped at it with both hands. *Finally*, I breathed, my chest and heart settling in that quietude I was constantly seeking and found so easily in her.

"You did well," she told me. Her eyes locked with mine and she smiled. "I'm proud of you, Ethan." This filled me with an honor I'd honestly not felt in years. Finley lifted up on her toes, bringing her soft lips to my cheek.

Finley

The harshness of his stubble-covered skin against the creaminess of my own sent a thrill down my spine. My stomach dropped to my feet and my mouth went dry. I leaned my lips against his cheek, the corner of my lip meeting the corner of his by accident. I lingered there, tempting a dangerous game, swallowed, and closed my eyes, my lashes brushing against the bone at his temple.

I expected Ethan to back away from me at that intimate distance but he surprised me by standing stock-still, his face against mine. His warm breath fanned across my face, making my eyes burn with a desperation for him. It was a torturous game we played, our back and forth, and we rode the line between friendship and love with precarious steps. I expected, no, *wanted* so badly for a misstep.

Bend to me, Ethan. Because I will not.

He balanced on the boundary once again, burying his face into my neck, and the restless ache that resided in my belly flamed brighter for him. He inhaled, bringing one hand up into the back of my hair, entangling his fingers in its length. He bent my head to the side for better access and I felt my knees threaten to buckle. How could he not know the power he had over me? How could he not know?

His lips remained at my neck, idling there, successfully succeeding in tormenting me. My body begged me to reach up to him, grab his hair and bring him into me, but I dared not move an inch.

He cleared his throat, the rumbling movement echoing against my own doling out a sweet agony. *Pull the trigger*, I silently begged him.

"You-you always smell so good," he told me, my mouth opening involuntarily at his sexy observation.

"I do?" I asked him, my voice raspy in unexpected emotion.

"Yes," he answered, his lips and his voice still at the side of my throat.

But neither of us dared to move in that ultimate cat-and-mouse game. A game I would have happily been the mouse in, the game in which I would have surrendered to him with just one word, one simple action.

But the worst thing happened instead. Instead, he pulled back from me and smiled sweetly, piercing my heart with how handsome he was. I hated the reminder. He tortured me.

He swallowed once more, his Adam's apple bobbing up and down with the movement.

"Should we check on them?" I asked him, desperate for a change in tone, anything to distract me from Ethan Moonsong and his obliviously punishing ways.

He looked shocked I'd asked him that but quickly fixed his expression. "Oh-oh, yeah," he answered me.

We walked down the street toward the hidden passage Ethan had been shown by the trafficker and found Phong, pulling him aside near a busy food shop.

"What's going on?" Ethan asked him.

"We've got the warrant, finally, but Detective Tran is having trouble getting men to assemble for the raid."

"Gosh damn it," Ethan exclaimed. "We just cannot catch a break."

"Can we not just raid it without them?" I asked him.

"Detective Tran won't risk us getting hurt."

Although we'd had two successful raids since Ethan and I had come to Vietnam, we'd had seven unsuccessful raids and most of those were because they were thwarted by the traffickers' purchased members of the police force. It was beyond frustrating and unbelievably disheartening at times.

Just then a loud bang sounded from the short alleyway and out poured everyone inside. Young, frightened children and armed traffickers came spilling out into the street, scattering around us.

"Someone must have tipped them off!" Detective Tran yelled to us over the screaming people clambering to get cover.

A trafficker, recognizing Father, smiled viciously at him and began to charge at him.

"No," Ethan whispered, watching the man take aim with his gun.

And then I was witness to that transformation, that quit of thought and abandonment to instinct again. Like the day Kim Banh died, something glazed over Ethan's eyes and he lunged forward, chasing after the armed man and the child he carried, resolute in saving Father.

As if in slow motion, I screamed, grasping at him but only catching the tip of the nón lá that laid against his back, loosening the leaf hat as it tumbled to the street. He turned toward me, his expression all mission, all duty.

"Don't worry, my love," he told me softly before turning back toward his task.

Time continued to stand still as I watched him, too mesmerized by the evolution of his movements to take cover. I followed his effortless shift of muscle and limb as he tackled the man, plucking his gun from him. Ethan spun him around while pegging him in the temple with the butt of it. Both the man and the gun fell in a heap onto the street. The girl he'd been holding screamed then ran toward Detective Tran, who was busy trying to disarm a trafficker. Father interceded just in time for the girl to avoid getting trampled by them, gathering her and two other girls who'd gotten free, taking them toward a shop, and settling them inside before running to a volunteer's aid.

Ethan whirled around the street, plucking up scattered traffickers with an ease I'd never seen the equal to. I knew no one would believe me if I'd told them, even if I had to recount for every movement and I could have as well. I memorized every second of that fight. How could I not? It was burned into my memory as the most insane, most harrowing thing I had ever witnessed.

Ethan Moonsong was a born warrior.

Ethan

Breathe.

Breathe.

Breathe.

Right. Right. Jab. Uppercut. Lay him out.

232

"Run to the shop," I told the girl I'd just saved as softly as I could. It's a purposeful tone. One that completely negates the chaos that surrounded us, but I knew she needed some sort of stability, some sort of security, especially then, and I was determined to start at that moment despite her very fresh, very raw past. I was determined for her to begin the wretched forget. And as soon as possible.

She nodded just as softly and ran toward the shop I pointed toward.

Breathe.

Breathe.

Breathe.

A man charged me but I twisted away from him then threw my elbow into the back of his neck. He stumbled forward and fell face-first into the cement. I flipped him over before raining down a fist into his face, knocking him out cold.

I stood, scanning my immediate horizon, memorizing the positions of every man I wanted stopped and swiftly decided the best route to finish them off as efficiently as possible. Two at nine o'clock fighting Detective Tran, one at twelve, one at two o'clock fighting Phong, and two men held Father's arms while the guy who tried to sell the girls to me punched at his gut and face. Seven men total. Five armed. I smiled to myself.

Pouncing on Father's attackers, kicking the solicitor's legs out from underneath him, I took them all by surprise. The men holding Father's arms dropped him at once and were on me but it was already too late. I ran my elbow into the one at my right's face, felling him where he stood. The puncher gained footing. Before the one on my left could reach me, I grabbed at him, swinging him into my chest to protect me from the knife the puncher was swinging my direction. A blood-curdling scream came from the man's throat as the knife entered his chest. The puncher's eyes bulged and he hesitated. *Mistake.* I popped the knife from his hand with one brisk movement and smiled, making the panic wear all over his face in awareness. I threw the hardest part of my skull into his face and the man sagged onto the street in one limp drop. I noted that Father was unconscious amongst the heap, but I knew I needed to come back.

Two o'clock was easy work as Phong distracted him. So was twelve. The two at nine o'clock saw me coming, stopped fighting Tran, and ran. And just like that, it was over.

Adrenaline took over and my immediate thought was Fin. I scanned the street and saw her staring at me, her mouth agape, her chest working furiously for air.

Are you okay? I mouthed.

She swallowed and nodded.

"Get them out of here!" Tran yelled at my left. I looked on him. His eyes were wide and desperate. "Police are coming and I won't have any of you here! Leave this instant!"

The adrenaline kicked into high gear and I pulled Father up and threw him over my shoulder, tossing his cane at Phong's feet. He picked it up and I ran with Father to Fin, grabbing her hand and running flat-out for several blocks, Phong just behind us until we reached the tea shop.

I ducked into An's and she screamed at the sight of us.

"It's okay," Phong yelled her way. "We're just running from a little danger," he downplayed.

I set Father on the most comfortable seat I could find, a little upholstered arm chair. He was still unconscious. An and her father ran to us, towels in their hands. An started administering to Father but briefly looked at me. Her eyes narrowed. She tossed me a towel then turned back to Father.

I picked the towel off the floor, eyeing it.

"Here," Fin said, reaching for it. Her hands were trembling as she fisted her fingers around it.

"Are you all right?" I asked her, closing the distance between us. I loomed over her, my height further accentuating the juxtaposition between my size and hers. Her eyes bulged and she began trembling harder. "Do I scare you?" I asked gently. My hands longed to reach for her, envelop her, but I tucked them at my sides instead, clenching my fists.

"N-no," she stammered, her stutter contradicting her answer.

I didn't want to scare Finley but I had no idea what to say to her. Suddenly I was aware of every move I'd made in front of her, every block, every punch, every dodge, every violent move.

"I'm sorry," I told her.

"For what?" she whispered, her trembling hand swiping the towel across the bloody knuckles I just became aware of.

"Excuse me," I told her quietly.

I left her there, standing with her frightened stare, and walked toward the restroom. I punched through the swinging door and found my reflection in the mirror.

I was a bloody mess. Literally and figuratively. My right eye was swollen, the light grey color of my left looked a darker grey probably, I thought, from the adrenaline. The ivory of my skin was marred with splatters of my own blood mixed with so many others. I turned the water on, pouring it over the skin of my arms, hands, neck, and face. My hair had fallen out of its wrap and fell into the sink. I stood up and pulled it back again. I bent and scrubbed my sensitive face with soap and when I felt it was clean, I stood and took myself in all at once. Free of blood, I noticed that my right eye was swelling shut, my lip was fat with a split, and I was already sporting a pretty deep bruise across my left cheekbone.

But at least you're not covered in blood.

I came back out to a conscious Father and was happy I'd cleaned myself up.

"Ach! Lad! Ya look like ya been dragged 'cross a grate, ya have. That angelic face marred. Ach! Sister will never let ya back out now. What made ya do it, son?"

"I wasn't going to let them kill you, Father."

He shook his head. "Well, I canna thank ya 'nough, lad. Ya saved me loife."

"I would do it a hundred times over," I told him. "I would do it for anyone."

"I'm startin' ta see that," he said, smiling but it pained him and his usual happy grin fell.

"We're ta go back to the house now, boyo. Not a word of this ta Sister 'til morn. No sense worryin' her."

I nodded.

We thanked An and her father. He still eyed me with obvious contempt but I'd found I didn't care anymore. My mind was occupied elsewhere.

I watched Fin, memorized her every movement, scrutinized her reactions to me.

"Don't look at me like that," she told me as she climbed on to the back of the scooter. I averted my gaze and closed my eyes in the pain her fear brought me.

Her hands quivered against my stomach as they wrapped around my sides. I dared not touch her. I knew I'd only scare her more. *Please don't hate me, Fin*, I silently begged her. *Be soft with her*, I ordered myself. I kept quiet on the way back to Slánaigh, careful not to make any sudden movements, and when we pulled across the loose shell drive and parked the scooter, I let her get off at her own pace even though my hands longed to help her off, to give myself that shot of relief her skin always gave me. It wasn't about me, though. If I was honest with myself, I was scared my touch no longer helped her in the same way. I was frightened, in fact, that my touch did the exact opposite. I didn't want to find out if I'd shattered that glass remedy, delicate in its nature yet had held us up so well thus far. I didn't want to hear the splinter, the tinkling fractured pieces as they cut me on their way back down to the earth.

"I'm to bed, ye' two. Tran'll be bringin' those girls Ethan saved in the mornin'. I'll need the rest ta help Sister and Dr. Nguyen," Father told us, leaving us behind on the shell drive.

I stood from the bike a few feet in front of Finley. The cool breeze from the ocean swept past us and back again, our hair and clothing shifting as it did so. We breathed. We studied one another. We did nothing else. My heart began to race harder and harder as the time passed on. I silently begged her to say something, anything, but she was deadly quiet, making me nervous. Her eyes followed the lines of my body down from my face to my T-shirt. She winced at the sight of the blood on my shirt. I tore it off without thinking, tossing it to the side.

"Better?" I asked softly. She closed her eyes briefly then met my own, nodding once. "Are you afraid of me, Fin?"

"A—" she began but her voice cracked. She cleared it. "A little," she admitted with a slight smile.

Her confession sent my heart into my throat. "That devastates me," I declared, meaning it.

"Why?" she asked, her head tilted to the side, as if she could have gleaned it from me with the gesture alone.

"Because I want you to be able to run to me without thought," I admitted, a memory of my past reeling up with a vengeance then settling back down into oblivion. "I want no hesitation from you. It pains me to know that I frighten you."

She swallowed, bit her bottom lip once, then said quietly, "You've always frightened me, Ethan."

That statement hung in the air a moment before it circulated around me, settled on my skin, stinging me.

She walked away from me but not toward the staircase as I had expected. When her foot hit the sandy path that led through the dense brush, trees, and the beach, she abandoned her flip-flops as she always did. I followed her hesitantly at first but picked up my pace when I lost her in the trees.

When I emerged from the canopy of trees, I found her as I had that night by the lake. The night that felt like a million years ago. The night she'd told me of her tragic birthday. The night she'd hugged herself, rocking back and forth on the balls of her feet.

I chose a spot next to her but a few feet to her right.

"I've always frightened you?" I asked her, guarded.

She turned her face toward me, her arms still wrapped around herself. That same bay breeze blew her hair around her face. "Always," she confirmed. My shoulders sagged, unwilling to bear any more of her truths. "But not in the way you might think," she whispered, shocking me.

"How?" I whispered back, edging slowly, painfully slowly her direction half a step in anticipation of I didn't know what.

She looked out into the vast, dark cove. "You represent suffering to me, Ethan."

"Why?" I begged her softly, taking another easy, heavy step toward her.

"You are the one I cannot ever have," she began, and my mouth went dry. "You are the untouchable one for me, and I hate it." I eased ever closer, not even realizing in that moment I had been moving. "I have pride, Ethan," she continued, "and I'm not one to want, to-to seek after, to crave without equal return. I want—no, *deserve* to be loved and wanted with the same ferocity. I know you want to stay friends," she said, making my chest burn. I could not believe this woman, this *incredible* woman, wanted me as much as I wanted her. "I can do that. I really can," she explained to me, unaware how badly I was fighting the need to stop her lips with my own, but I dared not stop her, not when she so obviously had so much to say. "I don't think I will ever get over you, not really. I know how pathetic that makes me look, but I am such the perfect combination of vulnerable and raw right now that all my secrets are spilling out of me without a thought as to the damage they may cause. It feels good to tell you anyway," she confessed. "Maybe this will help me build that envied effortless barrier I've strived so tirelessly to keep up these past few months." She turned toward me. "So to truthfully answer your earlier question, I was frightened for you, not of you, and though the way you handled yourself with those men was daunting and, to be honest, dangerously enthralling, I was more intimidated than afraid. So yes, I'm more *frightened* of you now than I ever have been," she confided.

She stopped talking, content she'd said all she needed to say, I assumed. Her eyes rose to meet the blue moon above us. She didn't appear to have regretted divulging her secret, which bolstered me.

I stepped nearer yet again. There was only a foot between us. I stared up at her moon. Her moon, because I decided then that it belonged to her with its beautiful flaws and its peaceful light. The moon and Finley were synonymous.

And I leapt.

I cleared my throat, trying to swallow down my heart. It beat so quickly, I was convinced it was going to burst from my chest. "I-Finley?"

"Hmm?" she asked with such an unconcerned air I felt my confidence falter.

Do it.

"Do you know how often I prayed that Cricket would have changed her mind and come back to me?" A pained expression flitted across her face and it wounded me knowing I put it there. "Just hear me, Finley." She looked at me and nodded, giving in to my request with her usual sweet generosity, despite the cost to herself. "So often. Daily, hourly, sometimes by the minute. It became my obsession. I was begging God to give her back, begging Him. I just wanted my world to become normal once again. I wanted my stability back." She nodded. "But He refused the obsessive request...and now I cannot thank Him enough, Fin." Her hands fell to her side and she turned toward me, curiosity filling her face. "Fin," I spoke her name softly, making her eyes turn glassy. I took her hand and that soothing warmth crept up my arm and I sighed my *finally* as always, but this time where she could hear it. A tear rolled down her cheek at my declaration. "Fin," I said again, "I can't say that life would have been as it was meant to be if we'd chosen to be with each other back then. I'd like to think we would have done well with one another, but I don't think we would have. No, in fact, I think we would have eaten one another alive. We needed too much then. You needed security I couldn't give, and I needed a mother you couldn't be. It's why I struck out to find someone to take care of me. I'm happy to have been blind to what you are then only because I couldn't have been what you deserved. We would have been each other's crutches. That's not what a love like this is meant for, Fin. Not the kind of love I feel for you right now.

"This love is reserved for nothing but adoration, intense attraction, for a different, singular type of devotion. This love I feel for you I feel because I love you just as you are and not for what you can give me. It's an unselfish love. And oh my God but I love you, Fin. So, so much." A soft sob broke from her so I buried her face in my naked chest and wrapped my arms around her. "I want you for you. I want you, Fin. I want you. Because I love you."

I drew her back from me. Her eyes searched my face. *Yes*, my eyes answered her, *tonight you will become mine. From this moment on, you belong to me, Finley Dyer.* I slammed my mouth against hers, twining my fingers through her gorgeous, soft hair, tilting her head opposite mine. I sucked in a breath through my nose, furious to have her near me, convinced I could inhale her as well as taste her, whatever got her closer to me, whatever further dissolved me into her. I groaned into her mouth at the burning sensation in my gut and limbs. It was drugging, her kiss. It was everything in me not to collapse at her feet in that heavy peace you feel when you've abandoned the world around you for the person you're touching. Under the influence of Finley Dyer. Oh my God, she was perfect. So, so perfect for me.

I had never in my life kissed anyone like that. I knew then that no one ever could, ever would, be able to taste me back the way that Finley Dyer tasted me then. In every brush of her tongue against mine, she took me to heights unimaginable. She owned me then, occupied my heart, soul, body.

The fevered, desperate kiss turned languid. We volleyed back and forth, learning one another, tasting one another, savoring one another, and I wanted to know her. Know her as this new Finley and no other Finley.

We were broken, the both of us, apart, but together we were whole, perfect, flawless, and intact. Collectively we were absolute. Together we were conclusive. Period.

Finley

Ethan bent his head toward me and married his mouth to mine. I sighed into his lips every held on to, suppressed, restrained, contused, crushed, and bleeding agony that'd taken residence in my soul for so many years. I released it into him and he took it from me happily, but the burden was just as quickly released from him and into the air around us, dissipating with the briny gusts encircling us under the flowery moon.

I was free.

And yet bound all in the same breath. Bound to Ethan, happily, with words I never knew could belong to me. Bound because he loved me the same way I loved him.

"Ethan," I breathed as he brushed the line of my jaw with his mouth.

"Yes," he breathed back between kisses.

"Look at me," I told him.

He broke away and stared down at me. His hair had slipped from its knot and had fallen around his bare shoulders.

I took a deep breath and laid my shaking hands at his sides. I could feel his ribs and the lean, corded muscle there and my hands shook with the knowledge that there was no longer a barrier there. Before, I'd touched skin as well as the finite idea that I his skin could never really be mine. I realized his skin no longer belonged to the forbidden, that it belonged to me and only me.

With this understanding, my gaze followed my hand as I memorized the porcelain skin covering his ribs. Sweeping my thumb along the ridges of muscle, I moved the palm of my hand so it rested over his taut stomach. I felt the muscle tense as I did this and looked up into his eyes.

He smiled at me, brought his defined arms up and wrapped his hands around the back of my neck.

I swallowed. "I'm happy God didn't answer your earlier prayer," I told him quietly, and his smile grew wider. "I'm happy I found you at the bar that night. I'm happy you pursued a friendship with me. I'm happy you disobeyed me and followed me here. I'm so utterly happy, Ethan." Tears streamed down my cheeks despite the smile on my face. "I can't believe it. I never thought that could have been possible. Never, ever, ever thought it would have been attainable, Ethan."

He kissed me and laughed into my lips. "If you'll let me," he began, "it will be my heart's goal to keep you so."

I pulled back and looked into his eyes. "I love you, Ethan Moonsong."
One of his hands fell off my shoulder and he brought it to his chest. He closed his eyes briefly before staring at me, smiling.

"Say it again," he begged, his hand still over his heart.

"I love you," I told him. "I love you because I can, because it's my right to. I love you because I want to. I love you because it was my choice. You are my choice, Ethan."

We were tumbling toward the sand, the both of us, falling over one another as we dropped toward the earth. Ethan turned his body so that we rested side by side.

His tongue met mine once more, warm and honeyed. He pulled away from me, burying his face into my hair and inhaling, blowing out his breath, fanning the hair around my face.

"Oh my God, you are so incredible, Finley Dyer," he told me, voice rough.

He tugged at my hair gingerly, sending a thrill down my spine and pulled my head closer to him, before he ran his lips up the line of my throat, his tongue peeking out softly every other kiss. He blew across my neck and the places where his tongue had met skin chilled me, sending my eyes into the back of my head.

He crushed his mouth over mine once more, drawing my bottom lip into his teeth, and bit down tenderly before pulling it brazenly then kissing it gently. I smiled into his mouth. He smiled back.

"Like sugar," he said, his voice thick as syrup. "Never tasted anything as sweet as you Finley Dyer."

He stood then bent down and offered his hand. I took it and he lifted me as if I weighed nothing, throwing his arm under my knees and lifting me against his chest.

"You're in a world of trouble, you know," his soothing voice promised.

"I am," I stated as he walked us back to Slánaigh.

He grinned flirtatiously. "Yes," he confirmed.

He set me down by my flip-flops but stopped me from slipping them on. Instead, he crouched on his haunches, bracing a hot hand at the back of my knee, slipping each shoe onto each foot. It was, needless to say, incredibly sexy in its coyness. He stood, clutching a hand at the small of my back and bringing me into him for the most fascinating kiss goodnight I would ever get. My whole body bent against him as he pressed himself into me, like he couldn't get close enough. He broke the kiss, and I thought it was over, but his hands found my face and he kissed me again quickly before placing his mouth against my ear.

"I'll see you tomorrow," he rasped.

I stumbled back, dazed at the turn of events, at the shift in Ethan, at the unbelievable way he could kiss, at the skill in which he handled me, at the love he declared.

CHAPTER TWENTY-THREE

Finley

I woke with a stupid grin on my face and it never left apparently, because the girls, Dr. Nguyen, as well as Sister teased me, though I was willing to bet that Sister and Dr. Nguyen were the only ones who knew why it was there.

That morning there were a few errands to run for Slánaigh and Sister, I believe on purpose, because she winked at me when she paired Ethan and me to run them. She called Father to see if she could "borrow" Ethan for a bit. She had to fight Father on it a little because Father said he needed Ethan to repair the dock on the boathouse that afternoon, but he relented as he always did if Sister requested something, though it usually came with a bit of grumbling.

I waited for Ethan outside, the morning sun bright and orange as it rose over the green bay. The butterflies in my stomach refused to settle, so I shifted my flip-flop-clad feet side to side over the shell gravel, my arms tucked into my sides, smiling at the ground like an idiot, just to give myself something to do.

My head shot up when I'd heard Ethan's boots hit gravel near the sand path. I knew it was Ethan because, as ashamed as I am to admit it, I'd memorized everything about him. I knew the sounds of his boots, the swish of his jeans, the clang of his chain. I knew the movement of his hands when he would push his thermal sleeves up his forearms and the toss of his head to get his hair out of his grey eyes. I knew the flex of his muscle when he carried me, the sly grin he kept to himself when he thought of something clever, the seductive stare I'd had no idea belonged to me, the width of his unbelievable shoulders, the sweetness of his deep, soothing voice, the careful choice of his words, and that night, I'd learned the drug of his kiss.

His hands found his pockets and his head hung low, but his smile told me everything I wanted to know. His eyes found mine and I bit my bottom lip to keep from smiling too widely. He didn't hide his, though, and let it shine at me with the brilliance of a thousand suns.

Slánaigh's door opened and he tossed his head toward it, taking his hand out of his pocket long enough to wave at Sister and for her to wave back before putting it back and crossing the rest of the drive to meet me at the bikes.

"Hello, beautiful," he said, his deep voice resonating across my skin, sending a shiver down my arms and legs.

"Hello, my love."

He smiled at that. "I'd kiss you right now but I can feel Sister Marguerite's stare.

"I'd let you kiss me but the gaze you feel is real and I don't want to answer for it later."
An enticing glint appeared in his eyes. He reached for his helmet and unhooked the chin strap.

"If I could have kissed you," he said coolly, "you'd have felt my hands at your back and neck." I swallowed at his words and nearly stumbled backward. He met my gaze, the helmet resting at his hip. "I'd try very, very hard not to slip my hands under the bottom hem of your shirt just so I could feel the skin at your hip." My breath rushed out in one heady punch. He smiled, knowing exactly what he was doing. He handed me my helmet and I took it but it laid limply at my side. "And then I'd try something I thought about the entire night last night," he explained, straddling the bike, never breaking my stare. "I'd taste that pretty earlobe of yours just to watch your skin raise," he whispered.

He took my helmet from me and placed it on my head before dragging me across the back of the seat behind him. My thighs met his and he brought my dangling hands from my side and wrapped them around his stomach. He put his own helmet on before starting the bike in one swift kick. As we backed out, he waved at a giggling Sister, and we sped out, casting shell debris and any presence of mind I'd had behind us.

We rode in silence, my cheek resting against his broad back, my hands at his sides. He'd disarmed me back there.

"Who are you?" I asked him, smiling to myself. His chest shook in answer.

Ethan

We rode into the city proper to the street market, found a place to park, removed our helmets, and stood on either side of the bike.

We stared for several minutes. My eyes felt heavy as I counted each breath she took, each rise and fall of her beautiful chest. It was so different to look on her since I was no longer confined to being in love with her from afar, no longer subjected to looking but not touching.

"I can touch you now," I announced to her.

"You've always touched me," she responded.

"Not like this," I whispered, reaching across the bike. I wrapped one hand around her neck, slid it up and rested her cheek on my palm. She turned into it and it made me smile. "It's never felt like this."

"It's much different now," she drowsily replied, her lids half closed, making my gut ache for her.

"So different," I told her, leaning into her face, kissing her cheek. I felt it raise with her smile, so I kissed along her jawline until I met the corner of her mouth. I lingered there.

"This feels familiar," she stated, making me smirk.

"Come to me," I begged her, wishing she would meet her lips with mine.

"No, Ethan," she quieted, "*you* come to *me*."
So I obeyed her. How could I not? I'd have taken orders from her willingly and forever if she was so inclined.

I kissed her softly, sweetly, slowly. I greeted the day with her with that kiss. I told her I loved her with that kiss, that I was going to learn her mouth with mine, that I was going to be her perpetual student. I told her she was the only one with that kiss. I told her she was made for me with that kiss.

I pulled from her and her breaths matched mine, her pouty, pink mouth raw and bruised from the night's discovery. My hand raised to her chin. My thumb grazed her bottom lip.

"Did I hurt you?" I asked her, my brows furrowed.

"No, Ethan," she said, her hand gripping my forearm near her face. "They're sensitive, but they don't hurt. I don't ever want them any other way."

My eyes narrowed, as my thumb brushed her lip over and over.

"Did you hear me?" she asked. I looked into her eyes. "I want to wear your kiss always."

I bent toward her and kissed them softly.

I held her hand, something I'd been dying to do for months, as we perused the aisles for the list Sister had given Fin.

"We're going back out tomorrow night," I told her, as she purchased several limes.

A man in a nón lá with a well-honed plank of wood setting on his shoulders balancing two hanging baskets from each end, full of a strange fruit I couldn't name, passed by reminding me I was not in America.

"Where are we focusing on?" she asked, distracted by a table full of live shellfish. She cringed into my side when one flopped off the table onto the street below, making me laugh. I held my hand out for her shopping bag and she gave it to me with a smile that dropped my stomach to my feet. I knew right then that I'd do anything, any menial task, if it meant I'd get a smile like that.

"I think we're going to Hanoi again," I told her.

We finished our errands and decided to eat a bowl of Phở at a nearby street vendor. We set our bags at our feet and leaned against the wall outside the busy shop.

"I'm pretty impressed at how well you can operate those chopsticks, dude," she complimented.

"I know, right? Who knew a hick boy from Montana could be this stealthy."

She choked on her broth, laughing. "Are you trying to be funny?" she asked me.

"What? No."

"Jesus, Ethan, do you even know what you look like when you fight?" I took a bite and shrugged my shoulders. She dropped her sticks in her bowl and stared at me. "You don't even look real," she explained. "Your eyes become clearer than I've ever seen them, almost translucent, as if you can see through anything." She paused and stared off somewhere over my shoulder. She was somewhere else. She whispered, "You move like your mind's decision is five steps ahead of everyone around you, as if you can see others' decisions before they themselves know them and your body moves deliberately, like it's only catching up to your patient mind. You move like no one else I've ever seen, Ethan. No one," she said, meeting my gaze once more. "Stealth isn't a disbelief, Ethan. Stealth is very much a truth."

I swallowed, unsure of how I should respond. I'd never thought of my ability as anything other than practiced genetics. The training sessions with my mom's brother Akule were meant to build character, a way to defend myself. I'd never once considered them a talent.

"You're exaggerating," I said with a smile.

"No," she said with seriousness. "I am not."

I nodded at her, afraid there was a side of me she saw that I couldn't and, frankly, never wanted to know because the man she described sounded horrible, and I was tired of horror.

CHAPTER TWENTY-FOUR

Ethan

The trip to Hanoi for the bust that night was amazing, as Fin shared a bike with me. I came close to losing control of it many times because I kept concentrating on the hand I had resting on her thigh instead of the road in front of me. I found myself applying the slightest bit of pressure just to relieve the temptation I had of palming it with sincerity. It was an exercise in futility as it only made me want to touch her all the more. Eventually, I had to remove my hand altogether or risked getting both of us to Hanoi in several pieces.

"In here!" Father yelled over the din of motors surrounding us. We'd arrived in Hanoi in record time, a group of about fifteen of us, including An this time. We were headed down a residential street and idled outside the large, sliding gate of someone's private drive. Eventually I could see the feet of someone behind it and it began to slide open for us. An elderly woman stepped back so we could motor inside and when we were all in, she closed it behind us.

I turned off our motor and looked over my shoulder. "Who is that?" I asked Finley.

"She's this badass old lady who helps out Father. Apparently she's got family money and she uses a lot of it to fund Slánaigh. She's just as wanted by Khanh and his men as Father himself."

I looked at the old woman and guessed she was probably in her late seventies. She had grey hair, was thin, but dressed stylishly. Her skin was remarkably young looking. The only thing that gave her away was her hair.

Father and the woman greeted one another warmly. She said hello to everyone she was familiar with before stopping in front of Finley and me, still sitting on our bike. We got off and removed our helmets.

"Hello," she said, with a thick Vietnamese accent. "I am Kim." She offered her hand.

I took it with both of mine and my hands swallowed hers. She was so tiny, maybe four and a half foot tall, but there was something in the raise of her chin, in the way she carried herself that told me she was bigger than life itself.

"Nice to meet you, Kim," I told her, which earned me a kind smile. "I'm Ethan, and this is Finley Dyer," I said, touching Finley's shoulder.

She turned to Finley and they shook hands as well. "Nice to meet you, Kim," Finley told her.

They began talking to one another but I wasn't listening. I couldn't help myself. Instead, I watched Finley's mouth speak, smile, laugh. She mesmerized me, this new Finley. This Finley not limited to restrictions, to boundaries. This Finley I was in love with. This Finley I would die for, tornado the world for, kill for. This Finley I would do *anything* for.

I watched how the glittering sun and the aimless shades from the hanging trees surrounding the drive played across her ceramic skin, her plump, crimson lips, her straight nose with just the slightest, charming slope, her defined, tempting cheekbones. Cheekbones I longed in that moment to run my thumbs across. I watched her bright blue eyes dance as she spoke as if they held hidden secrets bursting to divulge. Her hair swung about her shoulders, soft and inviting in its bombshell waves, its titian glow framing her brilliant face.

I shook off her narcotic, shedding it with an affirmation. *I am decisively and inescapably in love with Finley Dyer.* I felt like a complete fool. Not because of what I felt for Fin but because I had been so convinced that I had ever been in love with Caroline Hunt. Because I hadn't been. At least not anything like how I felt for Finley Dyer.

The hate I'd held for Spencer that had eventually graduated to an annoying opinion of him vanished. If he'd felt even one tenth for Caroline what I felt for Fin, I'd found him justified. I knew if I ever returned to Bitterroot, I was going to shake that guy's hand and thank him for freeing me. He'd cured my blindness. He'd made it so I could find *her*. *Her*, who stood before me. The elegant, striking, impressive woman who stood beside me.

With a trembling hand, I reached for Finley, grazed my palm against the small of her back and settled it there in that indent that seemed made for my hand. The warmth from her body reminded me of life, that she was real, human, and yet perfect for me. I wondered how in the world I had become so fortunate as to have earned her attention, her affection, her love, and desperately wanted to know what it was I needed to do to keep her. Always.

"Isn't that right, Ethan?" Finley asked, shocking me back to the present.

I cleared my throat, having no idea what she was asking me but answered anyway, "Yes."

She continued on, satisfied with my response it seemed, and I, satisfied she even acknowledged me.

Finley

"I'm sorry, Kim, will you excuse me? I just remembered something I wanted to discuss with Ethan."

"Of course, of course. Go on," she said with a smile, "I'll just see if Father needs anything." Kim turned and walked toward a distracted group of volunteers, deep in lively discussion with Father.

"What's up?" I asked him.
I brought my palms to his cheeks.

His eyes closed and he swallowed. "*Finally,*" he breathed, giving me butterflies.
Every time I touched him and gave him that reaction it resulted in my heart dropping and my stomach filling with anticipation of something, though I didn't know what. I don't think I ever wanted to find out.

I reached up and kissed his cheek, refraining from kissing his mouth in front of the group, not that they'd care, but it was out of respect for what we were doing that day. Though, to be honest with you, it took incredible self-control.

He smiled at me, apparently calmed down.

"You cool?"

"Yeah, I'm fine," he hedged. "Just wanted you to touch me."

My hands fell from his face to find his forearm. My thumbs rubbed the skin there, the soothing contact remedying that part of ourselves that needed constant touch. In this, among so many things, I knew we were made for the other. To so many others, I would have been clingy, irritating, but not in Ethan. Ethan needed my skin just as much as I needed his. We were kismet, a gift from the heavens above left to stumble about all those years until that altogether healing declaration, that single utterance. It was a phrase so many repeated, so many humans expressed, but I knew differently of it. I knew a side of it no one else had seen.

Because we pitched that creed at one another's feet hoping the other would scrape up the holy words, damaged, bent, and marred by the pasts we carried though they were, and tend to the declaration with a devotion and service only we would have been able to lend them. He safeguarded mine and I safeguarded his. His words were knit inside me then, to evoke them out would have meant my death. And the same could be said for Ethan; I knew it. We, together, were as settled a conclusion as the rising and falling of the sun.

CHAPTER TWENTY-FIVE

Ethan

We rode out from Kim's in three groups with the plan that the second or third bands would ring Father and Kim if any of us had a confirmed lead and location. In turn, they would contact Detective Tran, who was with the first set of volunteers.

Finley and I were in the second group along with Phong and An.

I rang Fin on the cell phone they'd given me and she answered. "I got you," she said, smiling at me.

"Yeah, ya do," I told her, kissing her temple and lingering there. I moved my mouth to her ear. "Stay near Phong, Fin."

"I will," she whispered back, killing me.
That girl.

I reluctantly withdrew from her and tied my hair back. I'd forgotten the leaf hat so was forced to use my hoodie instead. I tossed the hood over my head, pulling as much of it over my face as possible.

"Can you see me?" I asked her.

"Barely," Fin answered.

What Finley *didn't know* was that I'd brought my knives with me that evening. I didn't know why I did it. I'd never brought them before, but for some reason I felt like I'd feel safer if I had them near me. They were tucked inside my brown leather chest holster and zipped inside the thick hoodie so it wouldn't scare Fin.

"Ready?" she asked me.

"As I'll ever be," I teased.

She smiled at me but it fell slowly. "You're a good man," she told me.

"No, I'm not, but someday I hope I will be. I'm going to earn you," I told her.

Her brows furrowed. "You can't earn someone who's already given themselves to you," she explained.

"I'm just so grateful for you, Fin. I only meant that I intend to deserve you one day."

Her mouth fell open and her eyes narrowed at me. "Ethan, that is ridiculous—" she began, but I interrupted her.

"I know. I know, dude. I know, but I'm aware of how much better you are and I only want to give you someone to be proud of too."

She shook her head the entire time I spoke. "Ethan," she said, but before she could continue, she noticed that Phong and An were focused on us. "Uh, we'll talk about it later," she told me.

I smiled at her and kissed the top of her head.

I turned toward them and An smiled in understanding at me. My face flushed. I couldn't help the shit-eating grin that shot across my face. I turned my smile away from them to try to hide it, but I wasn't fooling her. She shook her head at me, and I choked on a laugh then cleared my throat trying to conceal it.

"Okay," Phong sang out in that way people did when they didn't fully understand what was happening. "Uh, let's head west from here." He turned toward Fin and me. "You guys can hear one another?" We tested the Bluetooth headset and I gave him a thumbs up. "All right, we'll follow as usual, Ethan. Just let us know if you have any trouble or if you have a lead."

I nodded, very aware we were on the job, and shed all thoughts except for those that belonged to the task at hand. We walked west toward the Old Quarter.

The Old Quarter was a feast for the eyes, with random cubed stacked modern buildings mixed together with the hundreds of vintage builds from a hundred years prior when the French had occupied. The shops at street level with residences above were an odd mix of Asian with French influence. It was alive with people teeming everywhere. Every direction I turned I was in the thick of a crowd. The little sidewalk restaurants were full to the brim with happy, laughing groups of friends, and the shops with their lights fully bright bustled with patrons.

I took a right on Hàng Dầu, one of the oldest streets in the Old Quarter and meandered around the groups of tourists mixed in with the locals loitering on the sidewalks underneath the shop canopies. The shops there were open front, butting right up against the walks and full to capacity with merchandise.

I took in my surroundings and was flabbergasted at the sheer number of bookstores the Vietnamese had and how packed they all were. Their

261

love for reading was like nothing I'd ever seen and was a testament, I thought, to the people of Vietnam.

I took a left on Hàng Bè, glancing behind me to make sure Fin was close and still with Phong. All the streets in the Old Quarter began with Hàng, which can be translated to street or shop. Hàng was always followed up by the market that street catered to. So, for instance, Hàng Dầu was the street belonging to the silk merchants because *Dầu* means silk. This practice altered as the years progressed, but you could still find many ancient silk shops on Hàng Dầu side by side with their modern shop neighbors.

In the evenings, the night markets emerged, popping up their makeshift tents and tables and setting up shop in the middle of the streets, making an already crowded area almost impossible to navigate, especially if you were trying to keep tabs on your girlfriend—*Oh my God, Finley is my girlfriend*—to keep her safe on your dangerous mission of finding the criminals who sold little girls for money.

We'd noticed that the traffickers in Hanoi followed a specific pattern. They'd start by haunting high tourist areas but changing positions and men frequently so you could never gain a true idea of who was a solicitor. The only way we could combat this was by using singular men as bait to draw them out. Since we didn't have their resources or the number of people they had, it felt like we could never chip away at the damage they were doing. Not that that would have stopped any of us, but it was discouraging at times. With two million international tourists coming into Hanoi every year, the demand would need their supply, we just needed to figure out how to choke them at the neck.

I coughed twice into my hand, the signal Fin and I had worked out when I wanted her to acknowledge me, to let me know she was okay.

"Gotcha, sailor," she teased. "You okay? Nod once, I can see you." I nodded. "Good. There's a lot of people out tonight, huh? More than we've seen before, I think." She paused. I could hear Phong talking to her. "Oh! Oh, really?" she said to him. "I guess there's a huge festival going on right now, love," she explained, distracting me for a moment with her term of endearment. "Ethan," she called to me low, fervently. "Him," she whispered, "the one on the corner there. Do you see him?" I searched for him, nodded once. "He's one of them. I can just tell. There's something about him, something I don't trust."

I stepped from the curb, narrowly missing a motorcyclist rambling through the crowd. I crossed between two street shops and aimed for the walk on the other side. The man on the corner was unusually tall for a local, probably six foot, with broad shoulders, and a cold, blank stare that belonged to every single trafficker I'd come across. I took a deep breath, rolled my shoulders, and stalked his direction.

I knew the second he saw me coming that I was his next target, which sent a thrill and a sadness through me.

"You like girls?" he said, his head cocked to the side.

Up close, I recognized that vacant, almost black expression in his eyes. I'd seen this in another man's eyes once before. When I was twelve, back in Kalispell, there was a man hooked on meth who beat up his wife regularly and when Dad and I had gone grocery shopping once, he'd just happened to be there at the same time. I was trying to fetch something near the pharmacy and I accidentally ran into him. He'd looked down at me and that's when I saw his eyes. Something about him elicited the most chilling shiver from my body.

I remember asking my dad what was wrong with the guy's eyes and my dad explained, "He's sold his soul, son. Whenever you see that look in another person, you run like hell. You hear me?"

In retrospect, I realized it was a strange thing to tell a kid, but in that moment I understood what he'd meant, why he'd warned me.

The trafficker smiled at me, but it wasn't at all friendly. He was a man who'd answered a call from the devil himself and he'd relished in it.

"Maybe," I told him. "What you got?" I asked.

"Do you have money?" he asked me, his English perfect.

"I don't know," I played back. "I guess that all depends on what it costs."

"A hundred," he said, testing me out. He was trying to figure out how schooled I was.

"No way," I said, walking away.

I got five steps away before he called out to me.

"Sixty," he said, done playing games.

I stopped, took another deep, steadying breath and turned around. "Sold," I told him.

"This way," he said.

He'd pointed down a busy shopping alley, full of people.

"You first," I said.

He smiled again, creeping me the hell out, and led me down the hectic alley. My heart pounded in my ears, the adrenaline kicking up to an uncomfortable degree. In response, my muscles grew tight against the constraints of my hoodie. The leather of my knife sheath dug into my ribs.

He took me to a shop full of women's clothing and hats. I hesitated at the store's entrance.

When he'd noticed I wasn't going any farther he said, "It's through the back here."

If I'd really thought it through, I'd have told him no and walked away in search of another opportunity, but there was something about him that told me whatever girls he'd held were desperate for me to find them, so I followed him.

"Ethan," I heard on the Bluetooth, making my heart race. "Don't do it," Finley said, a desperate tinge to her voice. "Gosh damn it, Ethan! Don't—" I heard before I cut the signal.

It's too late, I thought. *Keep going.*

He led me up a winding staircase behind the storefront and as we ascended, I nonchalantly unzipped my jacket but kept the hood up. At the top sat a small hall with a door at the end. He opened it and I shakily let out a breath as I took in what was behind the door.

There was a long hallway with deep red carpet and commercial-looking sconces with very sheer light peppering the length of it. It looked and felt like a carnival haunted house. I nervously followed him as he led me down the hall, stopping at a door in the center.

"The money," he said, holding out his palm. With jittery hands, I pulled my wallet out and handed him sixty dollars. "First time?" he asked, gesturing to my hands.

"Yes," I told him.

"Don't worry. It'll be fun," he explained, making my blood run cold at his careless, horrifying comment.

"How-how old is she?" I stuttered.

"Eleven, I think," he said flippantly and walked off toward the end of the hall. "Someone will be here when you're through to guide you back out," he explained, his back still toward me.

I fought the urge to throw one of my knives at his neck. Instead, I turned toward the door, my hands trembling, and turned the knob. I opened the door.

Inside was an eleven-year-old girl, her face and hair dirty, her clothes too big for her tiny body. I pulled down my hood.

She stood up and silently walked toward me, reaching her hands out toward my zipper.

"Stop," I whispered to her, pushing her hands away. "No," I said, when her hands grasped for me again. I grabbed them and held them away, pushing her back toward a chair at the side of the room. "Sit," I told her, trying to think. "Okay, okay, okay," I spoke aloud. "How the fuck do I get you out of here?" I said. "Think, Ethan, think!"

"I cannot leave," she said with a thick Vietnamese accent.

My head whipped her direction. "You speak English?"
She nodded.

"Sorry for cursing," I told her like an idiot, but her face remained blank, despondent. I paced the floor, adrenaline pouring out in droves. *Stop*, I ordered myself. *Efficient, safe, covert*, I told myself, remembering everything my Uncle Akule had taught me.

I turned toward the girl. "I'm going to help you escape here. I'm going to take you to a place called Slánaigh. Do you know it?"

Her mouth dropped and her eyes began to water.

"No," I told her, my gut aching for, her but I didn't have time for that. "No tears. I need you quiet. I need you to obey me. Do you understand?"

"Yes," she answered desperately.

"Stand behind this door. Do not *move* from behind this door until I tell you to. When I give you the order, you close it as quietly as you can."

She nodded and ran behind the door. Her tiny hands wrung themselves.

I popped my hood back into place and took a deep, steadying breath. *Mom,* I thought. *Mom, please, please help me.* I opened the door and popped my head out. As if on cue, another man opened the door at the end of the hall.

Breathe.

"Done?" he asked me, looking out.

"Uh, yeah," I said, but immediately sank back into the confines of the room.

I heard the man walking down the hall and I spared a glance at the eleven-year-old behind the door. Her eyes were wide with fear. I shook my head at her, reminding her to be brave. She nodded at me, her lips tensing in preparation for an order from me.

Breathe.

The man came through, looked around, and appeared confused that there was no girl within view. He opened his mouth, but I didn't give him an opportunity to speak. I grabbed for him. "Now," I whispered, and the girl closed the door softly. I spun the surprised man around, his back to my chest, before stepping out then swinging my elbow toward the back of the head just above the neck, hitting him on the occipital bone.

The man's knees buckled beneath him. I reached out, caught him before he could land with any sound, and laid him across the floor. The entire thing took less than thirty seconds. I looked over at the girl, her mouth gaping, her eyes huge in her head.

"He's only knocked out," I told her, "so we must move quickly. Stay directly behind me. Stay as soundless as possible. Listen for my instructions. Obey without hesitation."

She nodded her answer.

Breathe.

I opened the door as noiselessly as possible, peered through the doorway, noted there was no one around, and slipped through, with my young victim close behind me. I walked toward the door with the staircase, tucked the girl against the same wall, opened the door quietly, and scanned the stairs. *Clear.* I signaled for the girl to follow me and she did. We descended to the ground floor. I scoured the walls for any escape other than the storefront but found none. I took a deep breath and moved the curtain that separated the back from the front and quickly examined it. No one in the immediate vicinity. I crouched down low, running to the opening to the street. I searched the street for the trafficker who'd brought me up, but it took a second longer than I felt comfortable to find him. He was standing on the same corner.

Breathe.

I swung the girl up unexpectedly but she kept her mouth shut. I folded her into my chest as snugly as possible and walked the opposite direction of the solicitor, heading toward the opposite side of the street, getting lost in the crowd, but I knew I wasn't clear until I'd left the street itself. I went left, followed by two more, knowing Finley would be most likely waiting for me there. I found her, An, and Phong pacing outside a shop. Phong was talking animatedly on his own cell. An's hand was on Fin's shoulders as Fin furiously pounded her fingers against the cell phone she carried to connect to the Bluetooth.

I walked up behind them.

"Fin!" I yelled.

Time seemed to stand still as she whipped around my direction, bursting into tears. I put the girl down next to An, who began attending to her. I zipped my hoodie up as Fin rushed me, tears streaming.

She pounded at my chest. "Why would you do that to me?!" she yelled. "*Why?*" she bawled. "I thought you were dead, Ethan!"

She broke down, sobbing into the fabric of my jacket, and I wrapped my arms around her. She kept hitting me, but it was losing steam. The adrenaline left my body with considerable quickness, making my body tremble. I was afraid to talk in the moment. I needed to calm her first. Calm myself as well. I smashed her hard against my body, laying my hands at the skin just underneath her shirt, at the small of her back, as she cried into my shoulder, repeatedly asking why.

I kissed her at the temple and pulled back just enough to look into her face.

"I'm so sorry," I told her. Her eyes were red, tinged with a sadness I'd never seen, and my heart

FISHER AMELIE

broke for her. "So sorry," I told her, my voice dropping an octave in sincerity.

She swiped at her eyes and sucked in a breath. She looked left and her eyes swelled open at An checking the girl over and speaking to her softly, at Phong talking on the phone in Vietnamese.

"Did you save her?" she asked, pointing at the girl.

I nodded.

"Oh my God," she said. She inhaled and brought her hand up to her chest. The other reached for my hand.

Unexpectedly, shouting came from the direction of the shop that fronted for the illegal activities involving my poor little girl, and my head followed the direction of the drama. I became aware of myself once more, yanking Fin close to me. I got ready to run but noticed the poor girl didn't have shoes on so I was forced to let go of Fin so I could pick up the girl once more.

"We have to go," I told the group.

In a flash, all five of us barrelled through the crowd, running toward our original meeting spot.

CHAPTER TWENTY-SIX

Ethan

"Here! Take a left here!" I looked down at the jostling young girl in my arms. "You okay, kid?" She nodded, though her eyes were wide. "Almost there," I assured her, cutting right on Kim's street. "Finley!" I yelled when she fell back out of my view.

"What!" she said from behind me.

"Keep up, Fin!"

"I'm trying!" she said, irritated.

I glanced back. She rolled her eyes but sprinted forward, falling in step beside me.

We arrived at Kim's three minutes later, breathless. Phong, An, and Fin banged on the gates until they opened. Father and Kim were on the other side, a look of bewilderment on both their faces.

When Kim's eyes shifted to the girl in my arms, she yelled, "Trời ơi!" *Oh my God!*
She rushed up to us as I set the girl on the ground, and she assisted the girl inside her home. An followed her to help, which left Fin, Phong, Father, and myself standing there in silence.

"What happened, boyo?" Father asked quietly, the shock still on his face.

"The man invited me in," I said. "I couldn't help myself. He seemed like the devil incarnate and I couldn't leave without saving at least one of them," I explained, my heart racing.

Fin, apparently reliving the moment, started trembling.

"How-how'd ya get 'er out, son?" he asked, stunned.

My eyes shot to Fin's, silently pleading with her to understand.

"Fin told me not to go in," I began. She looked away, her eyes glassy, and bit her quivering bottom lip. "There was just something so off about the guy that I felt desperate to help any girl I could, so I walked in. He took me upstairs to this shady-looking hall full of closed doors," I told them, the memory making me queasy.

"What was your plan?" Phong asked, unable to help himself.

"I, uh, didn't have a plan," I answered him. Finley let out a choking sob so I grabbed her without thinking and swung her head into my chest.

"It's upsettin' the lass. No more," Father said.

"No!" Finley tore away from me to face him. "No," she said lightly, "I want to hear this too." Father nodded at her and their faces turned toward me.

"I paid him the money and went into the room. The girl," I began, but my voice broke. I cleared my throat. "The girl," I said again, "she-she was *altered*. Something awful has happened to her, Father." I squeezed Finley as close to me as possible. "I couldn't leave her there." The emotion in my voice dropping my tone. "I had to take her."

Father placed a hand on my shoulder as we stood under the lamplight over Kim's drive, the night pitch black around us save for the blazing band of light encircling us. A dichotomy of light and dark.

"I understand, o' course, son," he told me, squeezing my shoulder. Kim called for Father from her door. "'Scuse me," he said.

He turned and walked toward the house. Phong followed, leaving Fin and me under the spotlight.

I kissed Fin's tear-stained cheeks, eyes, chin, forehead, jaw—all the while breathing her name. I kissed her until I felt her sigh.

"I saw you in her," I told her. "I saw you, and I just could not leave her, Fin."

"I see that now," she said. "I see it."

"Are you still upset with me?"
She shook her head, her hair falling around her shoulders and over my embracing arms.

"I don't like you risking your life like that. I hate it, actually, but I know why you did it. I *feel* why you did it, Ethan. It's why I came here. I came here to save them," she said, a hitch in her throat, "because I couldn't save myself. So thank you for saving her." She placed her hands on my cheeks. "Saving her *feels* like you've saved me. A little piece of me feels like I'm one step closer to saying goodbye to that cracked Finley, that fragile Finley."

I grasped her to me. "God, what I wouldn't give to have saved you then, Fin."

She pulled away so she could see my face. "Can't you see?" she asked. "You *are* saving me."

273

We all rode back to Hạ Long Bay with lighter hearts, yet the triumph felt marred as we could feel the shadows of all the other children we weren't able to steal away that night.

I walked Finley up the Slánaigh winding staircase, her head at my shoulder and my hand at the small of her back. Reluctantly, I kissed her chastely at the door and with pins and needles in my hands, ran as fast as I could to my room of the boathouse, but not for rest.

No, I had plans.

I was going to earn the honor of loving Finley Dyer, and I knew just how to do it.

CHAPTER TWENTY-SEVEN

I said goodnight to Father so he knew I was there and it gave him the pretense I was in for the night. One foot in front of the other, I scaled the small dock walkway to my room, and sat at the edge of the bed, waiting for Father to fall asleep.

When an hour had passed, I checked for my knives in their sheaths and for the key to the bike on Slánaigh's shell drive. Very carefully, I exited my room, shutting the door as quietly as I could. I stepped into the small boat tethered to the room I stayed in, took the paddle, and made my way to the little shore. I did this so my body weight didn't shift the dock walkway to the shore and wake Father when I left.

It didn't take me long to get to the beach, and when the boat breached the water, I jumped out, pulling it up farther on to the shore, before tucking it behind some foliage to avoid questions in case someone from Slánaigh came along. I prayed they'd miss it wasn't in the water if they did.

My adrenaline pumped in my veins when I pushed the hanging plant-fall hiding the cove the boathouse was in. I wondered to myself, curious if I was making the best decision in leaving once more.

The rush I got from saving the little girl that night was too incredible not to do again. I'd never felt more accomplished than I had that moment I took her in my arms and physically left her hell behind us. I was so tired of our fruitless busts, overturned so easily by unfortunate circumstances or thwarted by bought police or judges. We'd saved only ten girls in the span that Fin and I had been at Slánaigh, and it just wasn't enough for me. I understood Father had to work within the parameters of the laws, even if those laws weren't being upheld unless it meant to do him damage. I understood a man in his position was bound by his vows. He was required a peaceful intervention, within reason…

But I wasn't.

I lifted the bike off its stand, pulled it back, and pushed it toward the end of the shell drive, not starting it until I'd been sure I was far enough away I couldn't be heard from Slánaigh. I drove until I found a space near the night market and parked, chaining it to a nearby tree.

I pulled up my hood, kept my head down, and started walking.

What are you doing? It's not too late to just turn around, dude. Just turn back around, go back to Slánaigh, and go to sleep. Work with them. Who knows? You might get a good bust tomorrow. I argued with myself for ten blocks, trying to convince myself what I was doing was beyond idiotic. Yet I never turned back. I was determined to see if my method would be more effective than Slánaigh's, because I had no intentions of working within the law.

You can always abandon the idea if it goes wrong anyway. If it doesn't go well, you just won't do it again.

"You like girls?" a man asked me.

I turned toward him and all my earlier doubts burned away with his one grotesque question.

"I love girls," I told him, my blood boiling. I tempered my facial expression. "What ya got?" I asked.

"Many ages," he explained. "Whateva you want."

My hands itched to remove a knife. "Take me to them," I told him.

His eyes brightened up. "Only hundred dolla," he said excitedly.

"Whatever," I said, no intention of letting it get that far.

He pointed toward an alley and gestured for me to follow him and I did, with no hesitation. I was as eager as he was it seemed but for very different reasons. I smiled to myself, pulling my hoodie farther over my face.

He knocked on a door situated in the middle of the alleyway, and I stuck my hands in my hoodie pockets to give them something to do. I breathed deeply, steadily.

One in front of me. Weak, easily overpowered. Breathe.

A man answered the knock. *Five foot six, maybe seven. Medium build. Squints. Bad eyesight. Nearsighted. Favors his right leg.*

Breathe.

I peered behind him and took in two more men, both sitting at a table playing cards.

Guy on left. Small build. Automatic weapon strapped to back. Holding cards with his right hand. He's left-handed. Gun's on the wrong shoulder for quick access.

Breathe.

Guy on right. Older. Mid-forties. Lean. Barefoot. Sipping coffee. Winced. Steaming cup.

Breathe.

Two exits including this door. Only one guaranteed street exit. Estimated guess the other door connects to the girls. Unknown number of men behind closed door.

"Right through here," the guy who opened the door said.

Breathe.

Go.

I pushed the street guy into the guy who answered the door, stunning them. Swiftly, I elbowed the solicitor in the back of the head, felling him with a sudden, dull thud. The other's eyes widened and he charged me, but I sidestepped him, tripping his bum leg, pushing his head against the jamb of the door, and slamming the door against his ear. He was out.

Breathe.

By this time, the men sitting were just realizing what was going on. I took two steps their direction, grabbed the guy's hot coffee and threw it in the face of the man with the gun. He screamed in agony.

Breathe.

While he scrambled, I pushed the heel of my boot into the bare foot of the man on the right, sending his head forward as he tried to tug his leg out from underneath my boot. I took advantage of the movement and slammed his forehead into the table, knocking him out cold. I spun around the gunman with ease, twisting the strap of his gun around his neck, effectively choking him off, keeping him quiet.

"Shhh. This will only hurt for a moment," I told him, before slamming his head into the table, knocking him out as well.

Breathe.

Without hesitation, I dragged the one in the doorway inside, and closed the door. In four steps, I was at the second door, bracing myself against the wall where the door would open into me.

I waited but no one came to their rescue, leading me to believe they were it. I reached for the handle just as it began to turn, though, so I laid flat once more. A white man peeked his head through.

"Uh, what's going on?" he stupidly asked the roomful of unconscious men.

Breathe.

"Nothing," I told him, smiling. He turned toward me, his eyes wide.
I grabbed the top of his head, grappling a handful of hair. He squealed like a pig as he pitched forward into my knee. He fell to the floor, passed out. I waited a moment for any others, but no one came.

Breathe.

I grabbed a bat leaning in the corner of the room closest to me before throwing open the door. I tossed it over my shoulder and propped myself against the jamb, looking through to gauge the environment.

Breathe.

One hall. Six doors. All interior. Only exit is the entrance I came through. Knowing this, I stalked to the end of the hall, anticipating that if any men might be hanging in their rooms like cowards came out, they'd automatically look toward the door that entered the main room.

Breathe.

I let the bat fall into my hand. With one swift kick, I dropkicked the last door.

Breathe.

Empty.

Breathe.

I kicked the second.

Breathe.

One girl. Seven or eight. Fearful eyes. Alone.

Breathe.

Third.

Breathe.

One girl. Ten. One man. White. Fifties.

My eyes blazed at him. "Get the fuck out," I gritted. He ran like the gutless piece of shit he was. "Stay," I told the girl.

Breathe.

Fourth. Empty.

Breathe.

Fifth. Two girls. Both around nine. No men.

Breathe.

Sixth. One girl. Seven. One white man. Forties.

Breathe.

He was trembling.

"Please!" he shrieked. "Please don't kill me," he begged. "Please," he whimpered. "I'll give you whatever you want," he cried. "Anything."

I tossed the ends of the bat back and forth on one hand. A habit I'd picked up when I was bored at baseball practice in high school. I did it carelessly. I wanted him to know I was just as eager to slam the end in his face as I was at playing.

"Leave," my voice grated after a moment. He scrambled up, buckling his pants, making me sick to my stomach. I caught him by his shirt collar when he tried to squeeze past me and threw him against the wall. I laid the thick part of the bat against his neck, using my forearm to drive it in painfully. "Come here again, touch another girl again and I'll know it. I know who you are," I lied. "I'll tell them all," I finished. I leaned my weight into the bat, cutting off his air. "Now get the fuck out."

I released him after a moment's pause. He shut the front room door behind him.

Breathe.

Breathe.

Breathe.

"Time to go," I said softly. I threw the bat to the ground and rounded up each of the five young girls. In all of their faces, I saw my Finley and felt ill. "Come on," I urged them. They obeyed, their faces devoid of life. They had no idea who I was or what I was. They only knew to obey.

I led them out, checking each man quickly before examining the alley for anything suspicious. When I was confident it was clear, I gathered two girls' hands and encouraged the remaining three to follow. I looked down and noticed blood running down one of their legs.

"I'm so sorry I didn't get here sooner," I told her.

She looked up at me, her face blank.

Breathe.

Shit. Where do I take them! I can't take them to Slánaigh!

Suddenly I remembered that Detective Tran was on duty that night. I had the girls follow me to the police station, thankful that the late hour kept people from noticing us. When we reached the street with the station, I pulled my hood as low as I could and bent to the oldest girl's level. I gave her the hands of the girls I'd held on the way there.

"Go. Take them there. Tran. Ask for Tran," I said, pointing to the small lit station in the middle of the block.

She nodded her head at me, tears streaming down her face, making my stomach clench. Then unexpectedly I was hugged around the neck. She pulled away just as quickly then ran with the girls away from me toward Tran's station.

I tucked myself back into the shadows and made sure they made it in. When they were inside, I was ready to run back to my bike but was stopped short by Tran himself, his hands on his hips. He came out into the street, looking back and forth, searching for whomever had brought the girls in, but I knew he would never find him. I wouldn't let it happen.

When Tran was back inside, I jogged back to my bike, satisfied I'd done something worth doing that night, confident I'd made the right decision. The memory of the little girl hugging my neck was answer enough.

CHAPTER TWENTY-EIGHT

Finley

When I saw Ethan coming up the drive, I practically sprinted to meet him.

"Hello, darlin'!" I shouted when I was a few feet from him.

He picked me up and swung me around, kissing the top of my head.

"Hello, my Finley," his deep voice resonated.

"What an awesome day, huh? The sun is shining, bright, and warm. The bay is gorgeously blue." I looked up at his beautiful face. "Your face is smiling. Certainly an awesome day," I told him.

He smiled even wider, his extraordinary teeth and mouth telling me everything I wanted to know about his heart and mind.

"You really are beautiful, you know that?" I asked him, my hands against his cheeks.

He smiled his crooked smile before running the palms of his hands across my forehead. "Finley Dyer," he sighed. "Don't talk to *me* about beautiful 'cause I *know* beautiful. I memorize it every chance I get," he said, studying my face then kissing my cheek.

I smiled at his flattering compliment. My cheeks felt warm as they flushed.

"God, I love that," he said, running his thumbs over my cheekbones.

"Stop," I said, embarrassed, turning my face away.

He grasped the sides of my neck and brought my gaze back to him. "Don't do that," he whispered.

"Do what?" I asked.

"Feel ashamed to show me how I affect you."

His words made me feel even more vulnerable and my cheeks turned warmer, but I kept my eyes locked on his.

"There it is," he said, clear admiration in his eyes. "There isn't a lovelier look than that one right there."

"Why?" I asked him.

"Because, Fin, there's nothing more revealing, more confessing. There's truth to that blush that words could never convey, never fully declare like the rush of color in your cheeks could. It chronicles your responses in the most attractive way."

He bent me backward and kissed my mouth, saving it from the gape that had been forming, dazing me almost unintelligent.

"Wow," I breathed stupidly when he broke contact.

"Damn straight," he told me, breathless.

He stood me up and held me there a moment while I steadied myself.

"Come on, sedated-version-of-Finley."

I blinked. "You know, you claim you're not good with words, but I beg to differ."

He took a deep breath and pierced me with his gaze. "Let's just say, I found a reason to find them."

As we walked up the winding staircase, I remembered myself, remembered my news. "Oh my God! I forgot to tell you!"

"What?" he asked, his eyes shifting to the right.

"Five girls somehow escaped one of Khanh's cells last night."

"No kidding," he said.

"Yeah! They showed up at Tran's door last night. Can you believe it? Such an amazing thing!"

"It really is," he observed. "Hey, what's on the docket for today?" he asked me, changing the subject.

I looked at him, confused. "Don't you want to at least know what happened? It's pretty fascinating."

He audibly swallowed. "Uh, okay. Yeah," he cleared his throat, "what happened?"

"According to the girls, some guy just showed up and took them away. The oldest girl said he spoke English and hand delivered them to Tran. When I first heard the story, I almost lost my mind. I'd thought it was you at first, but Father said he saw you go to your room and you never left."

"You all considered it was me?" he asked, his face white as a sheet.

"Yeah," I said, laughing at the expression on his face, "but don't worry. It was only a passing thought, babe." I rubbed his shoulder back and forth.

"Oh," he said, laughing disjointedly. "Good then."

I smiled at him. "We're just taking care of a few repairs around Slánaigh today. No busts planned because Dr. Nguyen is going to be seeing the girls who were rescued last night and Father is going to try and find their families so they can be reunited with them."

Ethan

I'm not going to lie, Fin's as well as everyone else's first assumption scared me. The fact they all so quickly brushed it away, though, made me realize how trusting they were of me, and I didn't know how I felt about that. *Don't worry about it now. You can't worry about it now. Just be more careful.*

Fin and I repaired a few of the shutters on the windows that had broken off or were hanging. When we were done, Sister brought a can of coral-tinted paint to us along with a tray of Phở. She smiled at us both and kissed us on the heads before swishing away, her skirts billowing behind her in her seemingly permanent haste, whistling as she went, obviously content with the tiny world around her.

We took a break and sat on a pair of beechwood rocking chairs at the back of Slánaigh facing the grove of trees that separated us from the beach, but we could hear the soothing waves and smell the sweet salt air.

As we rocked back and forth quietly sipping at the broths of our soups, the lapping of the water on the beach felt like the metronome of life, ticking in time to the rhythm of the earth. Finley, faintly at first, began singing. It was an ancient-feeling tune, reminiscent of something Celtic, I thought, coupled with a sweet melody with equally friendly lyrics despite its melancholy pitch. It was a love song.

My God did her voice do the song justice. I stopped rocking, set my bowl down, and watched her sing as she pushed and pulled her chair. She had no idea I was listening as intently as I was, I could tell, because her mouth lifted at the words she was pleased with and raised passionately when she reached the pensive ones. She was a sight to behold. *My sight to behold*, I thought. It was no surprise to me that her voice coordinated with her face. I felt it was only right that they matched so magnificently.

Finley stood from her chair, still singing, kissed my temple, gathered our bowls and set them on the tray. Her tune still spilling from her lips, Fin took the tray inside, leaving me alone in the quiet nature of that day.

To my dying day, though, I would remember how she sang that song. I would recall it in my time of need and her forever ago words would endlessly bring me comfort. Just knowing Finley Dyer and that song existed at one time on this earth was enough to give me breath.

CHAPTER TWENTY-NINE

Ethan

I spent the better part of three weeks saving little girls from fates worse than death at night, taking them to Tran, and stealing back into my room by way of the little boat. During the day, I would care for Finley, love her, kiss her, worship her, dare I say, honor her.

No one suspected me after that first day. Honestly, no one cared. The citizens of Hạ Long Bay called me "the guardian angel" in secret around town. I selfishly reveled in the nickname, thinking very highly of myself, naively convinced that the incredibly dangerous Khanh would let me continue robbing him of his product.

But life is nothing but unfair, is it not? Life is a punishing entity, to be truthful, just on its own without the influence of harmful decisions. Throw in a monstrous choice and you have a prescription for devastation.

It was a stormy night, that Saturday night, full of ominous sounds and elements designed for disaster. At one in the morning, I found myself circling the night market, an uneasy feeling in my gut, an instinct I foolishly ignored because I'd become so familiar with the rush of adrenaline and sick feeling in the pit of my stomach. I'd associated it incorrectly, disregarding everything my Uncle Akule had taught me, setting myself up for a fall that was the physical equivalent of tossing myself off the side of a cliff with no parachute.

A free fall to almost certain death.

A man I'd recognized as a trafficker from weeks earlier eyed me. There was something in his expression that told me I should have run, but I'd been walking for almost an hour with no interest from anyone. It seemed my heroic acts may have saved more than twenty-three girls, but they were also making it harder to find them. A few days after that first night, they'd become scarce. And the traffickers were very much aware of who I was, I was certain. Which is why I should have been on higher alert, but I was so desperate to save the girls I ignored the red flags.

"You like girls?" he asked slowly, his eyes raking me up and down.

Red flag.

"Yeah, I like girls," I told him, my head down, my face hidden in my hoodie.

"Right this way," he said, surprising me.

"How much?" I asked, my brows furrowing at his misstep.

Red flag.

"Forty dolla," he said, lowballing me.

Red flag.

"Done," I said, stupidly accepting his offer.

"This way," he said, keeping his distance.

He practically ran ahead of me and slammed his fist against the door three times. Without thinking, I unzipped my hoodie, crossed my arms, and palmed my knives. His breaths panted from his chest, his eyes wide on me.

"Don't do it," I told him, and his eyes blew wider. He began pounding on the door even harder.

I should have run then. I could have. I bet if I'd run at that moment, I could have gone back to Slánaigh and never needed to look back, working with Fin and Father and Tran in all Slánaigh's future endeavours and done so happily. But I didn't.

I studied the guy's hands and body, deciding he wasn't hiding anything. Instinctively, I rushed him, flipped his back toward mine and shoved his head hard into the concrete wall. He fell in a pile at my feet. It was too late to run. Too late because I heard the door being pulled open and knew in my gut that if I had run, I would have been gunned down.

Because it was a setup.

Breathe.

I flung myself against the wall. The door opened into the room and I recognized the tip of the gun almost immediately. It was an automatic. I grabbed it, taking advantage of his surprise, and swung it forward, yanking it from his hands. Gunshots rang out behind him. I ducked as the guy I'd stolen the gun from pitched forward with dead eyes. In order to get me, they'd killed one of their own.

Breathe.

Who are these soulless men? I wondered.

More gunshots rang out, and I dipped my head as they bit at the concrete of the wall opposite the door in the alley. My eyes shifted left and noticed shell casings. The shooter was close. Judging by the height he was spraying the bullets, he assumed I was standing.

Breathe.

I fell on my back in the middle of the doorway, rotated the gun and aimed up, intending to spray a wide path. I pulled the trigger. *Empty click. Mistake.* I'd never checked the gun. In a flash, I pulled out my knives while taking stock of the men in the room.

Breathe.

Gunman. Noticed I was on the floor. He aimed his gun at me. I planted a knife in his foot. He squealed in agony, dropping the gun, but it was slung around his chest and I wasn't able to reach it.

Breathe.

One armed man. Five feet to my left. He was standing but was unfamiliar with his weapon, clumsy, and struggled to get it in possession.

Breathe.

One unarmed man. Seven feet to my right and backed into the corner. He looked afraid, his shoulder pressing as far into the corner as possible, as if he could shove himself through.

Breathe.

The gunman reached for the knife in his foot.

Breathe.

I yanked the knife instead, sending him falling backward in one shrill scream.

Breathe.

"Put the gun down," I gritted from the floor at the second gunman.

Breathe.

"Die," he said instead.

Breathe.

"You first," I told him and heaved the knife, hitting my aim. He fell lifelessly to the floor.

Breathe.

Guy in corner cried out, pleading with me.

Breathe.

First gunman gritted his teeth. His eyes promised vengeance and soon. He reached for his gun yet again and aimed it at my face.

Breathe.

Without hesitation, I threw my second knife in his chest, straight for the heart. Dead.

Breathe.

I stood, yanking my bloody knife from the first man's chest then reached for the second.

Breathe.

The third man cried as I wiped the blades off on a nearby hand towel, sheathing both of them.

Breathe.

"Are there any more?" I asked him.

Breathe.

"Please don't kill me," he said.

Breathe.

"How many more?"

Breathe.

"Are there any more!"

Breathe.

"Spare me!"

Breathe.

I narrowed my eyes at him. It was a stall tactic.

Breathe.

There were two doors on opposite sides of the room. I chose the door nearest the crier. More than likely I knew he would probably pick the side with men and their weapons so he wouldn't get caught in any crossfire.

Breathe.

"Time's up," I told him.

Breathe.

His unpleasant, cowardly expression fell. A look of hatred built in its place. "Yes, your time *is* up," he answered. He shifted his body so that the handgun he'd been hiding came forward. I anticipated the movement and swung myself away as the first shot fired. One swift clip of the hand dislodged the gun. I caught it midair, pointing it at him.

Breathe.

"Open that door," I ordered.

Breathe.

A look of pure anger flitted across his face. I pushed him in front of it, reached forward, pulled the handle, tossed open the door, and stepped back. The man's hands went to his face as bullets assaulted him. I ducked low to the ground and into the corner. There was an incredible amount of screaming in Vietnamese, but none of the screams seemed to belong to any girls.

I knew then I would not be rescuing anyone that night because they'd not brought any girls with them. It was a witch hunt.

Breathe.

I positioned the handgun in my palms, used the jamb to brace myself, and took in the hall. Two men stood there with their automatics, fumbling with them and yelling at one another, gesturing to the dead men on the floor.

Breathe.

When they saw me, they took aim.

Breathe.

Two clear shots to their heads took them down easily.

Breathe.

Breathe.

Breathe.

CHAPTER THIRTY

Ethan

The lump in my throat was so large I felt like I couldn't breathe. My body trembled as I fled the alleyway for Slánaigh.

Just get home. You'll figure this out. Just get home. Get home, Ethan, I chanted to myself over and over until I reached my bike.

As calmly as I could, I tried to remove the chain. It took five attempts before I got it right. My shivering hands finally steadied enough to put the key in the lock. My heart constricted in my chest and I labored to breathe.

Just get to Fin. Find Finley. Just get to her. She'll fix this for you. She can fix anything.

I started the bike and tore out into the street, narrowly missing another driver. The guy honked his horn and yelled as he passed, making my blood pressure spike. I didn't know how much more I could take before I lost consciousness. I needed her touch.

Get to her hands. Just get to her hands.

I rushed back to Slánaigh as quickly as possible without arousing suspicion. I peered down at my hands. Every time I passed under a lamplight, they illuminated the bright red blood staining them. I cried out in anguish, wishing I could cleanse them, wishing I could rinse them, wishing I could *absolve* them. Lady Macbeth in the flesh. *She has light by her continually; 'tis her command.*

The nausea roiled in my stomach. I could smell the iron of their blood on not just my hands but on my clothing—*in my hair*. I shook from the release of the adrenaline. I felt confused, overwhelmed.

Their bodies. Their bodies. All those bodies. The blood! The blood! All their blood!

I could smell and taste the gunpowder as it lingered in the air, see their dead, uninhabited eyes, hear their deafening screams, feel their bitter, empty, yet desperate souls cry out in their unexpected and unprepared deaths.

I pulled as far as I could go into Slánaigh before shutting off the bike and hiking the remaining distance. I threw the bike's stand out and ran flat out until I reached the cove. I pulled back the foliage, sick to my stomach, and rode the boat to my room. I entered my room and rummaged through my things for my soap and shampoo.

When I had them, I quietly swam to the lagoon's waterfall, undressed, and vigorously, almost hysterically unburdened my skin of the dead men's blood. I laid my clothes flat against the rock floor, letting the fall of the water wash the blood from my clothes as well. I stood under that waterfall with its roaring, thundering ways, thankful for the reprieve from the guilt that racked my brain with loud, horrific accusations.

Somehow I knew that light would soon be cresting the bay, so I swam back and dressed in my room.

Get to Finley. Get to Finley.

I sprang out of my room, not caring if it woke Father. He'd only think I left earlier than him, which I did often in my eagerness to see Fin. I shot across the beach and up the trail through the canopy of trees. I bounded up the staircase, and scaled the narrow wraparound porch until I came upon Finley's room. I tapped on her window.

A groggy Finley came up to it and shoved it open.

"What are—" she began to say, but I cut off her words with a kiss.

I kissed her mouth, her cheeks, her neck. I kissed her everywhere there was skin to kiss with her hanging out of the window, a giggle sounded stuck in her throat.

"Finally," I breathed against her ear. I hugged her, fighting a burning sensation in my throat and eyes. "Finally," I said again, my heart beginning to beat steadily once more.

"Finley," I told her, my voice breaking. I cleared my throat. "Finley, you fix me."

"We fix each other," she told me with a rough voice, pulling back and smiling at me, her eyes puffy with sleep.

"Fin, before the sun rises completely, will you do me a favor?"

"Of course, Ethan. Anything."

I pulled my hair from its tie. "I need you to cut my hair."

Her eyes popped wide along with her mouth. "No," she said. "I won't do that."

I shook my head, the memory of the men's blood rinsing copper red from my hair onto the rocks of the waterfall. "No, it has it to be done. Either you do it or I will."

"But *why*?" she asked, a hitch in her voice. She ran both her hands throughout its length, making my heart ache.

"Because I-I need it to be gone. It's a reminder of awful things," I told her, not needing to embellish any further. She was so accepting of me. *What if she finds out? What if she figures it out and she detests you for it?* I shook my head of the inconceivable idea. She nodded her answer.

"Thank you, Fin."

She stood to get whatever she needed, and I slid down the side of the house. I looked out onto the dark horizon, breathing in the salt air, desperate for the stability of the tide. I listened carefully and was rewarded with the steady waves.

Suddenly Fin was there, climbing out the window barefoot, as usual, and sporting a T-shirt and cutoffs, her hair wavy and down around her shoulders.

"My God." The exclamation left my chest of its own accord. "Is it possible you've ever been more beautiful? Every time I see you, I can't help but think the same thing, but I think this time is quite possibly the most beautiful I've ever remembered."

She smiled shyly, making me all the more enchanted with her. She slid a small wood stool toward me, set it behind my back, and sat. I saw her

298

knees at my shoulders so I bent my arms slightly to hold her ankles as she worked. Her skin was soothing, warm, and alive. She ran her hands through the mass for a very long time as we looked out onto the moonlit bay. My chest ached as she did it, negating the effects of her skin, but I didn't say anything. This was a pain I couldn't share with her, refused to overwhelm her with. It was a cumbersome weight meant only to be carried by its inventor.

When she was done, she combed it several times then tied it in a band at the back of my head.

"Here goes nothin'," she told the wind. She took a pair of scissors and deftly removed my hair just above the band. "Oh my God," she whispered when she was done.

I turned her direction, my head already feeling so different, so light. It was such a foreign sensation, so alien and yet it felt *so right*. I needed an immediate change, to separate myself from *that* Ethan.

She handed me my hair and I took it in my hands, not sure what I was supposed to do with it. I laid it on the deck beside us wishing never to look at it again.

Finley took the sharp scissors and began cutting at my remaining hair. I had no idea what she was doing, nor did I ask. She rotated around me, making sure it was even, then sat back down and when she did, my hands found her ankles again. Not long after, I heard the click and buzz of a pair of shears. Every moment it took to cut my hair was gladly received, as it meant her gorgeous hands were on me at all times.

When she was done, the crack of the buzzing shears stopped, only the quiet waves and Finley's and my breathing could be heard. She swiped at my neck with her slender hands, removing the excess hair stuck there. She blew across the back of my neck, sending a shiver throughout my body.

She'd made me forget my night. Just like that. Finley was the calm *after* the storm.

She reached down near her feet and brought up a mirror, placing it in front of my face for me. I hardly recognized myself. I grabbed it from her and held it up.

"I, uh, gave you an undercut," she said, shifting around, sitting on her calves, and using her hand to flip the top half around. "I kept the top a little long so you could style it easily." She paused, dropping her hands to the deck. "Do you, uh, like it?"

I set the mirror on the wood below. I lifted her on top of my lap and wrapped my arms around her waist.

"It's amazing. Thank you so much, Fin."

"You're welcome, love," she said, kissing the top of my cut hair. She ran her fingers through the new length over and over and over. We sat in silence and waited for the sun to rise and as it did, my heart sank back into my chest.

A new day.

I would take the guilt of that night and carefully scar it over. I would always know it was there. I couldn't help but notice its thick, abrasive mark, but the wound would no longer open, no longer bleed. I made sure of that.

CHAPTER THIRTY-ONE

Finley

I held Ethan's hair in my hands, tucking it into an envelope to donate later. I didn't know why he had me cut it, but I knew it had to be done. I recognized he needed it as some form of therapy. I accepted it as it was because I owed Ethan that in equal exchange. He had secrets he wouldn't confide, I knew at least that, but I would wait for him to spill them when he was ready or when he wanted me to know.

I stepped back out of my window and joined Ethan again. The sun had almost completely risen, the morning that serene and brief limbo between light and dark, a cross between suffering and relief, strangely. The only hope was in the awareness that light would indefinitely arrive to wash out the pained darkness. But in the interim, there was peace in that murky shine and we soaked in that place, that place without hope or fear.

Ethan

I worked that entire day alongside Fin on edge, despite the mask I wore, in full anticipation that the bought police would come tearing up the shell drive looking for me, but they didn't. In fact, the four men who'd died at my hand and the two who'd died indirectly never even made the news.

I had two theories on that.

They had yet to be discovered.

or

They had been discovered by Khanh and he'd gotten rid of the bodies himself. He would still attempt his fishing expedition without the help of his bought police.

For now.

But I won't be falling for it, I'd thought. *No, my days of retrieving little girls without the help of legitimate law are over. Six men died because of me, because of my eagerness to save those helpless girls.*

But that's exactly the point, wasn't it? They're helpless girls. Those girls still need someone. They still need rescuing. They're so hard to find right now. Granted, it's your fault they're so difficult to track down, but what's done is done.

I fought with myself over the next four days. One minute determined to go back and the next condemning even the thought.

But each day that passed and there was no word from anyone about the deaths, the side of me that condemned the idea of stealing more girls quieted until it was muted.

The fifth night I paddled the boat to the cove's shore and hid it in the bushes. It was strange to feel the wind at the back of my neck, my hair gone now, my old life abandoned the second I'd made the decision to keep looking for girls. All except Finley, my lovely Finley. She was my permanent fixture.

I almost tripped over my own feet when a thought came rushing toward my mind.

And what if you're shot down by these men? You would devastate Finley. And even if you didn't die, could you risk killing any more men? Even if they deserve death? How could you face her knowing you'd willingly sought out trouble, willingly risked killing someone again?

I shook my head of the thoughts. "No, no. She will *never* find out. I wouldn't pour this on her."

But can you live with yourself knowing you were keeping secrets?

"Yes," I argued with myself, "I can do this. I can hide this one thing. I can handle it."

When I reached the bikes, I walked one halfway down the long drive before starting it up. I kept my hood down and reveled in my newfound purpose.

I was going to save children and earn Finley Dyer both at the same time.

CHAPTER THIRTY-TWO

Ethan

The night seemed eerily still, as if the city knew to stay in, could sense my mission and those who hunted me. Khanh, the man who ran the trafficking rings in northeast Vietnam, wanted me. Me, an American boy from Montana. Me, half Echo Tribe. Me, taught by Akule Moonsong. Me, my father's son. Me. Only half without Finley Dyer.

I pulled my black hood farther over my face and stayed near the buildings. I knew enough at that point not to expect solicitors to approach me. No, they knew who to look for. They'd gunned down a woman right in front of my eyes in the middle of a busy day on an equally busy street in Hanoi. They wouldn't hesitate to do the same thing to me.

So instead of exposing myself to becoming a potential target, I kept myself hidden, walking a fine line between the light from the moon and the shade of the buildings. I had every intention of exploring every alley I could.

They were like rats, the men in the trafficking cells. They sank into their dark, disgusting hiding spots. They chose the most bleak, soiled, offensive areas they could, as if they were frightened of the light, as if they were frightened of anything clean. As if they were afraid of what the exposure might do. As if the very idea of the moonlight was a risk they weren't willing to take, afraid they'd be gobbled up by the devil himself if their toes so much as traced that very visible line.

The line between heaven and hell.

A line I walked myself.

Careful, or you'll tip to the wrong side.

I captured the fear that thought brought me and shoved it away from me as quickly as possible. I imagined it shattered into a million pieces as it hit cobblestone and that those pieces grew legs like insects then crawled into the tight, dark spaces out of my sight. Out of my mind.

I came upon my first alley and edged the building nearest me, staying to the shadows. I glanced down and noticed a straight, smooth wall, void of any side entrances. I kept walking until I reached the next alley and did the same, yielding identical results. It wasn't until the fifth alley did I notice a door in the center of the building left of the alley. My gut instinct told me everything I needed to know.

It was the only door in the alley, ideal for privacy. The piles of trash usually piled high at the sides of the buildings were scarce, which would have been something they would have preferred so their customer base wasn't too revolted by their surroundings, as if they had the right to care. I scaled the wall toward the door. I could hear men's voices inside. They were arguing in Vietnamese, making me wish I could speak the language. They were yelling at each other, anxiety and anger prevalent in their tones, but there was an additional edge to their shouts I recognized. They were *afraid*.

As you should be, I thought.

I looked up. The alley was narrow enough I could push myself between the walls and scale up to the second-story window. It was an easy enough task, only ten to twelve feet above street level. When I got closer, I leaned my shoulder into the building housing the men and braced myself with a booted foot on the other wall.

Breathe.

Carefully, oh so carefully, I peered into the window, my heart pounding in my chest. The room was empty. I shifted so my left hand and that same booted foot held my weight, leaning my free knee under the sill so I could lift the window.

Breathe.

Quickly, I lifted myself, my fingers gripping the thin outside frame, then threw my feet inside, followed by the rest of me. I did this as quietly as possible, standing to my full height and unzipping my hoodie. I crossed my arms and palmed my knives, sliding them silently from their sheaths.

Breathe.

I noiselessly crossed the room and leaned my ear against the door but couldn't hear anything over the din of the men arguing below.

Breathe.

I cut across to the other side of the door and palmed the doorknob, turning the handle, and cracking the door.

Breathe.

When no one reacted, I pulled it open just enough to peer through.

Breathe.

There was no one there. Not in the halls, at least.

Breathe.

I listened for any distinguishing sounds, men walking up stairs or in the rooms, but I heard nothing. A moment's pause and I pulled the door open completely. I shoved myself back a bit, prepared for someone to invade the room but none came.

Breathe.

The hall was indeed deserted as I emerged a few steps from the door.

Breathe.

There were two doors besides the one I'd exited. I started at the one at the end, bending my ear but hearing nothing. I slid the knob, giving it a small nudge so it would fall open. There was no one there.

Breathe.

I bent my ear toward the second one and again heard nothing. I opened the door as I had the other and just like the other, it was empty.

Breathe.

Damn, I thought, *it was all for nothing.* I turned to flee when my eye caught the edge of a staircase leading to a third floor.

Breathe.

I had two choices. Leave. Or stay. *What the hell is the point of you risking breaking in here if you don't check all possibilities?* I stayed.

Breathe.

I headed toward the third floor as prudently as possible given that the stairs were wood. Every time one would creak, I'd still, my heart jumping into my throat and wait for the men to come barrelling up after me. But, it seemed, they were too busy arguing, which way was the best way to catch me or avoid me to notice I was already above their heads.

Breathe.

The third floor wasn't so much another level as a barren attic but in the back, tucked into a corner, was a room with a closed door that appeared recently constructed.

Breathe.

I twisted my way across the wood floor staying mindful of any sudden movements that could make a sound but also moving as efficiently as possible.

Breathe.

I listened against the door for any sounds but none came.

Breathe.

I slowly opened it, not sure what to expect.

Breathe.

Inside was a young girl, a very young girl. Her body trembled in automatic fear of me and my heart sank at the sight of her. She was newly abducted, I could tell. The other girls never shook the way this girl shook. They were accustomed to their horrors and had shed their despair along with their hope. But this young girl, she wore her trepidation with such distressed anguish I almost cried for her there on the spot.

I removed my hood and held my hands up in the air. I fixed my expression into something I tried to pass as composed, though I wasn't sure how well I'd done, since I was still reeling from the obvious dread rolling off her in panicked waves.

I shook my head back and forth and placed a finger over my lips to quiet her. She'd begun to whimper. As soon as I did this, she obeyed.

"Do you speak English?" I whispered. "Nod your head."
She nodded yes.

"I'm going to take you away from here," I told her. She shook her head vigorously. "Why not?" I asked her.

"They kill me," she answered. "If I leave, they kill me."

"No harm will come to you. Do you hear me? They will not touch a hair on your head as long as I am alive," I promised.
Her eyes blew wide.

"We have to hurry, though. Can you climb onto my back?"
She scurried over to my side and I bent down for her. She climbed on quickly and wrapped her baby arms around my neck as tightly as she could. I wrapped my arms underneath her legs and hurried back across the floor to the top of the staircase.

I leaned over. I could still hear the men yelling at one another. The girl was trembling but she held on with determination, making me proud of her.
Breathe.

I escaped down the stairs, crossed the hallway, and into the room I'd come through from the alley.

Breathe.

I set her down and signaled to her that I needed to crawl out of the window, brace myself, and that I needed her to climb onto my back again. She agreed.

Breathe.

Once through the window, I held myself up for her, my arms trembling from the effort. Nimbly, she obeyed me without hesitation.

Breathe.

We dangled fifteen feet above the concrete ground and although she shuddered with obvious fear, she held on.

Breathe.

I scaled the walls back down, careful not to shift so radically she fell.

Breathe.

When my toes hit surface, I exhaled in utter relief.

"Let's go," I said, turning my face to meet hers near my shoulder.

And so I ran.

CHAPTER THIRTY-THREE

Ethan

When I reached the end of the alley, I stopped to check for any lookouts at street level. *Clear.*

"Đến đây!" I heard behind us, startling me, and making my blood run cold.

Breathe.

I shifted the girl around, holding her like an infant, tucking her legs into my side and bracing her head on my shoulder.

Breathe.

"Hold on," I spoke.

She closed her eyes.

Breathe.

I ran in the direction of Tran's police station, hoping beyond hope that there were a few officers there who didn't reside in the back of Khanh's pocket.

Breathe.

I ran, my lungs pumping air. My body desperate for oxygen, desperate for relief, desperate for some sort of sign that he was losing momentum, but I could still hear his dull steps behind me. He yelled at me repeatedly in Vietnamese.

"He tells you to come," the small girl explained to me as we passed storefront after storefront, passing people with their strange looks but with no care other than to look upon us then carry on with their own business.

In the adrenaline rush, I made two split-second decisions that threw off my sense of direction and we ended up in an almost deserted part of the city, which I hadn't thought possible. It looked like a dumping ground for the locals' trash. Piles and piles of it lined the streets and the alleys.

Finally, the guy's steps seemed to fade a bit. In desperation for rest, I ducked between two buildings when I saw an opening through to the other side. I kept running, although slower, not for a second thinking he'd given up. I could tell the guy was built for endurance. He hadn't slowed because he needed to. He'd slowed because he wanted to.

When I reached the end of the byway, I had two choices. To my left, there was nothing but darkness and trash. To my right... the same. *Jesus! Which way! Which way!*

I heard what sounded like a metal can tumble across pavement a few yards behind us, maybe ten yards away.

Shit!

I sprinted right, running as fast and as hard as I could but was met with a dead end. *Oh, Jesus! I just killed us both!*

Breathe.

Breathe.

Breathe.

My chest burned with such intensity I could barely stomach it.

I glanced behind me. He was close. My eyes searched my surroundings. Pitch black and seemingly nowhere else to go. The smell of the trash amassed against the sides was atrocious, burning my nose.

I threw the girl onto the ground and tossed what I could over her.

"Don't move," I told her. "Don't say a word. Don't breathe." I peered over my shoulder. "And for the love of God, whatever you do, cover your ears and *don't look.*"

Her eyes widened to impossible breadth and she nodded. She obeyed me and faced the wall. I covered her face as best I could and waited.

Breathe.

Breathe.

Breathe.

My chest rose and fell violently. The rapid, thump, thump, thump of my heart drummed in my ears. Strapped to my sides rested my sharp blades. I unzipped my hoodie, crossed my arms, and palmed the knives' handles.

Breathe.

Breathe.

Breathe.

"Đến đây!" I heard again, making my pulse jump. My heart leapt into my throat. I crouched, bent my knees, readying for anything.

The speaker, the man chasing us, rushed around the edge of the building but came to a stop when he caught me standing. He smiled cruelly then spoke to me in Vietnamese, words I didn't understand, and made his way toward me. He stopped short once more. His head tilted to his right. His eyes narrowed.

"You messed up," he said in English, realizing I hadn't understood him before and made his way toward me once more. The look on his face was one of pure menace. "I'm going to skin you alive," he told me. "Then I'm going to take care of that girl personally. I'm going to *ruin* her," he finished. The word *ruin* sparked the memory of Fin's. "I'm ruined," she'd told me. My body shook with a wrathful terror.

Breathe.

I shook my head, my tongue too thick to speak.

He was big for a local. I suppose that's why they hired him to do what he did, but no matter. I was taller and built better. I also had something he didn't. I was trained to kill. Animals, yes, but to me he was just that. An animal.

My blood boiled in my veins and the anxious adrenaline was replaced with an absolute hatred, a fury so destructive it frightened me. My teeth gritted in my jaw and I reveled in the pressure.

I knew it the instant he'd made the decision, and all the breath I'd held whooshed from my lungs. A look of determination flitted across his face and I could only smile, content in my malice. This visibly confused him but he charged forward, regardless.

Two feet within striking distance, my short blades pealed with a beautiful ring and it brought me such serenity. The gun strapped to his back was useless and he knew it.

I plunged both blades into his sides near his ribs and his mouth opened in shock, his body leaned against mine in support. I held him up with the blades and bent into his ear.

"You messed up," I said, stealing his words.

Blood curdled from his mouth, and I removed my blades as he slid to the ground. I bent and wiped my knives off on his jacket. His mouth opened and shut like a fish out of water, but I couldn't conjure up any compassion for him. Instead, I stood over him and placed my boot over his heaving chest, pressing as much of my weight into him as possible.

"You will burn in fire so scorching you'll beg for this moment over and over again."

His last breath struggled from his lungs and his eyes went blank. I replaced my knives and kicked the corpse to the side, covering his body as much as I could with garbage, hoping the smell would hide him and no one would find him for several days.

I turned back to her, fished her from her hiding place, and threw her over my shoulder. "Don't look," I ordered, and she nodded her head.

CHAPTER THIRTY-FOUR

Finley

The morning came brilliant and dazzling. The day laid before me full of hope and gorgeousness. I was healing, helping those who were just like me, and in love with someone I never thought would love me back.

Don't get me wrong, I'd been okay with that. I knew my worth. Through soul-searching and heart-building, I'd built myself up. I'd chipped away at the hard exterior, rough sense of self, and years of built-up hate, and exposed myself to the woman I'd become. Yet with that cleansing came a vulnerability I didn't know I'd had, scars put upon me I did nothing to merit.

So, yes, I knew my worth. I knew I was worth anything and everything. I knew it. But I did need to make amends with those stripped-down burdens. I needed to shake them off, shed them at my feet, step out of them, and walk away without looking back.

It was a feat I could have done by myself. I was strong enough, but just because I could do it by myself, didn't mean I had to.

In walked Ethan. Someone I'd fought hard to forget. Someone I'd crushed so hard on at one point in my life, I'd been convinced I'd been in love with him then. But knowing what it meant to love and to be loved, I discovered I'd only really been at the tipping point. It was a beautiful house, the tipping point, with its stolen glances, butterfly-induced nearness, and intoxicating presences.

And Ethan *was* that house. I'd backed down his hill, tumbled and fell, and rolled my way back down to its understory depths, content to find a *different* tipping point, secure I would discover a new place to climb, but that was not what fate had laid out for me, it seemed. No matter how I fought her, she was a resolute mercenary.

And so, reluctantly at first, I hiked up my skirts and marched upward, but this time with the help of Ethan's hand. This time *he* pulled me to *him*, shouldered my weight, up to the tipping point, that place bright and that lived under the sun. He'd wrapped his arms around my shoulders and we both fell, on toward the other side. The side full of green, burgeoning love. The side with lush, verdant, and passionate adoration with its redwood possibilities.

I showered and dressed for the day as usual, but my heart felt heavy. I thought of the envelope full of Ethan's hair and took on that concern once more. *My poor Ethan*, I thought. *What secrets he must keep. What heavy concerns sit cumbersome on your shoulders?*

I helped Sister, who'd more than likely already been up for hours, finish laundry and set up the common room for school lessons. We laughed and joked with one another the entire time. She was eager to know the details of my "courtship," as she'd put it, with Ethan, and I was in no hurry to divulge. I told her of his sweet dedication and thoughtful considerations but kept our tortured business to ourselves, as it was just that.

She sighed appropriately and fanned herself at all the right parts.

"Do you like him?" I asked her as we set the dining tables for breakfast.

"I really do," she said but stopped folding a napkin.

"*But?*" I asked.

She continued with her task, remembering herself. "I can't place my finger on it," her French accent purred, "but there is something in that boy that gives me peace, security, but also frightens me." She looked at me, earnest. "Is that not rubbish?" she laughed.

I swallowed back the fear her words built upon my heart and tried to smile, but failed miserably.

"My dear, I did not mean to make you uneasy. Come," she said, extending her arms and rushing over to me, her skirts swishing about her. She bent me to her height and hugged me in that way a woman who knew how to love better than anyone in the world could hug. She ran her hands along my waves, smoothing it all out as she did so because she was a genuine mother at heart, despite her vows. Or, perhaps, because of them.

She released me and smiled so wide it didn't seem like it could fit in her petite face, yet it was a pretty smile, a feminine smile, full of kindness and wisdom, sweetness, and understanding.

Ethan came into the room at that moment, his height an imposing thing, his presence a little appalling. He looked run-down with bags beneath his beautiful grey eyes. His shoulders looked glutted, straining against his T-shirt. His hands were fisted at his side. He breathed as though he'd run the entire length of the beach to me. His eyes frantically searched the room and when he caught my gaze, he stilled.

"Finley," he gritted with that unbelievably deep voice that sent shivers up and down my body. He took one large, loud step with his boot, heading my direction, before noticing Sister was in the room.

"Oh," he started, "I'm sorry, Sister. Hello, how are you?" he asked, stopping short and tucking his muscular arms behind him.

"I'm well, thank you, Mister Moonsong," she answered back, but her eyes studied him anew. Finally, she smiled at him. "I'll leave you two to greet the other." She looked at us sternly. "Keep your hands clean," she told us, but her ornery grin appeared as she left through the door toward the common room.

"Ethan," I said, smiling at him.

I expected a smile in return, but he didn't give me one. Instead, he rushed me, threw his arms around my waist, and buried his face in my neck. We stayed like that for quite some time. I refused to pull away until he did, so I wrapped my arms around his own neck tightly, letting him know we could stay there all day if he needed to.

Finally, he pulled away but held my hands in his. "Good morning," he said.
I reached up and ran my thumbs beneath his eyes.

"You look so tired," I whispered. "Why don't you run back and get some rest. We don't have much to do anyway."

He shook his head. "No, I'll, uh, just stay here with you, if that's okay?"

"Okay, of course," I told him.

"What were we supposed to do today?" he asked me.

"Well, Father had another bust planned but it fell through. Our informant's told us the cell has no children they're aware of. So strange, right?"

He nodded. "Yes, strange," he parroted.

"Detective Tran called, though, says another girl was dropped off at his station early this morning. He can't locate her family so she's coming here."

"Cool," he said, but his face looked ill.

"Are you sure you don't want to lay down? I hope you didn't catch something."

"No, I'm fine. Really, Fin. Just glad to be near you."

We started walking toward the common room together.

"Tran is so bewildered by it all. He says he's going to try to install cameras."

"What does he want with the guy, I wonder?" he mused.

"Not sure. Maybe just to talk with him. Find out where he's getting all those girls?"

Ethan's face lit up with a large smile. "And how do they know it's not a woman who's dropping them off?"

"Because one of the first girls described a man, remember?"

"Yeah, but that could have been a fluke."

"I don't think so," I told him.

"Maybe the locals are seeing it can be done and they're finding and turning them in anonymously but as a collective."

I shook my head. "That's not likely."

"Why not?" he insisted. "It could happen."

I looked at him, confused.

"I-I guess," I answered, though not believing that for a second.

Ethan fixed his expression. "Well, you're right, that's probably not likely. Anyway, who cares how they got there. Let's just be glad they got there."

"You're right," I told him, squeezing his hand.

Ethan

I couldn't believe how careless I'd been. Akule would have been ashamed of me. I'd thought I was being vigilant, but the community that surrounded the traffickers was too tightly knit. I knew this. I was instantly recognizable too, which didn't help at all. Too tall to be mistaken for anyone else; it was only a matter of time before I was caught.

My hands trembled at the memory of sliding the trafficker's body off my knives. I knew why I'd needed to do it, knew the little girl had been my priority, but nothing could ever prepare you for taking another human's life.

I remember seeing an interview back home while watching TV with my dad about this soldier who'd been stationed in Iraq. He knew his job had to be done and he'd told the interviewer he felt he'd been prepared for that job, mentally aware of the task that had to be done, but then the soldier went on to speak about the feeling that first kill earned him.

There'd been a known terrorist they'd been monitoring by drone and by foot for quite some time. They'd followed him and caught him planting IEDs along well-used and well-known American tank and humvee roads but had yet to catch or kill him. He was shifty and intelligent.

The soldier had been tasked to watch those roads and one day, on his drone patrol, he'd recognized the terrorist. The man was burying a bomb set to detonate and kill American soldiers. Without thinking, the soldier said he painted his target and sent in a fighter pilot.

In less than thirty seconds, the terrorist was dust. There was much celebrating and backslapping, but that soldier said he'd never forget the haunting aches in his chest knowing he was responsible for taking another's life, even in defense of his fellow soldiers.

The interviewer asked him if he had a chance, would he do it all over again? The soldier, without hesitation, replied yes, but that it didn't mean he wasn't aware of the value of a human life.

See? Killing these men to save those girls is a necessary evil. They're killing themselves, really, just by being part of the operations, I thought. *Yeah, I'm just the instrument when you think about it. Those men needed to die. They needed death.*

I looked over at Finley. We'd gone outside to change a tire on one of the bikes that had gone flat. Her hair whipped around her face as she sat on her ankles, her hands tucked under her stomach, against her legs, waiting for me to ask for a tool. She was lovely. She was everything good that had ever happened to me, and I loved her with the fire of a million suns.

For her. I'll do it for her.

CHAPTER THIRTY-FIVE

Finley

We were given a few free hours while the girls were in lessons. We told Sister we'd be swimming in the cove right outside of Slánaigh if she needed us. She promised she'd try to bring the girls down for a swim later, if they all got their work done. This possibility sent the girls into a tizzy, making me laugh.

"Get your work done, my loves!" I told them. "I'll be waiting for you at the beach!"

Pen and paper went flying as Ethan and I made our way out the door. He hadn't brought his boardshorts so he improvised with a pair of cargos instead.

We walked toward the water. I fought the instinct to run.

"What's up with you?" I asked him.

"What?" he asked, distracted.

"You're actin' all weird. Seriously, what the hell is up?"

"I'm not acting weird," he answered, defensive. "*Ethan.*"

He kept silent and walked ahead of me, reaching the water before me and shedding his T-shirt.

"Whoa!" I said, examining his muscles. "What have you been doing?"

"What are you talking about?"

"Ethan, your muscles are, like, huge all of a sudden. Have you been working out when I'm not around or something?"

"A little," he said, sitting on the beach, resting his forearms on his knees.

"That's crazy. You're working all day with me, going on busts, and then working out? Tryin' to kill yourself or something?" I laughed.

He whipped his head my direction. "Why would you ask me that?"

"What?" My smiled dropped. "I just meant it's a little much for one person to do."

"Oh," he said.

"Ethan."

"Let's get in the water," he said, standing and walking into the bay.

"Don't do that, dude."

"Do what?" he asked.

"Ignore me like that, Ethan."

He turned toward me. "I'm not ignoring you, Fin."

"The hell you are. Is this about your hair?"

He laughed. "You think me that shallow?"

"Well, no, but, I mean, it was a huge part of your heritage and you'd had it for so many years. I'd thought-thought you'd kept it long because of your mom."

He was ankle deep in the water. His head hung when I mentioned his mom, making my gut ache. I wished I'd never said a word.

"I did," he answered, staring out into the bay.

"I shouldn't have mentioned your mom. I'm sorry."

"Why?" he asked, his face drawn in confusion. "I love talking about her. I loved her. I *love* her."

"I just thought I might have offended you was all."

"I could never be offended by that," he told me softly as I joined his side. "I did wear it long because of her. She always talked about her Echo Tribe ancestry, how it defined her in so many ways, how she cherished it, and how she wanted me to be familiar with it."
I grasped my throat. *Don't ask him why he'd cut it.*

He looked at me and smiled. The smile I'd been missing for a few days and didn't know how much I'd wanted back. A little piece of my heart set at ease when I saw that smile.

"Don't," he said, wrapping his arm around my shoulder, his eyes still on the water.

"Don't what?"

"Don't pretend like you're not owed an explanation anymore. I belong to you, Fin. You know this. You have a right to know anything and everything about me." He swallowed and dropped his arm, leaving me feeling ill to my stomach for some reason. "You just have to ask."

"*Okay*. So why did you cut your hair?" I asked him.

He looked at me with severe eyes. "I was shedding an old skin when you cut my hair. Ridding myself of an old Ethan."

"I don't like the way that sounds," I told him. "I liked that *old Ethan*, as you put it. *I loved him*."

"Well, you'll have to settle for this new one then because he's long gone, Fin." He paused. "He's forever gone."

"You're so confusing right now."

He turned toward me and shook his head. "I'm sorry. I'm being an asshole." His hands found my shoulders. "Let's test these waters, shall we?" he asked cryptically.

I eyed him, trying to figure him out.

He's off.

CHAPTER THIRTY-SIX

Ethan

That night, despite how worn out I was, I decided I needed to go out, to gauge the problems I'd caused by trying to help. I'd considered stopping altogether but quickly disregarded this option for several reasons. One, on Slánaigh's regular busts, I'd be recognizable and I'd have to explain why, something I would never, ever do. Two, I knew if I didn't take care of Khanh, find him, and *take care of him*, he'd expose me to the police, ultimately putting Slánaigh in danger, also something I would never, ever do.

I'd never thought in a million years taking things into my own hands would have snowballed as it had. It seemed every time I set out to do one right, I was forced into ten wrongs. I was struggling with my conscience as well. On one hand, I was saving girls, saving them from continued and terrible fates. On the other, I'd been forced to kill seven men.

Seven lives. I lined their blank, frozen-in-terror expressions in my mind and felt an overwhelming nausea.

To combat the unease, I lined up the sweet, angelic faces of every girl I'd saved and my heart steadied, my stomach settled.

But how can I get rid of Khanh? And what's to stop someone from just rising in place and continuing where he'd left off?

I knew the answer, and I also knew exactly what I needed to do. *Your hands are about to get a lot bloodier.* I needed to disarm, disassemble, weaken to the point of deterioration Khanh's traffic ring. The only way to do that was to find Khanh himself. Khanh would surround himself with his most powerful men, men who were in charge of the small cells he kept around North Vietnam. I needed to devastate their operations so badly it couldn't revive.

Resolved in my plan, I set out that night with every intention of getting information from the smaller cells that would lead me to Khanh himself.

I stayed to the shadows as I'd done the night before, searching the alleys, again as I'd done the night before, passing groups of people laughing and talking, passing lively storefronts, and street markets full of people bustling to and fro either working or buying.

Without realizing, I'd stumbled upon the store that posed as the front for the den above, the one I'd stolen my first girl from. Resolute, I ducked and entered the store, quickly crossing behind the curtains into the shadows of the little room with the winding staircase.

Breathe.

There was no one there so I made my way up, struck with a sense of déjà vu as I unzipped my hoodie and removed a knife. I pulled back my hood, no longer afraid of being recognized.

Breathe.

I entered the hall boldly, half not expecting anyone to be there, and half not caring anymore. *Bad sign, Ethan. Whatever.*

Breathe.

I edged up to every door before opening each one. They were all empty. I didn't bother closing them.

Breathe.

I made a beeline for the door at the end, the one full of men the last time I'd been there.

Breathe.

I leaned an ear against it and recognized low voices deep in discussion. I deciphered three men. I listened a little while longer, confident there were truly only three.

Breathe.

"Anyone there?" I asked facetiously at the door, tucking myself into the corner of the hall as far as I could get away from the door, smiling to myself.

Breathe.

There was an instant of silence followed by a barrage of bullets through the door. I ducked down as low as I could get. With my boot, I slammed the hall floor as hard as I could, attempting to give the impression they'd gotten me and that I'd fallen, eliciting another private smile.

Breathe.

When the bullets ceased, I stood swiftly, gathering my second knife and standing defensively as Akule had taught me.

Breathe.

There was a brief moment they waited before charging through.

Breathe.

My knife shot out, puncturing the first man's throat. He fell where he'd stood.

Breathe.

I reached for the first man's hand as he did and snatched the handgun from him. I pressed it against the second man's temple and fired once before the third man even had time to register what was happening.

Breathe.

I pointed it at his head just as he fumbled with his own automatic, trying to aim it at me. I brought the gun down and shot him twice. Once in each arm, disabling him. He cried out in pain, groaning and mumbling in Vietnamese.

Breathe.

"Quiet," I rasped. He cried out so I smacked him across the head with the butt of the gun. "Quiet." He whimpered but obeyed for the most part. Tears streamed down his face. "Now," I said, leaning over and removing my knife from the first man's throat. I wiped the blade on his clothing. I sheathed both knives. "You are going to tell me where I can find Khanh."

He said something in Vietnamese. I could only guess he was trying to tell me he had no idea who Khanh was or that he didn't know where I could find him. Either way, I didn't have time for it. In a flash, I pulled a knife from my holster and slammed it into his upper thigh. He screamed so harshly I lifted his shirt and shoved it over his mouth to deafen the effects.

When he'd controlled himself enough to stop screaming, I lifted my hand and the shirt fell. He cried in streaming tears.

"Stop," I ordered and he obeyed. "Khanh. Where is he?"

"Don't know," he panted in perfect English. I twisted the knife in his leg and he screamed out. "I don't know! I really don't know! I swear! I swear!" I lifted my fingers from the knife's handle. "Please, please, I promise. We're not allowed to know. I only know my boss. Name is Dai."

"And where can I find Dai?" I asked him.

"Nineteen Kim Mã. Hanoi."

"Thank you," I told him.

"Are you going to kill me?" he asked.

"Are you going to tell 'em I'm coming?" I asked for my own entertainment.

"No! No! I swear! I swear! I won't say a word!"

I snorted. "Yeah, right," I told him, yanking the knife from his leg.

This time he gritted his teeth through the pain, afraid to piss me off, I thought. I wiped the blood off my blade with his shirt.

"Please," he begged.

"I'm going to let you go but only because I want you to tell them that I'm coming. I want them to know I'm out for blood and they are going to pay. Tell them I'm coming for them and they're all going to die."

He whimpered like an animal.

"And when I do, if I see you, the last face you will ever know *is mine*."

CHAPTER THIRTY-SEVEN

Finley

Ethan was ignoring me, acting strangely, and so incredibly distracted. He wouldn't talk to me even when I pried and demanded he answer, which only yielded me short, one-word replies. He was no longer playful. He'd lost tenderness, even compassion.

I didn't know where he'd put himself, stored himself away at, but I wasn't going to let him get too far.

Because I was afraid he wouldn't come back.

Ethan

Detective Tran had come to Slánaigh the following afternoon and I'd made myself scarce, too many thoughts scattered around my head. I didn't trust myself from blurting a confession, so I busied myself fixing the plumbing issues on Father's houseboat.

"What 'tis 'ye hands busied wit', moiy son?" Father asked, startling me from my thoughts.

I cleared my throat. "Oh, uh, just having a look at your pipes. I think I can fix them. I'll just need pop into town and visit a hardware store." I looked at his expectant face. "Unless you have something else for me to do?"

"No, no, nothin' else, boyo. Go on' wit' ya. I've a lead on one o' the girls' families an' I mean ta' go 'bout foindin' 'em." He smiled at me and my stomach plummeted. I swallowed the satisfaction I felt knowing I helped that girl escape as well as the guilt from the murders that helped her get there.

It's fine. It's fine. Carry it all on your own. Carry it and keep it to yourself. Carry it and find solace in their freedoms.

I breathed deeply, trying very hard to obey myself. "Okay, cool, uh, I'll just head to town then." I stood and sidled my way past him. As I did this, though, his eyes narrowed on me.

"Ya roight, son? Ya need nothin' while ya here? Ya look toired. I'd no' begrudge ya toime off. Ya know this?"

I tried my best to smile at him. "I know, Father. Thank you."

I practically sprinted out of the boathouse and down the dock, not bothering to look back. I knew he was watching me. I could feel his scrutiny. Being in his presence sent me into a deep, almost drowning guilt. Made all the worse in knowing I was lying to him. He trusted me implicitly.

I ran down the beach, forgoing my usual hoodie. I'd come to hate the thing. It meant death, that hood. That dark, foreboding hood. I ran up the incline toward the canopy of trees and through the grove, over the path, hitting the shell gravel, my aim stood

334

there but along with it came the sweetest yet most intimidating view.

I slid to a stop in front of the bike. "Hello, Finley."

Her face was reserved, devoid of anything telling. "Hello, Ethan."

"I'm, uh, headed into town."

She straightened her back and folded her arms across her chest. "Oh yeah? For what?"

"Gotta get a few parts for Father's houseboat. It's, uh, it's fallin' apart."

"Is it?"

"Yup," I said, shoving my hand into my pocket for the key to the bike. I memorized her face. That face. That face. That *face*. "You wanna come with me?" I asked, devastated by her, but not trying to show it. I climbed on and the entire bike sank lower with my weight as if in sync with my heart.

Her brows furrowed. "Do you want me to?"

My jaw clenched and I stared at her. "Of course I do. I want you with me. Always."

Her face softened a little but no words came as she straddled the bike, sitting behind me. My breaths sped up in preparation for her hands. *Please,* I thought. Her fingers found my sides and I clenched the muscles there to keep from trembling. *Finally.*

I brought my right palm up and rested it on top of her left hand. I looked down and spoke in a low-pitched tone toward the earth. "I love you."

She hugged herself closer to me, wrapped her hands around me, and rested her cheek against my shoulder. "Do you?" she asked, making my heart break.

"How could you ask me that?"

She paused. "I love you too," she declared softly, setting me back to rights.

My hand left hers, found the key to the ignition, and turned. We rode into the town proper in search of a hardware store, not that I had any idea where one would be. We rode down the streetways, examining the shops around us in hopes of finding something that even remotely resembled one. We rode for almost an hour and by the end of that hour, I'd lost complete awareness of myself. I no longer cared for the repair shop. I cared for nothing but Fin.

On a side glance, I noticed a tea shop tucked into a corner of an intersection and pulled over, parking my bike next to hundreds of others that lined the sides of the street. I turned the bike off but neither of us made a move to get off.

"I'm very tired," I told her.

"Tired can mean so many things," she replied. She got off the bike and headed into the small five-by-ten-foot tea shop. I found myself running my hands down both walls as I followed her through the narrow shop to the counter in the back. She ordered our teas in Vietnamese, paid quickly, then left me where I stood to sit at a table nearest the front of the shop. I walked back to the wide, exposed entrance open to the street and sat next to her.

Her hands were folded on the table in front of her, her purple nail polish and many rings glistening in the noonday sun next to our teas. She turned to me, smiled sadly, then returned her gaze toward her hands. The thumb of her left hand began to trace the curling edges of the shop's plastic menu.

"Finley," I spoke.

Her thumb stilled. "Yes?"

"Are you upset?"

"Without a doubt," she said without hesitation.

"What about?" I asked, my heart racing in my chest. The palm of my hand found the pounding there and pressed.

"You're keeping something," she said, watching my hand. I dropped it at my side. "I can't figure it out because I can't get close to you. You won't let me."

"I'm right here," I told her, sinking into my chair a little. I stared out into the street and observed the passersby.

"You're a million miles away," she said.

I turned my head her direction. "I'm here," I said and sat up. I grabbed one of her hands with both of mine and brought it to my chest. "I'm right here."

She tugged her hand from mine. "No, I don't think you are."

"I am," I told her, running my hands through my short hair. I stared at her; my eyes pierced through hers. "What more do you want from me?"

She smiled knowingly. "I don't want anything from you at all," she told me, wounding me.

She stood, never having taken a single sip of her tea, and began to walk the sidewalk toward the day market. Something about our conversation scared me. So little had been said, yet there was something so final lying underneath it, like a venomous snake waiting to attack.

I left my cup behind, its contents untouched, and pursued her. She walked briskly, as if her destination was a settled place, and I wondered where she was going.

I sped up, determined to catch her. *Don't lose her. Don't lose her.* When I was near, I reached out and grabbed her elbow, staying her in her place in the middle of the busy sidewalk. People parted around us. We were jutting rocks in river rapids.

"Every step you take away from me, Finley Dyer, is a knife to my chest!" I yelled over the din of voices and traffic. "I don't know why! Why does this feel so painful?"

She turned toward me, her eyes glassy. "This is what it feels like to be torn apart, Ethan, that's why," she yelled, not out of anger, but to be heard.

I yanked her into me and hugged her to keep her near me. "Why do you think that?" I asked in her ear.

"I can feel you," she said, clutching my shirt at my shoulders. "I can touch you, feel you, smell you, see you, but you—" she said, pressing her palm into my chest, my heart, "*this* you is somewhere else, Ethan. I've been looking for you, searching for you, calling for you, but you don't answer me. You're living somewhere else and I feel the distance, smell the distance, see the distance. I can *taste* the distance, Ethan, and my God, is it bitter." She let go of me and I detested the absence. "Come back to me, Ethan," she whispered. "Come back. Come back. Come to me, Ethan," she said, her hands fisting the fabric at her stomach. Tears spilled from her eyes.

"I'm trying. Can't you see that I'm trying? God!" I said, gripping the hair at the top of my head. "This was never my intention. I just wanted to earn you," I foolishly admitted. "I wanted to earn you."

"How?" she asked, mistaking my meaning. "How could you earn me when I've given myself so freely to you, Ethan! How many times do I have to tell you that I already belong to you. You've already got me, Ethan. I'm yours," she said, extending her arms at her side, making the unthinking, passing people bend to her whim, like leaves swirling with the wind.

I made a move to grab her, but she let her arms fall before I could do so.

Her eyes narrowed. "When you say it was never your intention. What do you mean?"

"Nothing," I said, remembering myself.

"Why so many secrets, Ethan?"

"Listen, these-these troubles I'm in, these issues I'm dealing with. They're my own to handle. I need to handle them on my own."

"If you remember, I've said those very words," she said. "I thought the same thing, the very same thing."

"It's different."

"Not possible."

"Yes, it's different."

"I assure you, there is nothing, no grievance, no sin, no offense in this entire world that can be solved better alone than not."

Do not tell her!

"I can't."

"You can. When I said no, when I pushed you away trying to shoulder the weight of my difficulties on my own, when I thought I was strong enough, you came in and saved me, Ethan, when I hadn't even known I was falling. Sometimes you can carry something so heavy you aren't even aware of the millstone. It crushes you, leaving you unaware of it until it's almost too late. Open your eyes, Ethan."

My chest panted. "Even if I wanted to tell you, even if I wanted to share this with you, with Father, with Sister, with-with God," I swallowed, "I could never be forgiven. Not by you, not by anyone else, and certainly not by God. *I'm* the ruined one, Fin. I ruined myself. And there is no going back," I told her. "I am going to finish what I started because I have created a monster that needs to be destroyed. My carelessness has created that monster, and I am the *only* one who can defeat it!"

"Ethan," she began, her voice trembling, "when you say monster—" Her face went blank. "Ethan, Tran was at Slánaigh earlier today. He was looking for you. Said he wanted to speak with you. Does-does this have something to do with-with *that*?" she asked with slight hesitation.

I walked around her, left her standing there. I had work to do and it would no longer keep. I felt for my knives fitted in the back of my jeans and felt a sense of relief.

"What monster?" she screamed, desperate. "What are you talking about, Ethan?!" She grasped at my clothing in an attempt to get me to stop, but I trudged on back toward the bike. "Ethan!" she cried, her voice rising an extraordinary octave. "Ethan! Stop!" she said, yanking my arm. "Ethan, stop!"

When we reached the bike, I threw my hand in my pocket and pulled out the key. "Here," I said, handing it to her.

"No—" she began, but I wouldn't let her continue.

"Go back to Slánaigh, Finley. I won't be back for several days."

I stuck the key in her hand without asking.

"Ethan," she said, her voice frantic. "Where are you going?"

"I promised myself I'd protect you, and this is me protecting you."

"Jesus! Ethan! What are you talking about?! Fill me in! Is this about Tran? Did-did you do something. Does this have something to do with the girls after all? Did you take those girls, Ethan?" I sighed but refused to answer. "Oh my God, you did. You did take them. Oh my God. Okay. Okay. This is okay. See, we can just escape back to Montana. Father will fix everything here," she rambled hysterically, her eyes shifting side to side as she wrung her hands.

"No, my love," I told her. "He cannot fix this."

"He can fix anything," she said, her eyes wide with fear.

"Not this, Fin. Trust me."

"What do you mean? What do you *mean*?"

I ran both my hands down the sides of her hair, my thumbs across her cheekbones. "My God, do I love you, Fin." I let go of her, so she grabbed my forearms, her nails biting into my skin.

"Wait," she cried. "Wait! Jesus, please, just wait!"

"Get on the bike, Fin," I ordered.

"No. You owe me an explanation, Ethan. I deserve more than orders."

"If I told you, I could endanger you. Just please get on the bike and head back to Slánaigh."

"Endanger me? I understand you taking the girls has created an issue, but Khanh has dealt with much worse than just a few girls being taken, Ethan. You're blowing this out of proportion!"

"Get on the damn bike, Fin!" I shouted, shocking her silent.

Her face settled into something that resembled calculation, her body relaxed. She climbed onto the bike and started it up, kicking the kickstand up. "You're a fool," she said, staring at me as the bike idled. "I'm here, giving myself to you, making myself vulnerable to you in order to help you, to love you, and you keep pushing me away. You're such a bloody fool," she finished. She backed up and sped away, her last sentence lingering in the air around me before settling on my clothes, staining them red.

I was a *bloody* fool.

CHAPTER THIRTY-EIGHT

Ethan

I took the bus to Hanoi with no intention of returning to Hạ Long Bay any time soon. I had a few hundred American dollars in my pocket and retribution on my mind. I was going to finish what I'd started because I'd considered my soul, my mind damned and knew I had nothing to lose.

I was going to decimate Khanh, his cells, every single person who bought from him or even *thought* about buying from him. When I was done with them, those hands, all those dirty, filthy hands that left the beautiful spoiled and extinguished their lovely would be in a fitful sleep. Not even the crawling, slithering creatures within the dirt they lived beneath would eat their flesh when I was done with them.

To save girls. To save Slánaigh. To save Finley Dyer. If I had to die trying, I was going to protect her from the damage I'd done. Even if it meant I would lose her forever.

CHAPTER THIRTY-NINE

Ethan

I arrived in Hanoi around seven in the evening, spotted a shop that sold men's clothing for tourists, and found a black hoodie that fit me. I paid for my purchase and found a taxi almost immediately.

"Nineteen Kim Mã," I told the driver, and he took off.

I was looking for Dai.

When he pulled up to the building, I entered without a single thought to the danger I could be in. The first floor was empty and short with a narrow staircase taking up almost the entire length to the second floor. I yanked my folded leather holster out of the side of my boot and put it on over my T-shirt. I removed my knives, sheathed them, then zipped my new hoodie.

"There, that's better," I told no one. "Dai!" I screamed out.

Two doors shot open and five men spilled out of them, flanking one very small man.

I smiled at him. "You Dai?"

He smiled back. "Who are you?" he asked.

"I was sent here," I told him, recognizing the stabbing victim I left alive. I looked him dead in the eye. I tsked three times. "I warned you, did I not?"

His eyes blew wide and his body began to tremble. Before long, a wet spot started at his crotch before a puddle surrounded his feet. The men beside him shuffled away from him, eyeing him, then eyeing me. Realization dawned on them.

They all threw their automatics up, pointing them directly at me.

Breathe.

Dai turned to the man who'd given him up. He screamed something in Vietnamese.

"Let me guess," I told Dai, "he didn't tell you I was coming?" I leaned my shoulder against the wall, wrapped my arms across my chest for better access to my knives. I did this as casually as possible. "How embarrassing. Excuse me just dropping by unannounced then. I apologize."

Dai laughed then tilted his head, examining me. "You're the killer."

I lifted my right hand and saluted him. "At your service."

Dai laughed again. "I'm going to kill you, you know."

"You are?" I asked jovially.

"Yes, I'm going to cut your head from your body, feed that body to my pigs, and parade your head around on a pole for all to see, to warn anyone who ever tries to oppose us again."

His men started laughing at his gruesome depiction of my death. I was done playing.

Breathe.

"I'm so sorry, Dai, but I'm afraid I have my own plans."

Breathe.

"You do, do you? I can't wait to hear these plans."

Breathe.

"Here, let me show them to you," I said, and without a second thought I bounded up the stairs, yanking off a spindle I'd noted was loose when I'd entered the hall.

Breathe.

They weren't expecting me to jump up the stairs and although their bullets were quick, their movements were not. The spray was too slow. I swung myself over the railing, kicking the two men in the back in their heads, stunning them.

Breathe.

I whirled the spindle around, hitting the man to Dai's right, knocking him down to his knees.

Breathe.

I continued with the rotation and caught the other two men in front, stunning them as well.

Breathe.

Dai's eyes and mouth widened in disbelief. He reached, probably for a handgun tucked into the back of his pants, but I beat him there, smiling when he realized his hand reached too late.

Breathe.

I swung just as the two men in the back stood, pointing their weapons my direction. First shot. Second shot. They were down.

Breathe.

As the three men in front of Dai started to stand, I shot the first two as they too reached for their weapons,

346

ready to turn them on me. They fell in a heap on the floor.

Breathe.

Dai's hands flew up in surrender.

Breathe.

I left my stabbing victim for last.

"What did I tell you?" I asked him.

Breathe.

He fell to his knees, his hands clasped together. "Please!" he begged, "I just sell the girls! I don't do anything to them!"

Breathe.

"Convincing," I told him, raising my gun to his forehead. "The last face you'll ever see," I reminded him. His expression turned panicked. I pulled the trigger, his face stuck in fear.

Breathe.

I turned the gun toward Dai.

Breathe.

"I'll give you whatever you want."

Breathe.

"*Now* you play the good host!" I shook my head sarcastically. I smiled at him. "I'm afraid it's too late, though."

Breathe.

"I'll give you anything. Anything."

Breathe.

"Bargaining. Very manly. Okay, let's do this," I said, my feet spread apart. I settled the gun against my forearm as I crossed my arms. "How about you give all the little girls you've stolen from back their innocence? How does that sound?"

He began to pant like a coward.

"You want money?" he countered. "I have lots of money. I'll give it all to you."

Breathe.

"Nope. No money. Give them back their innocence and we have a deal."

Breathe.

"I-I can't," he whimpered.

Breathe.

"Why not?" I asked.

Breathe.

"You are strange. I don't understand why you are asking me this."

Breathe.

"I'm asking because I want to hear your answer out loud, Dai."

Breathe.

"I can't give you that deal."

Breathe.

"And why not?"

Breathe.

"Because it is irreversible."

Breathe.

"Bingo! You know what else is irreversible?"

Breathe.

He started crying. "What?" he asked, blubbering.

Breathe.

"Death, Dai. Death is irreversible."

Breathe.

He began to sob uncontrollably.

Breathe.

I furrowed my brows. "Please, Dai, you can send innocent little girls into the dens of devils but you can't face a little thing like death?"

Breathe.

He fell to his knees and buried his head in his hands. "I don't want to die!"

Breathe.

"You want to know something, Dai?" I asked. "Only people like you fear death with the despair that you fear it now."

Breathe.

"Please," he begged. "Anything you want!"

"Tell you what," I said, "you tell me where Khanh is and I'll make your death quick."

He clawed at my feet, begging me to spare him.

"Did you hear me, Dai? Tell me where I can find Khanh."

Breathe.

"I will tell you if you spare me," he tried to arrange.

Breathe.

"How about this, you tell me where I can find Khanh and maybe I'll *think* about sparing you. Best offer."

Breathe.

"He's here in the Ba Dinh District."

Breathe.

He's close. My heart leapt into my throat. "Where?"

Breathe.

"Are you going to kill me?"

Breathe

"Take me to him," I told him. "How far is he?"

Breathe.

"Not far. Not far," he explained, seemingly relieved.

He thinks he's going to get away.

Breathe.

"Get up. Lead the way." When he stood, I placed the gun at his lower back and stood closely. "Run and I'll kill you on the spot. Do you understand?"

Breathe.

"Yes," he said, his body shaking.

Breathe.

Dai walked slowly out of the building toward the West Lake area. We walked for thirty minutes in silence. In that time, his breathing slowed, steadied.

"You think you're going to get away," I told him. His body went stiff. "I can tell in your body language. No one escapes me unless I want them to."

He gulped.

"Give me a time estimate."

"Another ten minutes."

"Where is it?"

Feeling comfortable, I assumed, because we were in public, he answered, "It's a nightclub on the water."

"Khanh owns a nightclub?"

Dai laughed. "He owns many. Lots of foreigners come in and partake of his offered *services.*"

Breathe.

"He sells little girls there?"

Dai laughed again. "He sells everything there. The girls aren't on the floor, of course, like the older prostitutes, but he has them there."

"Prostitutes?"

"When the girls grow old, he sticks them in the clubs to service patrons with an older taste."

"I see," I said, pissed beyond belief. My blood curdled in my veins. "The girls in the clubs," I

350

observed, "they are girls he's used since they were small?"

"Yes," he answered.

"Why don't they just run away?" I asked, feeling chatty.

"They grow—how do I say this—*accustomed* to their lifestyles. He pays them a percentage of their earnings. It becomes their job."

I shook my head at this. "They *willingly* do this?"

Dai turned his head toward me. "Many of them don't know any other kind of life."

That's tragic, I thought.

Dai took a left on Yên Phụ and I followed suit, pressing the gun into his back to let him know it was still there.

Within five minutes, he pointed at a building several stories high with a club on the bottom floor in the middle of the busy, foliage-covered street. Tall palm trees lined the street near the club's sidewalk. It was a newer building, designed to look old with architectural details reminiscent of ancient Vietnam. It appeared to own two large two-story wood arching doors with alternative entrances within each. The building was a yellow plaster and was flanked on either side with two deep red pagodas that reached up into the sky, taller than the building itself.

It'd grown exceptionally dark by the time we'd arrived and the club was thriving. Expensive-looking motorcycles lined the street outside the club's doors and seemingly stretched for miles.

Having become familiar with Vietnam's government, I knew regular citizens weren't its patrons. A regular Vietnamese couldn't have afforded them. Those motorcycles belonged to high government officials, their children, expats, and tourists.

"Ah, I see," I told no one, but Dai answered anyway.

"Yes."

I thought of something when he spoke. "Do you have children, Dai?"

"Yes, I do," he said.

"How old are they?"

"They are adults now with children of their own."

"Do you love your children? Your grandchildren?"

"Yes," he answered.

"Then how could you do this line of work?"

"I was very poor. I could not afford to eat, to feed my family. One day, one of Khanh's men approached me, told me he could help me. I knew what he did, so I refused him. The next day he came. Again, I told him no. I told him no for three weeks straight until one day my wife needed medicine so I gave in. I agreed to run errands for Khanh himself.

"It was easy at first. I never saw any of the girls he sold. I never saw anything but the pretty clubs. Gradually, I was introduced to *other* jobs, darker jobs. I became used to the sights, the sounds. Soon I did not notice any injustice. I was given a house, a car, a chance to make more money, so I took it."

"You have regrets?" I asked.

"Many."

"Do you regret this life? What you've done?"

"Yes."

"How do I know if you're lying?"

"I cannot prove it to you, but if helps you understand, I will tell you a story. My wife died last year. My children loved her very much. I would see them so often because of her. I only knew them because she alone brought them to our house. I did not know this until she had died. When she died, my children stopped showing up, they stopped knowing me. I would call them repeatedly, try to gift them money, but they refused me."

"Why?"

"Because they knew what I had become. They knew who I'd become to get our house, our car, our money. And they hated me for it."

"Then why continue?"

"It's too late for me," he said, reminding me of someone. *But who?*

It's never too late, I thought instinctively. *No, he's right. It is too late. For both of us.*

"If I let you go," I said, curious, "what would you do?"

"I would run to Khanh. I would tell him you were coming."

"And if I prevented you from doing that?"

"Nothing would prevent me other than death."

"Why, Dai?"

"Because I'm entrenched and I like it."

"Then you will die by my hand tonight, Dai. I will steal your soul."

He turned his head and smiled, the smile of the devil himself. "You can't steal something that's already been stolen."

Breathe.

We walked to the front of the club and inside without any trouble. I figured this was either because

353

they recognized Dai and thought nothing of it or they recognized Dai and played it cool until they could get to the hooded guy behind him. I was betting on the latter.

I let Dai move ahead before sinking into the crowd of people near the bar, pushing down my hoodie, and crouching to blend in better. I noticed Dai looked behind him to see if I was there. The look on his face was one of shock. He looked around him, searching for me. After a minute, he gave up and raced through the crowd to a pair of elevator doors at the back of the club.

I noticed he placed his thumb on a fingerprint reader and the doors opened for him.

Breathe.

I had no idea how I was going to follow him at that point. I watched the lit numbers above the elevator doors. Floor six. The top floor. I made a break for the elevator doors, raising my hood one more time. I unzipped my jacket, making sure the flaps still covered the knives.

There was a line of ten or so scantily clad women sitting at the bar wearing too much makeup and sporting way too much skin. The prostitutes.

Breathe.

I looked around for someone who looked like they belonged at the club and spotted a waitress with a very short skirt carrying a tray.

"You," I said, catching her attention.

"Drink?" she asked.

I shook my head and held up a folded fifty. "Open the elevator."

She casually walked forward toward the doors and placed her thumb on the pad. When the doors opened, I handed her the fifty and she left without another word.

Too easy.

I knew she would be notifying Khanh, but it was a moot point. Dai had beat her to it. I hit the button for the fifth floor, not wanting to risk an automatic sixth floor attack. Although I had no idea what was on five, I did know for a fact what was on six.

Breathe.

When the elevator car reached the fifth floor, I tucked myself against the button panel, laying flat against the wall.

Breathe.

The doors opened but nothing came barrelling toward me. I placed my left foot in front of the door and looked out. There was nothing but a large room with doors lining walls. I stuck my head out farther, left and right. It looked like some sort of spa. All white with wood accents. There was a comfortable-looking waiting area as well as an attractive woman sitting at a reception desk, which shocked me.

She got up with a smile on her face, ready to greet me. When she saw I came unaccompanied, though, her expression twisted into confusion.

"How did you get up here?" she asked, unafraid.

"I'm looking for Khanh," I told her.

Her eyes widened and she screamed something in Vietnamese, running toward her desk, no doubt to alert Khanh and his men.

Breathe.

I ran to her before she could, swooping an arm around her waist and tossing her away from her desk. She yelped and landed on the white marble floor.

"No, no," I told her. She opened her mouth to scream but abruptly closed it when I raised Dai's gun at her. "Stay," I ordered as I went around to each of the seven doors and opened them, keeping my gun trained on her at all times. They were all empty except for a bed and a bathroom in each. I decided they were private rooms for the girls from downstairs. They all had such a Western feel, I knew they were reserved for the high-dollar tourists. I walked back to her.

"Now, tell me everything you know about him. How tall he is, what he weighs, how many men he keeps around, what are his skill sets. I want to know *everything*. Now talk."

Breathe.

Her lips trembled. "He is a big man."

"How tall?"

"He would reach your shoulders."

"His weight?"

"Seventy-five kilograms. Give or take."

Okay, I've got about twenty-five pounds on him.

"How many men in the building work for him?"

She started crying. "Seventeen in security for Khanh, another eighty or so that come and go. They run his cells and drop off cash throughout the night."

"Does he keep a gun on him? Any weapons?"

"No, he keeps nothing on him."

Yeah, right.

"What else should I know about him?"

"He's going to kill you," she said without feeling.

"Thank you," I told her.

I walked to her desk and ripped the telephone cord and wire from the wall and phone. I walked back over to her as she began to whimper. I wrapped the cord around her ankles several times, hogtying her. With one swift movement, I lifted her up and carried her to the bed of the first room nearest the elevator. I ripped a piece of cloth from the sheet on it and stuffed it in her mouth.

"Go ahead and scream if you want."

She screamed a muffled sound but enough to gain someone's attention if they entered the fifth floor. Just what I'd wanted. I walked over to her desk and examined it until I discovered the silent alarm. Before pressing it, I checked for weapons and stumbled upon a loaded gun attached to velcro beneath the underside. I removed it from its holster and checked the clip. Full.

Absently whistling "Tighten Up" by The Black Keys, I triggered the silent alarm, closed every open door besides the girl's, and made my way to the room on the opposite side near the receptionist desk. I cracked open the door and pressed myself against the jamb.

Breathe.

I heard the ding of the elevator door. My jaw clamped.

Breathe.

Breathe.

Breathe.

Footsteps rang out, too many to count. The room I'd chosen was well hidden but also constricted my view.

Breathe.

They ran to the receptionist's room when they heard her struggle. They screamed in Vietnamese and I took advantage of their distraction, creeping out of my door

357

and setting up shop behind the desk. Seven men that I could see.

Breathe.

One shot. Down. Two shots. Down. Three shots. Down. They came running out, a look of complete surprise on each of their faces right before I fell them where they stood. Before long, no one else came out and the only sound was the receptionist's muffled bawling.

Breathe.

Whistling "Tighten Up" again, I hopscotched over the men's dead bodies and stuck my head through the door. "Try to stay calm."

I made my way toward the elevator but remembered something and turned back around. I gathered as many handguns as I could, shoving them inside the waistband of my jeans. I strapped two automatics around my chest. I unsheathed one of my short swords and bent down. I chopped off one of the men's thumbs and stuck it in my pocket. I needed a way to access the elevator.

"Sit tight," I told the girl. "Not much longer." She screamed into the sheet gagging her mouth.

When I got to the elevator, I pulled out the severed thumb and placed it against the electronic reader. The pad beeped and the doors opened.

I stepped inside, dropping the thumb at my feet by accident. I picked it back up and stuck it in my pocket.

I hit the button for floor two, intending to work my way back up.

Breathe.

I balanced the automatics on my hips, keeping both my hands on the triggers. The doors wouldn't open. They required electronic access through the thumb pad. I let go of one of the automatics and retrieved the thumb again, placing it on the access pad near the button panel. It beeped. I picked up the automatic again. The doors opened.

Breathe.

A holding room. At least twenty-five children, girls *and* boys, between the ages of five and fifteen sat wide-eyed on the floor of an open room, drinking broth from bowls. I set the guns down then looked around the doors and took in their guards. Three men. Far right corner. No children near them. Eating at a table.

Breathe.

"Khanh sent me to fetch you," I said.

Breathe.

They looked at one another, confused. "He's pissed! Come on! Get up there!" I yelled.
They scrambled up, convinced my presence had to be legitimate, despite the fact that I spoke in English. How else would I have gotten in their elevator? Why else would I be there?

Breathe.

They scurried onto the elevator and as the doors closed, I winked at them, stuck my handgun near the barely there opening and shot three times, killing all three. Not a single child screamed, shocking me.

Breathe.

I tucked the gun into the back of my waistband then turned around toward them. Their presence snapped something in me. Their faces reminded me of why I was there.

Breathe.

"Who can speak English?"

A girl, maybe fifteen years old, stood.

"I do, " she said.

"What's your name?" I said calmly.

"Vi."

"Vi, I'm Ethan."

"Ethan," she repeated softly.

"I, uh, I'm going to get you all out of here. I have some things to take care of first, though, so I need you all to remain here. Do *not* leave. Do not step foot on that elevator until I come back for you. Understood?"

She nodded. A few others who understood, nodded as well, then began to translate to those who didn't. Before long, lots of faces were nodding.

"I'll be back," I told them, using the thumb once more to open the elevator doors.

I stepped inside, stood amongst the three dead men, and pressed the button for the third floor.

Breathe.

When the doors opened and I stepped through, I discovered it was yet another "entertaining" floor. The receptionist smiled briefly before taking in my arsenal. She'd yet to be warned I was coming because I'd killed anyone who could have warned her.

"Hands up," I told her and she obeyed. "Do you have anyone behind these doors?" I asked. She nodded. "Which ones." She pointed at three of the six doors. I bounded up to her and tied her up as I had the first girl.

"Stay quiet," I told her. She nodded.

Breathe.

I went to the first door and walked in on a sixty-year-old man with what looked like a fourteen-year-old girl. The girl scurried to one side of the room when the man turned to see who had interrupted him, tears were in her eyes.

Breathe.

"Stay," I told the girl then yanked the man by his hair, dragging him through the door, and placed him inside an empty room. I killed him without hesitation.

Breathe

When I came out, the men in the other two occupied rooms had come out to see what had happened. I smiled at them.

"Gentlemen," I said raising two handguns at each of their faces, "this way."
I stepped aside, exposing the dead child molester in the room behind me.

They both screamed and ran for the elevator that wouldn't work for them. They didn't have the magic touch. *But I do.* Two swift shots to the head and they went down. I dragged their bodies, their lifeblood leaving trails behind them, and put them in the room with the first.

Breathe.

I took the three girls with me to the second floor and dropped them off.

"Remember, no one leaves until I come back. I *will* protect you," I told them.

I made my way toward the elevators, stuck the thumb on the fingerprinting pad, and entered, pressing the button for the fourth floor.

Breathe.

My heart beat wildly in my chest.

Breathe.

The doors opened. Straight ahead there was nothing, just stacks of old club furniture, but my peripheral was blocked. I crouched down. Took one of the handguns in my waistband, removed the clip, placed it in my pocket, then threw the useless gun out into the middle of the room.

Immediately, I heard gunshots.

Breathe.

I readied the automatics, threw myself out of the elevator, turning onto my back, and began spraying both sides of the room.

They returned fire.

Breathe.

Something burned, stung as I went sliding across the concrete floor, making me grit my teeth.

I was hit.

Breathe.

I continued to shoot until all men had fallen. I counted at least fifteen on each side. I stayed down for two reasons.

One, I had no idea if there were more. Hidden.

Two, my legs were in sudden agony.

Breathe.
Rise above it, I heard Akule's voice in my head. *Rise above it.*
Breathe.

Out of bullets, I tossed the automatics, and removed two of the four handguns I had left. I flipped over on my stomach, ignoring the fiery pain in my legs. Scanning through the furniture, I spotted two pairs of feet at the back of the room. I rolled myself against a stack of chairs and took aim with one gun.

Breathe.

First shot. One man fallen. Second shot. Second man fallen.

Breathe.

Both fell at eye level with me. Both saw me. Both pointed their weapons at me. Both died within a second.

Breathe.

Scanning the rest of the room, I found no other signs of life. Using one of the stacks of chairs, I lifted my body with an agonizing shout. I gnashed my teeth together to defeat the misery. I put my weight on my legs and almost fell back down. Razor-sharp torture shot down my legs then back up my body. I let out one final muted bellow, my body breaking out into an intense sweat from the effort. I wiped my eyes clear with the bottom of my T-shirt and made purposeful strides toward the elevator doors.

I rose above it.

CHAPTER FORTY

Ethan

Breathe.

The elevator door closed. I pressed the button for the sixth floor. The brief ride was peppered with images of Finley. I had a sickening feeling of finality I'd never see her again. I thought back on all of my bad decisions. The decisions that ultimately prevented my forever life with her. I thought back on what had motivated me to do it. *She* was that everything. She was my foundation, my supporting walls, my attic full of secrets, my sheltering roof. She was my home.

My eyes stung at the memory of her driving away from me. My last words to her should not have been my last. My last words to her should have been everything she'd deserved. They should have been private, astounding words spoken from a marital bed made undone by us. By us. By *us*.

Those should have been my last words... before I'd began new words, new promises.

I'd made such an incredible mess of our lives.
Of so many good people's lives. I had no regrets when
it came to saving the innocents I'd saved, but I should
have found another way. A way that didn't cause more
rife, more suffering, more difficulties. I should have
been patient. I should have quelled the fury that rose
so easily in my heart and soul and mind and hands.

Breathe.

The doors opened slowly. And there. Ten feet
from me, surrounded by a small army of armed men,
stood a man I couldn't have mistaken for anyone other
than who he was. He was grotesque, wearing a smile of
triumph, with the most hollow, malevolent eyes I'd
ever seen owned by another human being. My body
shuddered.

"Khanh."

Breathe.

"In the flesh," his voice grated, the tone oozing
something so profoundly disturbing it made me want
to claw away my ears. His arms extended from his
sides in presentation. I fought the urge to throw a knife
at his open target of a black heart. It was so dark I felt
it could be seen through his shirt, beating the irregular
rhythm only shared by those whose soul had been
sold.

Breathe.

"Come in," he said, gesturing me forward. He
was young, much younger than I would have thought,
maybe twenty-five. He did indeed reach my shoulders.
I'd guess five feet ten inches. He was not one hundred
percent Vietnamese, mixed with something else,

something European. He was barefoot, casual, in a very American look of jeans and a T-shirt, as if the men surrounding him hadn't weapons trained on me. I looked down. Red lasers painted the entire length of my body. I looked up and saw Dai's smiling face.

Breathe.

I stepped inside and absently noted that my boots were filling with blood from my legs.

Breathe.

"Take a seat," he said, pointing to a part of sectional opposite where he'd tossed himself onto like a little kid.

He picked up a controller and started playing a video game on the large flat screen perpendicular to the windows that faced the night lights of Hanoi I sat with my back to. I felt so confused, wondering why he hadn't killed me yet.

Breathe.

"You're so young," I observed.

He laughed as his fingers clicked the controller, his eyes stayed trained on the TV. "That I am."

"Did your parents get you into this?" I asked, trying to figure out how the young, seemingly normal guy in front of me had gotten into the business he'd gotten into.

"Nah, self-made, baby."

"No need to brag to me, asshole," I said, leaning back into the sofa, making myself comfortable. "I've seen your business firsthand."

He stared through me with his horrific eyes and threw the controller at his side.

"Yeah, you have."

He sat up a little and his men followed the movement.

Breathe.

"You've been a busy bee, haven't you?" He leaned in menacingly.

I met him face to face. "Not as busy as I'd have liked."

He stood abruptly. My hand went for one of my guns but he turned just as quickly and made his way toward the kitchen. His men's guns were still trained on me.

"Come in here," he said, rummaging through cabinets.

I stood, making my way toward him.

"Would you like some tea?" he asked, placing a kettle on his gigantic range.

"No," I told him, edging around the men there.

He turned toward me, placing his hands at the end of a long kitchen island. "I have a proposition for you," he said.

"No," I answered.

He laughed. "You haven't even heard what I had to say."

"There's nothing you could possibly say that would sway me from my task."

"That's too bad," he said. "Because I've never seen anyone like you," he explained, grabbing a packet of monk fruit and setting it on the surface of the island. He walked to his sub-zero and grabbed a bottle of whipping cream. When he placed it next to the monk fruit, he said, "Bad habit. Mother's French." He stared at me. "You would be quite the asset for me," he continued. "I would be unstoppable with someone like you."

"It is too bad, because I'd rather die than work for you."

The kettle whistled shrilly into the thick air around us. "Really?" he asked, taking it from the lit burner and pouring hot water over a silver tea strainer in his cup. He placed his hands on either side to let it steep. We sat in an eerie silence for two minutes, seven seconds. I'd counted.

He removed the strainer and set it on a dish to drain. He poured the sweetener and the cream in, stirring with a metal spoon. The metal grated the bottom of the ceramic and the sound filled the room. He clicked the side of the spoon on the rim of the cup then set the spoon down on the cup's saucer. He lifted the cup to take a sip. When he swallowed, he set the cup back down with a loud clink.

"Maybe *you* would rather die but would *she*?" he said, startling me. He pulled something from his pocket, unfolded it, and brought it up to eye level, flashing it at me. It was a picture of Fin and me.

Fury built within me with such rapid heat, I thought my hands would melt through the surface of the island. I gripped the edges, certain they would crumble under the strain.

"She's quite pretty," he said. "I might keep her to myself for a few weeks until I tire of her. Or I could sell her to the highest bidder. Many, many men are eager for tall, leggy, gorgeous Western women. They're always my biggest sellers on the auction blocks."

My body trembled with the need to abolish him, stamp him out, annihilate him.

"Or perhaps I'll cut her up in little pieces and feed her to the children," he said, his eyes blazing with intensity.

"You are going to die," I told him. I heard the men around me shift closer.

He laughed then sighed, picking up his cup, and leaning one hand on the countertop. He took a sip. "It's too bad. Just too bad," he repeated, shaking his head. He set the cup back down. "Kill him," he said, walking toward the sub-zero to put the cream back.

Breathe.

Breathe.

Breathe.
Burner still on. Ceramic teacup. Kettle. Boiling water. Metal magnet strip on kitchen wall. Chef's knife. Meat carver. Santoku knife. Slicing knife. Six steak knives.
Breathe.
Four handguns. Unknown number of bullets.
Breathe.
My *short swords*.
Breathe.
No immediate cover. Fridge door, maybe?

Breathe.

Breathe.
I reached for the kettle full of boiling water and scattered the contents on the men behind me. They dropped their guns as they reached for their eyes and faces. I bent to pick up one of the abandoned automatics, rolled across the island, and landed on the other side, nearest Khanh.

I smiled at him as his eyes widened, his hands flew up in the air. "No! No! Don't shoot! You'll hit me!" I laughed.

"Isn't it too bad?" I asked him. I raised a handgun and shot him in the foot. He fell to the ground, screaming. I rolled up, yanked open the sub-zero door, and stood behind it. Khanh began to crawl through the kitchen toward his men, but I yanked him back to me, pulling him up, using his body as a shield.

Breathe.

I walked Khanh toward his men and raised my weapon. I fired off two rounds, hitting two men, but the remaining men scattered into his open-floor apartment, hiding themselves behind furniture, effectively trapping me in the kitchen near the television wall.

Breathe.

Khanh began to fight me, struggled to get away so his men could take me out. I took my handgun and shot him in the thigh of his right leg. He screamed in agony.

"Stop moving," I gritted.

Breathe.

I took note of all the men in the room, all their guns raised and aimed at me.

Breathe.

Nothing to lose.

Breathe.

I readied the automatic and unleashed a spray of bullets. As if in slow motion, the windows shattered, tufts of stuffing from the couch went flying through the air, glass exploded all around us. And the men behind the furniture were dying with shrieks. They still refused to shoot upon us. Khanh was my leverage.

He struggled in my arms, but I held tightly to his neck.

Breathe.

My automatic ran out of bullets so I tossed it aside, reaching for one of my only three handguns left.

Breathe.

"Attack him!" Khanh yelled out to the ones who survived the spray, taking me by surprise.

Breathe.

Five men approached quickly. Too quickly. One of those men was Dai.

Breathe.

I pushed Khanh down toward the wood floor.

Breathe.

I pulled out another one of the handguns and raised both arms. One shot. One man down. Two shots. Second man down.

Breathe.

I'd run out of time.

Breathe.

The remaining two men along with Dai rushed me, overcoming me before I'd gotten a chance to shoot them. I dropped both of the guns. I crossed my arms within my hoodie and pulled out my knives. They whistled with the swiftness of their release and the sound was music to my ears. Knives I knew. Knives I was comfortable with. Knives were second nature to me.

Breathe.

I spun, holding the handle of one knife so the blade ran down my forearm. I let the blade slice across one man's chest before planting the other knife in his neck. He fell where he stood. Both knives met my side once more.

Breathe.
Two to go.
Breathe.

I turned fluidly but caught a fist to the face, unable to predict it. I saw stars for a split second and stumbled back against the wall. I used it to right myself once more.

Breathe.

Another fist found my stomach, my face, my chest, my head, my temple. My eyesight swam slowly. I was losing.

Breathe.

My short swords dropped to the ground at my feet as I struggled to get Dai and the unknown man off me.

Breathe.

From the corner of my eye, I saw Khanh pick himself up and limp toward the elevator.

Breathe.

"Khanh!" I choked out. "Khanh!"

Breathe.

He turned toward me and smiled. "I'm going for her," he said, enraging me.

Breathe.

Mom, I prayed silently, *please. If you can, help me. Please, Mom.*

Breathe.

An unexpected energy filled me from within. My arms exploded out from me, sending the men flying backward.

Breathe.

I bent, grabbed a handgun from the floor, and shot the unknown without thinking twice.

Breathe.

My chest heaved as I stomped forward, Khanh my ultimate destination.

Breathe.

Dai tried to run ahead of me as if to protect him.

Breathe.

He stopped in front of Khanh, using himself as a shield.

Breathe.

My breaths pounded from my lips in a cumbersome effort, but I found my smile anyway.

Breathe.

"You protect him with your life, Dai. Why?"

Breathe.

"He pays me to."

Breathe.

"Does he pay you to die for him? Because that is your fate as of this moment."

Breathe.

"He does," Dai confirmed.

Breathe.

"And you would die for this man you yourself recognized as horrific. You would willingly do this?"

Breathe.

"I have no choice," he explained. "If I do not and he still survives, he will murder my family."

Breathe.

I looked at Khanh and he shrugged his shoulders.

Breathe.

I took one solid breath, almost choking on it. They'd done damage to my lungs. One had collapsed.

Breathe.

"If I let you go, Dai, and promise to take care of Khanh, will you leave this life?"

Breathe.

Breathe.

"I would," Dai said. "My regrets are heavy. And I feel their weight now."

Breathe.

Breathe.

"Then go," I told him.

Breathe.

Breathe.

His eyes opened as well as his mouth but before he could respond, blood pooled in the middle of his chest. All the life drained from his eyes, and he fell to his knees before collapsing into a heap onto the floor.

Breathe.

"You killed him," I told Khanh. "What for? He was insignificant to you. You are going to die anyway."

Breathe.

"I'm still going to have his family murdered," Khanh told me calmly, holding a dripping knife in his hand.

Breathe.

An inexplicable urge to vomit rose in my throat at the sight of him holding his dripping knife. He reminded me too much of myself. Tall, pale, dark hair, mixed race, bloody knife. And no hesitation to kill.

Breathe.

"Oh my God," I said. "We are no different from each other."

Khanh lifted his hands, including the knife, as Dai's blood found the floor near his feet. "We are not," he said.

Breathe.

Breathe.

"Move," I told him, making my way for the elevator. "I'm done. I have done the unthinkable. I am leaving."

Breathe.

Breathe.

"You will do nothing of the sort," he said, lifting his arm, ready to toss his knife my way.

Breathe.

Breathe.

With one swift throw, he released the knife.

Breathe.

Breathe.

Instinct kicked in. My body shifting down and away, the knife grazed my throat but never made solid contact. I stood upright.

Breathe.

Breathe.

Khanh shook his head once. He ran toward the kitchen and I followed.

Breathe.

Breathe.

He went straight for the knives on the wall, his hand picking up the Santoku knife. He backed away from me.

Breathe.

Breathe.

I picked up my short swords from the floor and followed him slowly around the island.

Breathe.

Breathe.

"You're too far gone," Khanh said. "Come join my side. I will forget these men's deaths. We would be unstoppable," he said, circling the island.

Breathe.

Breathe.

"Never," I said without hesitation. The truth was, I thought I was too far gone as well. I thought there was no saving me, but that didn't mean I would allow myself to stoop to his revolting crimes. I would rather die than touch the horrors that were his sins against children.

Breathe.

Breathe.

The grip on his knife tightened as evidenced by the whitening of his knuckles. He was done.

Breathe.

Breathe.

He tried to toss his knife at me once more, but I anticipated the move again and spun around it, choosing next to hop the island, sliding to his side of the counter. My legs met his chest, pushing him over the stove, near the ignited burner.

Breathe.

Breathe.

He tried to raise himself up but I flipped him on his side instead, palming his hair and shoulder, and pushing his face into the burner.

Breathe.

Breathe.

He cried out in anguish. His hands found the stovetop and he pushed up, grabbing for a meat mallet in a ceramic jar.

Breathe.

Breathe.

I took advantage of the movement, slid my knife across his throat, then dropped his body on the kitchen floor.

Breathe.

Breathe.

His hands frantically tried to stop the bleeding, but he gulped at the air, drowning in his own blood.

Breathe.

Breathe.

"You should have stopped," I told him.

His breath rasped from his mouth. "I'll... see... you... in... hell," he spit out, laughing and gurgling on his own blood.

Breathe.

Breathe.

He died in that moment.

I let out one final breath.

I was done *breathing*.

CHAPTER FORTY-ONE

Ethan

I hobbled out of Khan's apartment, weaving my way around the carnage I'd created. With trembling hands, I fished the severed thumb from my pocket and placed it over the reader.

"Almost done," I told the room of dead.

I traveled down to the second floor, bloody, beaten to a pulp, and overwhelmed by the weight of my own sins. The doors opened. All the children were standing in a semicircle around the doors. They'd seen the elevator descending, it seemed, and had gathered.

I brought the first elevatorful down. Ten children. I'd need at least two more trips.

The ten children emerged into the clueless club, the music still blaring, the patrons still partying. I led them out and the club took notice. Dancers stopped dancing, drinkers stopped drinking.

The entire club stopped, including the music, to gaze upon the blood-covered man and the ten children at his side.

"These children were kidnapped and trafficked by the very man who owns- *owned* this club!" I yelled.

Eyes widened, mouths dropped, some men and women escaped, frightened by my appearance.

"I have more children up there. I'm going to retrieve them. If *any* of you lay a finger on *any* of them, I will *flay* the skin from your bodies. Do you understand?"

I was met with utter silence as my answer.

I pointed at two harmless-looking women amongst the dancers. "Make sure no one nears them."

I went back up twice and came back down twice. Once I'd gathered twenty-nine children, I led them all out. A dirty, bloody antithesis to the Pied Piper. They stared. I was certain they would never see the likes of anyone like me except in their nightmares.

"Remember this," I cautioned the crowd. "Never forget this. Now you have seen these children with your own eyes. Know their pain! Witness the theft of their lives," I bellowed, releasing every ounce of fury I had left in my body, irrupting it onto their shoulders. "Now you can never say you didn't know. You can choose only to dismiss the memory."

That was the last of my fury, the last of my wrath, my bitter, confused anger.

It belonged to them now.

CHAPTER FORTY-TWO

Somehow I walked with twenty-nine children without losing one of them. People, even those jaded by harsh Vietnamese life, looked at us twice, at the spectacle that we were. One bloody six-foot-three Echo Tribe-American boy and twenty-nine dirty, abused, torn children.

They all followed me without hesitation, though, which I found strange. Many of them insisted on taking turns holding my damaged, mangled hands, but I dared not refuse any of them.

The gunshot wounds in my legs, the collapsed lung, and the myriad cuts and scrapes were starting to wear on me. I needed to sit, lay, something and soon or I was going to pass out.

When we arrived at the bus stop to Hạ Long Bay, the driver opened the doors but when he glanced at me, he tried to close them. I struck my hands out and pulled them open.

"Don't even think about it," my shredded voice ordered.

I loaded children on the bus one by one, counting them as I went. When they were on, two patrons got off and scurried away from me as quickly as possible. I pulled my aching body onto the first step and nearly fell forward. The bus driver stood and helped me up the second and third step.

I took out my wallet and removed all the American money I had left.

"Eight-hundred twenty-six dollars," I said, handing it to him. "We need to get to Hạ Long Bay." I looked down at the blood on my legs. "And fast."

The driver nodded and closed the doors. I looked out into the sea of twenty-nine faces and felt a glimmer of hope.

But just a glimmer.

And then I fell face forward onto the bus floor and escaped into the blackness that had so longed to take me.

CHAPTER FORTY-THREE

Finley

I sat at one of An's outside tables with her. It had been thirteen hours, forty-three minutes, fifty-three... fifty-four... fifty-five seconds since I'd seen Ethan last. Detective Tran had been to and from Slánaigh with Father Connolly, trying to figure out where Ethan had gone to and how to bring him back. An's father kept muttering in Vietnamese. She told me he kept repeating, "I knew he was wrong. I knew he was wrong." We were all in a state of panic.

But I was beside myself with worry. I'd physically fought An and Tran as they tried to keep me at Slánaigh once they'd told me what he'd done there in Hạ Long Bay, and what Tran thought he was going to do in Hanoi.

"Will he die?" I asked An for the hundredth time that night.

Phong came out with a cup of tea, set it front of me, and sat next to An. I didn't touch the cup, too keyed up.

"I don't know, Finley," she told me, not looking to sugarcoat anything, which I appreciated and hated.

Tears gathered in my stinging eyes.

"God, just send me some sort of signal," I asked Him out loud. "I'm tormented."

A bus arriving from Hanoi came bustling down the narrow street. It's normal route called for a stop right in front of An's father's tea shop. I stood when it made its regular stop and watched as the doors opened.

I followed the steps up, expecting random patrons to come down, but instead was met with children huddled together. They looked burdened by something, their arms lifted at shoulder level.

Phong noticed the oddity that was that bus and stood as well. "What in the world?" he asked no one.

An followed suit and stood as well. "They're *children*," she observed, the tone of her voice leading from curiosity to bewilderment in one phrase.

They were chattering in Vietnamese as they awkwardly descended from the bus and onto the sidewalk. There was a line of children five deep and maybe four or five wide packed together. They were struggling with something. A few more children piled off, running around the group as if they could try to help as the bus tore off.

I took a closer look at them, studying them in the moonlight.

"It's a man," I realized out loud. My heart jumped into my throat. "It's a man," I whispered, turning my chair over, and ran, knocking a few more out of my way, eager to get to the group.

I rushed over to them and peered over their shoulders.

There, on their laboring shoulders, laid Ethan Moonsong. Bleeding. Eyes gone to black.

I screamed at the top of my lungs.

"Jesus! Ethan! Ethan! Oh my God, Ethan!"

I grabbed him from them and fell to the concrete walk. I laid him down as gently as I could, tears dripping down my face.

I brushed back his hair and with shaking hands leaned over his body to check for a pulse. I found one, but it was faint, making me queasy. I leaned over his face to check if he was breathing. He was but, again, faintly.

"Oh, Jesus! Ethan!" I cried. "An! Call Father! Get Dr. Nguyen! Phong! Come help me!"

An ran inside and Phong met me on the ground.

"Do you have a knife? A-a-a pocketknife, maybe?"

He handed me his pocketknife and I opened it. I tore Ethan's shirt off his body, laying it at his sides and examining his torso. Large purple, hideous bruises tainted the skin there, making me cry out in agony.

Carefully, but with trembling fingers, I slowly cut down his soaked-in-blood jeans, laying the fabric aside. His legs were so bloody I couldn't find whatever wounds were doing the bleeding.

"Phong," I said, frantic, "I-I need, uh, water, lots of water and, uh, towels."

He ran without hesitation to gather what I'd asked for.

I moved up Ethan's body, nearer to his face, his broken face, and soothed into his ear, "Come back to me, Ethan," I said, laying my hands over his forehead, neck, and shoulders. I ran my skin over his again and again and again. "Please, my love. Please come back to me."

Phong hovered over me in that moment, his eyes wide in terror.

"What?"

"Don't worry about it now. Tend to Ethan," he said, handing me the water and towels.

I ran the water over Ethan's legs, using the towel to clean as much of it off as possible. I'd gotten it just clear enough to recognize bullet wounds. Seven total. One awfully close to the femoral artery.

"Phong, apply pressure to the obvious wounds on that leg," I told him and did the same for my side. "An! Bring me a few chairs!"

She did and we elevated his legs while I took the towels and tied them around his legs near each wound as pressure bandages. I did the same for the one near the femoral, but the towel filled too quickly with blood, making my own run cold. I shredded another towel into strips and twisted two until I had a tourniquet, wrapping it around his leg, and coiling it to keep the bleeding at bay.

"Is Dr. Nguyen coming?" I asked An.

"I'm here!" Dr. Nguyen answered for her.

She bent at his side and looked him over.

"I have to take him to my office. He needs surgery," she said.

Detective Tran arrived in a compact car soon after, and I watched helplessly as they loaded him inside. I tried to jump into the front, but they insisted I follow them instead, which I didn't understand at the time. It wasn't until later I discovered they were trying to prevent me from getting killed just in case someone attacked their car.

I stood on the curb, decimated, and unaware of what I was supposed to do. The tears came more freely then, wracking sobs spilled from my chest and lips.

"Come with me," An said, leading me to her bike.

She got on and I sat behind her, hugging my friend. We sped through the streets of Hạ Long Bay to Dr. Nguyen's surgical office. My life seemed to speed past me as we rode along in vivid, striking memories—some horrifying and some extraordinary. The extraordinary painted the most beautiful images I'd ever seen, and they'd all involved Ethan in some way or another.

Swimming at Hungry Horse with our class from school. Ethan there, always in the background, jumping from the cliffs, or swimming alongside us all. High school football games with Holly Raye on the bleachers with a blanket and a bucket of popcorn made all the more sweet by Ethan's phenomenal abilities. Holly Raye and me at the eighth grade dance, brace-faced, and huddled in the corner commiserating over how lame eighth grade dances were, yet secretly dying of happiness inside. Wild, silly sleepovers with Holly Raye. *Daydreams* of sleepovers with Ethan Moonsong. Chemistry class with Ethan. Conversations with Ethan. Falling in "love" with Ethan. Falling out of "love" with Ethan. Befriending Ethan. Ethan saving me. Falling recklessly, deliriously, intensely in love with Ethan Moonsong. *Kissing* Ethan. Wanting Ethan. Owning Ethan. *Loving* Ethan.

The tears clouded my eyes, so I closed them to rid myself of the pain, but it would not stop coming, would not stop hurting.

When I thought I couldn't take much more, we pulled up a sharp incline and made our way through the winding slope until we reached Dr. Nguyen's office. I tore off the bike before An had really gotten a chance to slow down. I ran, abandoning my flip-flops as I did, and rushed into the building.

Tran was there, sitting in a chair outside of the operating room.

"Is he already in?" I asked.

"He's in. The nurses were already here, waiting."

I sank into a chair next to Tran, sitting right on the edge. My legs bounced with nervous energy.

"Can't sit," I said, standing and pacing outside the operating room. I looked up when An entered.

"Phong took the girls and the boys to Father and Sister," An said, holding up her phone.

"Where will they put them all?" I asked, thinking of Slánaigh's already cramped quarters.

"The girls are bunking with the others. The boys will be sleeping in the common room."

"Are they okay?" I asked.

"They seem fine, brave."

"Did-did they say anything about what happened?"

"I guess one of the older girls said Ethan just showed up on their floor and insisted to the three men watching over them that Khanh was looking for them. They didn't question him, and when they entered the elevator, he... uh, well, he killed them."

"Oh my God," I whispered, sitting down out of necessity instead of restlessness.

"I guess he told them to stay where they were and that he would return to them later. He promised to protect them."

"I believe he did," I said, unaware what it all really meant for Ethan.

"Did she know what happened while he'd been gone?"

An cleared her throat and looked at Tran. "Um, she said that he left for two to three hours and returned to them a bloody mess." I gulped. "The girl said there were many guards there that night but that none ever took the elevator down to get them, not even to escape."

My body shivered.

"How many?" I whispered.

"She thought at least fifty."

I felt faint. Sick, really.

Tran stood quickly and left the building. An and I listened for his car's engine and when it turned over, we both jumped. We heard him back the car out of his space then pull forward before the sound disappeared. He'd left.

I wanted to vomit. "What does that mean for Ethan?"

"I think it means you and Ethan need to get the hell out of Vietnam, Finley. And you need to do it fast."

"How can I do that if he's recovering from surgery?" I asked.

A loud shout came from the operating room, and my stomach dropped to my feet. Unable to help myself, I plastered my ear to the door. Clipped Vietnamese words were exchanged in rising octaves.

"What are they saying, An?"

She leaned in and stuck her ear to the door, facing me.

Her brows furrowed in concentration for a few moments before they shot up in alarm.

"What?" I spit out. "What?"

An swallowed.

"An, I swear to God. I swear to God, An! What is going on!"

"Sit down," she said, gently prodding me.

I yanked my body back.

"Tell me what's going on, An."

"They-he had lost a lot of blood, Fin. I guess his blood pressure was dropping and they couldn't get it back up."

"You say he *had*. What do you mean he *had*?"

"Come sit down with me."

"No. No, An. Don't just sit there and tell me what I think you're going to tell me, An. Don't just sit there, An!" I screamed. Tears streamed down my face, gathered beneath my chin and neck.

An's face had turned white as a sheet. "The nurses called time of death."

I fell to the ground, my backside landing with a hard thud. "*What?*" I asked in disbelief. "*What?*"

"I'm so sorry, Finley," she added quietly.

"No! No!" I said, standing and pointing accusingly at her.

I slammed through the operating room door and took in the pools of blood beneath Ethan's operating table. The nurses stood around, doing nothing, their arms tucked into their sides.

Dr. Nguyen placed a defibrillator at Ethan's chest, screaming at him to come back. She shocked him, but he wasn't responding. I ran to his other side. His eyes were dull, lifeless. His mouth slack. Blood and bruises covered the entire length of his beaten body.

"Jesus!" I said, my body shivering where I stood. "Jesus! Tell me what to do! Tell me what to do!" I demanded, frantic.

Dr. Nguyen looked up at me, her eyes crazed. Something dawned on her.

"I have one epinephrine shot left in one of the exam rooms. Room three. It's in a drawer. Long needle."

I tore through the operating room.

"Four. Three!"

I yanked open a drawer. It was there, sitting on top.

I grabbed the plastic sealed package and ran back to the operating room.

"I have it!"

"It's okay," Dr. Nguyen replied. "It's okay. He-it's a miracle but the defibrillator worked. It worked. His heart is beating. He's breathing."

I leaned against the nearest tile-covered wall and sank down onto the floor, my hand still gripping the adrenaline shot. Without thought, I started praying, thanking, praying, thanking.

When Dr. Nguyen got Ethan stabilized, she sank back from the table. "I can't believe it," she said. "I can't believe it. He was dead. I saw it. He was dead." She looked at me and smiled the most gloriously infectious smile. "He was dead, Finley. It's a miracle."

Pent-up anxiety, nerves, and emotions came flooding out all at once for me as my body came back down. My body shook with the final acceptance that I'd almost lost him, that I'd almost been forced to return to Montana with Ethan in a box.

I cried for the millionth time that night, but it had never been as sweet as the release that came with knowing that Ethan Moonsong was alive.

CHAPTER FORTY-FOUR

Ethan

When I woke, there were two things I was very aware of. Suffering. Acute suffering. And suffering's direct counter. Finley.

"Your. Hands." I was able to say but with great effort.

I heard a sharp intake before her hands found my arm.

I exhaled. "*Finally.*"

"Finally," she repeated aloud, making me want to smile but couldn't.

She ran her hands up and down my arm, warming me up from the inside. My lungs filled with air. I'd found I could breathe easier when she was touching me.

After a few minutes, I pried my eyes open.

She was blurry at first, but she came in true after a few blinks. I tried to raise my hand toward her face but my arms were too heavy.

"Why do you look so tired, my love?"

She laughed, but her eyes filled with tears. "Because you died, came back to life, and have been in a coma for ten days."

My eyes opened a little wider. "Are you okay? Is everyone okay? Are the children okay? Father? Sister?"

She smiled a watery smile. "They're all fine. Many of the children have been placed back in their loving family homes. For those whose families couldn't be found or for those whose families were unsuitable, they've placed in Slánaigh. The boys have been moved to another home about an hour away."

"That's good." I swallowed or tried to anyway. My throat was so dry and scratchy, it felt like nails scraping down the sides. "Water?"

Finley jumped up and poured water into a glass. She stuck a straw in the cup and brought it to my lips. I took a drink and although it didn't cure the pain, it did soothe it.

"Better?" she asked.
I nodded, my neck screaming in pain. I gritted through it.

"Have—" I began, but had to clear my throat. "Has anyone come after you or anyone at Slánaigh?"

Finley sighed. "That's the thing, Ethan. No one from Khanh's group has done anything to us or the girls, they have been actively hunting you down, though. I guess a few of Khanh's men were eager to take his place and a new organization has come up already, but they still want your head on a platter." She shivered. "They will stop at nothing to find you. We're hidden here at Dr. Nguyen's, but I don't know what we're going to have to do to escape."

This shamed me. Everything I'd done, every body I was responsible for draining the life from, every

393

violent effort, every single move I'd made, every risk to Slánaigh...

And the traffickers still continued. They were a house of cockroaches. See one and there were a thousand more hidden behind them. Kill one and those thousands were ready to fall into their empty place.

The guilt was sudden and overwhelming. The faces of each I'd killed revolved in my head at a rapid rate. I sat up, grabbed the ice bucket near my bed, but could only dry heave. There was nothing in my stomach to purge.

My body shook. "Finley," I told her beautiful face, "I've done awful things, *terrible* things."

She swallowed. "I-I know," she breathed. Her admittance, her awareness of what I'd done, was like a burning hot knife to my gut. I threw my legs over the side of the bed. They were screaming at me to lay back down. I cried out in pain, almost passing out from the effort.

"Ethan," she said anxiously and stood, "sit back."

I looked at her as my body trembled. A result of the cumbersome remorse, the devastating, crushing strain of irrevocable choices so final, so concluding I was in utter shock.

"Take me to Slánaigh, Finley."

She helped me stand and dress. My legs were so swollen I could barely fit them into my jeans. We walked out of Dr. Nguyen's small hospital, me leaning on Fin, and Fin, I was certain, leaning toward leaving me when all was said and done.

FURY

Because who could ever love someone like me?

CHAPTER FORTY-FIVE

Ethan

We made it to Slánaigh. I'd only sucked in a breath twice in pain when we'd hit unexpected dips. As gently as I could, I got off the bike. I turned around to face Slánaigh but was greeted instead by the sight of Father Connolly, his cassock billowing in the ocean wind, his white hair whipping about his face. He looked beaten down, utterly beaten down.

"Finley," I said. She turned to me. "Go on up to the house. I'll meet you there soon."

"I don't want to leave you," she said, her hand in mine.

"You don't?" I asked, just to hear her confirm it.

"No," she answered.

"I promise I'll come find you soon."

"Of course," she said, kissing my hand and heading toward the house. On her way, she placed a hand on Father's shoulder. His own found hers briefly before she bounded toward the winding staircase.

When the door shut behind her, I faced Father head-on.

"Confessor."

"Aye, son," he said, walking toward me. With glassy eyes, he hugged me. "I know it all."

"You do?" I asked, scared I'd ruined our friendship.

"Aye."

"I'm… Are you disappointed in me?"

"Aye," he said, nodding his head once. "I'm gutted, me."

I started to break down but sucked it back in. "Father, I," I began, but he held a hand to stay me.

"Tell me true. Ya did it for the youngins, ye did?"

"Yes, sir."

"Are ye sorry, son?"

"More than you could possibly imagine," I admitted, a single tear treading down my cheek. I shoved it away with the fabric at my shoulder.

He nodded his head. "Ye understan' why 'tis wrong, Ethan?"

"I know, sir."

"Ya stole them men's souls 'fore they could find absolution. Ya stole the possibility, Ethan."

I sucked in a quick, excruciating breath. "Yes, Father."

"I understan' ya motivation, son. An' t'at motivation might be honorable but 'tis not ya place to decoide their fates."

I let out a harsh breath, absorbing the gravity of what I'd done. I nodded, unable to answer without breaking my composure. I had no right to feel sorry for myself.

"Confessor," I repeated.

"Aye, son."

"I confess to the murders of countless men, and I am heartily sorry for what I've done."

I hung my head low but his frail hand picked it back up.

His brows furrowed in understanding and pity. "Ach, the war that must rage within an' outside ya, boyo." He dropped his hand. "I can see ya remorse, Ethan. I can *feel* it. Ye seek absolution an' ye shall receive it, but 'tis one condition."

My eyes found his. "And what condition is that?"

"Ya must turn yaself in to Tran."

My chest panted and I almost lost my balance. I righted myself. "Turn myself in to Tran."

"Aye. When we take revenge 'pon ourselves, 'tis too burdensome, too heavy for us ta carry alone. It only causes more fear, more violence, more war. The only thing that can save us is love, my son. God is Love an' Love conquers all, so take this 'pon ya breast, let it lie there an' permeate ya skin. An' obey Him by turnin' yaself in."

"I see," I said, accepting the hellacious fate I'd chosen for myself. "No more Finley. No more thoughts of married life. No more thoughts of children of my own. No more thoughts of a life of Finley." I looked up at Father Connolly. His hands were clasped together as if in prayer. "I see. I, uh, let me say goodbye to her tonight. I'll go to Tran in the morning."

"O' course, my son."

I wanted to run, to sprint to Finley so as not to waste a single minute of the precious time I had left with her. I'd deal with the idea of my future in a Vietnamese prison later. I knew that I just needed to get to her. I needed her. I wanted her.

I almost faltered when I reached the stairs. The idea of a future without Finley Dyer was punishment indeed. It was a hell on earth. I detested myself in that moment, detested everything I'd done with a fiery passion.

I looked up the staircase and called out Finley's name. I needed to be alone with her and that wasn't going to happen inside Slánaigh. I called out for her again and she emerged, her face expectant.

I cleared my throat to control the emotions threatening to boil over. I locked my knees to keep them from buckling beneath me.

"Yes?" she asked, a breathtaking smile on her face.

"Come here, Fin," I told her.

"Why so serious?" she teased. "It's over. You're alive. You're here. We're together. We will be all right!" she said, her arms extended out, her lips shouting toward the sun.

I choked on the words hovering on my tongue so I took her hand and led her down to the beach, down to the cove full of cerulean water and ragged, jutting cliffs. A juxtaposition of dismay and calm dispassion. It described our situation perfectly. It described *us* perfectly.

When we'd reached the shore, I kicked off my boots and she tossed away her flip-flops. We walked until our toes met the edge of the water.

"It's so beautiful," she said, admiring the cove.

I looked on her, desperate to memorize every feature, every tick of muscle, every breath she inhaled. "*You* are beautiful," I declared. "*You* are the beautiful one here. All of this," I said, gesturing to the earth and water surrounding us. "It is humbled by you, plain when it shares space with you. It could only beg to sit at your feet, this earth. That is how remarkable you are, Finley Dyer."

I sucked in an incredible breath. "I was so desperate to keep you that I lost you," I told her.

Her face fell at my last sentence. "What do you mean?" she quieted.

"Do you know how much I love you?" I asked her, ignoring her question. "Do you know what I wouldn't have done for you? I can tell you. It is nothing. I would have captured a speeding train, if you'd asked me. I would have torn down Everest for you, if you had even mentioned it in passing."
I fell to my knees in the sand, the pain not even registering within my body. I was too consumed by the loss of what could have been to have even noticed.

Finley kneeled beside me, resting her hands on my face. I grabbed them in my own and clasped them together, shoving them into my chest, wishing I could swallow them, swallow her, keep her in me, close to me, always with me.

I yelled at the top of my lungs, longing for a way to turn back the time, to erase what I had done.

I looked at her. *But now you must be yet another victim. You must suffer because of me.*

"Fin," I said, my eyes blurred with tears.

"Ethan, you're scaring me."

"Fin, I, uh, I'm not going to be able to return with you to Montana."

"Why not?" she asked, her chest rising and falling.

I wiped my eyes on the sleeves of my T-shirt. "Because I have to go to Tran. I have to turn myself in."

She took her hands back from me, resting them against her throat. "No, n-no you don't."

"Yes, I do," I said, gripping her face in my hands.

Tears spilled anew down her cheeks. "Ethan, what are you saying? What *exactly* are you saying?"

My face contorted with the effort to keep myself in check. "I have to turn myself in, Fin."

"No! You don't! And you will not, Ethan Moonsong. Over my dead body!"

"*Fin*," I said, trying to reason with her. But how could I reason? Would I be reasonable if the situation had been reversed? No. In fact, I would have thrown her over my shoulder and walked back to Montana.

She wept, her teeth gnashing in frustration and anger. She began to hit me, pelting me in the chest, and I took the pain, took her fists willingly. I let her hit me until she'd had enough, until her hands fell at her sides in defeat. I knew that defeat. I felt that defeat.

"I cannot believe you would do this to me," she told me. "Do you know how long I have wanted you? You cannot comprehend the solace the memory of your face brought me when I had needed it most, when I didn't think I could take a single minute more of my horrific life." She sat back on her heels and stared out into the water. "You were a reason to get up in the morning, Ethan. You still are. You will *always* be the reason I get up in the morning.

"When those men would touch me, when they would do vile, terrible things to me, Ethan," she said, turning her gaze on me, "yours is the face I'd always imagined saving me." Tears flowed down her face. "I didn't even know then why, but your face was something my mind unwillingly thrust upon me, a sort of shelter from the damage they were causing. You were a shelter I'd never even asked for. You are still my shelter, Ethan."

Her teeth gritted. She bellowed at the earth with venom, with a desperate, lonesome hurt. "I am not meant to be happy," she stated. "I have been destined for a life of torment. In a way, I guess I'd always known and now I can see it all so clearly and I feel like such a fool."

Her words devastated me and made a liar out of me.

"It's all my fault," I told her. "I'd promised you forever. I'd promised you love, and I failed you."

Her body sagged. "You have not failed me, Ethan Moonsong. I know why you did it. I look at the faces of all the innocents you saved and I cannot ever fault you for that. I know your reasons. I admire your reasons, but I *loathe* the execution," she declared, double meaning and all.

I fell forward, my hands finding sand. I captured thousands of grains in the palms of my hands and brought my fists up. Sand fell through, blowing away with the wind, and no matter how tightly I'd held on to it, it refused to hold there.

"I was so desperate to keep you that I lost you."

If someone gives themselves to you freely, you just have to accept the gift.

CHAPTER FORTY-SIX

Ethan

Finley and I stayed wrapped in one another's arms on the shore of the cove that belonged to Slánaigh, intertwined in such a way that you could not decipher what limb belonged to whom. There wasn't a single minute of that night wasted as we talked throughout, clinging to each other's words as well as our bodies bathed in the soft light of a full moon.

"Tell me what our lives would have been," she asked me.

My tongue felt too heavy but I answered anyway. "We would have left here," I began. "We would have gone back home but only until we'd had enough saved to move somewhere exotic, somewhere tropical, somewhere beautiful. We would have bought some land, built a pretty little house. Maybe our little plot of land somewhere allowed for a vegetable garden, been near the beach." I'd known for several weeks into our trip to Vietnam that I'd never wanted go back to Montana and its cold. I'd pitched the idea out in the air near Fin one day, hoping she'd latch on to the prospect with enthusiasm, and, of course, she had.

"Eventually we'd marry, share a room, *share a bed*. We'd maybe take up surfing, or paddleboarding, or whatever, and we'd live simply, learning the land around us when we weren't learning each other," I told her, clutching her to me. Regret laid heavily in my grasp. The what-could-have-beens laid heavily between us. Her body wracked with sobs. "Do you want me to stop?" I asked her.

"No. Please, keep going."

"We'd own a big, stupid dog with long hair that shed all over our furniture. Daily you'd complain about it, but you'd be the first one out the door with it when it was time for its walk. We'd eat mangos on our little covered porch and watch the sun as it set, our dog at our very bare feet." She laughed in spite of the tears. "We'd make our money any way it would come, and my dad would visit for weeks at a time." I took a deep breath. "Eventually we'd have a baby." She sniffed at this, her pain so evident in the simple sound. "Girl or boy we wouldn't care. I'd place my hands on your belly as he or she grew. Devour annoying and pointless books on having and raising a baby but realizing they were useless when it really came down to it because when you gave birth to our baby, we'd see everything we needed in their eyes.

"We'd take turns during the sleepless nights, switching off when one couldn't take it anymore and just needed sleep. I'd make you breakfast in bed just because I could. If you ever wanted for anything I would get it for you. I would have pleased you, I think, Finley."

"Yes, I believe you would have," she said as the sun rose over the cove.

I kissed Finley then—a kiss to cherish, a kiss to remember, a kiss of what could have been.

We stood together, both of us covered in sand, but neither of us cared. We made our way toward the beach, under the canopy of trees, and up the path to the shell gravel drive. We sat on the bike together, starting it up, and heading out toward the main road, not a single word spoken to one another. I, for fear I would change my mind and risk my soul, our souls. She, I believe, in fear that she'd let me.

We drove through town slowly and before either of us were ready, we'd arrived at Tran's police station.

Finley and I got off the bike and hugged one another so fiercely bones risked snapping.

Fin had tried to be brave but she failed when she saw me succumb to the anguish that was saying goodbye to the love of your life, knowing you would probably never see them ever again.

"I love you," she said, wounding me with her simple yet profound words.

"I love you," I secreted into her ear.

I kissed her my last goodbye, our last goodbye, and tore myself away from her, fighting myself with the strength of ten men, wrestling the demons who'd brought me there in the first place and heaving them into the street at my feet.

I refused to look back until the very last second. I made sure she'd gotten back on the bike and started to leave.

"Finley!" I shouted, and her head whipped my direction. I choked on the emotion settling in my throat. "Finally!" I told her. "Finally!"

She paused as if to collect herself. "I love you too," she declared, a hitch in her voice.
I turned to the door of the police station, unable to look on her it hurt so badly, and swung it open.

I didn't bother taking in my surroundings, as nothing mattered to me then. I knew nothing would ever matter to me ever again.

I was a murderer of child molesters and sex traffickers, and I was prepared to pay for my crimes that although bent toward the righteous were tainted with sin.

I stood at the entrance, my head hung low, and yelled for Tran. Without realizing anyone had been near me, I was yanked by my arm. I looked up and found Tran's face.

"This way," he said quietly, his head turning about his neck quickly, taking in his surroundings. I followed where he led, into a small office. He shut the door behind us.

Finley

I stood on Slánaigh's porch hugging Sister Marguerite, crying, and wishing the pain would stop, but I knew that it would not. I knew I was unspeakably altered.

"I feel like my purpose has been ripped out from underneath me," I told Sister.

"No, child, it has not," her French accent soothed. "If in this life you are not meant with Ethan, in the next you are."

This truth made me sob even harder. "Please, I hope you are right."

We broke down together, sat united at the end of the porch, near Slánaigh's door.

"He'd promised me the most glorious life, Sister. We were going to conquer the world together, and I believe it would have been the best life I could have ever had."

She took my hand, soothing me with her own delicate ones, and prayed under her breath for me.

We sat quietly for many minutes, maybe an hour, until Father had met us. He stood on the stairs facing us.

"Ach, my choild! I'm sorry for ya. So sorry for ya."

"I know, Father," I told him.

"'Spite it all, he's still the most wonderful boy, he is. That he is. I'm ta go ta him late this evenin', discover what 'tis Tran can do fer him."

Unable to speak, I only nodded my head.

I stood with every intention of going to my room, falling into my borrowed bed, and staying there for days. At least until I found out what could be done for Ethan. I knew I needed to call his father in Montana soon, but not until I could glean a little more information on what was to happen to him. The possibility of death haunted me and I refused to think of it, though I knew it was their favorite option, especially for someone who had hit their own dirty pocketbooks with such a vengeance.

I was afraid for Ethan. I was more afraid than I had ever been in my entire life.

And that's saying something.

Ethan

Tran's office owned a bland khaki color all over—from the floor, the chairs, the walls, the tile ceiling, even Tran's desk. He plopped into his tan chair and it creaked under his weight. He signaled toward a metal chair in front of his desk. I sat under his command.

"Ethan," he said.

"Detective Tran," I greeted.

We sat in silence for half a minute.

"I suppose you know why I'm here," I told him.

"You are here to confess to your crimes, I assume."

I swallowed. "Yes, sir."

"What crimes are these?" he asked, knowing the answer already.

I took three deep breaths, my heart sped to a dangerous rate. "I murdered *countless* men."

"Who were these men you murdered?" he asked.

"Sex traffickers and their customers."

"No, *who* were these men you murdered?"

"I don't understand."

"Describe these victims to me."

"Uh, men who kidnapped innocent children and sold them into sex slavery and the men who molested them."

Tran leaned back in his chair. He turned to where his side sat flush with the line of the front of the desk. His elbow met the surface. He brought his hand down and played with a rubber band, running it in circles with his index finger.

Tran's head met the back of his chair. "Did Father Connolly ever tell you why I became a detective, Ethan?" he asked the ceiling, baffling me.

"No. He mentioned once you'd been doing it for over fifteen years or something like that."

He sat up, turning to face me once more. He laid his forearms on the desktop and leaned forward.

"I have been a detective for sixteen years, three months, two weeks, two days," he admitted, startling me.

"Committed," I acknowledged, knowing the hell he got daily for being a straight cop in a crooked city.

"I decided to become a detective seventeen years, six months, three weeks, six days ago." My brows drew together, perplexed. "That was five days after my daughter had gone missing," he stated, astonishing me.

I shook my head in disbelief, not knowing what I could possibly say to him.

His eyes grew glassy. "She was beautiful," he said. He leaned back and grabbed a framed picture of a little girl. His fingers traced her face before setting the picture face down. "I can't look at her sometimes it's so painful," he explained. He took a deep breath. "She would have been just a little bit older than you. She would have been twenty-two this year." He grew quiet, searching precious memories, it seemed. "I never found her. I have no idea if she is still alive, whether she's happy or not. I have no idea if she is *alive*, Ethan," he said, his voice breaking. "What keeps me awake at night is knowing that if she *was*, I would think she would have come home by now."

"I am so sorry," I told him seriously, honestly.

"It was a beautiful day out. I'd sent Hanh to fetch some broth at the market. I'd expected her back a half hour prior so I left the house to look for her. I can admit it now, though for years I couldn't, but I had left our home furious with her. When I arrived at the market, I searched the ice cream shop, so sure she would have been there, but when I discovered that she wasn't, I moved to the shops that held jewelry since she loved to try on the different pieces, but I could not find her there either. Frantic at that point, I tore through the market yelling her name repeatedly but no answer came.

"I'd decided to circle the market once more when I came upon one of her friends from school. I'd greeted them and asked if they'd seen Hanh, they told me they'd seen her and a man get into a car."

My heart plummeted at my feet for Detective Tran.

"As you can imagine, at that moment I was crazy, overwrought. I'd refused to stop, refused to sleep, refused to eat. It was a frenzied search for my Hanh."

His head fell into his hands.

"You can't imagine my pain, my suffering, my torment. I started looking for Hanh the minute I knew she'd been taken, and I have not stopped since."

My chest constricted for him. I tried so hard to put myself in his shoes, imagine the suffering he knew so well. Yet, the horror I felt for him that took residence in my heart and chest, I knew, fell very, very short.

Tran fell back in his chair and ran his hands down his tired-looking face. "So you can imagine my predicament," he said, staring at me.

"What predicament?" I asked.

"The one I'm presented now. The one where I arrest a good man for misguided crimes against the most vile human beings that ever walked the earth."

My heart pounded. "You have to do what you have to do, Tran," I told him, letting him know I held no ill feelings toward him for having to do his job.

He stood up and walked around his desk, sitting on the corner nearest the door. "You know there hasn't been an official report done on what the crooked cops here are calling *the massacre*?"

"There hasn't?"

He looked me dead in the eye. "No, Ethan, there hasn't."

"Why not?"

"Because the traffickers know that the number of dead would not escape national media attention, possibly international. They can't cover something like that up. Instead," he said, pointing at the door of his office, "there are men I'm forced to call colleagues out there actively hunting side by side with men I'm forced to call *victims* by made-up crimes designed to get their opposer's hands tied. And do you know who they're hunting, Ethan?"

I swallowed.

"You. They're hunting you." He stood in front of the window facing out into the street. "As I see it, I have two choices." His finger found the slat of his metal blinds. He pulled it down to get a better view. The metal rang out with the effort and quieted quickly. "I can either create a report of a man who walked into my office confessing to crimes no one has any interest in persecuting him for other than the criminals he inconvenienced *or* I could pretend you never came, pretend I never heard of your so-called crimes."

My heart was in my throat then.

"Ethan," he said, turning around and facing me. "I'm afraid I have no record of these crimes you have confessed to."

I breathed out harshly. "You don't?"

"No, I do not."

"Oh my God," I said, my body trembling with the release of my future completely altered by a single man.

"And since I have no idea what you're talking about, I believe it's time for you to leave. Leave my office, leave this station, leave Slánaigh, leave Vietnam. You have done what you've had to do by God. Let me carry the weight from here on, son."

"I feel like I can't let you do that, sir," I told him.

"It is not your choice to make anymore, Ethan. I never got to give my daughter a second chance, so it is imperative that I not stand by and refuse you yours. It's over. Now find Finley Dyer and leave."

I stood. Stood tall, stood in disbelief, stood at the foot of my new fate.

I turned to leave but Tran stopped me by grabbing my arm. He stuck his hand out and I took it.

"Maybe one day I will see you again," he said, "but if I do not ever have that pleasure, have a glorious life, son. Live it for my daughter, for the children you rescued, and those you could not, live it for Finley. Live it for God."

CHAPTER FORTY-SEVEN

Finley

My hand found the door handle and turned when I heard the faint *crush, crush, crush* of someone running down the shell gravel that lead to Slánaigh. To this very day I will not forget the feeling I got from turning around to see whose feet were responsible for it.

My heart raced, my body rocked back landing with a thud against the front door. My chest rose and fell rapidly with breaths I didn't know I'd ever get back.

"*Ethan*," I breathed.

I tore down the porch, down the impossibly long winding staircase, pausing every few feet to check that he was still there, that he wasn't a figment of my imagination. When my feet met gravel, I ran as I'd never ran. I ran for my *life* because Ethan was my life.

"Ethan?" I screamed.

He ran for me, his face devoid of expression. He was a man with a duty, a pursuit so precise he could think of nothing else. I ran against the wind, the hollowness of the air drowning out the sounds of the ocean. It had rained that morning, a sign I thought meant the earth had learned of Ethan's handing himself over, but then it had inexplicably stopped, washing clear the dirt and grime and left behind it the delicate fragrance that was a newly laundered earth.

Each step, each intense, staggering step toward him I shed behind me every cumbersome grief that had ever plagued me.

We collided in a thundering crash, falling toward terra firma, both freed from our chains.

"Finally," I whispered into his ear.
"Finally," he whispered back.

EPILOGUE

Ethan

Finley and I had escaped that night from Vietnam, back to Montana. We promised both Sister Marguerite and Father Connolly that we would never stop fighting for them, that we would be their voices from afar.

Two days later, we were at my father's door.

He'd heard us coming up the drive in a taxi at three in the morning and stood on the porch, waiting for whomever was inside.

When I emerged first, I heard my name. I ran to my dad like a small boy would but couldn't seem to muster up any sense of shame.

"Dad," I said, breathing him in, and clutching him to me with everything I had. He hugged me back fiercely.

"Welcome home, son."

Finley and I explained to him everything that happened, not leaving out a single detail. Many of the things I'd described Finley had not even heard yet. And at the end, I felt ashamed and terrified she'd leave me.

And yet, instead, both she and my father embraced me.

Within six months, Finley and I had packed our bags for Nosara, Costa Rica. There, we purchased a plot of land on Playa Nosara, grew a vegetable garden, and learned to surf and paddleboard.

There, we fostered many victims sent from Slánaigh whose families could not be found and had grown older, having trouble supporting themselves. We taught them how to start a new life using real-life skills, helped them begin their forever lives. We were utterly fulfilled, Fin and I.

We couldn't have imagined being any happier...

"Uh, Ethan?" Fin asked from her chair on our porch facing the ocean.

"Yes, babe?" I asked, handing her a piece of mango.

"My fingers are so swollen," she said, taking it. "My wedding band is cutting off my circulation."

"Here," I said, taking her hand, examining the best way to take it off. "That's so weird," I observed.

She took a bite of the mango and her face contorted. "Ugh! That is awful! We must have gotten a bad one."

I looked at her strangely. "What are you talking about? I just took a bite of it and it was perfect."

"Really?" she asked.

"Yeah," I said, sitting up.

Finley sighed loudly. "Oh my God, I have to pee *again*!" She stood. "What is wrong with me?" she asked, turning to walk into our beach house.

Suddenly, she stopped and faced me with shimmering eyes.

"Oh my God," I said, standing up.

I rushed her and began kissing her all over her face.

"Finally," she said with a watery smile.

HELP STOP CHILD SEX EXPLOITATION AND TRAFFICKING

ONE BODY VILLAGE

DONATE TO
ONEBODYVILLAGE.ORG

FURY

PLAYLIST

FISHERAMELIE.COM/LIGHTMYFIRE

CONNECT WITH FISHER AMELIE

FISHERAMELIE.COM

FACEBOOK.COM/FISHERAMELIE

TWITTER.COM/FISHERAMELIE

INSTAGRAM.COM/FISHERAMELIE

YOUTUBE.COM/USER/FISHERAMELIE

GOODREADS.COM/FISHERAMELIE

SIGNUP

FOR FISHER'S NEWSLETTER

FISHERAMELIE.COM/NEWSLETTER

FISHER AMELIE

MORE
OF FISHER'S
WORK

BOOK TWO OF THE SEVEN DEADLY SERIES
FISHER AMELIE

7D

GREED

ACKNOWLEDGMENTS

I have to start off by thanking Hollie Westring. You put up with me, Hollie. I don't know why. I really don't, but I'm grateful for you all the same. Your talent is incredible and, if it was possible, you are incredible'er. That's a word, right? No red marks! Thanks for enduring my obsession with adverbs. Thanks for your loyal support. Thanks for tireless effort to help me get FURY out. You've been with me for so many novels now, I cannot imagine that anyone ever could, ever would care as much for my work as you do. Thank you to the moon and back a thousand times. Love you, Holls.

To those of you who let me borrow your names. Thank you.

To Mama. Thank you for helping me plot this one out. Thank you for standing behind me. Thank you for teaching me about God. Thank you for showing me by example His love. Thank you for teaching me what a good mother is. Thank you a million times over. Thank you.

To Court, my lovely Court. Court-is-in-session, baby. To M, my darling M. You're so Shaken-Not-Stirred, Agent M. To T, my lovely T. Breakfast-at-Tiffany's, T. I'm literally at a loss for words when it comes to describing what you all mean to me. For someone that bleeds words, you'd think that would be an impossibility but here I am, unable to convey to you that you are my forever friends. Forever you will be a part of me. Forever I will put you at the top of the heap of the most beautiful people I know. I'm so sorry I haven't been able to be more "present" but I promise you that my babies are growing (as much as I hate it) and there will be even more time for "us days." I love you three so much it hurts.

To Shelly, Nichole, A.L. Jackson, and Amy Bartol. There are many, many, MANY authors within this industry but you all are the most talented, most sincere, most lovely of them all. I have a knack for scouting out the best of the best and you, my loves, are the best of them all.

To my little ones, my wonderful little ones. I hope one day, if you ever read this, that you know how much you influence my writing. You all spur in me the desire to better the world around me. You are my catalysts. You are the reason I write. I am so in love with you and you are all so beautiful it doesn't seem fair that I get to call you mine. I'm undeserving of such sparkling beauty, but for some reason God has gifted you to me. And who am I to argue with Him?

To Matt. Finally. You are Ethan and I am Finley. I don't know how apparent it was to you but to me, it jumped off the page from word one. In the book, Finally is so multi-faceted. It is not just a simple word. It is synonymous with love. It is recognition of a release of pain and suffering. It is an acknowledgment that they have recognized their soul mates. It means so many, many things. Just like us. I'd saved a dedication to you for so many years because I felt that no other work was worthy of a dedication to you. You deserve my entire heart. And since this book has my entire heart splashed across its pages, it is yours. So, Finally, Matt. Finally.

FISHER AMELIE

PREVIEW

VAIN'S FIRST

CHAPTER

PROLOGUE

Vanity's a debilitating affliction. You're so absorbed in yourself it's impossible to love anyone *other* than oneself, leaving you weak without realization of it. It's quite sad. You've no idea what you're missing either. You will never know real love and your life will pass you by.

But you will see.

One day you will blink and the haze will dissipate. You'll discover that what once defined you has wilted into graying hair and wrinkled skin. Frantic, you'll glance around yourself, in hopes of finding those you swore adored you, but all you will find is empty picture frames.

CHAPTER ONE

Six weeks after graduation and Jerrick had been dead for three of them. You'd have thought it would've been enough for us all to take a breather from our *habits*, but it wasn't.

I bent to snort the line of coke in front of me.

"Brent looks very tempting tonight, doesn't he?" I asked Savannah, or Sav as I called her for short, when I lifted my head and wiped my nose.

Savannah turned her glassy eyes away from her Special K laced O.J., her head wavering from side to side. "Yeah," she lazily slurred out, "he looks hot tonight." Her glazed eyes perked up a bit but barely. "Why?"

"I'm thinking about saying hello to him." I smiled wickedly at my pseudo-best friend and she smiled deviously back.

"You're such a bitch," she teased, prodding my tanned leg with her perfectly manicured nail. "Ali will never forgive you for it."

"Yes, she will," I said, standing and smoothing out my pencil skirt.

I could've been considered a dichotomy of dressers. I never showed much in the way of skin because, well, my father would have killed me, but that didn't stop me from choosing pieces that kept the boys' tongues wagging. For instance, everything I owned was skin tight because I had the body for it, and because it *always* got me what I wanted. I loved the way the boys stared. I loved the way they wanted me. It felt powerful.

"How do you know?" Sav asked, her head heavily lolling back and forth on the back of the leather settee in her father's office.

No one was allowed in that room, party or no, but we didn't care. Sav's parents went to Italy on a whim, leaving her house as the inevitable destination for that weekend's "Hole," as we called them. The Hole was code for wherever we decided to "hole up" for the weekend. My group of friends was, at the risk of sounding garish, wealthy. That's an understatement. We were filthy, as we liked to tease one another, double meaning and all. Someone's house was always open some random weekend because all our parents traveled frequently, mine especially. In fact, almost every other weekend, the party was at my home. This isn't why I ruled the roost, so to speak. It wasn't even because I was the wealthiest. My dad was only number four on that list. No, I ruled because I was the hottest. You see, I'm one of the beautiful people. That truly sounds so odd to have to explain, but it's the truth nonetheless. I'm beautiful, and it's not because I have a healthy dose of self-esteem, though I have plenty of that. It's obvious in the way I look in the mirror, yes, but even more obvious in the way everyone treats me. I rule this roost because I'm the most wanted by all the guys, and all the *girls* want to be my friend *because of it.*

"How do you *know*?" she asked again, agitated I hadn't yet answered.

This made my blood boil. "Stuff it, Sav," I ordered. She'd forgotten who I was and I needed to remind her.

"Sorry," she said sheepishly, shrinking slightly into herself.

"I *know* because they always do. Besides, when I'm done with their boys, I give them back. They consider it their dues."

"Trust me," she said quietly toward the wall, "they do not consider it their dues."

"Is this about Brock, Sav?" I huffed. "God, you are such a whiny brat. If he was willing to cheat on you so easily, he wasn't worth it. Consider it a favor."

"Yeah, you're probably right," she conceded but didn't sound truly convinced. "You saved me, Soph."

"You're welcome, Sav," I replied sweetly and patted her head. "Now, I'm off to find Brent."

I stood in front of the mirror above her dad's desk and inspected myself.

Long, silky, straight brown hair down to my elbows. I had natural blonde highlights throughout its mass. I'd recently cut my bangs so that they fell straight across my forehead. I ruffled them so they lay softly over my brows. I studied them and felt my blood begin to boil. The majority of girls at Jerrick's funeral suddenly had the same cut and it royally pissed me off. *God! Get a clue, nimrods. You'll never look like me!* I puckered my lips and applied a little gloss over them. My lips were full and pink enough that I didn't need much color. My skin was tanned from lying by the pool too much after graduation, and I'd made a mental note to keep myself indoors for a bit. *Don't need wrinkles, Soph.* My light gold eyes were the color of amber and were perfect, but I noticed my lashes needed a touch more mascara. I did this only to darken them up a bit, not because they weren't long enough. Like I said, I was practically flawless.

"He won't know what hit him," I told myself in the mirror. Sav mistook this for speaking to her and I rolled my eyes when she responded.

"You play a sick game, Sophie Price."

"I know," I admitted, turning her direction, a fiendish expression on my unblemished face.

I sauntered from the room. As I passed the throngs of people lined against the sides of the hall that lead from the foyer to the massive den, I received the customary catcalls and ignored them with all the flirtatious charm that was my forte. I was the queen of subtlety. I could play a boy like a concert violinist. I was a master of my craft.

"Can I get you boys anything?" I asked as I approached the elite group of hotties that included Ali's Brent.

"I'm fine, baby," Graham flirted, as if I'd *ever* give him the time of day.

"You look it," I flirted back, just stifling the urge to roll my eyes.

"Since you're offering so nicely, Soph," Spencer said, "I believe we could all use a fresh round."

"But of course," I said, curtsying lightly and smiling seductively. I purposely turned to make my way toward the bar. I did this for two reasons. One, to make them all look at my ass. Two, to make them believe I'd only just thought of the next move on my playing board. I turned around quickly and caught them all staring, especially Brent. *Bingo.* "I'll need some help carrying them all back," I pouted.

"I'll go!" They all shouted at once, clamoring in front of the other like cattle.

"How about I choose?" I said. I circled the herd, running my hand along their shoulders as I passed each one. Spencer visibly shivered. *Point, Soph.* "Eeny, meeny, miny, *moe*," I said, stopping at Brent. I followed the line of his throat and caught a glimpse of him swallowing, hard. "Would you help me, Brent?" I asked nicely without any flirting.

"Uh, sure," he said, setting down his own glass.

I linked my arm through his as we walked to the bar.

"So how are you and Ali doing?" I asked him.

He gazed at me, not hearing a word I'd said. "What?" he asked.

Exactly.

Three hours later and Brent was mine. We'd ended up sprawled out on the ancient Turkish rug in Sav's parents' bedroom, our tongues in each other's throats. He threw me underneath him and hungrily kissed my neck but stopped suddenly.

"Sophie," he breathed sexily in my ear.

"Yes, Brent?" I asked, ecstatic I'd gotten what I wanted. He sat up and gazed down on me like he'd never really seen me before. I smiled lasciviously in return, tonguing my left eyetooth. "Jesus," he said, a trembling hand combed through his hair, "I am such a fool."

"*What?*" I asked, sitting up, stunned.

"I've made a horrible mistake," he told me, still wedged between my legs. No need to tell you how badly that stung. "I've had too much to drink," he said, shaking his head. "I'm sorry, Sophie. You being the most gorgeous girl I've ever met's clouded my judgment, badly. I've made a terrible mistake."

At that most fortunate of moments, we heard Ali calling out Brent's name in the hall outside the door and he tensed, his eyes going wide. I could only inwardly smile at what was to come. Before he'd had a chance to react to her calling to him, she'd walked into the room.

"*Brent?*" she asked him. She saw our position and the recognition I'd seen in all the others before her was so obviously written all over Ali. She wasn't going to fight it. "I'm sorry," she said politely, like I wasn't in a compromising position on the floor with her boyfriend. *She's so pathetic*, I thought. She closed the door. We heard her pounding the floor to the stairs, running toward Sav no doubt. Sav would have to pretend she had no idea.

He threw himself to his feet, abandoning me haphazardly on the carpet and immediately began chasing her. *Well, that's a first*, I thought to myself. Usually they went right back to business, but I suppose we hadn't gotten far enough. *Yeah, that's why he left you lying here, half-undressed, chasing after his girlfriend, Soph.*

I balked at my own idiocy and stood up.

I walked to Sav's parents' bathroom and leaned over her mother's side of the double sinks. I fixed my bristled hair and ran my nail along the line of my bottom lip, fixing any gloss smudges. I tucked my formfitting black-and-white V-striped silk button-up back into my pencil skirt and stared at myself.

A single tear ran down my cheek and I grimaced. *Not now*, I thought. I was my own worst enemy. That was my secret weakness. Rejection. Rejection of any kind, in fact. I hated it more than anything.

"You're too beautiful to be rejected," I told the reflection in front of me, but the tears wouldn't stop. I ran the tap and splashed a little water on my face before removing the small bag of coke I'd hidden in my strapless. I fumbled with the little plastic envelope, spilling it onto the marble counter and cursed at the mess I'd made. I scrambled for something to line it with, finally stumbling upon her father's medicine cabinet. I removed the blade from her father's old-fashioned razor and made my lines. I remembered her mom kept small stacks of stationery paper in her desk in the bedroom and I went straight for that, rolling the paper into a small tube.

The tears wouldn't stop and I knew I wouldn't be able to snort with a snotty nose. I went to her parents' toilet and tugged at a few squares of toilet paper, blew my nose, then flushed it down. I swiped at the tears on my cheeks and bent over my lines just about the time a policeman came rushing in, catching me right before the act for the second time that night.

"What are you doing? Put your hands on your head," I heard a man's deep voice say.

I languidly stood from my unfinished lines and stared into the mirror. Sharing its reflection with me was a young, rather hot cop. *Shit.* I dropped the rolled-up stationery that smelled like old lady lavender potpourri and lazily put my hands over my head.

"Turn around," he said, fingering the cuffs on his belt. I turned around and faced him, his eyes widened at the full sight of me. He stumbled a little, a hitch in his step, as he progressed my way. He brought my right hand

438

down slowly, then my left and swallowed just as Brent had earlier. *Gotcha.*

"What's your name?" I whispered, his face mere inches from mine. Beats Antique's *Dope Crunk* rang loudly from downstairs. *No wonder I hadn't heard them come in.*

"That's none of your concern," he said, but the hesitation in his voice told me he thought he'd like it to be.

"I'm Sophie," I told him as he clicked the first ring around my wrist.

He kept narrowing his eyes at me, but they would drop to my breasts then back up.

"N-nice to meet you, Sophie."

"Nice to meet you, too...," I drug out, waiting for his name.

"What are you doing?" he asked me, throwing glances over his shoulder, no doubt worried if more officers would be joining us.

"Nothing. Cross my heart," I appraised, taking my free hand from his and crossing my heart, which just so happened to be at the crest of my cleavage. His gaze flitted down and he started breathing harder.

"Casey," he told me.

"Casey," I said breathily, testing out his name. He fought a drowsy smile, apparently liking the way I said it, and I smiled.

"L-let me have your hand," he said.

I gave him my unconstrained hand without a fuss. He took it and restrained it with the other.

"All tied up now, Casey," I whispered, raising my fisted hands just as he closed his eyes, almost drifting forward a bit.

"Come with me," he said, pulling me from the

counter. His eyes glanced down at my lines and he shook his head. "What makes you do that shit?"

"Because it feels good," I told him, turning his direction and seductively running my tongue along my top teeth.

"Don't even," he said, "or I'll get you on propositioning an officer as well as possession."

"Suit yourself," I told him, shrugging my shoulders. "It might have been nice," I leaned forward and sang in his ear.

"I'm sure," he said. I could see the surprise on his face at his unexpected and candid response. I decided to run with it.

"I bet if you handcuffed me to the closet bar just beyond those doors, I'd be quiet as a mouse until you came back for me," I said, letting the double meaning sink in.

"Stop," he said. The breath he'd been holding whistled from his nose.

"How old are you, Casey?" I asked, leaning into him.

"Twen-twenty-two," he stuttered.

"Huh, I just happen to be into twenty-two-year-olds. They're currently my thing," I lied.

His eyes came right to mine and held there.

"Really?" he asked, skeptical, yet inadvertently leaned into me. The grim line that had held his face before turned into a slight grin. *Seal the deal, Sophie.*

"Mmmhmm," I said. I pushed farther into his chest, my breasts mashed against his armor plate.

I tentatively kissed the pulse at his neck, knowing full well that if he really wanted to, he could definitely get me on propositioning.

I just couldn't go to jail. Not again. I'd already been once for possession when Jerrick died, and the judge told me if I showed back up in his courtroom, I'd be toast. This was worth the risk.

"Jesus," he murmured.

I threaded my fingers through the belt loop at his waist and brought him closer to me. He fiercely took my face in his and kissed me like he was dying. *What an amateur*, I thought. *Thank God I got a dumb one.* His hands grappled all over my face as he had no grace whatsoever. If the guy wasn't so sexy, I don't think I could have put up the charade as long as I did.

"Officer Fratelli!" we heard come from downstairs and he broke the kiss. "Fratelli!"

"I'm-I'm up here," Casey said, flustered. He adjusted himself and wiped his mouth.

"Uncuff me," I said, almost panicked.

"I can't," he said.

"Yes, you can, Casey. Do it and I'll repay you exponentially."

He groaned but looked at me apologetically. "When you get out, come find me," he said quietly as the other officer entered the room.

"The rest of the upstairs is secure," Casey said as if he hadn't just kissed my face off. "She was the only straggler."

"Fine," the older officer said. I thought he was going to leave but instead came through and examined the bathroom around us. "What the hell is this?" he asked Casey.

"What?" Casey asked.

"This," the older man said, gesturing to the lines of coke.

"Uh, yes, she was attempting a line when I found her," Casey told his superior.

Fuck.

"I'll bag this up," the man said and waved Casey on.

"I'm sorry," Casey said when we were out of the room. "I had to tell him. He'd have known I was lying."

"It's okay, Casey," I said with saccharine ooze. I kissed his mouth, then bit his lip playfully. "It would have been the best ride of your life," I whispered. His eyes blew wide.

"Wait, what? We can still see each other," Casey desperately plied.

"Sure we can," I lied again.

"I wasn't going to tell him about the drugs," he said again, his voice quivering. "I had only planned on getting you on the party. That would have only been a ticket, a misdemeanor."

"I know, sweets," I told him, "but you still messed up."

Casey led me down the winding staircase and I felt as if time was standing still. All my friends, cuffed themselves, looked up at me as I descended over them. I smiled down at them bewitchingly and they almost cowered in my presence. I'd been the one who brought the coke, and my smile let them know that if they brought me down, I wouldn't be going down with the ship on my own. If they squealed like the pigs they were, I would make their lives miserable. There's a fine line between friend and foe in my world.

Casey placed me into the back of a squad car when we reached the winding drive and buckled me in.

"Tell me," I said softly against his ear near my mouth, "what exactly am I being charged with?"

"Sarge will probably get you on drugs, but if it's your first offense, you should be able to get off lightly."

"And what if it isn't?"

"Isn't what?" he asked, glancing over his shoulder.

"My first offense."

"Shit. If it's not, there's nothing I can do for you."

"Oh, well, there's nothing I can do for you then either," I said coldly, the heat in my seduction blasted cold with a bucket of ice water at the flip of a switch.

Casey's mouth grew wide and he could see that he'd been had. I turned my face away from his, done with my pawn.

Casey got into the front seat and I could see through the rearview that his face was painted red with humiliation and obvious disappointment in himself that he fell for my game. He stuck the key in the ignition and drove me to the station.

I was booked, processed and searched. I scoffed at the women who had to search me before placing me in my cell. Stripping naked for anyone of the female persuasion wasn't exactly what I'd had planned for the evening. They looked down on me, knowing my charges, like they were somehow better than me.

"My lingerie probably costs more than your entire wardrobe," I spit out at the short, stocky one who eyed me with disdain.

She could only shake her head at me.

"Well, it'll go nicely with *your* new wardrobe addition," the dark-haired one said, handing me a bright orange jumpsuit.

This made both the women laugh. I slipped the disgusting jumpsuit on and they filed me away into a cell.

I shivered in my cell, coming down from my

high. I was used to this part though. I only did coke on the weekends. Unlike most others I knew, I had enough self-control to only do it at the Holes. It was just enough to drown out whatever crappy week I'd had from being ignored by my mother and father.

My parents were strangely the only I knew of who married and stayed that way. Of course, my mother was fifteen years younger than my father, so I'm sure that helped and she stayed in incredible shape. If you pitched a pic of her then and now, you wouldn't be able to tell the difference, and she'd gifted those incredible genes to yours truly. That was about the only thing my mother ever bothered to give me. My mother and father were so absorbed in themselves I don't think they remembered me some days. I was born for one reason and one reason only. It was expected of my parents to give the impression of a family.

My mom was a "housewife," and I use that term loosely. My father was the founder and CEO of an electronics conglomerate, namely computers and software. His company was based in Silicon Valley, but when he married my gold-digging mother, she insisted on L.A., so he jetted the company plane there when he needed to. It was safe to say that one, if not two or three, of my father's products were in every single home in America. I'd had a five-thousand-dollar monthly allowance if I'd kept my grades up during prep school, and that's about as much acknowledgment I got from my parents.
I'd just graduated, which meant I had four years to earn a degree of some kind then move out. I would retain a monthly allowance of twenty thousand a

month, but I had to earn my degree first. That was my father in a nutshell.

"Keep appearances, Sophie Price, and I'll reward you handsomely," my father said to me starting at fifteen.

And it was a running mantra in my home once a week, usually before a dinner I was forced to attend when he was entertaining some competitor he was looking to buy out or possibly a political official he was trying to grease up. I would dress modestly, never speak unless spoken to. Timidity was the farce. If I looked sweet and acquiescent, my father gave the impression he knew how to run a home as well as a multinational, multibillion-dollar business. If I did this, I would get a nice little thousand-dollar bonus. I was an employee, not a child.

"Sophie Price," someone yelled outside the big steel door that was my cell. I could just make out the face of a young cop in the small window. The door came sliding open with a deafening thud. "You've made bail."

"Finally," I huffed out.

When I was released, I stood at a counter and waited for them to return the belongings I had walked in with.

"One pair of shoes, one skirt, one set of hose, one set of...," the guy began but eyed the garment with confusion.

"Garters," I spit out. "They're garters. God, just give them to me," I said, snatching them out of his hands.

He carelessly pushed the rest of my belongings in a pile over to me and I almost screamed at him that he was handling a ten-thousand-dollar outfit like it was from Wal-Mart.

"You can change in there," he said, pointing at an infinitesimal door.

The bathroom was small and I had to balance my belongings on a disgusting sink.

"Well, these are going in the incinerator," I said absently.

I got dressed sans hose, returned my ridiculous jumpsuit and entered the lobby. Repulsive, dirty men sat waiting for whatever jailed fool they bothered to bail. They eyed me with bawdy stares and I could only glare back, too tired to give them a piece of my mind.

Near the glass entry doors, the sun was just cresting the horizon and I made out the silhouette of the only person I would have expected to come to my rescue.

Standing more than six feet tall, so thin his bones protruded from his face, but with stylish, somewhat long hair, reminiscent of the nineteen-thirties, clad in a fitted Italian suit, stood Pembrook. "Hello, Pembrook," I greeted him with acid. "I see my father was too busy to come himself."

"Ah, so lovely to see you too, Sophie."

"Stop with the condescension," I sneered.

"Oh, but I'm not. It is the highlight of my week bailing you from this godforsaken pit of bacteria." He eyed me up and down with regret. "I suppose I needed to get the interior of my car cleaned anyway."

"You're so clever, Pembrook."

"I know," he said simply. "To comment on your earlier observation, your father *was* too busy to get you. He does want you to know that he is severely disappointed."

"Ah, I see. Well, I shall try harder next time not

to get caught."

Pembrook stopped and gritted his teeth before opening the passenger door for me. "You, young lady, are sorely unaware of the gravity of this charge."

"You're a brilliant attorney, Pembrook, with millions at your disposal," I said, settling into his Mercedes.

He walked around the front of the car and sat in the driver's seat.

"Sophie," he said softly, before turning the ignition. "There's not enough money in the world that can help you if Judge Reinhold is presiding over your case again."

"Drive, Pembrook," I demanded, ignoring his warning. *He'll get me off*, I thought.

My house, or I should say, my father's house, was built a year before I was born, but it had since been newly renovated on the outside as well as the inside so although I may have grown up in the home, it barely resembled anything like it did when I had been small. It was grotesquely large, sitting on three acres in Beverly Hills, California. It was French Chateau inspired and more than twenty-eight-thousand square feet. I was in the left wing, my parents were in the right. I could go days without seeing them, the only correspondence was out of necessity, usually to inform me that I was required to make a dinner appearance, and that was usually by note delivered by one of the staff. I had a nanny until fourteen, when I fired her for attempting to discipline me. My parents didn't realize for months and decided I was capable of caring for myself after and never bothered to replace the position.

Freedom is just that. Absolutely no restrictions. I abandoned myself to every whim I felt. Every want I fulfilled and every desire was quenched. I wanted for nothing.

Except attention.

And I got that, I'll admit, not in the healthiest of ways. I won't lie to you, it felt gratifying...in a sense. I was rather unrestrained with my time and body. I wasn't different from most girls I knew. Well, except the fact I was exponentially better looking, but why beat a dead horse? The only difference between them and myself was I kept them wanting more. I used many, many, *many* boys and tossed them aside, discarding them, ironically, like many of them did to so many other girls before me.

This is what kept them baited. I gave them but a glimpse of my taste and they tasted absinthe. They were hooked by *la fée verte* as I was so often called. I was "the green fairy." I flitted into your life, showed you ecstasy, and left you dependent. I did this for fun, for the hell of it, for attention. I wanted to be wanted, and my word, did they want me. Did they ever.